THE TREE IN CALLE SULACO

THE TREE IN CALLE SULACO

A Novel

JAMES DETTE

Full Court Press
Englewood Cliffs, New Jersey

First Edition

Copyright © 2011 by James Dette

Published in the United States of America
by Full Court Press, 601 Palisade Avenue
Englewood Cliffs, NJ 07632

ISBN 978-0-9833711-0-6
Library of Congress Control No. 2011922877

Editing and Book Design by Barry Sheinkopf for Bookshapers
(www.bookshapers.com)

Colophon by Liz Sedlack

DEDICATION

This novel is dedicated to the unsung Latin American union and cooperative leaders and North American missionaries and workers in the various aid organizations who have been murdered in their struggle for justice.

ACKNOWLEDGEMENTS

My heartfelt thanks to my wife Evelyn who shared my experience in Ecuador and knew many of the people who populate this work. She has also graciously contributed the artwork for the cover of the book. I would also like to thank Barry Sheinkopf, director of The Writing Center in Englewood Cliffs, New Jersey, for his moral support, and for editing and bringing my novel to its final published form.

AUTHOR'S NOTE

The Sixties were a time of hope for Latin America: The seeds of a more liberal society were being sown. There was no "movement" per se, but there was a stir among the people—an optimism, a naiveté that life could be better. The operating policy of the Alliance for Progress, at least in theory, was to provide technical assistance to developing nations in exchange for land reform, tax reform, and the establishment of democratic institutions such as cooperatives and trade unions. Young Americans were motivated by John F. Kennedy's inaugural speech, in which he made the famous *challenge,* "Ask not what your country can do for you; ask what you can do for your country." The Peace Corps, lay missionary groups, and USAID attracted many who wanted to make a difference in the lives of the downtrodden in these countries. Grassroots organizations were emboldened to act. Labor unions, cooperatives, students, Base Christian Communities, and political parties took heart that their day was approaching.

Underlying the altruism of the Alliance for Progress, however, lurked the Cold War and the "necessity" to extract support for "our side" in order to receive aid. Most of those working at the engaged level were either not aware of, or ignored, this aspect.

Fundamental changes occurred. The Latin American bishops of the Catholic Church, long aligned with the ruling oligarchies in support of the status quo, held a meeting in 1968 in Medellín, Colombia, at which they declared that the Church from that time on would make a "preferential option for the poor." This was confirmed at the 1979 meeting in Pueblo, Mexico.

From the beginning, reaction on the part of the oligarchies and their supporters developed; its intensity varied from country to country. The extremes are visible in the CIA-abetted overthrow of a freely elected president in Chile, followed by massive repression from which the country has only recently recovered, and in the bloody civil wars in El Salvador and Guatemala, but also in the mostly peaceable but still unrealized struggle of the people of Ecuador for universal social justice.

The conceit of this novel is the move of a Latin American country during the Sixties from cautious optimism to the edge of *tinieblas*—abysmal ignorance, darkness.

My story is set in Costaguana, an imaginary country invented by Joseph Conrad for his novel *Nostromo*. In his own author's note for *Nostromo* Conrad writes, "If anything could induce me to revisit Sulaco [the principal Pacific port of Costaguana] it would be Antonia." She was modeled on his first love, the older sister of his boyhood chum. "That's why I long sometimes for another glimpse of the 'beautiful Antonia'. . .going out serenely into the sunshine of the Plaza, with her white head, a relic of the past disregarded by men awaiting impatiently the dawns of other New Eras, the coming of more revolutions."

I have taken the liberty to revisit Sulaco "and the dawns of other New Eras, the coming of more revolutions." The beautiful Antonia, now in her eighties, plays a small but important part in my tale. Besides being faithful to the geography and history of Costaguana, there are other links to *Nostromo*: my protagonist, a second cousin twice removed of Nostromo, the *capataz* of *cargadores*; my owners of the coffee-processing plant, descendants of the founder who is described by Conrad as performing a yearly delivery of his coffee to the Amarilla Club of Sulaco and appears in a flashback; and Conrad's engineer-in-chief of the National Central Railway, who also appears in the flashback.

I am indebted to Conrad and hope he approves.

James Dette

Weehawken, New Jersey

May, 2011

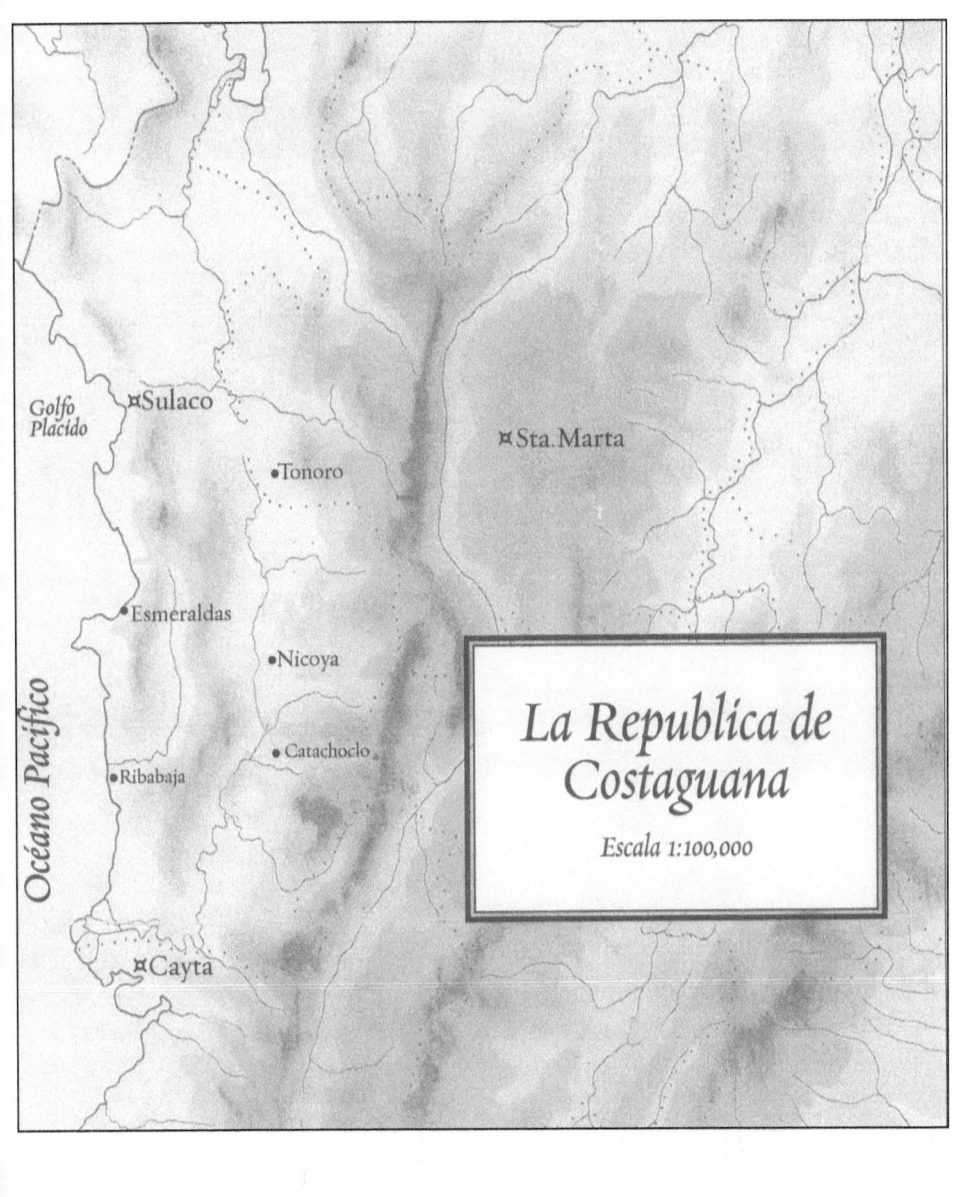

CHAPTER 1

S ERGIO FIDANZA, HIS HEAD PRESSED against the window, gazed at the passing coastline of Costaguana. Turning in the direction the plane was heading, to the range of mountains visible over the wing, he spied the majestic snow-capped Higuerota, Sultan of the Andes. He had prayed for a clear day, and it was spectacular. He stared for a moment, and then lowered his head into his hands and turned toward the window to hide his tears. But the gringo businessman in the olive green wash and wear suit, white shirt, and elaborate turquoise bola tie next to him was too busy making marginal notes on the papers he was reading to be interested in his surroundings. Sergio composed himself as he stared out the window, surreptitiously daubing his eyes with the cocktail napkin he had received with lunch after leaving Lima. After three years of exile he hoped that that would be his last emotional response. He remained fixed at the window.

In his mid-thirties, he had black curly hair and an ample but not bushy moustache. His broad shoulders strained the seams of a long-sleeved white guayabera. Julio Chang Crespo, Secretary General of the union federation FLOC, would be there to meet him. Julio was his one point of fixity in the universe. He'd gotten him out of the country three years before and been instrumental in getting him back. Julio was the older brother Sergio had never had.

The LAN Chile DC-6 began a wide turn over the Golfo Placido just west of the rocky peninsula of Azuera. As they passed Punta Mala at the northern end of the gulf Sergio had his last view of Sulaco, the second largest city in the country, before they landed. The airport had been constructed between the city and the harbor. The lights were coming on as a result of the short equatorial twilight, but he could still make out the cane shacks of the "suburbs," as the squatter neighborhoods were euphemistically called. As they made the final approach, the shadowy outlines of the Isabels, with the lighthouse on the promontory of Great Isabel, appeared to the right at eye level. He could make out the stationmaster's control tower when they passed over the railroad yards. The main line to the capital passed beneath them brief seconds before touchdown.

"Well, home sweet home," the gringo remarked in a heavy southern drawl as the wheels squawked, engaging the runway.

"Yes," Sergio replied, then turned quickly to the window.

"Somebody there to meet yuh?" The gringo hadn't had much to say since their small talk during lunch. It had been then that Sergio revealed his absence of three years. He turned back and nodded as he rubbed his forehead. The man mumbled something about the emotion Sergio must be feeling and busied himself arranging the papers in the briefcase that he had retrieved from beneath the seat in front of him.

As the plane came to a halt in front of the brand new terminal, the ground crew pushed the stairway towards the forward exit. Sergio, who had composed himself, leaned back against the seat with his eyes closed. "I'll be in town for a week," his suddenly very talkative companion was saying. "Stayin' at the Humbolt. It's the only one with a swimming pool."

"Yes," Sergio said. "They completed it just before I left."

"Maybe we could have a drink there after you get reacquainted?" the gringo offered.

"I'm not sure what my plans are."

"Well, here's my card. If you're free, just give me a call." Sergio read the card. *Dale (Bumpy) Cosgrove. Project Manager. Walker Tool Company. Equipment Sales & Rental.*

"Bumpy?" he remarked aloud.

"Yeah. In this business the roughnecks are likely to tag you with anything that comes to mind, and it has a way of stickin'."

They were in the third row of seats from the rear, so it would be a few minutes before the line started to move. Bumpy rose and retrieved his Stetson from the overhead bin. He held it in his hand after remembering that cabin height would not accommodate it and his six-foot plus frame. Peering through the window across the aisle, he remarked, "Looks like quite a reception committee for your ex-president."

"Ex-president?" Sergio excused himself as he squeezed across the aisle and slipped into the window seat of the empty row. A circle of men dressed in suits in spite of the muggy weather had formed at the bottom of the stairs. There he was in their midst: a tall, bald man with cavernous eyes. "El Dedo! On the same plane!" he exclaimed in Spanish. Turning to Bumpy, he explained, "Juan Carlos Vasquez Iturralde. That old bastard is the cause of all our problems. On the same plane! I can't believe it."

THE COMMOTION CAUSED BY THE return of the ex-president apparently distracted the immigration agents. Sergio received only a cursory review and was soon standing at a long low bench with his tattered suitcase in front of him. The uniformed customs agent was working his way down the line. During the British heyday of the maritime trade, the customs service had enjoyed special privileges in the port. They were smartly dressed in uniforms derived from the British, who, for all intents and purposes, still ran the port through the Oceanic Steam Navigation Company, the O.S.N., and commanded the respect of all who passed under their surveillance. Except for the upper echelons, navy blue trousers and a white short-sleeved shirt had replaced the uniform of navy blue kepi and tunic and white trousers with a navy blue tie. The kepi remained, except in the case of the agent who stopped and frowned at the businessman standing next to Sergio. His was under his arm, relieving its wearer from the oppressive heat of the low-ceilinged customs hall.

The agent murmured something. The businessman, obviously flustered, looked at Sergio, hoping for some assistance. Sergio leaned over and, pointing at the man's Gladstone bag, said, "He wants you to open it." Struggling with the latch, the man quickly complied. The agent rummaged through the contents; then, without further comment, he chalked a large X on the bag and the man's larger suitcase and turned to Sergio, who held his breath. The quarter-ounce bottle of Chanel Number 5 for his sister was in his pants pocket. The football for his nephew was in the shopping bag he had in his hand. The agent's frown eased slightly, and a flicker of a smile seemed to cross his face. He marked the suitcase with the X, and, turning to the next on the line, motioned with the chalk for Sergio to pick it up. As he did, Sergio turned to the still-shaken business-man and said, "It's all right. You can go now."

Sergio carried the bulging suitcase, secured with two leather belts, through the huge swinging door at the end of the hall. The high ceiling of the arrivals area offered immediate relief from the heat. He scanned the crowd as he continued toward the exit. The ex-president was at that moment being ushered by a huge contingent of hangers-on through the main door beneath the mural depicting the first flight between Sulaco and the capital.

"Sergio!" Julio was standing against a yet-to-be-occupied ticket counter not ten feet from the new arrival, with his arm on the shoulder of a dark-skinned boy of about ten years. The handsome face of the man, with his arms now outstretched, bore a strong hint of his Chinese heritage.

"Chinito!" Sergio dropped the suitcase, and the two embraced. Their heads pressed tightly together, they swayed slightly with the joy of the moment. Even the gruff secretary general had to blink back tears.

They finally parted. Sergio turned to the lad and asked, "Who's this?" Answering his own question, he bent over and embraced the boy. "Danny!" he exclaimed. He had recognized him from the photos his sister had sent him. Sergio held his nephew for a moment before he thought of the football. He reached for the shopping bag but stopped and looked at the boy. "Where's your mom?" The boy smiled shyly at the uncle he hardly remembered and glanced to his right. Petite Giovanna Fidanza de Arpe stood there, tears streaming down her cheeks.

Ten emotionally charged minutes later, the four were heading through the exit. Sergio was struck with the dank musty odor. It hung in the air, a sign that in three years the sanitary conditions of the suburbs had not improved. Julio carried the over-stuffed suitcase; Danny had his new prize in his right hand while his uncle held the other. Giovanna clutched Sergio's arm. She reached only to his shoulder, even in the high heels she was wearing. As they paused at the curb, a voice came from behind. "I see you found your friends." It was Bumpy Cosgrove, flanked by a not-so-tall American and a Costaguanero.

"Yes," Sergio answered.

"Well, if y'all get a chance give me a call." Cosgrove tipped his hat at Giovanna as he headed down the sidewalk.

"I will," Sergio said to the already turned back. Bumpy waved his acknowledgement.

"Who's that?" Julio asked, frowning. "He looks vaguely familiar. I think I've seen him around town. And the two with him."

"He was sitting next to me on the plane. Got on at Lima."

"With El Dedo," Chinito remarked, still frowning. He suddenly brightened. "You travel in fancy circles."

"Chinito! Over here," called a young Black from the other curb.

"Segundo, our driver," Chinito announced. He led them to the other side.

The wiry taxi driver stood waiting, ramrod straight with hands thrust into the pockets of his gray slacks. A slight puffiness of the face was in marked contrast to his lean body. As the four approached, he thrust out his hand to Sergio. "Compañero Chinito has told me all about you. Welcome home. You have your long-lost brother, eh, Doña Giovanna?" he added, smiling at the young woman who still had a tight grip on her brother's arm. "And you arrive with El Dedo. With all the people here to greet him, it's lucky there was any room in this poor excuse for a parking lot." Having taken charge of the overstuffed bag, he led them across an uneven field covered sporadically with gravel. "And look—I'm blocked in by some god-damn Vasquista. Pardon, Doña Giovanna." He indicated a tan Mercedes parked crosswise in front of his immaculate 1955 blue-and-gray Chevrolet Impala. He hoisted the suitcase above his head and squeezed between the cars. He reached the trunk of the taxi still furious at the lack of consideration of the followers of Vasquez Iturralde. After stowing the suitcase, he had a closer look at the Mercedes. "It's that priest-sucker, Licenciado Ribadeneira. He had the whole field to park in, but he didn't want to walk. Why the hell didn't he get here early like us? He's here with the rest of the Conservatives to see who can get their nose the farthest up El Dedo's—ay, pardon, Doña Giovanna, but I get so angry."

Sergio Fidanza knew at that moment he was home. Admiring the sentiments of the driver, he took in the whole scene with a smile.

"Calm yourself, Segundo. Vasquez has already left. The Licenciado'll be here any minute. Look, here he comes now." Julio indicated a short balding man in his mid-forties hurrying briskly across the field. "And hold your tongue. We don't want them to think we can't be civil." As he struggled to get into the driver's seat, the taxi driver grumbled something to the effect that the whole pack of them could go to the shit.

"Señor Chang Crespo, I do hope I haven't inconvenienced you."

"Not at all, Licenciado, we've only just arrived."

Shaking hands with Julio, Ribadeneira asked with a hint of incredulity, "Were you here to greet the president?"

"No. We had our own honored arrival. Do you know compañero Sergio Fidanza? He was Secretary of the Grievance Committee of the Port Workers. Only just arrived after three years abroad." Sergio's former post, and the length of his absence, made a statement that was not lost on the lawyer. Sergio shook the soft pudgy hand extended to him.

"I don't believe I've had the pleasure," the lawyer remarked without looking Sergio in the eye.

CHAPTER 2

GALO LUZURIAGA, GENERAL MANAGER of the Cooperative La Esperanza, was hurrying along Carretera del Valle, the road from the north. It paralleled the main commercial street of the town of Catachoclo, about a hundred meters to the east, and was indistinguishable from the other streets in the town. Catachoclo was at the end of the road—at least of the paved part. The road continued south in various states of disrepair to Cayta, there being little incentive to maintain it beyond the coffee plantations that extended ten kilometers or so from town. The road to the west had a gravel surface, extending for seven kilometers through coffee plantations and ending at the Chaco River. From that point on, people, material, and supplies were transported to the lands of the Arra'o Indians via a ferry rigged to a cable suspended over the river and anchored on two huge acacia trees. Of course the temporary bridge built upstream by the seismological investigation team might change that. The thought of change recalled to Galo the distressing news he'd heard on the broadcast from Nicoya the night before, recounting El Dedo's return that day from self-imposed exile. *That* might turn the whole *country* on its ear. Although born in Costaguana, the facial features of the general manager of the Cooperative La Esperanza revealed his pure European ancestry as did his height and slight build. His light brown, wavy hair was combed straight back from a receding forehead.

The sky was clear and offered some relief from the oppressive heat of the previous week. The few vendors on the side of the road eked out a living, selling watermelons, papayas, assorted soft drinks, cigarettes, and other sundries to the coffee truck drivers and occasional traveler. Their stands were of wood and cane with thatched roofs. The more substantial services, a mechanic, a tire vulcanizer, and the only gas pump within thirty miles were housed in concrete structures.

It had to be the day he didn't have one of the two co-op vehicles available to him that an early appointment with two Point IV advisors was scheduled: Charles Wiggins, the co-op specialist, who was a frequent visitor to Catachoclo, and a young engineer from that labor group. What was it called? Galo asked himself. Some long goddamn name that was even longer translated into Spanish. They were here to report on the status of the proposed coffee processing plant to be owned by the co-op.

He was picking up the pace when he heard his name called.

"Galito." It came from the direction of one of the stands. Germán Estevez, the general manager thought. He kept on walking without looking. "Galito!" The voice would not be denied. Galo turned and saw the man, in a straw hat, long-sleeved white shirt hanging outside a pair of duck trousers extending to the calves, and sandals, the typical dress of a day laborer, emerge from behind the crude stand. Compañero Estevez was one of the less successful members of La Esperanza. He had one of the smaller plots on which he grew, in addition to coffee, corn and vegetables for his own consumption and the watermelons he was now trying to sell. He probably earned just enough to pay for the permit for the stand.

"Germán, I'm in a big rush. I have a meeting with some Point IV people."

"They're already there," Germán advised.

"Already here?"

"I saw the green Jeep station wagon drive by about ten minutes ago. So there's no rush."

"No rush?" Galo took off at an even faster pace with Germán at his heels.

"Galito," Germán persisted, "I haven't heard about my loan."

Galo stopped and turned. "Look, the committee meets twice a month. The next meeting is a week from tomorrow. You'll know then." He continued on at close to a run.

"What's the hurry? Those Gringos will wait," Germán shouted at the retreating back of the manager. "What else do they have to do? And I'm *depending* on you, Galito!"

He's probably right on both counts, Galo thought. Managing the co-op was a responsibility that he took very seriously. Trained as an accountant, he'd gone to work right after university in 1953 for the Costaguanera Institute for Agrarian Reform and Colonization, ICRAC, the Spanish initials pronounced in typical Costaguana fashion, *ee-crack*. It had been created at the end of Camilo Bustamonte's first term. Many had seen it as a political ploy for his re-election. But the young graduates with socialist tendencies hired as staff, Galo among them, were committed to its success. Now in his late thirties, though he had left ICRAC to become the general manager of the Cooperative La Esperanza, agrarian reform was still his passion.

He turned down the side road, Calle Sucre. There stood the green wagon in the shade of an acacia tree alongside the canton administration building. Both doors were open. The two North Americans were standing in the shade of the tree, and the chauffeur was seated behind the wheel. The younger of the two waved as he approached.

"Señor Ingeniero Braun. Charles." Galo addressed them both, shaking hands. Then to the man in the Jeep, "Compañero Arias. . . . Sorry I'm late," he added.

"Not at all," Braun said. "We've just arrived ourselves. And please, call me Jim."

"Yes, of course. Please, come into my office." He turned to the chauffeur.

"I'll wait here," said Arias, anticipating the question.

"If it gets too hot, do come in. It is a bit cooler inside, I think." The chauffeur nodded in agreement.

The trio rounded the corner of the building facing the plaza: a dusty field about sixty meters on a side. The Church of San Agustín, an imposing brick structure with a bell tower over the main entrance, faced Calle Sucre, across from the northeast corner of the plaza. The rectory was to the left of the church. Behind the church on Calle Sulaco, the main commercial street, which separated the canton administration building from the plaza, was the convent and the clinic. A dozen or so palm trees had been planted in the plaza in what seemed to be in keeping with a plan for the future. Benches at the corners were the only other signs of the park it might one day become.

At that moment the roar of an airplane laboring to take off distracted them. "An airport right on the middle of town really amazes me," Braun remarked, pointing to the small air terminal with a short tower across the plaza. Beyond the building was the dirt strip of the municipal airport where the plane was coming into view over the church. In his mid-thirties, Braun sported a mustache a little darker brown than his close-cropped hair. About six feet tall, he was dressed in khaki pants and a khaki shirt with pinholes in the collar, suggesting prior military service. Charles Wiggins was about four inches shorter and twenty-five pounds heavier. He wore light cotton dress pants, a polo shirt, and loafers compared to the heavy work shoes of Braun.

"Yes. All the modern conveniences. Except we only have electricity from eight in the morning until noon and again from six in the evening until ten," observed the co-op manager. "How long was your trip?"

"About twelve hours driving, over two days," Wiggins replied.

"We stopped in Nogales," put in Braun.

"Well, you could have flown in one hour from Sulaco."

"Yes, I've done that before," said Wiggins, "but that would mean flying into Sulaco from the capital the night before. And the flight from Sulaco to here runs only once a week. A week is more time than we intended to spend."

"Well, the next time give us some warning, and we'll arrange a schedule that'll keep you busy," Galo proposed, thinking that with a week he might get some movement on the co-op's beneficio. "Or you could leave after four days by bus and catch a plane to Sulaco from Nicoya. They fly in there twice a week."

"Yes," observed Braun. "As matter of fact Charles is dropping me at the airport the day after tomorrow for the flight to Sulaco. I'm meeting my family there."

"But," said Galo, still thinking of the possibility of an extended stay, "you'd have to stay overnight in Nicoya. The plane leaves at nine-thirty in the morning." He shook his head. "It takes a week no matter how you look at it." Reflecting on Braun's comment, he added, "You'll have to be on the road by five-thirty."

"We're going to leave at five just to be sure," Wiggins said.

They walked through the entrance at the center of the windowless façade of the concrete block structure, which gave way onto a concrete-paved courtyard formed by the U-shaped building. A narrow arcade running the perimeter of the interior space protected rooms of varying sizes lining the courtyard. On the open side of the courtyard stood a wooden stage with a large sign, *Neighborhood Im-*

provement Board - Cantonal Council, across the top of the proscenium arch, and Costaguana folklore motifs on the sides. The structure at the far right corner of the U seemed an afterthought. It had two stories of wood construction with a porch on the second floor. Galo headed to that building. "Have you heard the news of the return of our esteemed ex-president yesterday?" Galo asked his visitors as they crossed the courtyard.

"Vasquez Iturralde?" Wiggins responded. "I'd heard some rumor that he might be returning."

"Well, the mischief-maker is back. We'll see what that portends for ICRAC." He led them into the back door and through the kitchen of the old house. It *was* cooler inside. They entered a large foyer with a desk near the door.

"Good morning, Licenciado," greeted the petite woman behind the desk. Gloria Manzano was the secretary for the ICRAC representative in Catachoclo. Hugo Robles, the previous representative, had resigned under a cloud three months before. So for all intents and purposes *Galo* was considered the representative, because a new one had yet to be named, and there was no one else to turn to. Galo made introductions, arranged for coffee, and proceeded upstairs. "I put the mail in your office," she called out before turning her attention to a squawking short wave radio mounted on the table to her right.

Galo Luzuriaga's office was a small room with two windows, furnished with a wooden desk, swivel chair, three straight-back chairs for visitors, and a three-drawer file cabinet.

"You're a lawyer?" asked Braun, having heard him addressed as Licenciado.

"No. I'm an accountant," Galo answered matter-of-factly as he sorted through the letters from his inbox.

"Like me, Jim," Wiggins noted, "but I haven't practiced it formally since I joined Point IV. I've gotten into cooperatives, or rather they kind of pushed me in that direction. I do enjoy the work, though, and the beneficio has us really excited," he added, glancing at Luzuriaga.

"Yes," replied Galo absentmindedly as he selected one envelope, laid it in front of him, and relegated the rest to the inbox. A knock at the door interrupted a comment he was about to make. A short muscular man entered, carrying a tray with three cups of steaming coffee and a sugar bowl. As he set a cup before each man, Galo introduced him to the visitors. "This is Pedro Varela, our porter." After shaking hands, Varela announced that the chauffeur was having coffee in the kitchen, and then asked Galo if there was anything else they needed.

"Thank you, no." Galo pushed the sugar bowl toward his guests as Pedro was closing the door behind him. Wiggins took a spoonful, Braun declined, and Galo stirred in three heaping spoonfuls. "Would you excuse me?" he asked, picking up the envelope on the desk before him. "This may be important." He opened the envelope bearing the seal and return address of ICRAC. It was addressed by hand in large bold letters. He smoothed out the letter, written in the same hand, and picked it up to read.

> *Friday, July 2, 1965*
>
> *Dear Galo,*
>
> *From what I've been able to find out, it's oil, but nobody's really saying it. Apparently some North American wildcatter with heavy financial and political backing. But something doesn't ring true. I wish I could tell you more. I'll keep nosing around.*
>
> *Sincerely,*
> *Margarita*
>
> *PS I'll be in Catachoclo the week after next.*

Galo looked at the date of the letter and decided that she would be arriving the following week. He folded the letter and returned it to the envelope. Removing a set of keys from his pocket, he opened the desk drawer and placed the letter inside, picked up his cup, looked at his visitors, and asked, "Well, gentlemen, what's new with our beneficio?"

Before either could respond, there came a knock at the door. "Excuse me, Licenciado," Gloria said, stepping into the doorway. "It's Hugo Rigpe. He's sorry to disturb you, but it's very important."

"Of course. Have him come up," Galo replied, and then to his visitors, "Charles, you know Rigpe. He's the chief of the Redheads." Wiggins nodded.

"Redheads. I've heard of them, but this'll be the first time I've met one," said Braun.

"The proper name of the tribe is Arra'o. You'll see why they have the nickname," said Galo. "This is getting a little dicey. He really should be talking to the ICRAC rep, but they haven't appointed a new one in three months, so he keeps coming to me to intervene. A very interesting guy, Braun. I'm sure you'll agree." As he was speaking, a short, barrel-chested Indian with a broad face, jet-black eyes, and prominent nose appeared at the door. In his late forties, his only clothing consisted of a rough cotton wrap-around skirt to his knees woven with broad brown and pale orange horizontal stripes and held in place with a wide leather belt from which hung a machete on one side and a leather purse on the other. A folded cloth of the same colors was draped over his left shoulder. He wore a necklace strung with bones, with matching strands tied below each knee, and woven straw slippers. His most bizarre feature was his hair, dyed red and plastered down to form a conical cap. He was probably the most exotic person Braun had met during his year in Costaguana.

"Welcome, Hugo," said Luzuriaga, rising to greet the newcomer.

"Thank you." The other two had also gotten to their feet and moved to permit the Indian to occupy the chair nearest the door.

"I think you know Charles Wiggins. And this is Señor Ingeniero Braun. I've asked them to hear what you have to say. They may be of some assistance." The manager of the cooperative never missed the chance to involve the gringos, even if it was not particularly within their scope of activity.

"Please to meet you," replied the Indian, offering his hand for each to shake. It was like grabbing a bunch of parsnips.

As he took the chair next to the door, Pedro arrived with another steaming coffee. "Strong," the porter announced, flexing the muscle of his right arm and winking at Galo.

Hugo immediately took a sip and smiled his approval, revealing four missing top teeth. They all watched quietly while the chief drank the coffee. When he finished, he smiled again and handed the cup to the waiting Pedro. "Good," he announced. Pedro took the cup, winked again at Galo, and retreated downstairs. The Indian's demeanor immediately turned serious. "Señor Galo, earthquake men break agreement."

"How so?"

"You remember many, many months past earthquake men come with ICRAC boss, Señor Chiriboga, for permission to cross river onto our land. Study earthquake, they say. See why earthquake come, they say. We say, we know why earthquake come. They say, that not scientific. They say, we build bridge in exchange for permission. We agree. But they build bridge five kilometers up river. Not convenient for us. Better here, at ferry crossing. They say river too wide, better upstream. They offer hire Arra'o men clear path in jungle. We agree." Looking at each of his listeners, the spokesman paused as if to let his words sink in. Before any of them could offer a response, he sat forward in his chair and continued. "Now they want go on Chiri Yacu. We say, no. *Never.*" With that he sat back in his chair, folded his arms, and awaited comment.

"What's Chiri Yacu?" asked Jim.

Galo explained. "About thirty kilometers west of here there's an ancient ruin. I'd been there several times after I first arrived, when I was younger. It's quite a trek. You take a path cut by the Arra'o. They're masters at this. You'd never know a path existed unless you stumbled upon it by accident. And even then without a guide you would soon lose it." He leaned forward and spoke in an almost reverential manner. "The ruin is quite remarkable. An archeologist who used to work for ICRAC and was with me on the second visit said it was pre-Columbian. There's a large square room about five meters on a side with walls formed by stone arches. One of them is still intact. Remnant foundations extend for about twenty meters from the main room. The Arra'o have done nothing to it but keep the jungle from taking over. That's all there is. . . . But it's the closest I've ever come to a mystical experience."

Hugo had been nodding in agreement as Galo described the ruin. Galo turned to the Indian and said, "Moving on the sacred land was forbidden from the beginning. The earthquake men said that it wasn't in their area of interest."

"Yes," the Indian agreed. "But now they say they must go on sacred land."

Braun, who had been listening with interest to the recounting of the Indian's tale, turned to Galo and asked, "What do the earthquake men do?" Galo turned to Hugo.

"They have big truck with big tall house on back," said the Indian, standing up and raising his arms to emphasize the enormity of the drill rig. "They make hole in earth." He bent over and moved his hand in a circle while making a growling noise. "Arra'o clear path in jungle and earthquake men pull wire like electric line through path. Then they make little earthquake in hole. Boom! They fold up big tall house and go down road made by bulldozer and make other hole."

"How long have they been at it?" Braun inquired.

"If you count the construction of the bridge, about three months," Galo answered.

"It doesn't sound like a seismicity. . .ah, earthquake study. Was there ever any mining in the area?"

"Only the silver mine near Sulaco, but that gave out about sixty years ago. I haven't heard of any other activity. Hugo, have you ever heard of any mining in the Arra'o land?"

Hugo, who had been listening intently, wrinkled his nose and asked, "Mining?"

"That's when they dig in the ground for something valuable, like silver or gold. Or even copper," Galo added.

The Indian smiled. "Only thing valuable is to eat, like ec'la."

"Ec'la? What's that?" asked the engineer.

"It's the Arra'o word for cassava. You know, it's the edible root of a small tree." Galo mulled the mining idea for a moment. "They'd be hard pressed to develop a mine in this part of the country. The area west of the Chaco belongs to the Arra'o, and it's thick jungle to the coast. Except for Rivabaja, which can only accommodate the coastal traders, there are no deep ports between Sulaco and Cayta."

"Well, it's not an earthquake investigation," Braun concluded. "I'm sure they're prospecting, and given what you say about the land, the only stuff that would pay off is oil. I'll bet that's what they're after."

Hugo had been following the conversation as best he could and had decided that his concern about the sacred land was not being addressed. "What ICRAC do about Chiri Yacu?" he asked very firmly but without any trace of anxiety. Hugo saw it very simply—ICRAC was the promoter of the deal, and now they were responsible to protect the Arra'o's interest.

"How many days before the earthquake men reach Chiri Yacu?" Galo asked.

Hugo stood up. "They must stop where they are. Go no farther." The others were taken aback by the sudden urgency of the matter. Galo rose and gestured for the Indian to be seated. He sat down but appeared agitated for the first time. Galo thought of Margarita's letter. But as a social worker she could do nothing, even if she arrived on the first flight the following week. He had to talk to Juan Chiriboga, Deputy Director for Colonization and his former boss.

"Hugo, I'm calling Chiriboga *immediately*."

THE GREEN JEEP MADE ITS WAY west of town on a road that traversed a gently sloping expanse of open land extending to low hills about ten kilometers to the north and as far as the eye could see to the south. Galo sat in the passenger seat so he could direct the chauffeur. Wiggins and Braun were in back with Hugo Rigpe in the middle. Galo had persuaded Braun to visit the drilling site. The young engineer, whose interest had been piqued by the Indian's story, didn't need much convincing. If time had permitted, he would have relished a visit to Chiri Yacu.

From the very edge of Catachoclo to the Chaco River the fields were planted in evergreen shrubs six to eight feet high, many with fragrant white flowers. "Coffee, Jim," Galo had said as they left the town. "What you see between here and the river is the result of seventy years of an agricultural development that began in the land around Catachoclo. That's why the town exists." A large rack truck speeding past in the opposite direction interrupted Galo's commentary.

"What's the hurry?" commented Braun, looking back at the retreating vehicle.

"He's taking coffee to the processing plant."

"The banana drivers in Tonoro are worse," observed the chauffeur.

"Can you imagine," observed Galo, "just thirty years ago they hauled the beans to the plant in ox carts. You might have seen six or eight of them in the road at one time."

"At least you wouldn't be taking your life in your hands," the engineer protested. "You were saying how it got started, Galo."

"Yes. Apparently before the turn of the century Catachoclo was a small center for the parrot and monkey trade with the Arra'o. A trader named Alfonso Palacios was making a regular visit to the area with a Colombian relative. The Colombian remarked that at an altitude of six hundred meters and with the gentle slope of the land, the area was perfect for coffee. Palacios took him at his word and decided to try his luck. Being well connected, he was granted thirty thousand hectares of land pretty much centered on Catachoclo. You passed through part of it on your way in yesterday." Galo turned to look at Hugo. "The fact that the Arra'o lived in this area didn't seem to stand in the way of the grant."

The Indian somberly nodded his head. "Arra'o live in all these parts," he said, making a sweeping gesture with his hand. "I born this side of river, but when little boy move to other side."

"Just like that?" the engineer asked incredulously. "They gave this guy thirty thousand hectares."

"Well, it wasn't exactly just like that. The government got a piece of the action. It was a good development scheme. They first exploited the timber both to clear the land and to finance the establishment of the coffee trees and construction of the processing plant."

"I'm surprised it isn't more prosperous, given the excellent conditions."

"Geography, Jim," said Galo.

"And politics," Charles added.

"You've got the coastal range," Galo said, pointing to the mountains straight ahead. "And no ports on the coast. The Rio Chaco would be a natural. It empties into the Pacific at Cayta. But there's a twenty-meter falls halfway there. There hasn't been any incentive to improve the road south, so everything goes north to Nicoya and beyond to Sulaco and the capital." He was interrupted by another truck roaring by.

"What's it like at night?" asked Jim. He was leaning away from the left side of the jeep.

"Fortunately," answered Galo, "they can't sort the beans at night, so the last truck is usually heading back to the plant before dark."

"What's the political problem, Charles?"

"There's more than one. Even though most of the original thirty-thousand-acre grant was distributed to the people who worked the land in the first agrarian reform, the family of the founder of the operation still owns the processing plant. Three years ago the UN established a worldwide quota system, and the government handed over the control of the Costaguana quota to the same family. This is renewed each year."

"And before too long, with Charles's help," Galo added, "we're going to take a piece of that quota right out of the pockets of those oligarchs for the co-op."

"It's the most exciting thing *I've* ever been involved in," Charles exclaimed.

1912

CHAPTER 3

T HE ENGINEER-IN-CHIEF OF THE National Central Railway has been trying to doze off. It is not an easy trick in a wagon drawn by four mules. But the unpaved back-country road is in fairly good condition, a tribute to the need to keep the region accessible to the ever-expanding population and the beginnings of a plantation economy. He gives up the attempt to nap and instead studies his driver and host, Don Alfonso Palacios Duque, sitting alongside of him. The plantation owner wears the suit of a businessman, albeit wrinkled, frayed, and dusty from the trip, complete with white shirt but without a tie. If he has any finer clothes, he is not wasting them on impressing the rustics who live in this corner of Costaguana. Though he does wear an elegant bowler tilted at a rakish angle, his pants are stuffed into very inelegant rubber boots. Except for the clothes he could have stepped out of an El Greco painting. He has the long thin visage, black hair, and somber expression of one of the attendants at the *Burial of the Count of Orgaz*.

As the wagon lurches through a stream-bed, Don Alfonso shouts, "There used to be a goddamn bridge here until the goddamn flood we had last year carried it away." They are the first words he has spoken since the end of his rant a half hour ago on the recent attempt to expropriate the 30,000-hectare plantation granted him by the honorable Don Vincente Ribiera, last president from before the War of Separation, by the goddamn Parliamentary Party now in control of the recently established Occidental Republic, for which he fought in the glorious defense of Sulaco, and in which the socialist and Italian bastards of the Democratic Party, even if they aren't in power, must have had some influence on the government's attempted expropriation.

The engineer wonders why he accepted the invitation to visit Don Alfonso's coffee plantation, thereby submitting himself to eight tortuous hours in a wagon with an obstreperous and volcanic rustic.

He is not the only passenger. Four Indians—two men and two women—have settled among sacks of flour, potatoes, garlic, and various other commodities for use in the household Don Alfonso maintains outside of Catachoclo. There is also feed for the mules and tools and equipment for the coffee processing plant. The two men, in their early thirties, are brothers. One of the women is the wife of the older of the two. They sit on the sacks of supplies and alternately converse in low voices or doze off when the road smooths out. The other, the teenage daughter of the couple, has just made her first trip away from home. She is sitting at the rear of the wagon with her legs hanging over, looking back. Her wavy black hair is pulled back in a long braid, which reaches down to the middle of her back. A round face with the bloom of youth still unscarred by the dreary life of the peasant bears a wistful expression as she ponders the wonders of the provincial capital of Nicoya. She cannot read or write, but her dark brown eyes reveal an innate intelligence. Now, after seeing a world heretofore beyond her dreams, she has begun to conceive of a different life.

Actually, the engineer knows why he accepted the invitation. The president of the National Central Railway made it part of the man's job to cultivate its future users. Don Alfonso is not high on the list of prospective clients, but he does present an interesting possibility. Coffee is a cargo that lends itself to transport by rail.

"Lunch!" shouts the driver as they pull up to a long, one-story building nestled under three huge cebu trees at the edge of a small hamlet. They have been following the Chaco River through a gap in the range of hills separating the Valley of Nicoya from the Valley of the Redheads, a tribe of hunter/gathers whose name comes from their dyed red hair. The government of Costaguana once regarded, and the government of The Occidental Republic continues to regard, the broad forested plain as the most feasible area for colonization. A dozen or so houses are scattered along both sides of the road. There are others closer to the river and out of view on the same side of the road as the hostelry where they've stopped.

The Indians jump off the wagon. The men are dressed in long-sleeved white shirts worn outside duck trousers that extend to their calves, typical of the Indians who have migrated from the sierra. The women also dress in costumes of the area, white cotton chemises to their knees with a dark blue outer skirt of wool. All four have brown fedora hats and are barefoot. The women disappear behind the building, and the men prepare to exchange the team of mules for fresh ones stabled at the hostelry. The engineer climbs down from his seat, leans back, and stretches his arms above his head to relieve the stiffness of the ride. His whipcord breeches are tucked into leather boots that reach to his knees. He has left his woolen jacket and brown fedora on the seat of the wagon. It is the first time off the wagon since they stopped to relieve themselves about two hours ago, the women scampering off into the trees on one side of the road and the men lining up on the other side.

"Don Alfonso!" The greeting comes from a large bearded man with curly black hair who has just stepped out of the low doorway at the end of the thatch-roofed adobe building.

"Jaime, I have with me the Engineer-in-Chief of the National Central Railway," announces the plantation owner. Bowing facetiously toward his traveling companion, he adds, "Treat him with respect. He is going to give us a railway."

"Wonderful!" shouts the bearded one. "I hope it runs right in front of my door. We will be ready when it comes, as we are now for such illustrious guests. Have the kindness to come in." Without further ado he ushers them into the cool, dark interior. The English engineer has to duck his head as he enters. Don Alfonso, a bit shorter than his guest, has his derby knocked off but deftly catches it before it hits the ground.

"I just paid five pesos for this," he growls, "and look at it." He brushes the mark left by the lintel with the sleeve of his jacket, leaving an even more unsightly smudge. "Shit. There's no remedy." They follow Jaime into a room with a dirt floor at the rear of the building. He directs them to a crude rectangular table with two long benches situated against the wall between two windows that nearly reach the ceiling and excuses himself. There are two other tables and benches in what serves as a dining room. The kitchen adjoins the dining room. The rest of the building houses a dormitory, storage rooms, and Jaime's living quarters.

Don Alfonso leans back against the wall and stretches his legs out under the table. "Some day, my friend, this valley is going to be pure coffee," he remarks with a wave of his hand, "but it won't happen if we don't have the railroad to bring the beans to market." He takes off the bowler and sets it down on the corner of the table.

The engineer leans forward, rests his elbow on the table, and considers his reply. He turns to face the other and asks, "Don Alfonso, if this valley will be all coffee, why will it take another three hours to reach your plantation?"

The older man mentally credits his companion for his astuteness. "It's all history now. I argued the same point with President Ribiera when I negotiated the grant. The bastards wanted to see if the valley could be developed. They knew I was very successful with my ranch in the sierra. Thank God, I still have it. I'd starve on the income from this operation." He is unusually frank *and* dispassionate in his analysis. "If I succeeded, then the President's *close* associates would have been given grants starting from here," he says, pointing to the floor. "Of course he didn't say all that to me. No. He said that it was important that Catachoclo prosper." He shakes his head in disbelief. "I haven't figured that out yet. It's just a shitty little town. The only reason for its existence is the parrot and monkey trade with the Redheads. The road beyond Catachoclo is barely a donkey path over the hills to Cayta." He pauses. "But now we are part of the Occidental Republic," he declares with both arms raised in a grand gesture. "Once the new government was formed, they recognized my grant, but they had different ideas on the development." He stops and looks at the floor, reflecting on his last comment. He looks up and says, "The only thing I could count on was Ribiera's promise to widen and maintain this road. And here's the man who's still in charge of keeping it in good condition." He points to Jaime, who has returned, carrying three pewter tankards.

"*Chicha*, gentlemen," he announces, setting a tankard of the homemade corn beer before each of the travelers, and one for himself. The engineer blanches. He's heard how it's made in the sierra. "I keep the barrel in the river. Nice and cool. Drink up." Alfonso raises his tankard in a toast to the engineer, who picks his up but is obviously not eager to return the pledge.

"Not to your taste, sir?" Jaime inquires, taking a seat on the bench opposite the engineer.

"Do they really make it—"

"By chewing the kernel and spitting it into a bucket?" Jaime finishes the engineer's question, and he and Alfonso roar with laughter. "Every gringo is told the same tale. The Indians used to make it that way a hundred years ago, and maybe they still do in the remotest areas, but we are not so uncivilized. We crush the corn, and add it to the water with just enough beer to start the fermenting process. I do have some beer, if you like?"

"No. This is fine," the Englishman responds, considerably relieved.

Alfonso takes a long draft and remarks, "Good stuff, Jaime." He sets the tankard down. "You must tell the engineer about your work on the roads. And while you're at it, when the hell are we going to get a new bridge back there?" he asks with a wave of the hand in the direction of the washout. Before Jaime can respond, Maria, the Indian woman, and her daughter, Gloria, enter the room with three plates heaped high with rice mixed with pieces of pork, black beans, and topped with a fried egg and a large basket of rolls. They set a plate before each of the men. As they turn to leave, Alfonso claps Gloria on the behind. They scamper out, giggling with embarrassment. "I think I'll get her to warm my bed one of these days." The Englishman's face betrays his dismay at the comment. Alfonso, not noticing, turns to the business at hand. "Good appetite!" he says.

The three dig in with gusto.

Jaime reaches for one of the rolls. "Courtesy of Don Alfonso," he says, displaying it for all to appreciate.

"There's no sense in the wagons coming back empty," retorts Alfonso. "But the trade in the goods we bring back from Nicoya barely pays for itself," he grumbles. "I have to plant a hundred hectares in hay and oats just to feed the mules."

"Listen to this, Señor Ingeniero," Jaime retorts, looking at the Englishman, "He pays nothing for the labor—"

"The hell I don't!" Don Alfonso slams his hand on the table. "I settle with them every year. . .on the feast of San Agustín."

"Yes. That gives it a certain air of sanctity," the big man observes with a smile. "But what do they end up with after you've deducted for the wood they gather, the water from the stream, and the grass their sheep eat?"

"They get what they deserve, Jaime," Alfonso shouts, emphasizing it with another blow to the table. "You're sounding more and more like one of those goddamn socialists. Besides, they're *my* Indians."

"*Your* Indians?" The engineer has been following the conversation with some incredulity.

"They came with the grant," he is informed matter-of-factly.

"What he means is," Jaime explains, "in return for the little piece of land they live on and farm, which happens to be on the land Don Alfonso was granted, they have to work a certain number of days each year for him. For which they are paid. once a year. . .on the feast of San Agustín," he adds.

"Where else would they go? What would they do?" Alfonso asks rhetorically through a mouth full of rice and beans. "I take good care of them. And how would you keep the road in shape if it weren't for the 'work party'?" Jaime nods in reluctant agreement.

"Work party?" After seven years in the country the engineer is still surprised by glimpses of the feudal society he finds himself in.

"All the residents—the Indians, that is," Jaime explains, qualifying the term, "are required to provide one month of labor each year to the government, which owns the land. The prefect of each canton keeps the records, and when we have repair work to do, he turns them out. Even Don Alfonso here has to provide his share."

"The government gives me the land, then extracts the profits right out of my pocket." He again slams the table.

"We could never build a railroad like that," observes the engineer.

"Speaking of the railroad," says Don Alfonso, raising the slamming hand, "my mules are getting tired of hauling coffee all the way to the station at Tonoro. It's 1912. I'm fifty-three years old. Can I look forward to it being shortened in my lifetime?" His voice rises with each comment.

"Well, we're about to finish the line to Santa Marta, and we've begun the work on the right-of-way from Tonoro to Nicoya," the engineer tells him. "But there are no plans right now to go any farther."

This time the plantation owner stands up and slams the table with both hands. The engineer winces. "We have the best goddamn coffee growing land in South America and no way to get it out. A river of no use to us because of the falls, Cayta is closer than Nicoya but it would take forever for oxen to haul the wagons over the hills, and the goddamn government's so shortsighted it won't provide what would turn this shit hole into *paradise*!" He sits down, grabs a roll from the basket, and resumes eating with a vengeance. His two companions do also. They finish the lunch in silence.

Jaime finally speaks. "A cup of coffee for the trip?" he asks with a twinkle in his eye.

Alfonso grumbles something incomprehensible.

"Tres de Mayo," Jaime adds. "The very best."

"Yes. The very best." Alfonso brightens a bit. "Every year on the third of May I deliver, *by mule*, escorted by my majordomo, three sacks of the very *best* of the best to the very patio of the Club Amarilla in Sulaco in honor of the glorious defense of the city against those Gamacho bastards."

"I know, Don Alfonso," the engineer recalls. "I myself have enjoyed many a cup of Tres de Mayo in the gallery of the Amarilla."

"Yes. The very spot from where we defended ourselves. Now

look at the thanks I get. They want to take my land from me."

"Calm down, Don Alfonso," Jaime cautions the older man. He turns and calls out, "Maria!" The older Indian woman, awaiting the call, rushes in with a steaming pitcher of coffee and a tray of cups. She sets them on the table and beats a hasty retreat. The three help themselves, reflecting on what has been said.

Alfonso finally breaks the silence. "We'd best be going. I don't want to arrive after dark." He seems to have followed Jaime's advice. He picks up his hat, places it on his head, and leads the way out. As he passes through the outside door, the bowler gets knocked off again. This time he doesn't catch it, but instead kicks it across the room and continues through without looking back. Jaime picks it up and hands it to Maria who has been clearing the table.

As they leave the building they shade their eyes from the sun, now high in the sky. A wagon similar to Alfonso's but drawn by only two mules pulls off the road under another cebu tree about a hundred meters farther in the direction they will be going. Enclosed with canvas fastened over a wooden frame, it is festooned with every kind of pot, pan, kettle, basket, container, farm implement, and assorted clothing. The driver dismounts and vigorously rings a bell.

The three men walk over to where Alfonso's Indians are busy checking the harness on the fresh team. "All ready to go, Su Merced," the older says, stroking the head of the lead mule. The women appear from behind the house. Maria hands the bowler to Jaime, and the two climb aboard the wagon. "It's not much worse for the wear," Jaime observes, as he presents it to its owner.

Alfonso puts it on his head and replies, "Five pesos shot to hell."

The two mount the wagon and, with a crack of the whip and a shout from the driver, the mules strain against the harness. By the time they reach the other wagon, a small group of villagers has gathered to inspect the wares.

NOW IT IS DON ALFONSO WHO is asleep, nestled among the sacks. The Indians, having ceded their places to the patron, are all seated at the rear of the wagon, except for Pedro, the husband of Maria and father of Gloria, who is driving the rig. The revised arrangements were made when they stopped to satisfy their biological needs. A compact man of medium height with short-cropped black hair, Pedro handles the mules with authority. The Englishman has decided that Pedro is the superior muleteer and discovered that he is the chief driver for Don Alfonso, making the trip to Tonoro at least once a month. The conversation is labored, Spanish being a second language for both. Pedro and his bride, Maria, migrated to the Valley of the Redheads sixteen years ago. Gloria was born a year later. Two other children died in infancy. The engineer is not sure of the chronology, but Don Alfonso apparently arrived shortly before or after the death of his third child. At that time Pedro became a planter of coffee and then a muleteer.

The road, which followed the river through the gap, has, since they left Don Jaime's hostelry, diverged to the east; it keeps to the center of the broad valley that slopes gently from the foothills of the Andes to the Chaco River now many kilometers to the west. Compared to the savannah north of the gap the area through which they are traveling is heavily forested. The absence of climbing plants and epiphytes, the number of deciduous trees suggest that the valley is subject to distinct dry and rainy seasons. They pass three hamlets located on shallow, braided tributaries of the Chaco. Don Alfonso barely stirs as they cross over the stony streambeds, a testament to Pedro's handling of the mules.

The road climbs a gentle grade. At the top of the ascent they are afforded a brief panorama of the valley stretching out before them. The driver points to a village about five kilometers off. "See, Su Merced? Catachoclo," he announces. As they descend, on either side of the road the undergrowth of the forest has been cleared and replaced with bushes two to three meters high, most of which are covered with white blossoms. The Englishman becomes aware of the strong fragrance of jasmine. Don Alfonso stirs, then sits up.

"We're home," he states, looking about. The mules seem to sense it as they pick up the pace without urging from Pedro. "Ha, ha! They can smell the barn," he remarks. He turns so that his head is between the two on the driver's bench. The blossoming coffee trees, planted on both sides of the road, stretch for another kilometer, after which an area of about ten hectares on the left side of the road has been cleared and the forest leveled. "There it is, the beneficio." He points to a huge wooden shed at the edge of the clearing nearest the road, where the pulp, membrane, and skin of the berries are removed from the beans. Just before the beneficio Pedro turns the team off the road through a large wooden arch with a sign declaring it the "Cafetero Tres de Mayo." They enter a driveway along the edge of the clearing. In one of the many drying grounds to the right of the driveway a half dozen men, using large wooden scoops, are pushing dried berries into a pile for the night.

The sun is just setting over the coastal range as they pull up under a huge mango tree in front of the main house, a rambling one-story adobe structure. The front façade has two large windows on either side of an entrance leading to an interior patio. To the left of the entrance lies a dining room, to the right, a combination living room and office. The left wing enclosing the interior patio contains the kitchen, storerooms, and quarters for the house servants. The bedrooms are in the one on the right. At the end of this wing stands a well with a pitcher pump and a screened washstand.

A man emerges from the entranceway. A woman has followed him but remains in the entrance. "Welcome, Don Alfonso. How was the trip?" Policarpo Zuñiga, the majordomo of the Cafetero Tres de Mayo, a swarthy, thin man with disheveled black hair and a large mustache, carries a black fedora in his hand. His dress is similar to his boss's but considerably less tidy. A mestizo, he was the majordomo on Alfonso's hacienda in the sierra.

"Uneventful," the boss answers. "I see you've made yourself to home in my absence."

"Not at all, Patrón. Just making sure everything is ready for your arrival."

"Consuelo not up to the job?" Don Alfonso adds, looking directly at his housekeeper in the entranceway. She stares back at her boss without comment. Not waiting for an answer, the patrón, realizing his hat is not on his head, looks around and finds that he had been sleeping on it. He picks up the crumpled derby from between the sacks and hurls it over the back of the wagon onto the driveway.

Maria, who has alighted with the others, runs after it and returns, attempting to straighten it out. She hands it up to Alfonso.

"Keep it!" he roars, climbing down from the wagon. "Five pesos shot to hell." Maria looks at the others, who remain noncommittal. She removes her fedora, puts on the derby, and beams with delight. The engineer has put on his hat and coat and retrieved his bag from the wagon. As he comes around to where Maria and her daughter are standing, he sees Alfonso and the majordomo in conversation. They both turn and look at Gloria. The majordomo shrugs, turns to the two men, and motions for them to move the wagon to the barn. As the women follow the wagon, he says to Maria, "There's work for the girl in the house tonight."

Maria nods. "Yes, Su Merced."

The Englishman is startled by the appearance of the housekeeper at his side. She relieves him of the bag and says, "I will put it in your room." She is a bit taller than Maria, but in other respects not very different in looks: the same chemise and wraparound skirt. Consuelo, however, wears straw slippers. "Dinner is ready, Su Merced," she announces to Don Alfonso and proceeds through the entrance.

"And we're ready for it. You are in your house, Señor Ingeniero," he adds, ushering his guest into the patio. He indicates the washstand at the end of the patio, where a young boy is lighting a lantern against the rapidly descending darkness. "We can get some of the road off us." The two men make use of the latrine and wash up. The lad is lighting a fourth lantern in front of the dining room as they return.

"Welcome, Su Merced," he says as he genuflects and kisses Don Alfonso's outstretched hand. The Englishman is not surprised at the reverence shown by the boy. It's a common sight on the haciendas in the sierra, with which he is familiar. He notes that his host is almost imperceptibly refining his coarse demeanor of the road to that of a landed gentleman. Almost but not quite.

"He's one of mine," the country gentleman remarks off-handedly as they enter the house.

The floor is paved with fired brick. The furniture has a certain country elegance. The dining table can seat ten but is set for two. There is a matching sideboard on the side opposite the window and a small worktable next to the door to the kitchen. A chandelier with three lanterns casts a soft light. Don Alfonso sits at the head of the table facing the kitchen; his guest faces the window.

The Englishman, yielding to his curiosity, asks rather abruptly, "Do you ever fill the table?"

"My family spends a month here during the dry season. The wife, two sons, and their families. I have four grandchildren. The wife refuses to spend more time unless Catachoclo gets an opera house." He laughs at the absurdity of the requirement. "She lives in Nicoya, which *doesn't* have an opera house. My oldest runs the hacienda in the sierra, and the other fancies himself a politician. That's what I get for sending him to university." This other side of his companion intrigues the Englishman, but the entrance of Consuelo followed by Gloria carrying a tray turns their attention to the dinner. Consuelo sets a plate of soup and a tankard of chicha before each, and they leave without a word.

Alfonso picks up his tankard and says, "Made here on the hacienda. Good health!" He salutes the other. Reassured, the guest returns the salute.

AFTER A DINNER OF RABBIT STEW and boiled cassava and a cup of Tres de Mayo coffee, Don Alfonso offers his guest a cigar. They light up and enjoy the smoke as they discuss a tour of the cafetero the next day and lunch with the pastor of San Agustín. Plans made, they retire for the night.

The engineer sets the candle on the table and closes the door of his room. It is plain, almost Spartan: an ample bed, the table with a chair, a chest with three drawers, a washstand, and a chamber pot under the bed. The louvered upper half of the door, with the window opposite, provides ventilation and admits the faint aroma of jasmine on the warm night air. Before removing his vest, he extracts his watch from its pocket and carefully stands it upright against the railing at the edge of the table. He notes the hour: ten o'clock. He takes off his boots and trousers and lies back on the bed. The events of the day finally overcome him. He sits up and blows out the candle. His last conscious impression is of the room bathed in the light of a gibbous moon shining through the window over his head. He is fast asleep before his head hits the pillow.

A moment later the moonlight reveals two figures bundling across the patio. Consuelo, with Gloria in tow, disappears behind the screen of the washstand. There is the squeak of the pitcher pump and the sound of the basin filling with water. A moment later the skirt of the girl followed by her chemise are draped over the screen. "Áchachay!" the girl exclaims, protesting the cold water on her body, and is hushed by the older woman. Minutes later the clothes disappear behind the screen and the women reappear. Consuelo leads her charge across the patio to the patrón's room. The door opens. Consuelo pushes the girl through the door and retreats back across the patio, extinguishing the lanterns before entering her own room.

The engineer awakes. His head rises from the pillow. He hears something and sits up. The moon has shifted so that the light streams through the louver in the door. Is that it again? he asks himself and gets up to investigate. Peering through the louver, he sees a figure go through the open door of the servants' quarters across the patio. The door closes and silence re-envelops the scene before him. He is unsettled for the moment but dismisses it and returns to bed.

CHAPTER 4

THE ENGINEER IS AWAKENED BY a knock at the door. "Yes?" he calls out.

"Patrón awaits you in dining room. I leave hot water for you." He gets up and goes to the door in time to see Consuelo entering the kitchen. He finds the pitcher of hot water on the ground outside the door, and decides that he will shave. Fifteen minutes later he enters the dining room. The air is still laden with the aroma of the cigars.

"Did you sleep well?" the host asks his guest. "And ready to receive the president of the republic, I see," he adds at the sight of the clean-shaven face. "I wish he were here to see how desperately we need that railroad."

Before his guest can comment, Consuelo enters from the kitchen, carrying a large tray with a bowl of rice, a large cube of cheese, a ham, a basket of rolls, and pitchers of coffee and hot milk. She places the food on the table and retreats without a word. "Good appetite," says the patrón.

The engineer pours the coffee and milk into his cup. "Have you thought of using trucks?" he asks matter-of-factly.

"Trucks? Over *these* roads?" The engineer is already sorry he made the suggestion. "Señor Ingeniero, we know mules. Mules are dependable. Mules eat oats and hay. We don't know automobiles, and we have no gasoline," Don Alfonso mutters, shaking his fork in front of his guest. "There aren't enough trucks in the whole country to carry one month's harvest to market. No. It's a *railroad* we must have." Having laid that preposterous proposal to rest, he returns to his breakfast. He takes his knife, slices off a piece of the ham, and chews it vigorously, extracts a piece of gristle from his mouth, and throws it to the floor. The engineer, resigning himself to three days of relentless pressure for a railroad to Catachoclo, helps himself to the ham and cheese.

Alfonso describes the process of preparing the beans for market, how the berries are picked, bagged, and brought to the drying beds. He points to the beds visible through the window. He goes into some detail about the operation inside the beneficio. "When all the chaff and other refuse are removed," he says, "the beans are packed into sacks for shipment. That's where your railroad comes in." The engineer nods in vague agreement. The housekeeper appears at the door to the kitchen and announces that the horses are ready. The patrón downs his cup of coffee. "Do you need anything?" the host asks. The engineer shakes his head. "Then let's be off."

Pablo, Pedro's brother, is standing with the horses under the mango tree across the driveway from the entrance. The engineer spots Don Alfonso's derby lying prominently on the ground in the entrance. Alfonso sees it and kicks it back through the entrance, shouting, "Consuelo, burn that goddamn hat!" The engineer is at a loss to explain the reaction, but the significance of the hat is not lost on Don Alfonso. He strides across to the horses. "Where's your brother?" he barks at the Indian holding the mounts.

"Tending the mules, Su Merced." The other cowers before the anger exhibited by the patrón, who mounts up without further comment. The engineer mounts the other horse, and they head toward the barn and corral about fifty meters farther up the drive.

A lad of about twelve years appears at the barn door. "Where's the muleteer?" he's asked.

"Don't know, Su Merced," he answers.

"And the majordomo?"

"He's at the harvest, Su Merced."

"Goddamn." The patrón stares at the blacksmith shop across the drive and then at the four mules of yesterday's team in the corral. "Goddamn," he repeats. He looks at his guest for a long moment and seems to change his demeanor. "We'll start the tour at the beneficio," he says in a more pleasant tone, then without further comment starts his horse at a quick trot down the drive. The engineer notices for the first time the canal that parallels it. They reach the large shed just as a worker is directing three oxcarts loaded with bags of berries arriving from the other direction to one of the drying beds. The two dismount and walk around to the side of the building where the water in the canal is turning a waterwheel. The patrón points out the gate on the downstream end of the sluice, which raises the stream of water, engaging the wheel, when power is needed. They enter the beneficio at the end, where sacks of coffee beans ready for shipping to market are stacked. Concrete walls four meters high support a timbered roof covered with thatch. The air is heavy with dust and the faint aroma of coffee. Along the far wall and in line with the shaft of the waterwheel are the machines that separate the pulp, membrane, and skin from the dried berries, and the ones that sort the beans until only the largest and best remain for shipment.

"This is quite impressive," the engineer remarks in a loud voice so as to be heard above the rumble of the wheel and shaft. "And particularly in such a remote area."

"And every last bit of material not found locally was brought in by mule: the cement, the machines. And these are the *only* machines in the whole process, beginning with the harvest and ending with the beans going out by mule, *not* railroad." Don Alfonso motions to one of the dozen or so men struggling with loaded baskets, charging and discharging the machines with dried berries and processed beans. The man snatches off his hat and comes over at a trot.

"Welcome back, Su Merced," he says, grasping and kissing the patrón's hand.

"This is the chief engineer of the National Central Railway," says Don Alfonso, gesturing to the engineer. "And he is arranging for the railroad to come to Catachoclo." The engineer grimaces as the worker takes his outstretched hand and kisses it. They spend the next half hour observing the operation. The engineer is taken up by the machines that separate the beans from the chaff and the relative simplicity with which they are engaged to the wheel shaft by the manipulation of a lever. The men go about their tasks without looking at the patrón. In the final step bags are placed on a crude balance, filled until they tip the balance, and sewn up.

"Is there anything else we can show you, Señor Ingeniero?"

"No," he answers. "*Very* impressive," the engineer says again as the two men leave the building.

"What you see took five years to build. But before that we had to clear some of the forest to plant the trees." They stand for a moment, surveying the scene before them. "I came here in '95. Let's see," says the patrón, putting his hand over his eyes. . . . "I was thirty-five. I left my brother with my father to run the hacienda. They were pissed when I took Policarpo with me. But it wasn't until '07 that we produced the first beans with these machines. By that time we were the Occidental Republic, and I had already delivered the *first* three bags to the Club Amarilla, *by mule*, and have been doing it every year since. Before that, we did *everything* by hand." As the two mount their horses, the oxcarts are making their way down the driveway, while the workers in the drying beds spread out the newly delivered berries. They pass the oxcarts, and the men stop and bow. The engineer smiles back, but the patrón ignores the whole display.

"The procedure isn't complicated. The main thing to keep in mind is to move as little weight as possible. It would be better to dry the berries near where they're picked, but that would require building drying beds." He turns in his saddle to face his guest and adds, "But first the railroad. . . . But what I need even *more* is more coffee *and* workers to pick it."

They reach the end of the drive just as the peddler's wagon from the day before enters through the arch. The driver waves but does not stop. Don Alfonso and his guest pass through the arch and turn left toward the village. The day is warm. Large puffy clouds drift across the sky, creating an occasional breeze. The horses, Don Alfonso riding a large gray stallion and his guest a smaller roan gelding, proceed at a leisurely pace, while the host describes the operation of the harvest. "It requires a lot of pickers as you will see."

About half a kilometer down the road, they hear voices and come upon a group of about two dozen men, women, and older children scattered down a wide lane perpendicular to the road, engaged in harvesting the berries. The pickers, with four-kilo waist baskets suspended from their shoulders, are the farthest off the road. One of the pickers, a young man with a strong tenor voice out of sight to the right of the lane, is singing, perhaps with one of the young women in mind.

> *The plowed fields, the planted soil,*
> *The harvest and his love*
> *Bring mirth to the Indio in this world*
> *in spite of his sadness.*
>
> *Wherever he may go, he sadly*
> *Plays his rondador*
> *Because in his heart there is*
> *but sorrow and pain.*

The words, in Quechua, are lost on the planter and engineer. Closer to the road a group of women and girls culls through berries spread on a cloth on the ground. Two men are filling a sack with the culled berries and sewing the top with coarse twine. They leave the sack on the ground with two others to await the return of the oxcarts. The voices subside at the arrival of the two, but the work continues. One of the sack fillers informs the patrón that the majordomo left some time back for another area closer to the village, which is also being harvested.

"Don Alfonso, are these the people you pay once a year?" asks the engineer. He tries to no avail to effect a tone of mild interest.

The planter bridles at his intent. "Don Jaime's socialist ramblings to the contrary, they get what they deserve," he retorts. "These people are *lazy*. It isn't *their* coffee, so they think there's no need to work hard." Unaware of the presence of his patrón, the singer starts another equally lugubrious song. The planter raises his hands in exasperation. "Even with Policarpo constantly at them, I can just barely keep the machines busy," Don Alfonso complains. "*And* if it weren't for the coffee, there'd be nothing to *pay* them," he concludes with an emphasis precluding further discussion. One of the returning oxcarts trundles into the lane. The other two keep heading south on the road. The driver and the two bag fillers load the three sacks onto the cart. "See!" the patrón snarls. "Now he has to wait until another six are filled." He pulls his horse around and, giving it a kick, heads to the road. The engineer follows.

Unintimidated, the Englishman continues the discussion as he pulls alongside the irate planter. "We have no problem with the workers on the railroad," he observes. "And I've heard of no complaints about the miners."

"You English are leaving yourselves open for trouble with your European attitudes," he shoots back. "I've heard that those Italian Socialist bastards you've got working for you are getting their syndicate ideas around. And they're talking to the port workers."

"I think it's only a matter of time before we recognize their union," the engineer informs him.

"Agh! *Stupidity!* Sheer *stupidity!*" Don Alfonso shouts, alarming the two cart drivers they've just caught up with. They snatch the hats off their heads. He pays them no heed. "I'd fire the lot of them."

"It won't work, Don Alfonso. It's a skilled work force. We'd never be able to replace them. But we can keep them in line. A few minor concessions are all it will take."

"A few concessions. Bah! If one of them ever shows up here, we'll concede to send him back in a box."

"They'll be here when the railroad comes," the engineer replies, rather pleased with the dilemma he's presented.

"Like the clap," observes the older man with a rueful smile.

PADRE ENRIQUE COLÓN, PASTOR OF SAN AGUSTÍN, wears a frayed cassock in need of a cleaning. His shoes are in similar disrepair, but his decidedly European features are clean-shaven. A shock of black hair with a tuft of white in the center grows low on his forehead. The second son of the former governor of the Entre Montes Province greets his visitors at the door of his residence, a small house stoutly constructed of brick with a tile roof. The engineer shakes his hand and notes the strong grip and the smoothness of his skin, which he attributes to its never having known a hard day's work.

"You are in your house, caballeros," says the padre as he leads them into a study in the front of the building. "Please, be so kind as to seat yourselves." He motions to two armchairs arranged before a desk and seats himself in a similar one behind it. At the priest's back a window opens onto the street and to what may become a plaza in some distant future. A silver pen, inkstand, and crucifix are arrayed on the desk. A breviary lies open in front of him with an unlit lamp to the side. There are a few more chairs behind those in which the guests are seated; the only other furniture is a bookcase on the outside wall next to the chair of the Englishman, who notes the titles on the top shelf: *The Bible, The Lives of the Saints,* Dante's *Inferno, The Way of Perfection, The Autobiography of Theresa of Avila,* and a thin leather-bound volume with *Rerum Novarum - Leo XIII* embossed on the spine. There are others on the lower shelves, but he cannot make out the titles in the dim light of the study.

"Well, Don Alfonso, it has been a while since you've graced our table. To what do we owe the honor of your visit?"

"I've come first and foremost to introduce to you the chief engineer of the National Central Railway, who, we anticipate, will grace *our town* with its services."

"May God hear you," the priest responds, nodding with approval to the engineer-in-chief. "And when might we expect this wonderful enterprise?"

"Well, there's much work yet to be done to bring the service to Nicoya," the engineer explains. "And traversing the gap will not be easy."

"Traversing the Andes to our former capital was certainly not easy," says Don Alfonso, not letting the Englishman off the hook.

"We will pray for your endeavors, Señor Ingeniero," the priest interjects. The engineer smiles at the reprieve.

There is knock at the door. A short, heavyset woman enters and announces, "Lunch is ready, Padre." She is about forty years old and has black hair worn in a long single braid, and she is dressed in the costume of the sierra, an embroidered chemise with a blue wraparound skirt. Over this she wears an apron.

"Thank you, Maria. Please, caballeros," says the host, rising and gesturing toward the door. They pass into the dining room across the hall. An undistinguished table seats six on equally humble chairs. Opposite the door stands a sideboard, above which hangs a nondescript painting of the Last Supper. The three occupy the chairs at the end nearest the window, with the priest at the head. A plate of quinoa soup with carrots and parsnips and a glass of naranjilla juice are already at each place. Padre Enrique says grace, adds a good appetite, and invites his guests to begin. The planter slurps his first spoonful and grunts his approval.

"And how are things at the beneficio, Don Alfonso?" the host asks.

"Barely tolerable," comes the answer accompanied with a frown and another slurp.

"Oh?"

"It's not that there aren't enough berries on the trees. I can't get these lazy good-for-nothings to get them picked. And our friend here is suggesting that they be paid. You might disabuse him of some of his socialist ideas."

"Well, he might have some support from our late Pope, Leo XIII of fond memory." Alfonso glares fiercely at the priest's remark. "Of course, I'm sure the Holy Father had our European brethren in mind," he quickly adds. "Yes, our Indians are but children in the eyes of the Lord. We must first teach them the ways of our civilized society."

"And that they'll get their reward in heaven," the planter says with finality.

"To be sure," the priest agrees.

"And when can I expect another shipment of *your* berries, Padre?" Don Alfonso asks his host.

"By the end of the week. . . . The church owns two hundred hectares just south of here," he says by way of answering the engineer's unasked question. He adds, "It's our only source of income, you know."

"Do you have tenants, and do you pay them once a year?" the engineer asks.

"Oh, no. We don't administer our land in that manner." He picks up a small bell from the table and rings it. "Our tenants are sharecroppers. We divide the income from the crop."

"And do you deduct for the water and the grazing?"

"Yes," he answers matter-of-factly, "and for the transportation of the berries. With the modest premium Don Alfonso pays us, we manage to get by."

Maria enters with a tray and places a plate containing a chicken leg and thigh, a boiled potato and an ear of corn before each of them. "The poor collation of a country priest," Padre Enrique says with a wave of his hand over the plate.

"Not at all," the engineer protests. "And the soup was quite good," he adds for Maria's benefit, who smiles as she places the bowls on the tray and leaves. The Englishman gazes at her retreating back.

"Our niece. A sad case," Padre Enrique adds, frowning and shaking his head. Alfonso rolls his eyes. "Señor Ingeniero, you must inspect the construction of our new church," the priest proposes, studiously ignoring Alfonso's wry smile.

AN HOUR LATER THE THREE MEN are standing in front of the adobe chapel that serves as the Church of San Agustín. The front wall, about seven meters across, is coated with stucco but still reveals the evenly spaced holes where the scaffolding had been secured. The wall narrows to a peak, forming a crude campanario, in which one bell hangs. The two wooden front doors are open, revealing an interior made barely visible by three glassless windows on each side of the chapel located near the roof. Three rows of pews arranged on either side of an ill-defined center aisle can accommodate thirty-six parishioners with room for many standees behind. Two women in black are kneeling, one behind the other, in the front left corner of the chapel, before an icon of Our Lady of Guadeloupe. The altar, a plain wooden table placed against an interior wall with a large wooden crucifix, behind which lies the sacristy, is separated from the congregation by a wooden communion rail. A lectern near the icon of the Virgin, fourteen wooden crosses hanging on the walls, seven to each side, and the sanctuary lamp provide the only other adornments.

Behind the chapel looms the north wall of the new church. "Our building fund is now sufficient to permit us to start the east and west walls next month," the priest announces with a certain amount of pride. "When we reach the middle of the chapel we will dedicate the new church and tear down the old. Come, let's take a closer look at our new wall," he says. As they reach the corner, a Redhead with a young, miniature version of the indian emerges from one of the shops that line the other side of the street.

The engineer stops. The two Indians proceed down the street, unaware of the interest they have engendered in the foreigner. "I've heard about these fellows, but this is the first time I've seen one." His companions follow his gaze.

"Oh. The Redheads," Alfonso remarks at the sight of the Indians. "You usually see a few in town. But on the first Saturday of every month they bring in the parrots and the monkeys they've caught for the traders who come in from Nicoya. That's how *I* first came here. With a second cousin from Colombia. He knew all about coffee, and the rest is history."

"Are any of the Redheads yours, Don Alfonso?"

"Hah! They belong to nobody," retorts the planter, missing the implication of the engineer's question. "Even Padre Enrique hasn't been able to evangelize them."

"Yes, it's true," the priest agrees. "One or two families attend mass on rare occasion. It's a bit of a scandal, since the women wear only a shawl around their shoulders. They speak no Spanish and very little Quechua, so it's hard to learn why they attend at all." The engineer ponders the response as he watches the two Indians in the distance.

"What do you think, Señor Ingeniero?" Padre Enrique asks as they reach the wall of the new church. Tall arched openings flank a semicircular apse. Pilasters together with temporary wooden struts braced against the rear of the chapel stabilize the single course of brick forming the wall.

"Buildings are not my area of expertise, but I'd say you were off to a good start."

"Wonderful," the priest exclaims. "We hope one day to have stained glass windows like the cathedral in Santa Marta," he comments, pointing to the two openings. "The sacristy will be here." He indicates an area on the west end of the wall. "And be connected to the rectory."

"Does this building belong to the church?" the engineer asks the priest, pointing to a thatch-roofed adobe structure behind the new wall.

"Yes. It's mostly used for the religious instruction of the children."

"Be sure they're taught to work hard for the salvation of their souls," the planter growls.

"As a matter of fact, two of my catechists are yours," the priest reports.

"Oh? Who?"

"They're brothers. Pedro and Pablo Quishpe."

THE LAMPS IN THE CHANDELIER, which had cast shadows of the two men on the plastered walls of the dining room, are hardly necessary as the day dawns. The engineer can easily distinguish the mango tree across the drive. As Pedro passes, leading the team of mules down to the beneficio, the guest pours himself another cup of coffee with milk and offers to fill his host's. Don Alfonso nods his assent. The planter adds two teaspoonfuls of sugar and takes a sip. "Señor Ingeniero," he begins with considerable gravitas. "I am concerned that you are not in agreement with the need for rail service to this valley."

The engineer lays his hand briefly on the arm of the planter. "Don Alfonso, let me summarize my position." He takes a sip of coffee. "My president did not encourage me to make this trip as a vacation in the countryside. We—that is, the company—are always interested in the possibility of extending our service." He holds up his hand as the planter starts to comment. "You've shown me everything there is to see of the operation of the cafetero. I've seen your production records. I can only marvel at the success you've achieved. But this is only the beginning. My president will have to meet with our accountants and eventually with the government in Sulaco."

"God help me! They'll certainly derail it," the planter interjects, shaking his head.

"Not at all. If it's economically feasible, we'll get the approval. But we can't get it on your petition alone."

Don Alfonso reflects only a moment, and then pulls out his watch. "We'd best get started. You don't want to arrive in Nicoya after dark."

"I'm ready. I believe they've taken my bag to the wagon."

The warm, damp breeze at their backs carries the smell of the barn and corral as they walk down the drive. They can see the men at the beneficio, hitching the team to the wagon. "One thought, Don Alfonso," the engineer starts to say, "if you ever need more men at the beneficio—".

"I need more *berry pickers*!" the planter shoots back.

"Well, perhaps this will help in that regard. I was going to say that there is talk that the silver mine is giving out. If it's true, you could recruit workers there."

"Troublemakers, you mean."

"Yes. But *talented* troublemakers."

"All I need is talk that the railroad is coming to Catachoclo." The planter kicks a stone and sends it flying into the millrace. "Not another dose of the clap."

The team is hitched and ready to go as the two men reach the beneficio. Pedro is standing on the far side of the rig. The engineer turns to his host and says, "Again, it's been a very informative trip, Don Alfonso. I've learned a lot, and I think my president will be very interested in my report." They shake hands. "My home is in Tonoro. Please be my guest whenever you are in the area." With that he climbs onto the driver's bench. Pedro mounts from the other side and takes up the reins. Without further ado, he calls out to the lead mule, and with a flick of the whip they are off. The wagon reaches the road just as the rising sun strikes the peaks of the coastal range. The barn odors give way to the jasmine aroma of the coffee blossoms, and the engineer resigns himself to the rigors of the long ride ahead.

The road is flat, and the team is moving at a good pace, even though the load is heavier than the one they pulled several days ago. The coffee is stacked six sacks high and covered with a tarpaulin to protect it from the dust of the road and any precipitation. They have traveled about a kilometer when the engineer turns to the driver and finds Pedro staring intently at him. Pedro quickly turns his gaze back to the road. A moment later Pedro rises to look behind. He resumes his seat in an obvious state of agitation.

He turns again to his passenger and, searching for the words, blurts out, "Su Merced, I beg you, please help me."

"What is the problem?" The engineer sees a look bordering on terror in the eyes of the muleteer.

"My child," he responds, pointing ahead to a figure on the edge of the road. "She comes with us." He stops the team, and the girl runs to the other side, throws up a small bag of clothes, and climbs up herself. Pedro turns and lifts a coffee sack from the middle of a row that has been stored on end behind the bench, exposing a space created by the bridging of the sacks above. The girl squeezes herself into the space and Pedro pushes her bag of clothes in and returns the coffee sack to its place. He calls to the team, and the mules strain against the harness. In a few moments the rig is moving at its former pace.

Pedro turns and looks at his passenger, who has said nothing during the entire incident. "Su Merced, I beg you—" he starts to say. The engineer nods assent, places his hand on the muleteer's shoulder, and extends the other to seal the unstated bargain. Pedro's joy is short-lived. The sudden sight of Policarpo, who has overtaken them, startles the two. The swarthy majordomo motions for Pedro to pull up. Words are exchanged in Quechua. Pedro remains stone-faced.

"Señor Ingeniero," Policarpo addresses the Englishman, "this indian's girl is gone, and some things are missing from the kitchen. The patron wants them returned."

"You can tell Don Alfonso that I've seen nothing of the girl," the Englishman replies, staring directly at the majordomo. The mestizo pulls at his mustache, contemplating a response. He circles the wagon, making a cursory inspection then, without another word, signals Pedro to resume the trip. The mules strain against the harness and begin the ascent of the hill that provided the first glimpse of Catachoclo several days before.

When they reach the top, Pedro stops the wagon and turns to scan the road behind. Assuring himself that the majordomo has not followed, he moves the sack of coffee blocking the hiding place. She sticks out her head, but her father cautions her to remain ready to get back in. They start the gentle descent on the other side of the hill. The engineer mulls the fitful sleep he had the first night in the house of Don Alfonso. "What will you do with her?" he asks the driver.

"I have a cousin who cooks in the home of a doctor in Nicoya. The doctor is a good man. She will stay with my cousin."

"But what will happen to you?"

The muleteer stares straight ahead. "I think nothing, Su Merced," he responds after some reflection. "I will have to pay for what he says is stolen. That is all. . .I think."

The engineer is angered by the thought of the muleteer paying for something that has *not* been stolen, just to satisfy the arrogance of a lecherous planter. He regrets offering the hospitality of his home to Don Alfonso.

1965

CHAPTER 5

SERGIO'S HEAD THROBBED. He lay on his back, observing his surroundings. The window in the loft bedroom of Julio's son faced west, sparing him the bright morning sun. The boy was staying with a friend while Sergio eased his way back into the world of Sulacan syndical intrigue. The room was spare. Other than the bed there were a chest of drawers, a table, and a chair against the wall opposite the hatch through which entry to the loft was gained. On the table lay the boy's books and school supplies; above it the only light, a bare bulb on a wire, hung from the ceiling.

He glanced at his watch, noted the late hour, and sprang to a sitting position. "*Oh,*" he groaned aloud, holding his head in his hands. He arose slowly and, taking his clothes from the back of the chair, dressed, then sank onto the chair to put on his shoes. After waiting a moment, he made his way gingerly to the hatch, descended to the floor below, entered the bathroom, and immediately relieved himself. He stood leaning on the wash basin for several minutes before splashing cold water on his face, sloshing it into his ears and on the back of his neck. Oh, that's good, he thought. He passed a comb through his hair and moustache and, briefly appraising his reflection, decided that he was presentable.

In the kitchen, Julio's wife, Luz, greeted him. "How's the

chuchaqui?" she asked, using the Quechua word for hangover, absolutely devastating at high altitude.

"Those guys haven't changed in three years. I haven't had so much to drink since I left here, and I swear to you it won't happen again," he promised as he sank into a chair.

"I've heard that before," she said, setting a cup and a cruet of coffee extract in front of him. "And here's some aspirin, but wait 'til you've had something to eat."

"No," he said, opening the bottle. "I mean it. After two months in Argentina, I gave it up altogether. *Those* people are crazy. Anyway, I think I must be allergic or something." He poured some of the extract into the cup and added two spoonfuls of sugar.

Luz took a pot from the stove and poured scalding milk into the cup. The aroma filled the room. "That'll fix you up." She was a small, attractive woman from a village in the Sierra. Her father had sent her to live with his sister in Sulaco after finishing elementary school, expecting that she'd get work and send some of her wages home. But the aunt had insisted that she finish secondary school, after which she went to work in the administrative office of the National Central Railway. It had been through her union activities with the railroad workers that she met Julio. When Sergio had first met her she had worn her jet-black hair Sierra fashion, in a long braid. Now it was cropped short, but still black and wavy. "Here, have some bread and jam," she said, pushing a plate with two rolls toward him. "How about some oatmeal?"

Sergio thought a moment, then said, "I think that's just what I need." She extracted a saucepan from the oven and a bag of rolled oats from the cabinet over the counter next to the rear entrance.

Julio's modest concrete home in the older suburb of El Milagro was built on the site of the cane shack he'd grown up in. The kitchen had just enough room for a small table and two chairs against the wall next to the entrance to the hallway. Sergio sat facing the rear door, with his back to the stove. The sink was to his right, under a window that opened onto the rear garden. He dunked a roll into the coffee and bit off a piece, then buttered the remainder and added a spoonful of orange marmalade. By the time Luz had cooked the oatmeal, he was feeling much better.

She poured herself a cup and sat down across from him. He dug a spoon into the cereal, took a mouthful, and then suddenly rested his head in his hand.

"The *chuchaqui?*" she asked.

"No," he said, not lifting his head. "This oatmeal reminds me of the farm in Italy. I think I ate it every morning for thirteen years."

"Farm in Italy?" She stared at him in disbelief.

"I grew up there. During the war." He wiped his eyes with his thumb and index finger. He wondered why he was so emotional. Ever since his arrival, he'd been moved to tears at every reminder of the past.

"I thought you were born *here*."

"I was. We went back when I was two." He dug into the oatmeal with renewed interest.

"I never knew," she exclaimed. "Why did you ever go back?"

"My father had a brother who was struck by lightning and killed. He had to run the farm until he could dispose of it. There were two cousins, but they weren't farmers. Before we knew it, the war started, and we couldn't leave until it was over." He took a long sip of the coffee. "We almost went to North America, but my mother's family was here, so we came back."

"I never knew," she exclaimed again. "What was it? Thirteen years in Italy, then three years in Argentina, and you still came back to Sulaco."

"The two cousins went to North America. They work in textiles near New York City."

"But you came back?"

Sergio shrugged. "It's in the blood. Once a Costaguanero, always a Costaguanero."

"The Tiger is glad you're back," she observed. "He was the first to arrive last night and the last to leave. Him and Iván Ramirez."

"Yes," the young man agreed. He finished the oatmeal and pushed the bowl to the center of the table. "That was good. The two of them were after me all night to take over the grievance committee again."

Luz picked up the bowl, put it in the sink, sat down, and lit a cigarette. "Will you?" she asked, waving out the match and throwing it in the sink.

He turned down her offer of a cigarette. "I'm here less than a week and they want me leading the charge. I'm still technically working for ORIT," he said, draining his cup. "They've told me there's a job for me here, if I want it. I need some time to think about it."

Luz stood up, reached over to the stove, and turned on the burner under the milk. "Those two are peas in a pod. Their whole life is syndicalism. They think everyone thinks as they do. My Julio's more like Antonio Bucci."

"Antonio Bucci!" he exclaimed. "I can't believe he's still alive, much less still head of the railroad workers. My father knew him. They came from the same province in Italy. Even courted the same girl. I'm told it took Antonio a few years to get over my mother marrying my father. He even quit playing dominoes in the saloon of an old Garibaldino where they congregated. My father was full of stories of those days." The feeling welled up again. Luz got up and shut off the burner.

"More coffee?" she asked. Sergio poured some of the extract into his cup and hers without looking up. Luz filled the two with milk and sat down.

"In the first years on the farm, in the evening, the hands and often the neighbors would stop in. He'd tell the stories of when he and my Mom were young. He was trying to keep her spirits up. They'd laugh. Sometimes she cried. Then he'd get her up and they'd dance around the kitchen. It worked. Mom got to know the neighbors, and we sort of settled in. But you're not interested in this," he said, catching himself up short.

"No, no. It reminds me of when I was a kid in the Sierra. We did the same things."

"Well, the war changed it all anyway. It was a rough three years. He was more apt to spend the evenings with close friends cursing the fascistas, and later the Nazis, when they confiscated the crops."

"I never knew," she said again, still surprised at the revelations of her friend. "Does Julio know about all this?"

He thought a moment. "Probably not. I'm not the storyteller my father was. And he's gone now fifteen years."

"And your mother?"

"She died within the year."

"Oh," she murmured in sympathy.

They each silently contemplated the meaning of Sergio's revelations. The hot coffee did wonders for the *chuchaqui*. "I never knew," she finally said.

An astute observer of people, the labor leader's wife launched into a commentary on the guests of the previous evening. But, the one person he wanted to hear about had not been at the party, nor had he had any reason to believe that she would: Margarita Bustamonte.

A FEW HOURS LATER, SERGIO was sitting at the bar in the Humbolt Hotel. The overhead fans did little to relieve the oppressive late morning Sulacan heat. "An Orangina," he said in reply to the bartender's inquiry. Cosgrove had said that he'd meet him in the bar at ten. He glanced at his watch. Five minutes after. The gringo's late, he thought. Julio had said to find out what the man was doing here. Don't offer any details about your work, but if he asks, tell him as little as possible. You've just returned. Not sure if you want to get into—uh-oh. Here he comes.

"Sergio, ole buddy." The man looked even taller than Sergio remembered, striding across the room with his arm outstretched. He had on jeans and an embroidered guayabera neatly tailored to fit his trim physique.

"Mr. Cosgrove," Sergio replied, shaking hands.

"Bumpy, Sergio. Everyone calls me 'Bumpy.' That looks good. Whattaya drinkin'?"

"Orangina."

"Oh? Well, I think I'll have something a little stronger." He turned to the bartender and ordered a gin and tonic. "And bring them out to the balcony," he added. "It's a lot cooler out there, Sergio." The two made their way to the railing where they could overlook a tree-lined boulevard that separated the hotel from the wharfs. "Who was the little lady I saw you with at the airport?" he asked.

"My sister," Sergio responded, frowning slightly. "They left for the capital two days after I arrived. It was all the time she could stay away from the business, and her son couldn't afford to miss any more school."

"The kid?"

"Yes." Next it'll be Julio, Sergio thought, glancing at his interrogator.

The hotel was located in the newer portion of the port, about three kilometers from the deep draft docks of the O. S. N. The coastal traders used the wharfs. Just below them, porters were unloading sacks of cacao from a barge. "Are they some of your guys?"

So much for the vague responses, thought Sergio. "My guys?"

"I heah you was with the port workers," Bumpy responded without diverting his gaze from the men on the barge.

"That was three years ago. It's no secret," Sergio added with a hint of annoyance, "but how did you know?"

"I haven't been spyin'," the other said. "It was really a coincidence. That Costaguanero that was with me at the airport? He happened to overhear a taxi driver speaking to some others about picking up a union leader that had been exiled for three years. When we saw you outside with the driver, he put it all together." Bumpy shrugged then added, "And *you* told me about being away for three years."

Before Sergio could comment, the waiter arrived with the drinks and a dish of olives. "Set them there," Bumpy said, indicating a wrought iron table next to the railing. "And put the tab on room two fifteen. And a dish of that popcorn." The waiter nodded.

"Where did you learn Spanish?" Sergio asked, going on the offensive.

"Well, I've been bouncing around these parts for four or five years now. I do pretty well getting around town, but when it comes to business I need some help. Where'd you learn your English?"

"At the university. And there were a few Englishmen still at the O. S. N. before I left." Sergio didn't mention the trips to the States when he worked for ORIT in Argentina. "As for the men unloading the barge, they're tough to organize. They wander the wharfs looking for jobs, do the work, get paid, and go to the bars and drink it up." The two sat. The wrought iron chairs made a clattering noise as they pulled them up to the table. Sergio took a sip and set the glass down. "About two years before I left, a nun was making some headway with them."

"A nun?" Bumpy pulled his head back, not sure he'd heard correctly.

"Yes. Sor Marillac. She was with a French order that ran a school that's just a few blocks from here," Sergio responded, waving in the general direction. "They still run it. After classes she got to wandering the wharfs, talking to the men. She got the order to let her use the courtyard for meetings after the kids left. She knew her stuff." The waiter arrived with the popcorn. Sergio picked a few olives from the dish, and the other helped himself to a handful of the corn.

"After about a year and a half getting their confidence, she came to us for assistance. All she wanted was money to buy them caps and badges. We were happy to help." Sergio stroked his moustache, smiling at the thought. "It's amazing. If one of our organizers was doing it, he'd have been spending money like a drunken sailor and getting nowhere."

"Is she still at it?"

"Well, about that time the military was beginning to stray from the barracks. With some reason. Our esteemed president, El Dedo, the one on our plane, was making a complete mess of it. The generals forced him out, leaving us a vice-president with a *big* drinking problem. The port workers and the teamsters called a general strike, and the iron fist came down right in the middle of Sulaco." He stood up as he made the last comment and stepped to the railing. Some of the workers below were opening the sacks and raking the beans out onto the cobblestone pavement of the wharf to dry in the sun. He leaned over for a moment before he turned to face his companion, who was draining his glass. Bumpy motioned to the bartender for another round then turned back to Sergio.

"Why'd they pick on you?" he asked matter-of-factly.

"Let's just say I was keeping bad company at the time," Sergio told him, cutting short any further revelations. He mentally chastised himself for being so forthright and wondered why he had been.

"No problem. I didn't mean to pry. And the nun?"

Sergio sat down again. The waiter replaced the empties and set down another dish of olives and a bowl of popcorn. "From what I'm told, the nuns decided to close down the activity. They were a foreign order and didn't want to jeopardize their welcome. They transferred her to a school in the Sierra. And the caps and badges gradually disappeared," he concluded, shaking his head. "She really knew what she was doing."

"Where I come from, the nuns stick to their prayin'."

Seizing the opportunity, Sergio asked, "And where *do* you come from?"

"Houston," he answered, grabbing another handful of popcorn. "Oil?"

"In the blood. My daddy was a wildcatter. Owned his own rig," the Texan added with more than a hint of pride. "He'd bring me out to the fields every chance he got. I remember my first gusher. Just like the movies. Rainin' oil on everybody. My daddy was furious. Runnin' around shoutin', watchin' that stuff goin' to waste." Bumpy took a pull on the drink. "Wouldn't let me work out there but summers. He sent me off to the A and M. I got me a degree in geology."

"What brings you here?" Sergio asked, determined to make up for lost time. "The little oil we have is in the Orient."

"Maybe so. My daddy had a knack of findin' it where everybody said it wasn't. I guess I've inherited some from him."

"Where're you looking?"

"Hey! That's the sixty-four dollar question. Let's just say it's somewhere south of the Mason-Dixon Line." Sergio gave him a quizzical look. "Oh, that's the line that marked the North from the South before the Civil War. I guess it still does. Old wounds never seem to heal."

"We've got a few of those here."

"How so?"

Before Sergio could answer they were interrupted by a group of Costaguaneros seating themselves at a nearby table, the clatter of chairs made it impossible to hear. One of the group nodded toward their table. It was the Licenciado with the Mercedes Benz. Sergio was struggling to remember his name when Bumpy got up to greet the newcomers. It seemed he knew the Licenciado and at least one of the others. Sergio, who had not gotten up, noted that his host was coping admirably with the Spanish. After a brief exchange Bumpy returned to the table with the lawyer. "Licenciado Ribadeneira, here, says he knows you." Sergio got up and shook the limp hand extended to him. He wondered how a man with such a handshake could do business, let alone convince a client that he had the ability to get out of his own way. The pudgy man apologized again for any inconvenience he might have caused that previous day and excused himself.

"He's helping me with—well, it don't matter. What were we talking about? Oh, yeah. You were saying that you had your own war wounds."

Bumpy's apparent guilelessness unnerved Sergio. He could not shake the feeling that he was being somehow—how did they say it?—suckered. He continued his Costaguana history lesson with the feeling that he was telling his companion something he already knew. "This whole coastal area was, for about fifteen years in the early nineteen hundreds, the Occidental Republic," he said with a verbal flourish. "But the War of Reunification ended that."

"Never heard of it."

"Most people aren't even aware of the Occidental War of Separation and the silver mine that started it. But if you've had any schooling in the littoral, *you know.*"

Sergio gave a brief account of the silver mine owned and operated by an Englishman, financed by U.S. bankers, and the fabulous wealth it generated. So much wealth that the Sulacans thought that it would be better all around if they set up an independent country. So they fought a war and won. After ten years or so the mine gave out as quickly as it had been developed. The president of Costaguana at the time, under pressure from the military, decided to reunite the country. Without the silver, most of which had wound up in England and the U.S., there was little resistance.

"So now we're one country again. There are those who, for reasons of personal wealth, or the lack of it, care very much. I don't. As far as I'm concerned, the history of this country has been written by the generals, whose only interest is to suck whatever they can out of it to fill their pockets." He stopped suddenly and frowned. "That's a simplification. If you're really interested, I can recommend one book that is fairly objective. It's a memoir written by Doña Antonia Avellanos. It's not even about the war, but it has more to say than any history book. If my father were alive, he could regale you with stories about a second cousin once removed who, he says, was a hero of the war of independence. But his name doesn't appear in any history book." Sergio drained his glass and began to chew on the ice cubes. He looked again at the other man, guessed that he was in his early fifties. That, and his blue eyes and graying black hair, wasn't enough to distinguish him from most of the other Texans who passed through Sulaco. "So much for my heroic cousin," he said, putting a period to the lesson.

They both sat quietly, watching a gull circle the balcony. It suddenly swooped down on the table of the licenciado and his friends, snatching a french fry from the plate in the middle. They all jumped and flailed the air to rid themselves of the intruder. Sergio laughed. "It's their sport, the hungry devils." The bartender came running and apologized profusely for something quite out of his control. He picked up the plate, promising to bring a fresh one immediately. Bumpy caught his eye and, after confirming that Sergio wasn't having another, asked to sign the check.

"I'm sure glad you called. It's always nice to know some of the folks when you're visiting." The strange feeling enveloped Sergio again. "And I got a history lesson, too. What was the name of that woman?"

"Doña Antonia Avellanos. You'll find it in any bookstore. It's one of our few classics."

After making their good-byes Sergio left immediately, but Cosgrove lingered at the bar signing the check. Licenciado Ribadeneira excused himself and came over to Bumpy. "Cosgrove," he said, "I'll be finishing up in half an hour. Would you like to meet here rather than in my office this afternoon?"

Bumpy looked at his watch. "Sounds like a good idea. Come up to my room when you're done." Without another word the two men parted.

SERGIO HAD MADE A DETOUR as he left the hotel that brought him to Escuela San Tomé, the school of the French nuns. The children were playing in the yard on their lunch hour. An ancient nun, overseeing the activity, was being hugged by two little girls standing at either side of her. "Good afternoon, sister," he greeted her from behind. The three pivoted around as one to see who was speaking.

"Good afternoon, sir," she replied. The girls giggled.

"I'm inquiring of a friend. Sor Marillac?"

"She's no longer here, sir. For three years now." The nun gave her charges an affectionate pat and sent them back to their comrades.

"Is she still in the country?"

"*Bien sûre, monsieur.* She is in our mission station at Catachoclo."

"Oh," Sergio replied. "I know the area. I knew Sor Marillac when she was active with the unions."

The nun glanced quickly in the direction of the school and then back at Sergio. "She's still at it," she offered, beaming with pride.

"COME ON IN," THE TEXAN called out in response to the knock on the door. "It's open." The lawyer entered the room and took a seat across from his client at the table that stood in front of open French doors leading to a very narrow balcony overlooking an indoor swimming pool. A faint odor of chlorine wafted through the doors. The room was modestly furnished with a double bed and two night stands on the wall adjacent to the doors, an ample credenza with a mirror opposite the bed, and the table with two chairs at which they sat. A tray on the table held two glasses, a bucket of ice, a bottle of Tanqueray, and two bottles of tonic.

"Can I offer you a drink?" Bumpy asked, motioning toward the bottle of gin.

"Just the tonic, thank you."

Bumpy put three cubes of ice in each glass and poured the soda. "Well, what do you heah?" he asked, as he added a splash of the gin to his. Ribadeneira took a long sip and returned his glass to the table without making eye contact.

"My associate is still working on it," he answered, fingering the briefcase he was still holding in his lap.

"Working on it?" Bumpy raised his voice ever so slightly. "They'll be ready to go on that land next week. It's key to the survey."

CHAPTER 6

IT HAD NOT BEEN HIS INTENT when he left the schoolyard after his brief chat with the old nun, but a half hour later Sergio found himself across the street from the port workers' union hall. The building, on Avenida de La Muelle one block from the main entrance of the Oceanic Steam Navigation Company, was no beauty, but it was functional. A sign twenty feet wide stretched above the doorway, read *The Port Workers' Union* in thirty-centimeter-high letters, and beneath, *Established 1916*. The union had been founded just before the end of the War of Reunification. The O.S.N. had not discouraged the movement, hoping that its existence would ameliorate any attempt to take over the company by the new government. Under the sign gaped the entrance to the commissary, the pride of the union. Just inside stood two refrigerated display cases that served as the counter, behind which steel shelves extended under a five-meter-high ceiling to the rear wall of what had formerly been a animal hide warehouse. The shelves were loaded with crates of eggs, sacks of rice, cartons of Maggi dried soup, cases of V-8 juice, cans of vegetables, jars of cooking oil, and more—basic foodstuffs at modest prices to the members. Behind the display cases stood Paco Fuentes, the chief clerk, cigarette dangling from his lip, pencil tucked behind his ear. He was attending to a girl of about twelve who stood in front of a large basket that Paco was filling with merchandise. He carefully placed a bag of eggs on top of a bag of rice he had just weighed out on the scale at the end of the display case, and two cans of pinto beans.

At a counter tucked in behind the wall to the right of the entrance, Sergio caught a glimpse of Magda Ponce next to the cash register. Her hair was still blonde but teased up in the latest fashion. He had started to cross the street, practically deserted in the heat of midday, when the now-familiar wave of nostalgia washed over him. He decided to wait until it passed. But the few steps he'd taken permitted him to observe that Magda was engaged in a conversation with a very pretty young woman who was gently rocking a stroller. She was wearing a sleeveless brown dress with a pleated skirt. Her hair was blonde, too, and swept up into what was called a "beehive" in Buenos Aires, apparently the rage in the United States. Standing next to her and holding her hand was a little girl of about three. They were Americans, he was sure. Strollers were not a common sight in Sulaco.

His nostalgia was quickly replaced by curiosity. He crossed the street and paused at the side of the huge doorway opposite the cash register. Paco was leaning over the counter, handing the basket to the girl, who took it over to Magda to pay for the groceries. The American pushed the stroller away from the cashier so the girl could complete her transaction. Paco turned to an older woman who had been waiting to be served. Glancing at Sergio, his jaw dropped. He boosted himself up onto the counter, swung his legs around, and jumped to the ground, shouting, "Magda! Look who's here!"

In the next moment he was vigorously shaking Sergio's hand and clapping him on the back. Magda, constrained from following Paco by her tight skirt, stood at her station, waving her hands and squealing, "*Oooooh.*"

Sergio leaned over the counter and embraced her. She hugged him without letting go until he finally cried, "You're strangling me!"

In the excitement of the reunion, the older child had sought the protection of her mother's skirt, and the little girl in the stroller began to suck rapidly on the pacifier that had been hanging from her mouth as she slept. As Sergio was released from Magda's grip he fell backward, bumping into the American. "I'm so sorry," he apologized.

Paco started the introduction but was cut short, having forgotten the strange name.

"Braun," the young woman put in, extending her hand.

Taking it, he said, "Sergio Fidanza. At your service."

"And her husband is upstairs, visiting the Tiger," added Magda.

"The Tiger?" Mrs. Braun asked quizzically.

"René Andrade. The Tiger is a nickname," Sergio explained. "What lovely children," he added, leaning over toward the older, who retreated a step farther into her mother's skirt.

"I'm afraid they're both a little tired. We've been walking around all morning."

"Where are you staying?"

"At the Humboldt. Just down The Malecón."

She speaks very good Spanish, he thought. "Oh? Have you run into Mr. Cosgrove? From Texas, I believe."

"Yes. My husband . . . . Oh, here he is." Jim Braun, the engineer from the American Institute for Free Labor Development, entered the commissary. The older girl immediately held out her arms to him. He picked her up as his wife said, "Jim, this is Sergio. . . . I'm afraid I've forgotten your last name."

"Fidanza. Pleased to meet you," said Sergio, extending his hand. Jim shifted the child to his left arm and shook hands. "You've been up with the Tiger. I hope he's in good humor."

"Quite good, I'd say. We were discussing some assistance he's giving us in a course in collective bargaining for the FLOC."

Collective bargaining? wondered Sergio. Whatever could René offer in the way of new thinking in that area? Bargaining had never been too confrontational between the union and the O.S.N. "FLOC? Then you must know my friend Julio Chang Crespo."

The child in his arms began to squirm. "Fidanza! You're his friend who's just returned from Argentina. I'm with The American

Institute for Free Labor Development."

"Daddy, when are we going?" the child asked.

"Right now," he answered, settling the girl in the jump seat behind her sister. "Look. We must be getting back to the hotel. The children are very tired. We'll be here for another day, though. Maybe we can get together."

"It will be my pleasure," Sergio responded. Extending his hand to Mrs. Braun, he said, "You have a lovely family." He watched the couple walk off in the direction of the hotel then turned back to Paco and Magda. "I met his former boss in Buenos Aires. He told me that I would probably run into him, but I didn't think it would be so soon."

"He's been here before, but it's the first time for the Missus," Paco noted.

"She's so nice, and she speaks such good Spanish, and the children are precious." Magda was obviously taken with the visitors.

"It looks like you're busy," Sergio said. A man and a young woman had joined the older woman and were waiting patiently for the visitors to leave. Another vigorous handshake and a clap on the back, and Paco boosted himself over the counter. Magda insisted on another hug before Sergio could leave for his inevitable meeting with the Tiger.

He climbed the long staircase, which opened onto a large hall with windows on three sides and a raised dais opposite the street on the fourth. The wall behind the dais was decorated with the flags of Costaguana and the Oceanic Steam Navigation Company on either side of a huge oil of bewhiskered patriots from the days of the War of Separation. Arrayed outboard of the flags hung ancient photographs of the port and the railroad loading area. The folding chairs, in place for a meeting, could accommodate a hundred and fifty.

The hall was also used for smaller social gatherings, but they had to rent the nuns' schoolyard on the other side of the school building for the huge annual dance. The nuns could use the generous stipend they received yet avoid witnessing the scandalous behavior of some of the membership, although Sergio had always suspected that the younger ones found an excuse for retrieving something from their classrooms during the affair.

He entered the door to the right of the dais. Hector Rivera sat at a typing stand behind a desk piled with files, a stack of correspondence trays, a carousel of rubber stamps, a stapler, and a litter of envelopes, some opened and some not. A black telephone hung on the wall within easy reach. Two filing cabinets, upon which rested a large wall clock that read 12:45, stood in the corner. Squeezed into the other corner was a small desk for the secretary next to the open floor-to-ceiling window that provided much needed ventilation. High ceilings and windows made life tolerable during the Sulacan dry season. The window faced east, with a view of Higuerota on rare clear days. Julio had mentioned that she was new and that typing was neither her forte nor her principal duty. Her chair was vacant. Out to lunch, Sergio suspected.

Hector, dressed in a short-sleeved white shirt and dark tie, looked up from the typewriter. "Sergio," he said, getting up and extending his hand. "The Tiger said that you were back. He's got your office ready for you."

"I know," Sergio replied, "but theoretically I'm still on the ORIT payroll."

"Two paychecks are better than one," the other observed.

"Until you get caught," Sergio said with a frown. "Is he in?"

"He's with the girl," said Hector, motioning towards the desk in the corner. "I'll let him know you're here." He picked up the phone and dialed. "It's Compañero Fidanza." Hector smiled, then hung up. "He said to go right in."

He couldn't be too involved. The gringo had just left, Sergio thought, as he opened the door at the far end of the office. He found himself in a large room with ten small desks and chairs arrayed in two rows. These constituted the "offices" of the various union officials, unoccupied at the moment. The officials also had responsibilities in the port. The walls were lined with file cabinets and shelves on which lay an assortment of books, pamphlets, files, and reports describing and recording the work of the port workers union on behalf of the membership. He had occupied the desk nearest the door of the Tiger's office, which opened as he approached.

She wore a dress not unlike the one worn by Mrs. Braun but lighter in color, which she was smoothing into place with her left hand. The other clutched a stenographer's note pad. Maybe Julio was a bit hasty in his judgment, he thought. Skimpier on top, the dress revealed the graceful figure of a coastal native. Grace was the word for everything about them: the way they walked, gestured, and spoke. "Good afternoon," she said with a certain self-assurance. The smile that accompanied the greeting lit up the light brown-complected features of her African ancestry. He'd observed these women walking along the country roads and felt that they would be just as much at home on a runway in one of those European fashion houses. He watched her as she retreated toward the outer office, then turned back to find the Tiger smiling at him.

"I hope I wasn't interrupting anything," Sergio said to deflect the certainty of a comment on his interest.

"No, no. Just some dictation. It can wait," the other assured him, shaking his head. "Come in! Come in! But before you do, that's your desk over there," he said, pointing to the one just outside his door. "It's all arranged," he added as Sergio raised his hand in protest. "Delgado will take correspondence and be our delegate to the federation, and you'll handle the grievance committee like before."

Grievance committee, Sergio thought. What was there to grieve? The union had become so tight with the O.S.N. management; it was hard to tell them apart.

The older man led the way into the office and sat down on the wooden swivel chair that squeaked as he leaned back. Sergio regarded him and the office. Spartan was the word: for the room and the occupant. The commodious wooden desk matched the swivel chair, as did the wooden chair Sergio sat in and its two mates. He remembered that they were castoffs from some departmental sub-chief of the O.S.N. The other furniture, a credenza along the wall behind René, a pew-like bench along the opposite wall, and a coffee table, were newer and of uncertain vintage and provenance. The walls were almost devoid of decoration. There was a large poster announcing the next meeting of the International Federation of Port

Workers which, on closer inspection had occurred the year before, and over the pew hung a group photograph of the current leadership. But the air-conditioner, in the window behind the secretary general of the union, was new. It practically obscured the view of the O.S.N. and the Golfo Placido beyond.

René Andrade, at six feet, was surprisingly tall for a Costaguanero. In his mid-fifties, he had the look of a longshoreman, broad-shouldered and with large, coarse hands that hung at his sides. He was not uneducated, had finished secondary school, but his major attribute as a union leader was his charisma; the workers loved him. In the early evenings he made a habit of standing on the sidewalk in front of the commissary. He greeted all the men by their first names and always had a word for the family members. Like Julio Chang Crespo, he lived in the nearby suburbs. He was also fortunate for having served under the founder of the union, Guillermo Andrade Jacome, who, although not related, had groomed him as a successor.

"Shut the door," René said, as Sergio was about to sit down. "I can't afford to overwork this damned machine."

"How long have you had it?"

"Four months. If I'm not careful, it'll blow a fuse. And when it does, I can't open the window, so I'm worse off than without it."

"Why don't you get rid of it?"

"I'm thinking of giving it to Ramirez and the girl. They're always running in here on any excuse."

"I didn't think the girl needed an excuse," Sergio said with a straight face.

"Listen!" the older man said, scowling, "I know what they're saying, but she does her job, and she's good at it." Sergio smiled. "I mean being a secretary," René quickly added.

Pretty sensitive, Sergio thought, and decided that the subject would be better dropped. "How about some lunch? I see that the Bar Litoral is still up the street."

"I can't. I've got a meeting in the port at two. In fact, I was getting stuff together when Hector called." René gestured at the papers on his desk, which was otherwise always clear except for the telephone and the correspondence trays.

Not wanting to let another day pass without telling his former boss what was on his mind, Sergio leaned forward and put his hands on the desk. "René, I want to be straight with you, and I'll be brief. I've been gone three years, a lot has happened, and I'm *not* going to jump right back into my old job without giving it a lot of thought." He held up his hand to ward off the protest. "And I'm still on the ORIT payroll." Having made this unadorned declaration, Sergio sat back and waited for the reply.

The older man pondered it for only a moment. "What the hell are you going to do for ORIT? That Cuban, what's his name—"

"Ricabarran."

"Yeah, him. He's got it under control. What's he need an assistant for?"

"I'm not his assistant. They want us to split up the work between the coast and the sierra. I would stay here, and he'll stay in the capital. And I haven't decided on that either," Sergio added. There was a long pause as René scowled and drummed the desk.

"Have you talked to Chinito about this? He's probably still trying to get you to work for him." Sergio smiled. "See? I was right," Andrade added.

"Whether it's the port workers, ORIT, or FLOC, the unions are just pawns in the struggle between the U.S. and Russia. I saw it in Argentina. And look at what they did to Goulart in Brazil. There's—"

"It's for that kind of shit that we snuck you on that freighter going to Santiago three years ago," René shouted, slamming his fist on the desk. "While we worked like asses trying to make it better for our people, the goddamned comrades with their workers' paradise got the generals on our necks, and they'll do it again." He rose and turned to look out the window above the air conditioner.

Three years and he hasn't changed, thought Sergio.

"What more could these guys want?" said René "Decent working conditions, collective bargaining that's a model for the movement—I just had a gringo from AIFLD in here," he added, turning back from the window. "We were talking about a course for FLOC."

"Yeah, I know. I met him and his family in front of the commissary."

"And a commissary!" René shouted. "What the hell can the commies offer that can beat our commissary? I'll bet they don't have it any better in Argentina." He sat down and absentmindedly toyed with the papers on the desk. Sergio felt a pang of remorse. He didn't want to upset the man, but the thought of slipping back into the same position that he had left three years before really disturbed him.

"They've got it, René. The unions there are a power to reckon with."

"And we're not?"

"*You* are," Sergio said, more to placate him than in agreement. "And the Teamsters and the railroad workers. And maybe the petroleum workers. But the rest? Mutual aid societies. You pay your dues, and they see that you get a decent burial."

"Chinito would have something to say about that," observed the Tiger. For a moment he had a kicked-dog look.

Sergio wondered what he really thought. "Chinito knows what he's up against." he replied.

The phone rang, and René picked it up. "Yes? . . . Shit!" He looked at his watch. "Tell them I'll be there in twenty minutes. And send in the girl. Look," he went on, glancing at Sergio, "I have to get going. You take your time thinking it out. But hurry up," he concluded with a smile. "I could use your help. We're going to have our hands full with The Dedo back and your comrade friends nipping at his heels."

It was the old Tiger. Sergio was relieved. They both rose. René came around and opened the door for his guest, as the girl was about to knock. "This is compañero Fidanza," he said, putting his arm around Sergio's shoulders. "Sergio, compañera Matilda Estevez."

"Pleased to meet you," she said, extending her hand. "Compañero Andrade was saying that you're coming back to work for us." She passed into the room without waiting for a response.

"Let's get together soon, Sergio. At the Litoral. Call me tomorrow."

CHAPTER 7

A T ONE FORTY-FIVE THE FORMER SECRETARY of the grievance committee found himself walking east on Avenida de La Muelle. There was little traffic; most of the citizens were at lunch or otherwise secluded from the oppressive midday sun. Dank, fetid air clung to the empty street. He wondered if growth and development would ever succeed in ridding the suburbs of it. Glancing over his shoulder, he spotted a bus heading up to the city center. He hesitated for just a moment in anticipation of boarding it but headed instead for the Bar Litoral for lunch. He wondered if Lucho was still waiting tables. He wondered if the bar still existed. But of course, he had invited René to lunch there, and *he* hadn't said anything. Sergio turned the corner into the Calle Noriega, and there it was. A ragged awning protected the tables outside from the sun, which by then had the sidewalk in shade. And there was Lucho, standing at the door with his tray under his arm, surveying the outdoor patio, ready to respond to any need of the four patrons at a table in the far corner. They were seated on plastic chairs that could be nested together for storage inside. The tables were also of plastic. They accommodated four if only drinks were being served. If the patrons were eating, even two would be crowded. This of course didn't stop the students from making their own arrangements of chairs and tables.

Sergio retreated back around the corner. The feeling of nostalgia had overcome him. The Bar Litoral had been the refuge the group sought, to no avail, that night three years before. They'd been forced to flee out the kitchen door and through the garden just as the soldiers were storming through the dining room. Lucho's nonchalant conversation with them had given the "conspirators" time to make their escape. *Conspirators*, Sergio thought—the brush they tarred everyone with who hadn't fallen into their narrow definition of "patriot."

He stood there a full five minutes as the memory of that night passed before him. They'd made their way through a hidden break in the rear wall of the garden, into the adjoining garden of a sympathizer. It hadn't been the first time they'd had to use that method of dispersal. There had been about ten of them. They'd split up as they entered the next street. It was the last time he saw Margarita Bustamonte. He had stayed with her until they reached the convent of Sor Marillac's Sisters of the Most Holy Redeemer. The nuns had hidden her until her father could make arrangements. Sergio had then made his way to Chinito's home and, ultimately, to the freighter bound for Chile.

As he approached the bar, the waiter turned in his direction and squinted. He was dressed in a white shirt and tight-fitting black pants. A few years older than Sergio, he was taller and very thin. As Sergio reached the shelter of the awning, the look of recognition blossomed on the waiter's face. He dropped his tray on the nearest table, hurried toward the newcomer, and embraced him with a whoop of surprise.

"When did you arrive?" he asked, clapping him affectionately on the back with a pair of large, bony hands.

"A few days ago."

"And you're only now paying us a visit?" Without waiting for a reply, Lucho added, "The last time you were here, it wasn't so pleasant. You had to sneak out the back, and without paying your check. But never mind, the lousy ten pesos you owed was nothing compared to the damage that military wrecking crew that was after you caused. It took us a week to clean it up."

Sergio looked in shock at the matter-of-fact disclosure Lucho was making in front of possible witnesses. The waiter noted his concern and dismissed it with a wave. "Don't worry, my friend. It's not the same that it was three years ago. It took a year for the dust to settle. Then everyone but the commies breathed a little easier, and we began to see that that sot of a president was the major cause and maybe they'd been right in chucking him out. What do I know?"

he added, noting the look of dismay on Sergio's face. "I didn't have to spend three years away from home. Me, I'm just an ignorant waiter. Come on! The boss'll be glad to see you. Business hasn't been so good lately. Maybe your gang will start coming around again."

"My gang?" They were the only words Sergio had been able to utter since their embrace. He'd always marveled at the rapid-fire pace of Lucho's conversation. He could just imagine the line he had fed the soldiers that permitted their escape.

"Anibal, look at the homeless pup that's wandered in," the waiter called out to the old man sitting behind the bar, slitting paper napkins into four pieces with a kitchen knife and arranging them in a circle in a glass. He carefully fanned the points out so that one piece could be easily grasped as the need of a patron arose. An espresso machine stood at one end of the bar, a beer tap on the other. The shelves on the wall contained a respectable variety of rums and their rough country cousins, *caña*, fruit brandies, two bottles of American whiskey, and one unopened fifth of Chivas Regal. A large neon-lit sign advertised the local beer. The motto, *Never Drink Water, Drink Solaco Beer*, was printed in an oval around an intricately fashioned logo, which upon close inspection depicted a boy peeing into a stream. The bar itself was about twelve feet long, with a brass rail. There were no stools.

Anibal Rincón was wearing his Montecristi hat, a classic jipijapa with a black band, and a long-sleeved guayabera. He put down the knife and turned toward the sound of the voice. "Compañero Fidanza!" he exclaimed, stretching over the bar to Sergio's extended hand. The old man shook it vigorously and grabbed Sergio behind the neck. "It's good to see you again." He released him and stood back, to take a look. Then he turned and examined a paper on the shelf above the cash register drawer. "By my records you owe twelve pesos," he said with a broad grin, displaying four missing upper teeth.

"I told him it was ten," Lucho said.

"It was ten three years ago. Now it's twelve," Anibal insisted. "And that's not counting the damage those bastards did. But because compañero Fidanza is a true patriot, not one of those priest-sucking

Conservatives, I am going to scratch off the whole debt," he added, making an elaborate show of eliminating the line from the paper above the cash drawer. "And now we are going to open the bottle of Chivas Regal in honor of the occasion." He removed the bottle from its place on the shelf and began to peel away the collar around the neck.

"No, *no!*" protested Sergio. "I don't want any whiskey."

"Don't worry. It's on me," the owner assured him. But Sergio would not have any. "Then a shot of *caña* to warm *your caña*," Anibal offered, reaching for a bottle of Pistola, a rustic caña made in Nicoya.

"No. Nothing, thanks," Sergio insisted, resting his foot on the rail. "Maybe an Orangina."

"An Orangina? How will I ever pay off the damages selling soft drinks? Besides, soft drinks are for women. How did you survive in Argentina?"

"I survived by not drinking. I don't know why exactly, but I'm allergic to alcohol. I get terrible hangovers. It's not worth it." Sergio had repeated this story countless times since his return and was beginning to regret he'd ever stopped by the bar.

The old man softened. "That *is* too bad. I hope it's not contagious. Well, we'll fix you a lunch. Javier," he called out to the cook. "A plate of haddock for our guest. Fresh from the docks," he said to Sergio. "Lucho, set a table for compañero Fidanza."

The skinny waiter brought a knife and fork to the table nearest the end of the bar with the espresso machine. He took a precut napkin from a glass on the table, folded it into a triangle, and placed it on the table with the fork on top of it. Sergio took a seat as Anibal came around the end of the bar with his Orangina and a beer for himself. He sat down facing the younger man. "Well, kidding aside, it's good to see you. The Tiger told us you were back, so we knew it was just a matter of time before you'd be coming around to visit the scenes of your past indiscretions." He smiled and lifted his glass to toast the occasion. Sergio did likewise with his Orangina. They took a long pull at their drinks and set the glasses down. Sergio slipped a square of paper from the glass to wipe his mustache.

"Have you seen a doctor?" Anibal asked.

"What about?"

"Those *chuchaquis?*"

"Look, Anibal, when I don't drink, I feel great. I don't need a doctor to tell me what I already know. I just don't drink, and that's that."

"Very bad for my business."

"You'll survive," Sergio remarked with a scowl. He wondered how long it would take for people to get used to the fact.

Lucho appeared with a steaming plate and a small bowl of chili sauce. "Good appetite," he said, setting it before Sergio. The strong aroma of cilantro wafted up from the boiled cassava that accompanied the fish.

Anibal, noting that there was no one else in the restaurant and that the four outside had left, said to the waiter, "Lucho, get yourself a beer and join us." Lucho returned with another round and a basket of bread. The two watched Sergio ladle a generous amount of the sauce onto the haddock and begin to eat. Anibal finished off his first beer. "And don't worry about the damage," he said, bringing the conversation back to that night three years before. "They did me a favor. I used the month they shut me down to redecorate." He smiled as he gazed around the room. Sergio followed the gaze in disbelief. If it had changed, he couldn't discern it.

Sergio cut a piece of the fish and was about to lift his fork when Lucho, out of the blue said, "That Margarita was a firebrand." The fork stopped half way to Sergio's mouth. He held it there for a moment, then put it back on his plate, hoping that his shaking hand hadn't been noticed. "Whenever I saw that . . . . What was that car she had?"

"An MG Salon," Sergio offered. He sat staring at his plate. It was the first time since his return that anyone had mentioned her name.

"Yeah. Whenever it was parked in front, I knew there'd be some excitement."

"Apparently it had the same reputation over at the university," observed the boss. "You got her to the nuns' that night, right?" he added, looking at Sergio, who'd broken off a piece of the cassava with his fork. He decided not pick it up but instead leaned back in the chair.

"It was the last time I saw her," he said and, testing the waters, added, "What happened to her?"

"Her old man got her out and sequestered her at his farm north of the capital."

"Well," said Sergio, trying to appear nonchalant, "ex-presidents do have some clout."

"I think after a few months it all blew over anyway," the boss observed. "But I haven't heard anything in particular." That ended the conversation about Margarita Bustamante, daughter of the thirty-first president of the republic.

THE NEWLY RETURNED EXILE rounded the corner of Avenida de la Muelle just in time to board a bus to the center of the city. The buses had wide wooden bodies mounted on imported chasses. The outsides were of a uniform drab green with the name of the company, *The Intercity Fleet,* emblazoned on the side and over the front windshield. The only other identifying mark was the route number, printed on a large piece of cardboard and placed in the front window. The insides of the buses were an entirely different matter. The drivers' creativity was in evidence there, particularly in the vicinity of his seat. Elaborate decoration around and over the windshield was *de rigueur.* It usually took the form of a shrine to a patron saint, complete with lights that blinked when the signal cord for a stop was pulled.

Sergio handed the driver thirty centavos and pushed through the turnstile. He ducked his head as he felt his curly black hair brush against the ceiling and took the seat just vacated by a young woman carrying a small, cross-eyed child. The tot smiled at him as her mother headed toward the rear door. He marveled at the happy youngster and wondered if she would still be smiling in ten years. He wondered if *he* would have a smiling child in ten years. He wondered if he would be alive in ten years, and then he decided that the prospects were not good on all counts.

Where the avenue passed through the suburbs, it had been recently paved with concrete, but the pretentious center island was still devoid of trees. The area bustled with commercial activity in the late afternoon. Merchandise from the shops spilled out onto the ten-meter dirt strip that separated the stores from the pavement. This empty expanse, planned for a row of trees, shrubbery, and sidewalks, also invited the parking of vehicles of all description. Schoolgirls in blue pinafores worn over nondescript dresses marched arm-in-arm down the edge of the pavement in groups of three or four, each clutching a pencil and notebook. Patrons sat at tables outside of bars that seemed to occupy every corner. He thought of the elegant restaurants that lined the Avenida 9 de Julio in Buenos Aires, reputed to be the widest boulevard in the world. Yes. Why *indeed* had he returned to Costaguana?

He knew, but did she?

As the bus approached the old walled city the concrete pavement became dressed stone, and trees were growing in the center island. The buildings were more substantial; some even boasted tile roofs. But it was still basically a commercial strip, lined with a hodgepodge of automobile agencies, gas stations, a furniture store, and a variety of appliance, hardware, and other establishments catering to a small, newly upwardly mobile middle-class. It wasn't until the bus passed through the wall via a gate that had been enlarged to accommodate the avenue that the colonial character of the former capital of the Occidental Republic could be appreciated.

The bus negotiated the Plaza Rembrandt immediately inside the wall and proceeded up the street on the opposite side, the Avenida de la Constitución. It was not as wide as the Avenida de La Muelle and led to the main square of the city. The narrow streets, originally designed to carry pedestrians, horsemen, and the occasional carriage had been laid out in a grid system, and all but the widest were now one-way. The wide bus made its way slowly. That it moved at all was a testimony to the traffic police. These stalwarts were mounted on platforms at each corner of the city center, each well within sight of his neighbor. They directed the flow by facing the traffic that had to stop and presented their side to the vehicles that had the right-of-way. At the change they blew a whistle, made a quarter turn, and swung a club, their only armament, in a circle. They accomplished what even the most sophisticated signal system never could have hoped to.

The bus made a left turn two blocks before the Alameda, the main square, and proceeded north. Sergio pulled the signal cord and set to blinking the lights surrounding the elaborate scene of St. Francis of Assisi preaching to the birds. He descended by the rear door onto the narrow sidewalk and continued in the same direction. The two-story buildings on either side threw the street into shadow. The fetid odor of the port area had given way to diesel exhaust with an overlay of cooking oil. A woman in the doorway of a humble eatery, the only establishment in the otherwise blank wall of a building fronting on Calle La Reina around the corner, was stirring a large, shallow copper pot filled with shredded pork. The tank on which it was mounted fueled the gas burner. The sidewalk, a meter and a half wide where he stepped off the bus, narrowed to about thirty centimeters at the corner where he turned right onto La Reina. The second cross street, Avenida Garcia Machado, formed the north side of the plaza one block to the right. It was wider and boasted arcaded sidewalks. Painted on the brick above the two arches at the end of the arcade was the faded sign that read *EL POR-VENIR*. The afternoon tabloid had since moved to a larger building in the area outside the old city that he had just traversed. The neighboring department store, Anazani's Emporium, had expanded into the space formerly occupied by the newspaper. A display of electrical appliances filled the corner window—another sign of the growing middle class. The store had a branch in the affluent neighborhood of the old city, The Anazani's North. Glancing again at the faded sign before crossing the street, Sergio was reminded of the memoir he'd recommended to Bumpy Cosgrove. *El Porvenir* had been founded by the family of Doña Antonia and was still run by a cousin's grandson. The generals had closed it down, but he'd heard that it had been allowed to reopen within the month.

A modest sign identifying the headquarters of FLOC hung over the sidewalk halfway up the block. He entered the ancient building and mounted the stairs on the right side of the passage that lead to an interior courtyard. At the end of the balcony that overlooked it on three sides stood the reception area. Maria Luisa Cizneros looked up and smiled at the former secretary of the grievance committee.

"Compañero Fidanza," she sighed. "Compañero Ricabarran has been with him since lunch." Turning very serious, she confided, "It's about that poor Spaniard who was lynched Saturday."

"Lynched?"

"In Nogales. He was the manager of a textile plant. Haven't you heard? It's in *El Semenario*." She reached to the table behind her and offered the Santa Marta morning paper to Sergio.

"I've heard nothing," he said as he took the paper and sat on the bench along the railing to read it. The meager details available were described under the headline *Spanish Manager Lynched*.

> *Nogales, July 10—The badly burned body of Sebastian Perez, the former manager of Textiles de La Sierra, was removed at noon today from the grounds of the factory where it had lain since the terrible events of the early morning. The police have concluded that it was the work of a group of employees of the factory dissatisfied with the outcome of events of the past week. The following account was pieced together from remarks heard in the village and the eyewitness report of Emilio Gonzales, the porter.*
>
> *Upon their arrival at work on Monday, Señor Perez had advised the workers that the factory was temporarily closed. Wages due would be paid on Wednesday. On Wednesday morning the workers were instructed to return at six in the evening at which time the gates were locked and a posted notice advised that payment would be made on Saturday morning. No one responded to the shouts of those assembled.*
>
> *Workers began to arrive at five o'clock this morning. Señor Perez arrived in his car at six and forced his way to his office through the crowd that had grown to about twenty. A short time later the porter came to the gate with the message that the owners were at that time meeting in*

the capital and arranging the affairs of the company. He could offer no more information and returned to the building.

The workers, incensed at the treatment they were afforded, stormed the gate and gathered at the door of the office. Much shouting and threatening ensued. Then, according to the porter, without further warning they broke down the door, dragged out the poor man, beat him, doused him with gasoline, and set him afire. As the mob was threatening outside the door the porter reported that the manager's last words were, "Barking dogs don't bite."

Sergio looked up. "Barking dogs don't bite," he said, shaking his head.

"It's awful. His poor wife is so distraught." Maria Luisa was from a family well connected in the country's commercial circles. Her union proclivities, much to her family's chagrin, stemmed from her university years. She had well defined social justice beliefs but exhibited a genuine and heartfelt sensitivity for anyone in Señora Perez's circumstances. "Shall I tell them you're here?" she asked without further comment.

Sergio nodded and started down a hallway as Maria Luisa was making the announcement. The door to the left led to a meeting room. He proceeded to the one straight ahead.

"Just the man!" exclaimed Julio Chang Crespo as Sergio entered an office thick with smoke and took the outstretched hand of the tall, balding man who was smoking the cigar, seated in front of the desk, then Chang Crespo's.

The office of the secretary general of FLOC was about the same size as that of the secretary general of the Port Workers' Union but a bit warmer in appearance. The building had been a residence in the post-colonial era, this probably a bedroom. The window to the right as you entered faced the west. The spire of the cathedral in the Alameda could be seen through the one facing south. The wall on the east separated the office from the meeting room and could be entered through a door at the far end; on it hung the requisite pictures of official activities and former officers. But there were two that stood out from the others. They were of the founders of FLOC, both women: Doctora Golda Lederer de Saenz and Doña Antonia Avellanos Corbelàn.

"What's up?" asked Sergio as he sank into the chair next to Jorge Ricabarran, the regional representative of ORIT. Ricabarran was a Cuban refugee, a union leader not in sympathy with Castro. ORIT had picked him up in Mexico, where he had fled, and assigned him to the Postal and Telegraph Workers Union. Over six feet tall, he could have easily been taken for a rich hacienda owner from Monterey. This was not lost on him. He enjoyed the reputation of being a ladies' man, although on the job he was all business.

"You heard about that incident up in Nogales?" Chinito asked without further ado.

"Just now." Sergio motioned toward the reception area.

"Well, we were talking about Jorge goin' up and nosin' around."

"I'm glad you didn't have me in mind."

"No, I have *another* job for you."

"Listen to this, Jorge," Sergio replied, looking directly at his nominal boss. "I'm on *your* payroll, The Tiger has my desk all ready, and *he's* got a job for me."

"Only if you want to," Chinito said, raising his hands in a gesture of acquiescence. "I thought it would good for you to get out of here for a while instead of moping around."

"Moping around? Who's moping around? I've been gone for three years. I just want to get my feet on the ground, is all." Sergio added in all seriousness, "But this lynching, it's terrible. How could those guys do such a thing?"

"It's been brewing for about six months," Chinito answered. "Ever since they brought in the new machinery. That move alone resulted in reducing the workforce by half, after having been completely shut down for a month to install it."

"And they brought that Spaniard along with the new machinery," Ricabarran put in, blowing a cloud of blue smoke into the air.

"Tell him, Jorge."

The ORIT representative nodded. "I ran into him in Mexico.

He managed a plant for them there, and he had a reputation for union busting. He tried to keep the leadership from being hired back."

"The membership was solid behind Zuñiga," Chinito added.

"So what got them to this point?" Sergio asked, still trying to make some sense out of it.

The other two looked at each other. "You tell him, Chinito," the older man said, getting up and walking over to the window. "You know the details better than I do."

"Well, it seems pretty simple on the surface. Textiles de la Sierra has been operating in the capital for fifty years now. They built the facility in Nogales about ten years ago, and we capitalized on our work in the area to unionize the new plant. From day one."

"With ORIT's help," Jorge added, flicking an ash out the window.

"It was a joint effort," Chinito agreed. "ORIT got that gringo union. . . . What's the name?"

"The ILGWU. International Ladies Garment Workers' Union."

"Yeah. They still support the work." Chinito leaned back and slapped his hand against his forehead. "God. Wait'til they find out about this." Recovering, he added, "That's why you've got to get up there, Jorge." He reflected a moment on his sudden realization before going on. "Anyway, about a year ago they bought that old factory off the Avenida de la Muelle and started installing the same machinery here as in Nogales. In fact, the Spaniard was managing both operations. Apparently the business didn't materialize, and they decided that the Nogales plant was the less efficient and began shutting it down whenever the orders dropped off. It's been pretty chaotic, especially with the pay. What happened last week has been going on for months."

"But a lynching? How did Zuñiga ever let it happen?"

"He wasn't there. His mother died, and he was at the funeral."

"Do we know who was involved?" Sergio was getting embroiled in spite of himself.

Ricabarran returned to his seat. "All we know is from the account in *El Semenario*. We haven't been able to reach anyone, including Zuñiga. We understand he's on his way back, but that's all."

"There's nothing more we can do until Jorge gets up there," the secretary general concluded. They sat in silence, Sergio staring at the floor. Finally, Chinito spoke. "Well?"

"Well, what?" Sergio asked, without looking up.

"The assignment down in Catachoclo."

Sergio looked at his boss. The Cuban responded to the unasked question, "It's fine by me."

"Okay," said the former exile. He got up and walked over to the window. "I guess I do need to get around a little more."

"It's settled, then," Chinito said.

"Good," said Ricabarran, as he got out of his chair. "I'll go to Nogales tomorrow. Meanwhile I've got a meeting with the Tiger." As he crushed the stub of his cigar in an ashtray on the desk, he remarked off-handedly, "This is the only thing that bastard Castro has going for him."

"René was leaving for the port when I left his office," Sergio remarked, turning from the window.

"Yeah. He told me, but he'll be back by the time I get there," Ricabarran said, then added, looking at the two of them, "Shall I mention anything about this?"

"Go ahead," said Sergio. "He's got to understand that I'm not going back to my old job. Maybe this will start him thinking along these lines."

As the door closed behind the Cuban, Chinito, elbows on his desk, buried his face in his hands. "Now maybe I can get that lynching out of my head," he murmured.

"I thought for a minute that you had me in mind for that job."

"No. There's nothing you could do. Probably nothing anyone can do." He leaned back, staring at the ceiling, and then added, "Jorge'll sort it out. But this business in the south, it's going to take someone who really knows Catachoclo. The history of the area. Jorge Quishpe and the beneficio workers. I don't have anyone with your savvy, Sergio. That's why I think you're the one for the job."

Sergio resumed his seat without responding. He looked up at

the photos of the two women, who had founded FLOC, the Litoral Federation of Christian Workers, in 1938. He then regarded his friend, who was leaning back in his chair. Since Julio Chang Crespo became Secretary General in 1957, he had been engaged in holding up their vision, a constant struggle at the margins of the labor movement. The years had exacted their toll.

"And I can't afford to lose the help of the—what is it? LIG? Whatever, those New York textile workers." His thoughts had returned to Nogales. "You know they're run mostly by Eastern European Jews, so it was a big step for them to get involved with us. It was really Doctora Lederer who brought it off. Did you know she was a Jewish lawyer from Czechoslovakia?" Sergio shook his head. "But you know her?"

"Sure, we all do. The founder of FLOC," Sergio answered, looking up at the picture. "We met a few times at meetings. But I didn't know where she was from."

"Yeah. Apparently got out just in time. Imagine. And then meeting up with Doña Antonia?" Chang Crespo reflected on this for only a moment. "I was thinking of asking her to go with Jorge, but she doesn't need that. Jorge can get the information she needs. Well, anyway, my man, you get the picture."

Sergio wasn't sure what he was getting, except an assignment that was just prolonging his final decision. "And that's the trouble," he finally said, "I'm not your man." Then he added, after seeing the dismayed look on his friend's face, "Julio, I'm glad to do this for you. I owe it to you. But your man? I was the Tiger's man for how many years? And he's got me assigned to my old desk right outside his door, ready for me to be *his* man again." He rose suddenly and looked out the window at nothing in particular. "I've got to be my own man."

Julio smiled. "Who is she? An Argentine you left behind?"

Sergio turned to face his surrogate older brother and replied, "No. She's a Costaguanera, as a matter of fact, and I don't know if she even remembers me or knows I'm alive." Looking back out the window, he murmured to himself, "Or cares."

IN THE EARLY EVENING THE SUBDUED LIGHT of the shop windows and the occasional incandescent bulb glowing from the peak of an arch seemed almost to cast a spell on the pedestrians strolling the arcaded sidewalk of Avenida Garcia Machado. The street was quiet, and the sidewalk, though crowded, lacked the hubbub of the mornings. Instead, there were the hushed conversations and the genial companionship of the Sulacans. To the observer with the least bit of a romantic bent it exuded an enchantment that was palpable. Two young women, probably office mates, stood arm-in-arm, gazing at bolts of material whose ends were draped over a bamboo pole running the length of one of the shop windows at Anazani's Emporium. A lottery saleswoman ambled along the street side of the arcade, waving her sheets of coupons at the passersby. A group of three men stopped her to examine the numbers with an air of expertise that belied the astronomical odds against winning. A shoeshine boy had soon cajoled one of the trio into availing himself of his services. The man leaned against a column and put his foot on the boy's box while his friends concluded their selection. Near the corner a figure stood in the shadows, arms draped with finely woven woolen tablecloths. He wore the distinctive garb of the Otovalo Indian from the Ecuadorian Andes: straw slippers, white duck pants, a cotton shirt, a blue poncho to his knees in spite of the heat, and a fine Borsalino hat on a head of black hair done in a single long braid. A gringo tourist couple was looking over his wares. He seemed almost not to notice. The bell in the cathedral tower tolled seven.

A decidedly unromantic Sergio Fidanza nevertheless took in the lightheartedness reflected in the faces that materialized before him in the gloaming as he made his way from the office of FLOC toward the main square. He remembered similar evenings with Margarita after a meeting. It had been the only time she wasn't fired up over some issue, the only time she had talked about everyday family happenings or any other subject similarly unrelated to the movement. It was infectious. Sergio had almost forgotten that he was secretary of the grievance committee, a Socialist Party member, and a fellow traveler. What had it been about that time of day that put aside the burning issues that otherwise fired their passions? They would sit at a table in the Bar Austral just off the Alameda and exchange almost forgotten experiences of their youth. The complete disparity of their backgrounds had seemed to fade with the parting daylight. During these moments, completely unaware of her classic beauty and oblivious to the glances of the passersby, she would listen attentively to Sergio's tales of farm life in Italy during the war and respond with her child's-eye view of presidential palace intrigue. How many of these occasions had there been? Just the one? How long had he really known her? Months? A year at the most, yet it seemed at times they were childhood friends, neighbors.

Julio was right. Instead of moping around, Sergio had determined to find out where she was and resign himself to the inevitable fact that she was married. But he had no idea where to begin. Julio hardly remembered her. University politics were of no interest to him. He tended to lump them in with the machinations of the equally volatile port workers—a lot of smoke but no fire. "Her family has a farm outside the capital," he'd said. "Ask your sister to look into it." It was probably the way to go, but Sergio was reluctant to broach the subject with her. He *could* couch it in terms of a political inquiry. Yes. That was it! He would call her the next day. Julio had arranged the trip to Catachoclo for the following day.

Catachoclo. The thought snapped him out of his reverie. He was looking forward to going. It had been at least four years. He was feeling energized already. Sor Marillac was there. Maybe she knows something. He reached the Alameda and continued diagonally across, in the direction of the pension where he then resided.

CHAPTER 8

"FIDANZA," BRAUN CALLED OUT as his visitor entered the bar of the Humboldt Hotel. The engineer was seated on the same stool Sergio had occupied the day before. "I'm glad you could make it," he said as they shook hands. "With our afternoon flight, I didn't have the time to meet you in the center."

"Quite all right—I have nothing but time today." Sergio looked around the bar, hoping not to see Bumpy Cosgrove. "Mr. Cosgrove still around?"

"No. As a matter of fact, he left for the capital on the morning flight."

"Oh. And your family?"

"They're having breakfast in the room, and they'll be going to the pool for a dip before we leave. I'm having breakfast here. Can I offer you something?"

"Just coffee."

Braun gave the order to the bartender and asked to have it be served on the balcony. They took a table overlooking the Malecón.

"I hope you've enjoyed your stay here in Sulaco," Sergio said above the clatter of the chairs being dragged over the concrete floor.

"We have. Yesterday we went to that fishing village, Zapiga. What a lovely beach! And the water's so calm. It lives up to its name."

"Yes. Golfo Placido. The village used to be notorious for smuggling," Sergio remarked. "There's probably a bit of it still going on." The waiter arrived with a plate of fruit, a basket of rolls, a pitcher of steamed milk, and a cruet of coffee extract. Sergio helped himself to the coffee and milk as Braun dug into the fruit. "How old are your daughters?"

"Lisa's three, and Jenny's eleven months. She was born in Santa Marta—a Costaguanera!" he added with a hint of pride.

"Watch out. She'll be coming back here one day. I was two when my family went back to Italy, and we returned after thirteen years. Now I'm back again after three years in the Argentine. It's in the blood." The engineer thought about it for a moment and smiled without commenting. Sergio continued, "I met your former boss while I was in Buenos Aires."

"Joey Ramirez?"

"Yes. He told me to look you up. I didn't expect it would be so soon."

"He left three months after we got here. I was in charge for a month and a half before John Pendleton, my new boss, showed up."

He shook his head. "Talk about a baptism of fire. I'm glad to be dealing with just the social projects." Braun poured some extract into his cup, topped it off with the hot milk, and helped himself to a roll.

"What are you involved in?" Sergio asked. He figured that they were about the same age. That and mustaches were all they had in common, but he was developing a liking for the engineer.

"I came here to develop housing projects," Braun told him, "but the unions don't have a nickel's worth of savings, and no land. So I'm involved in credit unions and savings and loan co-ops. We *do* have a self-help housing project with a professional union outside Santa Marta, and we might get something going with the port workers. At least they've got the credit union." The former secretary of the grievance committee thought of his long-dormant account and wondered how it was faring. "And I was just in Catachoclo with a Point IV advisor."

"Catachoclo?" Sergio set his cup down. "I'm going there tomorrow. Did you meet Jorge Quishpe of the beneficio workers?"

"As a matter of fact, that was the main reason for me going," Jim answered, obviously pleased at the connection. "We're going to set up a course for them in credit unions. I was with a guy from Point IV who's a specialist in it."

"He mention any problems at the beneficio?"

"No—these guys tend not to discuss union business with me. I guess they see me more as a social projects person. Oh, by the way, I met a Redhead for the first time," Jim added. "It seems they're being harassed by some exploration activity."

ELIZABETH BRAUN WAS SITTING on the steps leading into the shallow end of the pool when the two men arrived. Lisa, girded with an inflated life preserver, was happily splashing around while her sister slept in the nearby stroller. "I wish you a safe trip back to the capital. And you must look up my sister," Sergio added, taking Elizabeth's outstretched hand. "I've given her address to Jim."

"I'm pleased to have met you, Sergio, and I look forward to meeting her." She turned quickly to the older girl, who was beginning to float away. "Say 'good-bye,' Lisa." The child returned Sergio's wave and went back to splashing.

Braun accompanied him to the hotel entrance. "I hope you can do something for those guys."

"If it's oil, the Redheads will have their work cut out for them. I'll keep you posted," Sergio added, and started up the Malecón toward Avenida de la Muelle.

When Braun returned to the pool, Elizabeth was toweling off the older girl. "She's getting hungry," she remarked, looking at the younger child rocking herself in the stroller. She finished drying Lisa and put on a short robe.

"Time to go to the room," the father announced, and grasped Lisa by the hand. They headed for the elevator in the lobby.

Their room was similar in layout to the one Cosgrove had occupied. Two cribs had been squeezed into the corner, next to the small balcony that faced the Malecón rather than the pool. Elizabeth sat down in one of the chairs and proceeded to nurse the younger child. "He's a very nice man," she observed, "but he seems a bit melancholy."

"I know what you mean," replied Jim as he helped Lisa, who was more interested in jumping on the bed than getting dressed for the trip. "From what he's said, it seems that, having just returned after being away for three years, he has no idea of what *he* wants to do, while everyone else is making plans for him."

Elizabeth reflected upon this for a moment. "*I* think he's in love."

WHILE ELIZABETH AND JIM BRAUN were speculating on the reasons for Sergio Fidanza's melancholy, the daily bus from Nicoya was turning off the Carrera del Valle onto Calle Sucre in Catachoclo. It lumbered down to the canton administration building and turned right onto Calle Sulaco, the cobble-stoned main commercial street in the town. The curbs and sidewalks were of concrete, and the buildings on the east side, farthest from the landing strip, had a wooden gallery extending to the curb. With a long blast of the horn the bus pulled to the curb in front of a grocery store that also served as the depot. A small knot of people was milling around the entrance, and on a bench in front of the establishment sat Galo Luzuriaga, manager of the Co-operative La Esperanza. As the bus came to a halt, a porter in blue trousers and a short-sleeved shirt scrambled up the ladder on the rear of the vehicle and began untying the ropes securing the assorted belongings of the passengers. A young man who had arrived in a black Ford station wagon greeted the first of the desembarking passengers, two middle-aged women. They waited to the side while the porter handed down the baggage to a co-worker at the rear of the bus. People who had been visiting either in Nicoya or one of the villages along the route, or were coming to Catachoclo on business, followed the two women off the bus and looked for their belongings at the curb.

One of the last to leave was a young woman whose striking beauty set her apart from her rustic fellow passengers. Her wavy black hair, cut in a fashionable style off the shoulders, framed a wide face with high cheekbones and dark brown eyes. She was wearing a gray cotton skirt that showed off an athletic figure to perfection, and a short-sleeved ruffled blouse. She held a child a little over a year old in her arms.

Galo rose from the bench as soon as he spotted Margarita Bustamonte. A peasant woman leading a three-year-old girl by the hand followed her off the bus. When Margarita reached an open space on the sidewalk, she handed the child she was carrying to the awaiting mother. The woman was profuse in her thanks. Margarita greeted Galo warmly and turned to the two men who were the last off the bus. Galo shook Juan Chiriboga's hand and said, "I'm glad you were able to get here so soon. Rigpe was adamant."

"It's a very delicate matter, Galo. Indigenous rights and. . .ah, scientific imperatives can make for a volatile mix." The Deputy Director for Colonization, of medium height with straight black hair and a mustache to match, had a swarthy complexion ravaged by smallpox. Like his tall companion, at least one meter-eighty, and blond, he wore dress pants, a short-sleeved white shirt, and a tie. They probably had jackets packed in their suitcases.

"It wouldn't be so volatile if basic civil rights were being respected!" Margarita had made the comment in a soft, measured voice, but her eyes lent it a different tone.

"Yes, Margarita, I take your point, and we've had ample opportunity to discuss it," Chiriboga replied, and then to Galo, "We appreciate your help in this matter, Galo. You know Felipe Krueger?" he added, gesturing to his companion. "From our legal department." Without another word Margarita left the group to claim her valise from the curb where the porter had placed it. Galo excused himself and joined her.

"They think the Arra'o are just in the way. I suspect they're going to try to buy them off," she commented in the same measured voice as she reached down to pick up her valise. Galo made an attempt to help her. "That's all right, I'm not going far."

"Where are you staying?"

"Since I'm here for our quarterly review of the social services, the nuns have been kind enough to invite me to stay with them. It beats that dungeon, Hotel Sulaco. And they *are* pleasant company, especially Sor Marillac."

"You're always welcome to stay with us," said Galo. "Maruja gives her regards. She says we should get together."

"Yes. Let's do," she added quickly as her two traveling companions approached. "Let me know if there's anything I can do," she said to the three men, and without waiting for an answer, strode off in the direction of the clinic. A boy came out of a small shop next to the depot where patrons paid a fee to read whatever was available and suited to their tastes on racks of magazines, newspapers, comic books, and other types of reading material. He came up to Margarita and offered to carry the valise. She handed it over to him, whereupon he hoisted it on his shoulder and fell in step behind her.

"She's a lot like her old man," commented Chiriboga. "He had a very, very savvy way with the 'great unwashed.' She had us move when that woman with the two kids got on. But it was a blessing in disguise. We didn't have to listen to any more of her opinion on the treatment of the indigenous peoples."

Felipe, who had been quiet up to that time, pointed at the retreating back of a fellow passenger about sixty meters up toward the plaza and asked, "Do you know who he is? He got on with us in

Nicoya."

Galo, who kept his own counsel in matters involving the press, recognized Victor Hugo Ramirez, the stringer for *El Porvenir* in Nicoya, by his slight limp and long black hair, protruding from under the jipijapa perched on his head. "Ah. He looks familiar, but I can't say for sure from here. . . . I made arrangements for you at the Flamenco."

"It was just a restaurant the last time I was here," said the deputy director.

"He did the second floor over into three rooms. And he has his own generator, so your lights won't go out at ten." Glancing at his watch, Galo added, "We'll still be in time for lunch." He picked up their bags and put them in the back of a rusty brown Chevy pickup of pre-war vintage parked in front of the reading room. Two boys were huddled on a bench, absorbed in a comic book.

"HOW'S THE ROOM?" GALO ASKED as the ICRAC representatives joined him at the table in the dining room. The Flamenco was a shiny oasis in an otherwise drab provincial market town made more prosperous by the beneficio, located at the edge of a slightly more prosperous residential neighborhood. The clientele tended to be government functionaries, such as Chiriboga and Krueger, businessmen visiting the coffee processing plant east of town, or the occasional tourist looking for the "authentic" Costaguana. Prior to the renovation, these people would have lodged at the Hotel Sulaco. With only three rooms and a total capacity of seven, it was only the ones who were booked in advance by their local friends who could avoid staying at the much older hotel.

"Not bad. It's the only one with a private bath."

"It's the only room in the whole *town* with a private bath," Galo reminded them.

The owner, Yapa Flores, had followed them into the dining room. He had thick, close-cropped black hair with a mustache to match. A soiled white bib apron covered dungarees and a white shirt. When they had seated themselves, he gestured to a blackboard on which was noted *Lunch. Chicken stew with rice.* They all nodded.

Chiriboga ordered three bottles of Sulaco beer.

"Well, Galo, what can you tell us?" Chiriboga asked without further ado.

"After I spoke to you by radio about the meeting with Rigpe, I enticed the gringos to drive out to where the drilling was going on. It didn't take much convincing. The engineer was quite interested."

"Did Rigpe join you?"

"Only to the ferry crossing. He got out there."

"Did he say why?"

"As far as he's concerned, the talking is *over*. Either ICRAC does something, or they take matters into their own hands."

The deputy director lightly drummed the table while he sorted out the chronology. "That was Wednesday of last week," he finally said. "Well, fortunately the head of the drilling operation had just returned to Sulaco from Argentina the day before. I was able to get him on the phone the next day, Thursday." Yapa Flores returned with the beer. As he was serving them, Chiriboga continued, "He thought it had all been arranged. He assured me that they wouldn't proceed until we could work out the problem, but they only had a few days work before having to move ahead." He took a sip of the beer and added ominously, "He was adamant about getting on the land." He extracted a napkin from the glass holder at the center of the table to wipe his mustache.

MARGARITA BUSTAMONTE, DAUGHTER of the thirty-first president of the republic, was surveying the street from the door of the convent. She saw Galo load the bags of her traveling companions into the bed of the pickup. The three squeezed into the cab and drove up the Calle Sulaco. Galo waved as they passed. The lad had set down Margarita's bag and was waiting patiently for a response to the senorita's tug at the bell rope.

"Margarita! How nice to see you again!" exclaimed the exuberant nun as she opened the door. "We were beginning to wonder if there had been a delay."

"Just a short wait at some construction outside of town, Sor Beatrice," the young woman reported as she embraced her greeter.

"Excuse me." She turned to the boy and handed him a coin.

"Thank you, senorita," he said, and scampered off in the direction of the reading room. The nun picked up the bag and ushered her guest into the cooler interior. She was as tall as Margarita and wore the white work habit of a nurse of the order, which extended to her ankles and barely exposed her white tennis shoes.

"We've been awaiting your arrival before starting lunch," the nun said as they crossed a small anteroom just inside the door into a large space with a low-beamed ceiling. It was furnished, in an aesthetic manner suitable to the modest lives of the occupants, to serve various purposes: a large table in the center with eight chairs for dining and meetings of the community, five of the places set for lunch; a sideboard between the doors to the kitchen and the dormitory wing, with covered bowls of food ready for the lunch buffet; two desks on the interior wall, each before a window that faced the clinic across the courtyard; several chairs at the far end with reading lamps; and a shrine in the far corner dedicated to Saint Therese of Lisieux. The only other religious decoration, a framed reproduction of Leonardo's *Last Supper*, hung on the windowless wall facing the street.

"Sor Marillac! Look who's here!" she called out to the kitchen.

The bright blue eyes of the nun who appeared at the door lit up when Margarita entered. In the light gray habit of the sisters who are not nurses, it was hard to judge her age, because the white wimple that surrounded her face gave her a youthful appearance belying her forty-five years. She wore black oxfords and a gray veil that came to her shoulders.

"*Bienvenue*, Margarita. How nice it is to see you again!" she declared as she embraced the guest. "How long has it been?"

"Three months since the last review."

"Oh, it seems much longer." The nun was obviously delighted with the visit. "We are just ready to sit down. Would you like to freshen up?"

"I'll just wash my hands."

"You know where it is." Sor Marillac indicated the hallway that led to the sleeping quarters and the bathroom. "Sor Beatrice, please show our guest to her room," she said to the nun who had answered the door.

As the two left for the dormitory wing, Sor Marillac busied herself uncovering the bowls. Two nuns in white entered from the kitchen in conversation about a case they had just treated in the clinic. "Has our guest arrived?" asked Sor Therese, the older of the two—the superior of the community and head of the clinic. Her companion was dark-complected and spoke the unaccented Spanish of Costaguana.

"She's washing up," said Sor Marillac. "They should be with us— Here they are now!" she remarked as the two returned from the dormitory wing.

"*Bienvenue*, Margarita," the mother superior said.

"It's always a pleasure to be with you, Sor Therese. And I'm glad for the respite from the altitude."

Without further formality Sor Therese invited all to serve themselves from the simple buffet: a salad of tomatoes, lettuce, and sliced avocado, hot rice and beans with shredded chicken. A pitcher of lemonade, a basket of rolls, and a tray of condiments lay on the table. As soon as everyone was seated Sor Lourdes, the Costaguanera, offered grace.

No sooner had they begun to eat then the doorbell rang. Sor Beatrice returned with a telegram for the superior, who opened it, as the others watched. Telegrams to the convent were a rarity.

"We have another guest, arriving tomorrow," she announced. "Doctora Golda Lederer. Sor Beatrice, please have them reply that we look forward to her visit."

THE ONLY ONES IN THE CAMP when Galo and the two ICRAC functionaries arrived were the geologist and the cook. The former was in a tent that served as the field office; he was poring over a long sheet of graph paper that he had rolled out on a drafting table. Slight and not very tall, his khaki pants and short-sleeved plaid cotton shirt were neatly pressed and looked as fresh as when he had dressed that morning. The remaining furniture in the three-by-four-meter shelter consisted of a stool, a gray steel desk and chair, a three-drawer file cabinet, and a plan rack, all sitting on the packed earth. A Coleman lantern hung from the ridgepole. The afternoon was seasonably hot, so the side flaps had been rolled up to permit what little breeze there was to circulate. He looked up as the pickup approached and glanced at his watch. By the time the three men had gotten out of the vehicle, he was on a walkie-talkie radio. "Walter is in the field," he responded to Galo's inquiry. "I call him," he said, holding up the instrument. "He is coming. Ten minutes." The young man's Spanish was very limited.

"We'll wait outside," Galo said, not wishing to strain the fellow's facility. The camp was compact: two side-by-side dormitory tents, a latrine and washstand behind the sleeping quarters, an open-sided kitchen with two picnic benches under a canopy, and a large van for parts, tools, and storage. Sacks of driller's mud and other bulk supplies were stored on the ground next to the van. Some twenty meters behind the van and even farther from the tents stood a strange-looking cube about a meter on a side, constructed of woven three quarter-inch steel cable on a frame of angle iron. On a hatch constructed of the same material ran the legend in English, *Danger —Dynamite*.

The men ambled down to the river. A pair of burros led by a Redhead approached from the direction of the ferry and crossed the river on the new bridge constructed by the drilling company. "You know, this bridge is quite something," Galo observed. "All they did was stabilize both shores and drop this truss in place. It's an English invention. It only took a month to transport it from Sulaco and install. As you can see, some of the Redheads find it more convenient then the ferry." He stopped speaking when they heard the sound of a vehicle in the distance. In a minute the bridge was creaking under the weight of it. The foreman waved as he passed them and proceeded to the office, where he parked next to Galo's pickup. He was in his mid-thirties, just under a meter-eighty, with wavy blond hair framing a round face. He got out of the black Ford pickup and said something to the geologist as the three were returning to the tent.

"Luzuriaga," he said, thrusting his hand toward Galo, and then turning to greet the other two. "Walter Wagner," he said by way of introduction.

"Juan Chiriboga," said the deputy director, shaking the foreman's hand. "And this is Felipe Krueger, from our legal department."

Without further ado Walter gestured toward the tent and said, "I think I can explain the problem to you." He introduced the ICRAC men to George Fuller, his geologist, who had just laid a set of plans on the table. He thumbed through the set and opened it to a map of the study area. The ICRAC men stood on either side of Walter, Galo and the geologist facing him. "This is the river," he said, running his fingers along its location on the sheet. "Here's the ferry, and we're here," he added, placing an index finger on each spot. "Now, here's where the ruins are located, except. . . ." He paused for effect. "They're *not*. They're *here*, just inside the area they agreed we could work in," he added, pointing to a penciled-in square about five kilometers closer to the river and within the line denoting the boundary of the study area.

"Where are you working now?" asked the deputy director.

"We've been working on a transect to the main line here," the other replied, pointing to the location, "since last Thursday. That's when our boys refused to clear the main line any closer to the ruins. We're stuck until we get this straightened out, and my bosses are pissed."

THE STREET LIGHTS, SUCH AS THEY WERE, had just come on: bare incandescent bulbs hanging by their wires from wooden poles planted at irregular intervals around the plaza, along Calle Sulaco as far as the hotel, and down Calle Sucre and Calle Maldonaldo to the Avenida del Valle. As darkness descended, the lights were enough to fill the street with a pale yellowish aura. At the sidewalks, those shops illuminated by electricity augmented the street lamps. But all the shops had kerosene lamps to serve when the power went off at ten, or failed altogether.

It was a quiet time. People strolled Calle Sulaco singly or in small groups, Margarita and Sor Marillac among them. They walked slowly: the nun with her hands thrust into the pockets of her habit, and her companion with her arms folded across her chest. Margarita was particularly pensive. She was thinking of evenings in Sulaco, years before, when she attended university, and remembering how the mood of the early evening had always charmed her. The two reached a point on Calle Sulaco where a tree grew in the middle of the widened roadway, with a small patio around it. A circular bench of concrete had been constructed around the tree, with wooden benches on four sides of the pavement facing it. Four ornamental lamps, the only ones in town, lit the area. Margarita sat on the circular bench. The nun took the wooden one, turned to her companion, and asked, "Margarita, why is an attractive woman like you not married?" the question forthright but not offensive. The two had become good friends since that night in Sulaco three years before, but the nun had never broached the subject.

"*Sor Marillac*! You sound like my mother."

"I can imagine why. It's hard to believe that there isn't a parade of suitors at your door. Does your father loose the dogs on them?"

"*No*," she protested.

"Then you must be too fussy."

"I guess that's it." Margarita frowned as she examined her shoe, then added, "They never seem to measure up."

"*So*, you have a *beau ideal*." The nun's eyes brightened as she closed in on her quarry. "Do I know him?"

Margarita blushed and turned away.

The nun thought for just a moment and, with a sudden inspiration, exclaimed, "Fidanza!"

Margarita blushed a deeper red. "Oh, I hardly knew him." She dismissed the suggestion with a wave of her hand.

Sor Marillac would not be dissuaded. "That night. *Le beau geste. Ah, oui*. . . . But where is he?"

Margarita relented. "It was months before I learned they'd smuggled him onto a ship bound for Chile, that he'd gone on to Argentina," she murmured. "He may still be there. Married, for all I know." After three years, it was a French nun in whom she would finally confide.

"But we will find out!" The nun rose. "We have a province in

Argentina. I have a friend in Buenos Aires." Her voice rose with each point. "And Doctora Lederer, who's coming tomorrow, *she* will know!" She was suddenly on a mission, as was obvious to the group sitting at the adjacent bench. Margarita, finally unburdened, did not protest. "But we must get back," the nun said, looking at her watch. "And if he's married, we'll find that out, too. We can't have you spending the rest of your life. . . . Well, none of that. Come! Dinner will put a different perspective on the thing."

"THE RUINS *ARE* WHERE THEY *ARE*," Chiriboga declared, "regardless of their location on a map." He took a sip of the beer Yapa Flores had just set before him. "And that's the fact all parties have to deal with."

The comment was music to Galo's ears. "How do you think the drillers are going to take this?" he asked.

"Well, there's going to be a rather large group here tomorrow to make it pretty evident how they intend to take it," Chiriboga responded dryly. "I'm sure they'll object. Point to the map and say that that's what they'd agreed to."

The owner brought over the blackboard on which was noted, *Dinner. Loin of beef with french fries.* They all nodded, and Yapa retreated to the kitchen. They were the only patrons in the restaurant, but Yapa had reported he had a full house booked for the next day.

"Who's going to be here?" Galo asked. He was beginning to feel a little heartened by Chiriboga's apparent warming to a fight, or at least an initial stand in favor of the Redheads.

"One of their managers and a lawyer are flying in from Sulaco, and the big boss, Cosgrove, is coming by private plane from the capital."

"That should cause a stir in the town," Galo observed. "The last time we had any plane other than a TAMC DC-3 was when the president inaugurated the new coffee-processing plant. Maybe you can get a ride back with him." The co-op manager smiled at the idea.

"That depends on how the meeting ends," the deputy director remarked sardonically.

Luzuriaga turned serious. "Juan, what the hell is this all about? I mean, all this commotion over an earthquake study?" Galo paused, then added, "*I* hear it's oil." The two ICRAC men exchanged glances.

"Is this a guess, Galo? Or do you know something we don't?" Felipe, who'd had precious little to say the whole afternoon, had asked the question.

Galo thought for a moment before responding. "An American engineer was visiting here last week with Wiggins—the Point Four guy?—when Rigpe was telling his story about the drilling operation. Braun, that's his name, had done seismicity studies in the United States, and he didn't think this was one. He said it sounded like prospecting. Probably for oil." Galo thought of Margarita's letter but added nothing. Flores returned with the steaks and asked if they wanted another round. Galo declined. The other two decided to split a beer.

"It's all so goddamn hush-hush," the lawyer muttered. "The rumors have been flying. The director seems to be under the gun, but nobody will say anything." Krueger was obviously upset. "Our only orders were to 'find a way.' Find a way. Hah!"

"Take it easy, Felipe." Juan was solicitous of his young companion. "It's not going to be settled tomorrow."

"Is Rigpe going to be there?" asked Galo.

"Not unless you invited him."

"Me!" exclaimed the co-op manager. "*I'm* not even going to be there. You guys are on your own." He waved off any thought of getting more involved.

"We know that! I was just pulling your leg," Juan assured him with a smile. Galo wasn't sure if it was the beer, or was the deputy director not as stiff as he'd thought? "And by the way, Galo, we really do appreciate your pitching in. I'm hoping to recruit a replacement for Robles within a month. But don't hold your breath. Again, I appreciate your help. As for Rigpe, his not being there will assure it won't be settled tomorrow."

"They're sure bringing in enough power to settle it tomorrow," offered Felipe, not satisfied with these assurances.

"It's just round one, Felipe, just round one."

The discussion turned to soccer, and Galo for one decided that he had heard enough that day about Chiri Yacu. It was after nine when they got up from the table. Galo bade them goodnight and decided that it was too late to stop by the convent.

CHAPTER 9

EXCEPT FOR SEGUNDO'S TAXI, the pitch-black street in front of the pension was deserted. Sergio could barely make out the car and the dark-skinned figure standing beside it.

"Fidanza. Good morning," the driver called out in a loud whisper. He opened the back door.

Sergio muttered a reply, put his recently purchased valise on the back seat, opened the front door, and got in. He was wearing only a short-sleeved guayabera in anticipation of the cool, moist morning air giving way to the heat of the day. "Sorry to get you up so early," he said, as the chauffeur got in and started the engine.

"I'm always up this early, but I'm usually at my stand at the Humboldt. There's always some businessman going to the airport or train station. I like the gringos. They're good tippers." His rapid-fire speech left little opportunity for comment. "The worst are the Argentines. I hope you didn't pick up their bad habits." Before Sergio could defend himself the driver added, "Don't worry. This is on Chinito's bill."

"Thank God he saved me from any embarrassment," Sergio replied.

The street took shape in the headlights. Three blocks up, the lights from the Alameda to the right faintly illuminated the corner. They turned toward the plaza, where large ornamental lamps cast numinous shadows on the paths. A small bell in the cathedral tower struck a half dozen times, announcing the mass at five forty-five as three figures in black, with black shawls draped over their heads, entered the street just in front of them. Segundo hit the brakes. The women didn't even look around, much less hurry their gait.

"Look at them! Already beatified!" the chauffeur cried, throwing his hands into the air. "On their way to Mass. They'll be on their way to heaven if they don't watch out."

"Calm down, Segundo." They continued around the plaza and turned onto Avenida de La Constitución. They did not encounter any other vehicles until they were in the Plaza Rembrandt, at the old wall. The Avenida de La Muelle was showing the first signs of life. The cafes were lighted, and the waiters were preparing for the early morning patrons.

"Do you want to stop for a coffee?" the chauffeur asked.

"No," the passenger answered. "We'll get something at the terminal." The road was still relatively empty as they turned onto Camino al Aeropuerto. Five minutes later they were at the main entrance. It took another five on the perimeter road before they reached the Quonset hut that served as the terminal for the Costaguana Military Air Transport, known by the initials in Spanish, TAMC. Except for the DC-6s used between Sulaco and the capital, the rest of the service consisted of ancient DC-3s. Sergio hopped out of the car and retrieved his valise from the rear seat. "We made good time," he observed. "I've got over half an hour. How about that coffee?"

Segundo looked at his watch. "I think I'll just get over to the hotel. With some luck I'll pick up fare before the other drivers. I was out to the train station yesterday with Compañero Ricabarran. I don't envy him his trip," he said, shaking his head. "Those guys are in big trouble. Probably'd been sucking the bottle. I understand the police have rounded up a half dozen. The porter fingered them. Well, what could *he* do? A grisly business." He looked at the ground, reached out for Sergio's hand, and added, "Have a good trip. With any luck you should be there by lunch." Without further ado he left, turning to wave as he got into the car.

Sergio picked up the bag and pushed through the door to the cavernous interior. There were two almost indistinguishable areas. The section to the right, serving the arriving passengers, was divided by a low counter for the incoming baggage, brought from the planes on a cart train to garage doors on the opposite wall. The arrival gate was in the far right wall. Two ticket counters were located in the area to the left. Several passengers were already in the waiting area just behind the counters. The door straight ahead led to the plane, which was already parked on the hardstand. The area served a DC-3 complement well but got pretty crowded before the two daily DC-6 flights to the capital. Even with additional seats around the perimeter, only about half of the passengers could be accommodated.

With only one of the two ticket counters attended and the sparse number of passengers in evidence, Sergio suspected that that day's flight to Catachoclo was a *mixta*, carrying mostly cargo in the forward part with canvas bucket seats along the aft sides for the passengers. The man behind the small bar to the left of the entrance was laying out baskets of rolls. One person was waiting at the bar. There was no one at the counter, so Sergio went there first. He set his bag on the scale and produced his ticket. The agent ripped off the flight coupon, returned the remainder with a boarding pass, and checked the bag without uttering a word. He managed to nod when Sergio asked if the flight was leaving at six-thirty as scheduled. Sergio started for the bar on the opposite side of the waiting room. As promised, the temperature had risen with the sun.

He had just seated himself on a stool when he became aware of someone on his left. He turned to face a petite woman in her early sixties. Close-cropped, wavy gray hair crowned a round face with large, watery blue eyes and high cheekbones. Dressed in a gray skirt and white short-sleeved blouse with a dark blue cravat, she was quite attractive. Setting down a small leather briefcase, she held out her hand and smiled. "Sergio Fidanza?" she asked. The voice was surprisingly deep, coming from such a tiny woman. "It's been a long time."

Sergio only hesitated for a moment before exclaiming, "Doctora Lederer! It's a pleasure to see you again. Yes. It's got to've been at least three years," he added, smiling. "Compañero Chang Crespo wasn't sure you'd be able to make it." He was quite pleased by the appearance of Doctora Golda Lederer de Saenz, the founder of FLOC.

"He called a little late, but I was able to arrange it. He even got my ticket for me," she replied, holding up an envelope.

"Do you have any other luggage?" Sergio asked. The briefcase didn't seem large enough for even an overnight stay.

"Yes," she said, turning toward the door. "Here he is now," she added, waving at a balding man of medium height carrying a valise about the size of Sergio's. "Fidanza, I don't think you've ever met my husband, Luis. Luis, this is Sergio Fidanza." The man smiled as he set the bag down and shook the other's hand.

"Pleased to meet you," Sergio said, and added, "I was just going to have a coffee. Can I offer you something?"

Golda looked at her husband. He glanced at the clock on the wall above the departure door and said, "Not for me, thanks. I'm working at the clinic today, and I must be off." Luis Saenz was a dentist and worked one day a week at the Port Workers' Clinic and one day every other week for FLOC. He embraced his wife, kissing her lightly on the lips, and said to Sergio, "Take good care of my Golda." Sergio nodded.

She waved at her husband as he looked back before passing through the door. "He's a little nervous. I haven't traveled on union business for several years now." Sergio picked up the valise and carried it to the counter. The agent repeated the routine as before, in silence.

"Shall we have a coffee, Doctora?"

The question was answered by the announcement of the flight's departure.

"OH, DEAR," REMARKED THE LAWYER as they entered the plane. "I'd hoped it wasn't going to be one of these affairs." They took the first two bucket seats opposite the entrance. A North American took a seat up forward on the side of the entrance, leaving one empty between him and the cargo. By the look of him—pointy boots, blue jeans, plaid shirt, and a Stetson—Sergio had the ominous feeling that he was somehow connected with Bumpy Cosgrove. All but three of the seats were quickly filled. Sergio recognized a functionary of O.S.N., taking a seat next to the gringo. Doctora Lederer nodded to a man she identified as the accountant for the coffee processing plant. He sat next to the cargo on their side. The gringo kept turning to peer out of the window at his back. A young man in an air force uniform made sure that all passengers had their seat belts securely fastened, pointed out the airsick bags in pockets under the seats, and was about to pull up the ladder and close the hatch when the gringo, who had been peering out of the window, exclaimed, "Heah he comes!" A moment later Licenciado Ribadeneira was laboring up the ladder, breathing heavily. He looked directly at Sergio but seemed not to recognize him. Surveying the rest of the passengers, he spotted his traveling companion and collapsed into the seat next to him.

Golda turned to her companion and muttered, "Alfredo Ribadeneira. The plot thickens." The cabin attendant finished closing the door, checked the licenciado's seat belt, and folded down his seat from the rear wall of the cabin. It was then that Ribadeneira realized who Sergio was and gestured toward him. Sergio nodded back. Golda, seated closer to him, also nodded.

As the captain turned over the engines, an announcement was made to the effect that the flight would take one hour and five minutes. In minutes they were airborne and banking to the southeast as the plane gained altitude. Five minutes later they reached the coastal range, where they were suddenly buffeted by strong updrafts. At one point Golda let out a soft cry as all of the passengers were lifted about six inches in the air. A woman sitting directly across from her reached for the airsick bag and got it open just in time. No one spoke during the continued lurching of the plane. When, after what seemed like an eternity, they reached the intermountain valley where the air was considerably smoother and the passengers had begun to relax, the attendant folded up his seat and opened a cabinet.

"Ah. Here comes the coffee," said Golda, eyeing the tray full of cups the attendant had extracted from the cabinet. They each took one. The attendant produced a thermos and promptly filled the cups. Golda retrieved from her briefcase two large rolls generously slathered with Camembert cheese, cut in half, and wrapped in wax paper. Sergio smiled at the sight. "And you thought we only carried important papers in these things."

"Thank you, Doctora," he said, accepting the proffered sandwich. They ate in silence, engrossed in thought. Sergio decided to wait for the lawyer to broach the subject of the trip. She ate slowly. When she offered him the uneaten half of her sandwich, he declined. "No, thank you, Doctora." She put it in her briefcase and turned to look at him. He returned her gaze but then looked away.

"Fidanza." She paused and looked down at her hands clasped in her lap. Her traveling companion followed her gaze, expecting her to begin discussing a plan of action once they reached Catachoclo. It was moments before she resumed. "Fidanza," she repeated in her deep voice. "We have such a thing with titles. It's Doctor this, Señor Ingeniero that, Licenciado the other." She paused to sip her coffee. Sergio was more than a little taken aback by the unexpected discourse. "What is it? Are we in such awe of education? Or is it low self-esteem? Of course a certain respect is appropriate," she added, gesturing with her hand, "as when children address their teachers as 'maestro.' But the labor movement in some ways is the worst offender. Everyone is addressed as 'compañero.' Very egalitarian. But when *I'm* at a meeting, it's always '*Doctora* Lederer.'" She shook her head. "I sort of understood it at the beginning. We were dealing with people with very little education. They looked up to Antonia and me." She turned to look directly at Sergio. "But now? You've been to university. So has Chang Crespo." She leaned back in the seat and looked straight ahead.

He didn't know quite what to make of this sudden turn. Then without thinking, he said, "With your permission, Doctora. . .I mean, ah. . .*I* will call you compañera. 'compañera *Golda*,'" he added with emphasis.

She threw back her head and laughed. She seemed almost embarrassed at his reaction. He was nonplussed, not sure if he'd said the right thing. She was quick to put him at ease. Looking directly at him, she said, "Compañera Golda. I would like that. Compañera Golda," she repeated it, smiling. "Well, now that we have the formalities settled, we'd better get to the business at hand."

They first exchanged what meager information each had on the Nogales affair. Sergio's was limited to the account in the paper.

Golda had learned from Chang Crespo that Zuñiga had returned from his mother's funeral, to find six workers locked up in the local jail. Based on the little Zuñiga could tell to Chang Crespo, Golda was of the opinion that the only thing FLOC could do was see that they had a fair trial. Since the victim had been a foreigner, there wasn't much feeling on the part of the townsfolk one way or the other. The owners would press for the toughest sentence, and no matter what happened the wife and family of the Spaniard could never recover their loss. "A pity," she said. "He didn't deserve it, no matter how ill-used those men were. The bloody system grinds the humanity out of people." They both reflected for a moment on Golda's observation. "But our business is with the beneficio workers in Catachoclo." She reached into her briefcase and withdrew a file folder. "You know, Fidanza, they're one of the oldest unions in FLOC outside of the Sulaco area. Antonia and I came out here in '42 to organize them. By train to Nicoya and by bus from there. It took *two days*," she added for emphasis. "We stayed over in Nicoya. And now we do it in an hour." She opened the folder and studied its contents. "Do you know Jorge Quishpe?"

"Yes. I met him the first time in 1955 at a congress in Sulaco, and again when I made several visits to Catachoclo for Julio a year or two before I left." He briefly explained the troubles over a lockout the union was having with the new manager, who had taken over upon the death of his uncle. "By the way, compañera Golda, I met with an American yesterday who works for the American Institute for Free Labor Development. Do you know them?"

"Yes. AIFLD. We've had some dealings with them. They're always pressuring us to join the World Confederation of Free Trade Unions." She frowned and observed, "Those gringos are always choosing up sides."

"He'd just been in Catachoclo and met with Quishpe. He says that they're setting up a course in credit unions for them."

"Good! I hope joining the WCFTU isn't part of the price," she said with her deep throaty laugh.

"He also mentioned that, while he was meeting with the head of a coffee grower co-op, a spokesman for the Redheads came in and created a stir about some drilling company moving in on their land. He was quite taken up with the story and hoping that we could do something."

"Who was he meeting with?"

"Galo Luzuriaga." Gazing off into the distance, Sergio added, "I think I may know him."

"He's a good man, Fidanza. He'll do something, if anybody can. But FLOC has never had any dealings with the Redheads. As you know, we decided years ago that we were going to concentrate on the industrial workers. ICRAC has the responsibility for the indigenous population."

"The AIFLD guy said that Luzuriaga called ICRAC. That may be why our friend across the way is with us," he said, leaning over and looking straight at his companion to preserve the confidentiality of the observation. However, the loud drone of the engines made their conversation inaudible to the other passengers, as the others' were to them.

"I'm not sure how really hard they'll advocate for the Redheads." She thought about it for a few moments. "Well, we'll see what we can do," she said with a sigh of resignation. "Getting back to Quishpe. When we were here in '42, he was a thirty-year-old firebrand, ready to take on the world." Golda smiled and nodded. "He worked in the beneficio. His mother, a firebrand in her own right, was from Catachoclo, but, as it happened, worked as a cook for my brother-in-law, a doctor in Nicoya. Jorge grew up in his house. With no children of their own, they treated him like a son. That's how we met." The loudspeaker was activated, and the voice of the pilot announced that they would be landing in ten minutes. Golda returned the file to her briefcase.

"I remember him telling me once," recalled Sergio, "that he was the illegitimate son of the founder of the original beneficio. A fellow named Alfonso Palacios. Imagine."

"Having heard the story from his mother, I don't doubt it myself," Golda replied. "But there's an old Czech proverb—'You might as well believe it as look for proof.' In any case, he founded the original union with our help, and he's going to meet us at the airport."

"Where are you staying, compañera Golda?" Sergio asked as the plane began its descent into the valley of the Redheads. He was becoming more comfortable with the familiar address.

"With the Sisters of the Holy Redeemer."

"I understand that Sor Marillac is stationed there."

"You know. . .?" Golda looked at her companion in surprise, but for only a moment. "Of *course*. From her porter organizing days on the Sulaco wharves! . . . She's still at it. She's our eyes and ears in the town."

"And was of great help to us during the night of our fall from grace," Sergio recalled.

The plane circled around to the south for its final approach. The rapid descent after clearing the low mountains caused Sergio's ears to stop up. He held his nose and blew gently to clear them. Golda did the same while reflecting on the plight of the Redheads. Looking at Sergio, she said, "Yes. We must do something."

1942

CHAPTER 10

T HE MAN IN HIS MID-FIFTIES, standing on the platform of the
Nicoya train terminal, pulls a watch from the vest pocket of
his white linen suit. It is three o'clock in the afternoon, and the locomotive of the train from Tonoro rumbles by, enveloping the platform in steam whooshing from the cylinder at each slowing stroke
of the piston. With a shrill blast of the whistle the train screeches to
a halt. He waits beneath the wooden arcade as passengers begin to
alight. An attractive woman with wavy brown hair, cut just above
the shoulders, steps off the second car and searches the crowd. After
recognizing the man in the linen suit, she turns to assist her traveling
companion. The tall woman's light step belies her sixty-two years.
They advance toward the gentleman, who lifts his jipijapa and extends his hand to the older woman. Her austere visage changes completely when she smiles. "Doña Antonia, how pleased I am to have
you visit us." The pressure of Antonia's hand confirms the strength
of a woman who has withstood Costaguana political intrigue for over
forty years. Then he turns to her companion. "Golda, the news of
your visit with Doña Antonia was most welcome," he says, kissing
her on the cheek. "But I hope you will grace us with your presence
for more than one night."

"We must go on to Catachoclo tomorrow, Paco. But Luis says

that we should stay a few days upon our return."

"Well, you tell my little brother that his indulgence is appreciated, and that a visit from *him* is long overdue." A porter arrives with the baggage, and, as he follows, the three leave the station for Paco's awaiting car. "And you, Doña Antonia, active as ever?"

"No, not really. Golda has assumed most of the responsibility for FLOC, and my cousin's son is now publisher of *El Porvenir*. I'm just a contributing editor."

"*Just* a contributing editor?" A deep laugh erupts from the petite Golda, and her blue eyes twinkle. "A column every week and trips like this on a regular basis. Yes. Antonia is in semiretirement, sitting in her living room and tatting altar cloths for the cathedral." She laughs again. They reach the car. Paco tips the porter after he places the baggage in the trunk of the 1936 Chevrolet sedan parked at the corner.

DOCTOR FRANCISCO SAENZ'S HOUSE lies in a residential neighborhood not far from the train station. The housekeeper, an Indian woman of about forty-five years is seated at a table under a window in the large kitchen. She wears her hair in the single braid of the sierra but is dressed in a European-styled pleated skirt and cotton blouse. The window opens onto a garden shaded from the afternoon sun by a huge eucalyptus tree, across from which lie the servants' quarters: an arcaded building with two bedrooms, a toilet, a storage room, and a laundry stand. The woman is rereading a letter she has just finished writing. She puts the letter down and looks out the window. A teenage girl is retrieving bed linens from a wash line stretched between the laundry stand and the eucalyptus tree. A round face, with the bloom of youth unscarred by the dreary peasant life she has left behind, bears a wistful expression. After removing each sheet the girl carefully folds it and places it in one of two baskets on the grass. In the other, an infant of about six months stirs and opens his eyes. He kicks his feet and begins to cry. The girl places the last pillowcase in the basket, picks up the child, and, cradling it gently in her arms, sits on the bench next to the laundry stand. She unbuttons her blouse. The crying stops as the baby clutches his mother's breast and begins to nurse. She leans her head against the wall. A smile of contentment illuminates her face. The woman in the kitchen feels the tug of the baby at her breast. She looks down at his two black eyes returning her gaze as a small stream of milk escapes his lips. She strokes the infant's wispy black hair. She looks up as the car pulls into the driveway, announcing the return of the doctor with his guests. When she looks back, the baby's gone and the garden is empty. She folds the letter and puts it into the pocket of her apron.

Paco is opening the trunk as the housekeeper comes down the steps to greet the guests. She opens the car door and extends her hand to assist. "Welcome, Doña Golda. How was the trip?"

"Uneventful thank you, Gloria. You remember Doña Antonia Avellanos?"

"Of course. Welcome!" she greets the older woman and turns to take the two suitcases Paco has retrieved from the trunk. "I will take these to your rooms." Gloria Quishpe rushes off into the house without another word.

THE TABLE HAS BEEN CLEARED of the supper dishes, and night has settled on the city. A dog barking in the distance is the only sound drifting through the open window on a breeze with the faint scent of eucalyptus. The three are enjoying a postprandial cup of coffee.

"Will Leticia be back from the capital when we return?" Golda asks.

"If you grace us with a few days, she will be here before you leave." Paco gets up, fetches a box from the buffet behind him inlaid in the style of Andalusia, opens it, and offers a cigar to Golda.

"No," she says, "I'll stick to my cigarettes."

"Antonia?"

She declines. "But please go ahead. It reminds me of my father. He enjoyed a cigar with his coffee, as did my uncle."

"The cardinal?"

"Yes. The first and last cardinal of Sulaco."

"They probably drank the same coffee, Tres de Mayo," Paco says as he lights Golda's cigarette and his cigar.

"Yes. I recall in those days Don Alfonso Palacios would have his majordomo deliver three sacks to the Club Amarillo every year on the anniversary of the defense. They say he was among the defenders, but I don't remember the man." She frowns as she sips her coffee and reflects on the events of forty years ago. Returning the cup to its saucer, she remarks, "I never would have dreamed it, but here we are, organizing the workers of his beneficio." A faint smile crosses her lips. "Well, if we are going to have an early start, I think I'll retire."

As she rises, Paco calls to the housekeeper, who enters from the kitchen. "Gloria, please light the way for Doña Antonia."

He leans forward and taps the ash from his cigar as he watches them leave. Then he turns to his sister-in-law. "When Luis wrote to me of your coming, he urged me to accompany you to Catachoclo."

"Luis worries too much," Golda remarks with a wave of her hand. "This is not a land of brigands, some backwater of ignoramuses. These landowners and cafeteros repress their workers because it's always been done, and they think that it's the only way. We are here to disabuse them of this thinking."

Paco smiles at the flip retort. "But a union? They scarcely know what the term means."

"I'm sure they know exactly what it means."

"They will try to intimidate you."

"Paco, Antonia was in Sulaco when it was under siege by the Gamachos during the War of Separation. The daughter of Don Carlos Avellanos and the niece of the former cardinal of Sulaco is fully capable of her own intimidating." She takes a long drag on the cigarette and then snuffs it out. "And I am no stranger to intimidation." The low moan of a horn announces the night watch making his rounds. The security it proclaims belies the turmoil in the world of 1942.

"And still no news of your family?" Paco asks, knowing the answer.

The petite woman appears even more fragile as she shakes her head. "Nothing since two years. I wanted to go back but. . . ." She shrugs. Brightening a bit, she adds, "So we cope. Antonia prays, and we throw ourselves into the work. . . . I wish I had her faith."

Gloria returns to the room and picks up a tray from the sideboard next to the kitchen door. She retrieves the coffee service from the table before asking, "Is there anything else, Don Francisco?"

"No, Gloria. That will be all. Oh—and breakfast at six. The señoras will be taking the bus at nine."

"At six." She nods, confirming the hour. "Goodnight, Doña Golda, Don Francisco," she says and leaves, closing the kitchen door behind her.

"It's a strange string of events that brings us here, Paco," Golda observes. "But that's the way life plays out."

"Yes. Her father dropped her on our doorstep, so to speak. And when I learned of the circumstances, how could I say no?"

"There are many who would have."

"I suppose. But we needed a laundress, so it worked out."

"Doctors don't deliver their laundress's babies."

"Leticia is the heroine, Golda. She taught her to read and write and do figures." Paco goes over to the buffet. "Would you like a brandy?"

"With some soda. Thank you."

Paco pours the drinks and resumes his seat. "She reads almost at the university level, but she never wanted anything more than her work in the house. She took over as housekeeper when her aunt died—a breast cancer, sad to say. And when the baby came, Leticia doted on him. Like it was our own." He raises his glass. "To your health. . . . And success."

"Thank you. With Jorge there, it will certainly be a success."

"Yes, Jorge. Jorge Washington Quishpe. We would have sent him to university. But I think it was a *fait accompli*. When he was ten or eleven, during the school vacation, he started riding the coffee wagons with Pedro, his grandfather. By that time Don Alfonso had died, and his sons had no inkling of who Jorge was. By the end of the second summer, even at the age of thirteen or so, he began to understand the life at the cafetero for what it was. That's where you enter the story."

"I remember it well," Golda says. She takes a sip of her brandy and returns the glass to the table. "We were recently married and visiting you and Leticia for the first time. I think Gloria had over-heard us speaking of my work with the unions in Sulaco. The next day I was sitting in the garden when she asked if she might speak to me. It was then I heard of Jorge and the working conditions at the beneficio. It was an opportunity to extend our work out of the city, so I told her I would send her some books to read. When we got back to Sulaco, I sent her the encyclical, *Quadragesimo Anno*, the one on the reconstruction of the social order, and a biography of Samuel Gompers." She takes a sip of the brandy and smiles. "Within the month Jorge was on my doorstep."

DRESSED IN THE CLOTHES THEY ARRIVED IN, the two women wait in the living room for the return of Paco from an early call at the clinic. It has been raining lightly since breakfast. Gloria enters, clutching an envelope. "Doña Golda, I have a letter for my son." She holds it out cautiously.

"Of course, Gloria." Golda reaches out for it. "I'm sure you're concerned about Jorge, but he's planned it very well," she says, put-ting the letter in her black briefcase.

"He's been more than two years gathering the group and devel-oping the mutual trust," Antonia explains. "Once the declaration is signed and notarized, there's nothing the patrón can do."

"If it were Don Alfonso, there'd be something done," Gloria ob-serves matter-of-factly. "But he's been dead these twenty-five years. Don Carlos may not be the tyrant the old man was, but the apple has not fallen far from the tree. And who will notarize it?" she asks with a note of foreboding.

"That's what *we're* here for, Gloria," says Antonia. "We'll witness the charter, bring it to the prefect of the canton for his stamp, then file it here in Nicoya. The law is clear on the matter. There should be no trouble."

"May God hear you, Doña Antonia," Gloria murmurs. "I worry, but I would have it no other way. Perhaps we will finally find jus-tice."

At the sound of the car in the driveway Golda glances at her watch. "Oh, it's late." Gloria takes the bags and leads the way out to the car. The women each take an umbrella from the stand next to the door.

"I'm sorry for the delay," Paco shouts, opening the trunk lid for Gloria. "But we'll make it, even if I have to chase him out of town."

"Go with God," says Gloria as she embraces each woman. She stands stone-faced as the car speeds out the drive, oblivious to the rain.

1965

CHAPTER 11

G OLDA AND SERGIO, FIRST OFF THE PLANE, were astounded by
the number of people milling in and around the small aerodrome. Although much smaller than the TAMC terminal in Sulaco,
it was a bit more elegant, of concrete block construction and sport-
ing a two-story control tower. The two led the line of a dozen passengers into the crowded waiting room. Golda spotted Jorge
Quishpe standing near Juan Chiriboga and Felipe Krueger, who were
there to meet Ribadeneira and his associate. "There he is, Fidanza,"
she said, pointing to a man in his early fifties. Quishpe was a head
taller than most of the others waiting to receive the passengers. The
black hair that grew low on his forehead was combed straight back.
His brown pants, a white shirt open at the collar, and polished brown
loafers suggested a certain urbanity not common among his peers.
His severe countenance lightened considerably as he recognized
Doctora Lederer. The head of the Beneficio Workers Union removed
a tan straw hat as the two visitors approached.

"Doctora Lederer, what a surprise!" he exclaimed. "I didn't
know you were coming. And Compañero Fidanza!" he added, shaking the younger man's hand and then embracing him. "I was happy
to hear from compañero Chang Crespo that it was *you*, coming to
help in our planning. But Doctora Lederer is a welcome bonus."

Chiriboga and Krueger, dressed in shirts and ties, moved toward
the arrival door to receive Licenciado Ribadeneira and his gringo as-

sociate. The ICRAC men greeted Ribadeneira, who introduced the senior geologist. "Pleased to meetcha," he responded in English.

"Is FLOC involved in this?" asked the licenciado, glancing at the three still in conversation while they waited for the baggage delivery. "Doctora Lederer and a guy named Fidanza were on the plane with us." The two ICRAC men followed Ribadeneira's glance. Chiriboga shook his head. "I don't know them. Who is she?"

"One of the founders of FLOC. And Fidanza had been with the port workers." He frowned as he pondered the possibilities. "It must be union business," he decided. A voice on a loudspeaker announced that the baggage could be retrieved on the sidewalk in front of the terminal. Golda, Sergio, and Quishpe were the first through the entranceway. A cart containing the baggage had been pushed around to the curb. Not seeing their bags on the side toward the terminal they walked around the cart, where they encountered Ribadeneira coming from the other direction.

"What brings you to Catachoclo, Licenciado?" Golda asked with deliberate nonchalance.

"A meeting with the deputy director of ICRAC," he answered, nodding in the direction of Chiriboga, who was helping the gringo with his baggage.

"Here in little Catachoclo?" she asked, smiling sweetly.

At that moment, a small plane, touching down in front of the terminal, distracted them. "I'm afraid you'll have to excuse me, Doctora. We're expecting another participant on that plane."

"Would it be Bumpy Cosgrove, by any chance?" asked Sergio, who had remained silent up to that time.

The pudgy man winced and then answered, "As a matter of fact, it would." Without waiting for a comment, he rushed off toward the terminal.

"Well done, Fidanza. You caught him good."

"Jorge," Sergio asked, "do you know anything about the drilling across the river?"

The union leader shrugged. "They say it's an earthquake study."

"If it's Cosgrove, it's oil," Sergio told him, grabbing the two valises.

"Where are you staying, Doctora?" Jorge asked, taking Golda's valise from Sergio.

"At the convent."

"Good choice. And you, Compañero? The Sulaco?"

"You guessed it."

"Well, it's had some improvements since your last visit," Jorge reported as he led them across the road in front of the airport. "They serve a breakfast of sorts, and there are toilets and a bathroom on the second floor. Of course," he added, "they still have the washstands in the rooms, in case there's a line at the bathroom."

The accountant for the coffee processor was being ushered into a blue Chevrolet sedan parked behind a rack truck on the other side of the road. He nodded to the doctora as she and her companions slipped between the two vehicles and entered the plaza. They proceeded across the dusty expanse in the direction of the church.

"Doctora Lederer!" The voice was coming from behind them. They turned to see a man in his late thirties, wearing a white guayabera and a jipijapa covering long black hair. He limped slightly as he hurried to catch up, removing his hat as he approached. "Doctora Lederer," he repeated as he reached them. "I don't know if you remember me. Victor Hugo Ramirez," he said, shaking her hand.

"Of course. You're from *El Porvenir*. This is Jorge Quishpe."

"Yes, we've met," the other acknowledged, shaking the union leader's hand.

"And this is Sergio Fidanza."

"Pleased to meet you," said Ramirez frowning, and then added, with a smile of recognition, "You're with the port workers."

"Was," Sergio corrected him.

"Oh?" he said. After making a mental note, Ramirez addressed them all. "Do you have any comment on the earthquake study they're doing on the land of the Redheads?"

"We're very concerned that their rights be observed," Golda remarked, "and we support them to that end. But we're here on union business."

"You should be talking to the gentleman who's just arrived on that private plane," Sergio offered. "His name is Dale Cosgrove."

The reporter pulled a notebook from his back pocket and a pen from the breast pocket of the guayabera. "Could you spell that for me?" he asked.

Sergio obliged him and added, "We've heard it's for oil."

"*Oh*? Well, thank you very much. I'd better be going," Ramirez said, as he turned without further formalities and rushed off toward the aerodrome.

"*Ramirez!*" Golda called out to the retreating back of the reporter. "You didn't hear that from *us!*" He waved his hand in agreement without turning around. "Well," she observed in her throaty laugh, "the fat will soon be in the fire."

Ramirez arrived back at the aerodrome as two workmen in blue uniforms were towing the luggage cart back behind the building. Chiriboga, Krueger, Ribadeneira, and the gringo were just leaving the building with the newly arrived Bumpy Cosgrove. The reporter, correctly guessing who Cosgrove was, planted himself directly in his path, and asked, "Señor Cosgrove, can you tell us anything about the oil prospecting going on across the river?"

A SHORT, ROUND INDIAN WOMAN, wearing a white apron over her blue wrap-around skirt, opened the door of the convent. She stared at the two men, and then smiled when she recognized Quishpe. He gestured toward Golda and said something to her in Quechua. "Yes, yes. Come in, Señora Golda," she said, grabbing the valise from Jorge and beckoning them to enter the anteroom. She opened the door to the dining room and held it for her. As Golda passed through, the cook waved her finger at the two men and said, "No, no." She pointed to two straight-backed chairs opposite the inside door. "Wait here." Once inside she motioned for Golda to have a seat at the table and excused herself. "I will get Sor Marillac."

A minute later Golda rose from her seat as the beaming nun entered the room. "*Bienvenue*, Doctora," the nun said as she embraced the visitor. "Did you arrive here alone?"

"No. My companions are waiting," Golda replied, pointing to the door. "You know Jorge Quishpe. And there is another from Sulaco, whom I think you also know—Sergio Fidanza."

The nun's eyes widened, and her hand flew to her mouth. "Fidanza? *Mon dieu!*" she exclaimed. She turned toward the kitchen then as quickly turned back. "*Ooo, la-la!* Fidanza!"

The Doctora was completely surprised by the reaction. "I *thought* you knew him," she remarked rather tentatively.

"Yes, yes. But here? In Catachoclo?" The nun took a deep breath and composed herself. "Just last night we were talking about him. Wondering where he was. *Mon dieu!* Here in Catachoclo. *Incroyable.* Maria!" she called out to the kitchen. The cook appeared in the doorway. "Maria, take the gentlemen around to the clinic." Then she turned to her guest and said, "Come. I will show you to your room."

A few minutes later the two women returned to the dining room. "So you can see, Doctora, why I was so surprised when you said that he was with you." As they proceeded through the kitchen on the way to the clinic, the nun asked, "Will you be having lunch with us?"

"No. We'll be meeting at the union headquarters all day."

They entered the courtyard between the buildings. The clinic was quite substantial. Built in the late fifties, it had its own water well and elevated storage tank on the roof. The tank, which also served the convent, was charged every morning, and occasionally during the day, by two porters using a hand-operated two-man pump. A small generator was available, sparingly, to provide light on overcast days and to run the emergency equipment. Waiting clients already filled benches along the wall of a colonnade running half the length of the long, low structure. A young woman, in a postulant's habit and holding a clipboard, was keeping reasonable order. There were several examining rooms—one with a table for emergency procedures, the most serious of which had been a leg amputation the year before—a consultation room, which doubled as a meeting room and extra examining room, a storage room, and a general office/pharmacy. The double-sloped roof was open at both ends, providing ventilation that made the interior reasonably comfortable except for the hottest days.

"I wonder what we should do," said the nun, thrusting her hands into the pockets of her habit as they strolled across the courtyard.

"I think nothing," Golda advised. "You know what they say, 'What will be, will be.'" She was not about to be drawn into any conspiracy.

They reached the entrance as the postulant was escorting a young mother with an infant to one of the examining rooms. The child did not look well. Sor Marillac addressed the mother by name and asked what was wrong. The woman explained that the child had had diarrhea for a day. Sor Marillac went with her to the first room on the left where Sor Beatrice was readying the examining table for the next patient and, after a brief discussion with the older nun, took the baby from the mother and laid her on the table. "She's lucky to have gotten the infant here so quickly," the nun said to Golda. "If they wait too long, there isn't much we can do. Diarrhea is one of the biggest killers of the babies."

They walked down the white-walled central hall and into the conference room. Sergio rose from the chair nearest the door as they entered. "Fidanza!" the nun exclaimed. Sergio shook her outstretched hand. "How long has it been? Three years, no?"

"Three years last month," he confirmed, obviously happy to renew their friendship.

Unable to restrain herself, she announced, "And Fidanza, you will never guess who is visiting us—the young woman you deposited on our doorstep that night!"

Sergio could feel the hair on his arms and the back of his neck rise. He almost wished he hadn't heard. He felt, rightly so, that all three in the room were staring at him and smiling. He looked about, fully expecting that she might materialize in their midst. He was dumbfounded but finally managed to blurt out, "Margarita."

Golda had walked around the table to an empty chair. "Are you all right, Fidanza?" she inquired. "You look a little pale."

"Yes. Fine." He sank into his seat. "Margarita Bustamante," he murmured, half dazed, looking at the floor.

"The very same," said the nun. "She is visiting our station in San Miguel with Sor Lourdes and Sor Maryse. They will be back this evening, if you'd. . .like to stop by?"

"Yes," he said, still looking at the floor. "It would be. . .nice to see her."

"Are you married?" the nun asked. The words were hardly uttered when her hand flew to her mouth. Golda could barely suppress a chuckle.

Sergio, still staring at the floor, muttered, "No. I'm still. . .single." The import of the question had completely eluded him.

"I think we'd better get moving," Golda suggested. "We have a lot of work to do."

A flicker of understanding began to show in Jorge's eyes as he rose at the suggestion. "Yes. The others are waiting at the headquarters," he said. By the time they had reached the street and made their good-byes to Sor Marillac, Sergio seemed to have regained his interest in the business at hand.

VICTOR HUGO RAMIREZ HAD FOLLOWED the group over to the canton administration building after Cosgrove insisted, in answer to his question, that the drilling was not for oil but was rather a seismicity study. He'd maintained this to all of Ramirez's subsequent questions, fired at his back as the group hurried across the plaza. When they reached the building, Cosgrove turned on the reporter and in no uncertain terms declared, "You'll have to excuse us, Señor—what'd you say your name was?"

"Ramirez."

"Señor Ramirez. We have some important things to discuss."

Without another word he proceeded to the assembly hall at the corner of the courtyard opposite the office of Galo Luzuriaga. Ramirez watched them until the last was inside before turning in the direction of Galo's office.

THE ASSEMBLY HALL WAS ABOUT SEVEN meters wide and nine meters long. A raised platform about three meters wide extended across the width of the room to the right of the entry door. A long table draped in dark brocade, with five chairs behind it, sat in the center of the platform. A painting of a military man dominated the room from the wall behind the table. The man was dressed in white trousers and a navy blue tunic piped in gold, with ornately fringed gold epaulets. Two large medals adorned his left breast. The most striking thing about him was his fierce expression, augmented by a wide, luxuriant black beard trimmed level just below his chin, and two heavy black eyebrows that joined over the bridge of his nose. The life-size painting had an ornate wooden frame two-and-a-half meters high and a meter wide. Just in front of the platform, a small desk with two chairs faced about fifty chairs, arranged in rows of six each.

As they entered, Walter Wagner and George Fuller rose to greet them from a bench situated against the wall next to the portrait. On the table they had already unrolled the plan that Chiriboga and Krueger had reviewed the day before. They arranged the chairs and the bench around the table and took seats.

"First thing I want to say," Bumpy barked without further introduction, "is that all that stuff about oil prospecting is bullshit, and I don't want to heah any more of it. We've got enough with these Indians to deal with. I don't need more trouble." He pointed to the center of the table and added for emphasis, "It stays with us."

Chiriboga, sitting opposite Bumpy, stiffened. "I'm afraid the rumor is out and—"

"Let it *be* out!" Bumpy shot back. "But I don't want any of *us* feeding it." He paused to let the idea sink in. "That Redhead gonna be heah?"

"*We're* representing the Arra'o, Señor Cosgrove," Chiriboga told him. "As far as they're concerned, they've agreed to everything they're going to."

"Well, that's just fine with us," said Bumpy. "They agreed to that area," he added, leaning over the map and gesturing to the terrain marked for the study, "and that's exactly what we intend to study."

"The Arra'o stipulated that the ruins were not to be desecrated," Chiriboga said clearly and dispassionately, "and *you* agreed to *that*."

"Yeah. We agreed to the ruins being over there. . . . Who the hell made this map, anyway?" Bumpy's displeasure was becoming apparent.

"I checked into that before we came down," said Krueger. "It's part of the military coverage of the country. This area is based on a

boundary survey conducted after the Occidental War of Separation."
He consulted a notebook he had opened on the table in front of him.
"It was updated in 1955, using aerial photos."

"They seemed to have missed the ruins by a country mile,"
Bumpy observed with a wry smile bordering on a sneer.

"The jungle is pretty thick," observed the lawyer. "They probably
couldn't confirm them and just used the original location."

"'*Just used the original location*'!" Bumpy was irate. "We got a lot
riding on your 'just used the original location'."

Chiriboga raised a cautioning hand to calm him. "I'm sure,
Señor Cosgrove, we can sort this out. Surveys like the one you're
performing cover a lot of ground. I'm sure your engineers can come
up with an alternative," he said, gesturing toward the two seated to
his left. They both looked at Cosgrove, who stared for a long moment at the plan on the table. When he finally spoke, his voice was
calm.

"Señor Chiriboga, I came down heah to discuss a political solution. Something that'd get these Redheads' attention."

"I think you've gotten their attention, Señor Cosgrove, as I think
they have yours." Having made his point, Chiriboga leaned back in
his chair.

The deputy director's response had unnerved Bumpy Cosgrove,
but he kept his temper under control. He'd expected a supportive
ICRAC. "The only thing that's got my attention is their refusal to
clear the jungle for my crew."

"I believe they're refusing to clear in the direction of the ruins,"
Chiriboga replied. "I think you should explore your other options."

"Yes, I do have another option. There's plenty of these coffee
growers around here who'd jump at the chance to work for the
money we're paying and not be concerned about what they was *encroaching* on."

Bumpy's wry grin turned to a frown when Chiriboga, leaning
forward in his chair, replied, "*That* would be a grave mistake." Licenciado Ribadeneira and the senior geologist, who had said nothing
up to the moment, squirmed in their chairs. The two technicians
stared at the drawing, and Bumpy, maintaining an aggressive air, kept

his eyes on the deputy director.

Chiriboga broke the silence. "Señor Cosgrove, perhaps we should give you a chance to discuss this with your colleagues. We can leave. You're welcome to stay here, and we can reconvene after lunch."

Bumpy turned and swung his left arm over the back of the chair. Drumming the table with his right hand, he pondered the offer. The Texan looked hard at Ribadeneira, who was perspiring profusely, then turned to the ICRAC men and said, "Good idea. But unless you have other plans, let's make it tomorrow morning."

Chiriboga glanced at Krueger, who nodded. "That's fine with us." The two rose and, shaking hands all around, prepared to leave.

Bumpy got up and escorted them to the door. "You might want to check with your people in Santa Marta," Bumpy advised. The deputy director gave a noncommittal nod. Bumpy watched for a moment as the two crossed the courtyard in the direction of Galo Luzuriaga's office, then returned to his seat, leaving the door open.

The corpulent lawyer was mopping his face with his handkerchief, expecting the obvious. He was not disappointed. Switching to English, Bumpy asked, "Well, Licenciado, what's your opinion?" He again draped his arm over the back of the chair and, hooking the right heel of his cowboy boot on the rung of the chair, seemed ready to hear a detailed discourse, which, in the end, would probably not influence his decision.

The licenciado's fleshy fingers momentarily fussed with the clasp of the briefcase lying on the table before him. He made a final pass with the handkerchief over his drenched face and began. He summed up in lawyerly fashion the sudden turn of events, allowing as how the prevailing opinion had been that ICRAC would support the drilling in spite of the erroneous location of the ruins. He ended with the recommendation that they consider an alternate drilling program.

Bumpy, seemingly determined to see what he considered a ridiculous charade to completion, turned to the senior geologist. "George, what do you think of changing our drilling program?"

George Mitchell, broad-shouldered and a little older than Cosgrove, whose tanned and craggy features reflected years spent in the oil fields, leaned forward, put his elbows on the table and tapped his fingers together. "Bumpy," he began, "we've done a mess of prospecting in our day. We've had our share of good luck and our share of dry holes. But when I look at the records we got so far, and Fuller here says that the latest just confirms it, I get the shivers." He paused for a moment and seemed to be mentally reviewing the data he had been receiving from Fuller. He held up a gnarled index finger and said, "I'm not quite ready to take it to the bank, but. . . ."

"What would it take, George?" Bumpy asked.

"We'd have to finish the line," the other answered and leaned back in his chair.

"What about doglegging around the ruins?" Bumpy was intent on looking at all of the options.

George thought about it for a moment. "We'd have to see what the results were on the other side. *And* we'd have to deal with the eleven-kilometer gap."

Bumpy turned to the drilling foreman. "How long would it take to do that, Walter?"

"I estimate six to eight weeks," the young man said without hesitation.

"Six to eight weeks just so these Redheads can hunker down on that pile of rock when the spirit moves them," Bumpy observed, shaking his head. "When do we have to make the decision?"

The drilling foreman rose, leafed through the plans on the table, and pulling one out, placed it on top. "We're working on this transect," he said, pointing to the location. "We have another, here, we can do before we have to move ahead. It should take us about two weeks. Three at the most." He remained standing and turned to look directly at his boss. "There's another consideration."

"Oh. What's that?" Bumpy asked.

"The drill rig is due for an overhaul." Wagner ran a hand through his wavy blond hair. "If we pushed through as originally planned, I'd chance it. But making a dogleg, I'd like to get that replacement rig in from the main camp in the Orient. That'd take two weeks. That is, if they started tomorrow. Of course, we'd keep going here."

"Well, with all that," the boss asked, with a touch of impatience, "when will you have to know?"

Wagner thought for a moment. "Three weeks," he answered, praying that he was right.

Cosgrove spent another half hour grilling Ribadeneira about the legal issues. The lawyer thought that the law was on the drillers' side, but that the political climate was such that a court decision was not likely to be had before, and without, every potential presidential candidate, including the recently returned Juan Carlos Vasquez Iturralde, weighing in. Having explored all the issues, Cosgrove adjourned the meeting and announced that he would be spending the night with the owners of the Cafetero Tres de Mayo. Wagner said that they were prepared to have them all to lunch at the campsite. Ribadeneira was not as keen as the others to take up the offer.

THE UNION HEADQUARTERS WAS a five-minute walk from the clinic: up Calle Sulaco, a right turn just past the hotel, then left, before reaching the Flamenco, onto Calle San Martin. The narrow, cobbled pavement was badly eroded, but the concrete sidewalks under the wooden arcade were in good condition. The office, next door to a tailor, who, according to his sign, catered to 'Elegant Youth,' sported its own sign, *The Beneficio Workers' Union*. They entered through a wide double door that had been left open to permit air to circulate. The arcade and the thick walls kept the inside temperature about ten degrees below that of the street. Backless benches lined the walls of the room, which was illuminated by a single bulb hanging by its wire from the center of the ceiling. The wire ran along the ceiling and then down the far wall to a switch next to a door that led to another room. A table with four chairs sat beneath the light. Andrés Puíg, the secretary of the finance committee, came around the desk he had been seated at to greet the arrivals. Puíg was five years older than Quishpe, almost as tall, and similarly dressed: khaki trousers, pleated in the front, a long sleeved white shirt, and a straw hat with a leather band. He had the ascetic frame of a friar but an almost aristocratic physiognomy. With a dark suit and tie, he would not have looked out of place in the philosophy department of the university.

"Doctora Lederer! I had no idea you were coming." He removed the straw hat and held out his arm in a way that required Golda to grasp it by the wrist. "We were expecting—ah, yes. compañero Fidanza," he said, recognizing Sergio. "How long has it been since you were here?"

"Over four years."

"Yes. When Don Juan Carlos was killed in the accident and his cousin, Don Luis, took over the Cafetero Tres de Mayo." Puíg looked off into the distance, conjuring up that time. "He tried to break us, but thanks to you, we prevailed. Are you back with the port workers?"

Sergio was about to comment when a young man hurried in from the back room, hastily wiping his hands on his pants. Looking hard, Sergio suddenly identified him as the one who had stood fast when the owner tried to lock the workers out of the beneficio. "Compañero Castro!" he exclaimed. "What a pleasure to see you." The man, in his early thirties, was clean-shaven and wore a loose t-shirt outside jeans. The two embraced. Sergio turned to his traveling companion and said, "Compañera Golda, this is Compañero Rubén Castro." Quishpe and Puíg looked at each other in astonishment at Sergio's use of the informal address. Castro seemed to take it in stride. "He's the one I spoke of on the plane." Golda took Ruben's proffered forearm.

After they arranged themselves around the table, Quishpe began, "Doctora Lederer—"

He stopped and looked strangely at Sergio who, sensing his discomfort, said, "Compañera Golda feels that it's not in keeping with union fraternity to address her as 'Doctora.'"

"Of course," Quishpe quietly responded. He thought about it for a moment. "Of course," he repeated with animation. "It's like when I stopped addressing the bosses as 'su merced.' They beat me at first. But they got used to it. . .or tired of beating me. As long as compañera Lederer won't beat us, we will be happy to oblige." A deep laugh erupted from the petite Golda. Soon they were all laughing at Jorge's remark.

"Good." Jorge brushed a fly away from his face. "But now we must get to what brought you here." He looked intently at the two visitors. "Before we discuss the coffee growers, we have two concerns. One is specific, the other more of a. . . ." He paused, grasping for the right word.

"A suspicion of trouble to come," Andrés put in.

"Yes. Suspicion. But first the teamsters. You know, compañeros, that our drivers are all part of our union. They joined with us right from the beginning."

"You worked very hard to make that happen, Jorge," said Golda.

"Yes. And there hasn't been any trouble. We struggle as hard for their benefits as we do our own. But now they tell us that every time they stop in Nicoya or Tonoro, someone from the National Drivers' Union will try to sign them up. These guys tell our drivers that they can do much better with the National." Jorge lowered his voice. "Lately it's been getting a little hot. There are subtle threats."

"Threats? What's with these guys?" Sergio looked at Golda, then back at Jorge. "Is Mario Puentes going to come down to Catachoclo to negotiate with Don Luis Palacios? . . . Just because the teamsters played a key role in dumping the junta. . . ." His voice trailed off in frustration. "And the Tiger will have something to say," he added. "They tried that with the drivers inside the port. I can't *believe* it!"

"Jorge," Golda said quietly, "you've nothing to worry about. I'll call Puentes as soon as we get back. He owes us."

"Good, I hope that's settled."

"It is," Sergio emphasized. "Now, what's the 'suspicion?'"

Both Jorge and Andrés turned their gaze to Rubén Castro, secretary of the grievance committee. "Compañero Castro, tell our friends what we've learned."

"Shall I tell them about the new construction?" the young man asked.

"Yes, yes. Just as you described it to us." Jorge turned toward Rubén, who was seated at the end of the table facing the street.

He cleared his throat before continuing. "They are constructing several large buildings along the road to Nicoya," he explained, waving his hands to indicate the size. "We heard that they're going to roast beans and make powdered coffee for sale in the country."

"It sounds like more workers to organize," Sergio noted.

"Yes. But listen to this," said Jorge. "Go on Rubén."

"*First*, they built a barracks."

"A *barracks?*" Sergio could barely contain himself, his union in-
stincts rising to the surface. "Aren't they going to hire local people
for the work?"

"We believe they will," answered Jorge. "But they seem to have
something else in mind for the barracks. Rubén?"

Before the younger man could continue, a woman entered from
the door at the rear, carrying a tray of steaming mugs.

"Coffee, señores," she announced, setting the tray on the corner
of the table.

"This is Magda, our caretaker," Andrés said by way of introduction.

"And is that little Magda?" asked Golda, indicating a small child
who had appeared in the doorway. Magda waved the child away in
embarrassment. "No, no. It's all right. Come, child, let's have a
look at you." The girl came over to Golda without hesitation.
"What's your name?" The girl looked at her mother.

"Olga," the mother answered, beaming with pride as she distributed the mugs among those at the table.

"And how old are you, Olga?" Golda asked.

"Three," the girl answered, holding up three fingers.

"Ah. And when are you going to school?"

"In two years," the mother answered, as she picked up the tray
and took Olga by the hand. "Come. The señores have work to do."

"Good bye, Olga." Golda waved at the child and, turning back
to her companions, remarked, "She's very sweet, and *bright.*"

The sugar bowl was passed around. "Tres de Mayo?" asked Sergio, taking a sip.

"No. We buy it from the growers," Andrés said. "It saves us the
middleman."

"The co-op has its own beneficio," Jorge noted. "It's very rudi-
mentary and a thorn in the side of the patrón. He sees it as competition. It isn't now, but it will be. And," he added, holding up a

forefinger, "it's the main reason for your visit."

"First, the barracks," Sergio reminded him.

"Ah, yes. Rubén?"

The secretary of the grievance committee put down his cup and wiped his mouth with the back of his hand. "As soon as it was finished, three men who had been living in one of the workers' cottages moved in. It'll hold about ten or twelve. There are four or five in it now, and *none* are from here."

"What do they do?" asked Golda.

"They're guards."

"Guards?" asked Sergio. "What the hell do they guard? Excuse me, compañera Golda. Is coffee disappearing? Is someone shearing his sheep while he's not looking? Milking his cows?"

"Being unjustly accused of thievery is not unusual, compañero Fidanza," said Quishpe. "I can attest to that personally." He turned back to Rubén.

The young man continued. "There's always one of these guys by the main gate now, where the workers have to enter, and they patrol at night with dogs. They've even been seen riding through the plantation." Just then the bulb went out. Rubén stood on his chair to light the lantern hanging next to the bulb, even though the room had not been thrown into darkness. Sunlight was filtering in through the door and a large window, reflecting a gray aura off the walls onto those seated at the table.

As Rubén was resuming his seat, Andrés remarked, "In the old days the patrón and the majordomo were the law. If a worker was caught with a handful of beans in his pocket, he'd get the stick. We gradually got over our fear. But now this." With a somber face, he held his hands, palms up, over the table, as if to lay the problem out for all to see.

". . .Have you tried to sign them up?" asked Sergio.

"Of course," replied Jorge. "Rafael, the big guy with the teeth, just laughed. He said, 'We don't need no shitty union.' Excuse me, Doctora Lederer."

Golda, who had been listening grim-faced to the account, said, "This is *not* a good sign. You must keep an eye on them. If it's just a security measure, it's one thing. If it looks like a move to break us, we'll get help." She paused, searching her mind for some words of reassurance, but found none. "I'll discuss it with Chang Crespo," she finally said. Sergio drained his cup and set it back on the table, while the three leaders of the Beneficio Workers' Union mulled Golda's words.

"We will do that, Doctora—ah, *compañera* Lederer," Jorge said, nodding and smiling. "But now we must prepare for our meeting this afternoon with the Co-operative La Esperanza."

CHAPTER 12

T HAT WAS QUICK," REMARKED GOLDA as Fidanza reentered the lobby, such as it was, of the Hotel Sulaco. He laid his key on the counter, the only furniture other than the bench on the opposite wall, on which three of his companions were seated. Behind the counter hung a set of boxes with a hook above for each of the rooms. A short, bald man followed Sergio into the lobby, took the key, and hung it on its appropriate hook, number 6.

"What was there for me to do, go in the room, put my bag on the floor, and come back down?"

"Do you want breakfast?" asked the bald clerk.

"Yes, if you're ready at seven."

"We start at six-thirty."

"Fine," Sergio answered, and to the others, "I guess we're ready."

Rubén, who had been standing by the door, led the way out. When they reached the sidewalk, he reminded them of business he had back at the beneficio and headed off up the street. The others went down Calle Sulaco toward the plaza, walking under the arcade on the shady side. At one-thirty the street was deserted except for a small pig rooting for something in the opposite gutter. What there could be of value was a mystery. As they approached the tree in the middle of the street, they spotted two men sitting on one of the benches. They were greeted with a nod, which they returned. When they passed, Golda turned to Fidanza and said, "They're the ones who were with Ribadeneira in the aerodrome."

Sergio glanced back. "Yes, you're right. I wonder where they left Cosgrove and the others. D'you know them, Jorge?"

"The one with the mustache is from ICRAC. I don't recall ever seeing the other guy."

"It's got to be the drilling on the Redheads' land," Sergio decided.

"Luzuriaga will know," said Jorge.

They were just opposite the convent when a green Jeep station wagon, coming toward them on Calle Sulaco, sped past and stopped at the tree in the road. Sergio, glancing back, saw the two men, who had been seated there, get up and engage in a conversation with the occupants of the Jeep. Quishpe led his companions to the street entrance of the building housing the office of the co-op.

"Good afternoon, señores," declared Gloria Manzano, secretary to the ICRAC representative, when they appeared at her desk. "Licenciado Luzuriaga is expecting you." Barely five feet tall, she rose to indicate the stairs, adding, "You know the way, Señor Quishpe."

The group mounted the stairs. The co-op manager met them at the top, shaking hands with the two local union leaders. Jorge turned to Golda. "You know Doctora Lederer—" he paused, then decided to leave it as 'Doctora'"—of FLOC."

"Of course. How are you, Doctora? It's been a while." He bent over slightly, taking Golda's hand. His fair complexion and wavy brown hair contrasted with those of the other men, underscoring his European lineage.

"And this is Compañero Sergio Fidanza, who is here at the request of FLOC." As Galo shook Sergio's hand, a sense of recognition passed between them.

"We're waiting for the appointment of a new ICRAC representative, so we can use his old office. It's roomier than mine." He ushered them into the room across from his. It was obviously unoccupied. The only decoration—a large map of the environs of Catachoclo extending to the river to the west, about twenty kilometers to the south, and to Boca del Valle to the north—hung on the wall opposite an empty desk. He indicated a table with four chairs at the far end of the room in front of two windows that opened onto a balcony overlooking the courtyard. The ubiquitous aroma of jasmine drifted in on the breeze. Galo pulled over the chair from behind the desk and joined them.

As they seated themselves, Pedro poked his head through the doorway. "Coffee, señores?" They all declined.

"We have soda that's fairly cool," Galo offered.

Only Sergio took him up. "Orangina, if you have it."

"Yes, sir," said the porter, before disappearing from view.

Galo leaned forward and clasped his hands on the table. "First, I'd like to thank you both for coming to Catachoclo," he began, looking at each of the visitors in turn. "As you'll see, it's very important to us. And you're very acquainted with the area. Doctora Lederer, you were first here in '42? That must have been an adventure."

Golda nodded. "I was telling Sergio on the plane. Two days from Sulaco. But I haven't been here since '63."

"And you, Sergio, four years ago?" He looked at Fidanza. He was sure he knew him. "I'm surprised that we didn't meet then. When exactly was it?"

"In August of '62."

"OK. That's when I got married." He paused a moment before continuing, still trying to recall where he knew Sergio from. "Well, I don't have to remind either of you that the Valley of the Redheads is the most neglected area in the country."

"And *still* the most difficult to get to," Golda put in.

"That's a major factor in the problem. What you see here is the result of the industry of the Palacios family and the backbreaking work of the peasants. The only difference is that all of the benefits have accrued to the Palacioses. And if it weren't for the work of you around this table, the peasants'd still be living like serfs."

"And we'd still be beaten by the majordomo." Andrés's eyes spoke volumes.

"With your help, and the solidarity of the workers you represent," declared the manager of the Co-operative La Esperanza, "we mean to change that."

Sergio's Orangina arrived as Galo began to outline a plan that would make a reality of his dream. It centered on a proposed Point IV project to construct another beneficio farther south in the valley, in which the co-op would participate as the major shareholder. The plan included acquiring a piece of the coffee export quota as well, which was, at that time, in the hands of the Palacioses and two other families. "It'll be like taking the money right out of their pockets," Sergio observed.

Although not a part of the plan *per se*, Galo explained that, in one of its last acts, the military junta had approved the extension of the railroad from Nicoya to Catachoclo. "Changing this area from a backwater to. . .well, a railroad terminal," Luzuriaga concluded, "will be the most compelling factor in the success of the undertaking. And just a week ago the co-op expert from Point IV was here. He's really excited about it." Galo was showing a considerable amount of excitement himself. He got up and walked over to the map. "This whole area is ripe for colonization," he said, sweeping his hand from a point south of Catachoclo to Boca del Valle. "But we've got to make sure it isn't just exploited by the goddamn oligarchs." After ten years of struggle Galo had before him a vision of the future, a vision he was sure the four in front of him shared, which energized him even more. "The Point IV people like Wiggins, the co-op expert, see it as a great demonstration project. Anybody in the government who can think sees it as an escape valve for the growing sierra population, and ICRAC sees it as work and patronage."

"What will the Palacioses see it as when they get wind of it?" asked Sergio.

"They already have. You can't keep any secrets in this country." Galo's elated mood turned serious, but after a moment he regained his momentum. "But there's too much at stake for the country. They can't stop it. They'll try to get their cronies in on the ground floor, but it won't work," he insisted, gesturing dramatically with each declaration. "The gringos will fight for it. They need a winner just as much as we do. And all of the candidates will be for it just for the votes." He turned serious again. "How it sorts out after the election is another story." With that he sat down. "In the end, you know, the stupid oligarchs can only benefit from the project. But the bastards aren't satisfied with benefiting. They want the whole pie." His voice trailed off.

"Galo," said Golda, "you can count on us." In her soft, low voice she went on, "If I might make a recommendation? You were with ICRAC, were you not?" Galo nodded. "Wouldn't you be more effective sitting behind that desk over there?"

"I don't know if I could take it again. Or if they would even give it to me, if I asked."

"You should think hard on it," Golda urged.

Luzuriaga did, for a long moment—of his three years, choking on the bureaucracy. "No, Doctora," he finally said. "I've got too much invested in the co-op. And I love the work," he added, looking around at the others. "How about *you*, Sergio?" The sudden inspiration surprised everyone including himself. There was silence as all eyes turned to Sergio. "You could *do* it," Galo went on, warming to the possibilities. "ICRAC supports the new beneficio. You could look after the union's interests at the same time. You're a natural."

"Well, it's certainly worth looking into," Sergio finally said.

"I can mention it to the deputy director. He's in town right now."

"*That's* him," said Jorge. They turned to the secretary general of the Beneficio Workers' Union.

"We just saw him and another guy sitting under the tree when we walked over," Jorge explained.

"They're staying at the Flamenco. After our meeting, Sergio, I'll go over there and propose that you two get together tonight or tomorrow, before you all leave."

"Tomorrow would be better," Sergio said, realizing that he would be meeting Margarita in an hour or so.

"Fine. If it doesn't work out, you can arrange a meeting next week in the capital. I think it's a great idea," he added, looking around for support.

"I agree," said Golda. "I'm sure both you and Jorge could use the help. As long as Sergio is interested." They all turned their attention to Sergio.

"Well, as I said, 'It's certainly worth looking into.'"

"Before I forget, Galo," said Sergio, putting aside for the moment thoughts of yet another job, "when you met with Wiggins, there was an American engineer with him?"

"Yes. Jim Braun. He's a nice chap but a little naïve."

"Yes, he is," Sergio agreed. "But he's a good person to have on your side. I saw him yesterday in Sulaco. He seemed more concerned about the harassment those drillers are giving the Redheads." He drained his Orangina and set it down on the table, adding, "He thinks it's for oil."

"Everyone thinks it's for oil," Galo observed, "in spite of the boss driller's adamant denial." He had recalled his earlier conversation with Victor Hugo Ramirez.

"Unfortunately," Sergio muttered, "it's the wild card in your whole enterprise."

"Yes. I even got a letter last week from a former colleague in ICRAC suggesting it was oil." At that moment Galo knew where he had met Sergio. "You may know her. Margarita Bustamonte."

LUIS PALACIOS STRODE FROM THE DIRECTION of the barn as the green Jeep station wagon pulled up to the entrance of the residence of the Cafetero Tres de Mayo. A second floor accommodating three bedrooms and a bath had been added to the front of the residence since the days of Don Alfonso. A brick patio extended from the entrance to the newly cobbled driveway now lined with eucalyptus trees, including the point opposite the entranceway where the large mango tree had been. A brilliant purple bougainvillea covered the front of the house. Don Luis called out to Bumpy as he descended from the passenger side of the vehicle, "Welcome, Señor Bumpy, welcome to Tres de Mayo. And how long has it been? Since before the holidays last year, no?"

"That'd be 'bout right," replied Bumpy, taking the outstretched hand of his host. "We were just finishing the preparations for the drilling."

"Yes. You must tell me all about our enterprise. But first let's get you settled."

Walter Wagner, who had driven Bumpy from town, jumped out, opened the rear hatch of the wagon, and removed Cosgrove's leather Gladstone bag.

"What time shall I pick you up tomorrow?" he asked his boss.

"No need for that," interjected Luis. "I'll have one of my men take you in." Walter looked at his boss.

"Much obliged, Luis," said Bumpy, and then to Walter, "I'll see you all at the town hall at nine, then." Walter got back in and drove off.

"Teresita," Don Luis called to a woman standing in the doorway, "take Señor Cosgrove's bag to Paco's room." The woman, wearing a pinafore apron over a long-sleeved white blouse and blue skirt, scurried down to where Walter had left the bag.

"Right away, Don Luis."

"The family not heah?"

"No. They come for the holidays and maybe for a week or so during the dry season. Family lore has it that my grandmother refused to move to Catachoclo until they built an opera house. It now seems to have become a tradition. Neither my uncle's wife nor my cousin's wife would live here when they ran the cafetero—and, as you see," he added, gesturing toward the town, "we still have no opera house."

"Yeah," mused the Texan. "I guess that's why I never married. Those buildings up the drive are new, aren't they?"

Don Luis followed his guest's gaze. "The smaller is our office. We were overflowing the study," he said, pointing to the right side of the house.

"And the other long one?"

"My security group."

"Oh? Interesting."

"Yes. But first, let's have a drink. It's Tanqueray, isn't it?"

"Yes, it is, but I've been sitting and absorbing bad news all day, I'd rather stretch my legs." Cosgrove pulled a bandana from his hip pocket and, removing his Stetson, wiped his brow. Replacing the hat, he added, "How 'bout a look at your new construction? Security, you say?" He stuffed the bandana back in his pocket. "Might come in handy."

The patrón called over a young man with a scraggly moustache who had been standing near the end of the house, apparently waiting for orders. He came at a trot. After a few words with his boss, he was off. Bumpy and Luis started up the drive. The young man reappeared, rushing from the barn toward one of the new buildings, accompanied by an older and larger man. They entered the building. "I've sent them ahead to make sure the place is fit for a visit. With six men living together. . .well, you know. It's like a bunk house in those cowboy movies."

"I've lived in some oilfield bunkhouses in my day," Bumpy confided.

"There you have it."

"Like goin' home."

Six bunk beds were lined up on one side of a room wide enough to hold another row on the opposite side. In the absence of beds the space was partially occupied by a table with four chairs and six footlockers strung out against the wall beneath the four windows. Some nails had been driven into the wall between the beds to hold a ragged collection of clothes. One of the occupants was sitting on the last bed, struggling with a pair of shoes that had no laces. The other two appeared to have just awakened. "Rafael, this is Señor Cosgrove. His company is doing the drilling across the river."

Rafael was a brute. A large, unkempt, graying moustache covered a harelip and a mouth drawn down in a perpetual frown. His lined, weather-beaten face and hunched back showed the years spent sleeping in the small thatched tent of a hacienda field guard. When he replied to the introduction, he revealed a set of large teeth accented by two gold incisors. He wore a flannel shirt and dungarees that had the smell of the barn. "Señor Cosgrove may have need of your services," the patrón said, although unaware of the specific interest.

"Glad to oblige," said the brute, with a voice that corresponded to his general appearance.

The three others gazed at their visitors as they crossed the room and left by the other door. A long, low trough was affixed to the outside of the wall below three water faucets. A large piece of broken mirror had been attached to the wall above one of the faucets. An outhouse stood about five meters off the corner of the bunkhouse. "Pretty nice accommodations," observed Bumpy. Luis, who wasn't quite sure how to take the comment, decided to describe the office building they were approaching.

"I'm glad to have it out of the house. The work was overflowing into the other rooms." He extracted a bundle of keys from his pocket, selected one, and unlocked the door. They stepped inside the large, unoccupied room. Three desks and a row of filing cabinets provided the only furnishings. "That one is mine," he said, indicating the slightly larger desk in the far right corner. "My accountant sits here." He pointed to the desk to the left of the door. "And the majordomo's here."

"Where're they now?" asked Bumpy.

"They live in town and are off on their lunch. They should be back any minute," Luis added. "Do you want to talk with them?"

"Not especially," the oilman replied and, stepping outside of the door, added, "That Tanqueray would taste pretty good about now."

LUIS ADDED A SPLASH OF TONIC to his guest's drink and a larger amount to his own. He placed the bottle on the table before them and took the seat adjacent to Bumpy. The square table with four chairs occupied the corner of the room away from the windows that faced the patio in front of the house. Glass-enclosed bookshelves, devoid of books, lined the walls behind them. An imposing mahogany desk with the shield of Costaguana carved into the front panel stood before the windows. On the far side of the room a leather-upholstered couch, with two matching chairs in front of more, and equally empty, bookshelves completed the decor.

The patrón took a long pull on his drink and set the glass down. "Do you play bridge, Bumpy?"

"No. Poker's my game." Bumpy took a handful of popcorn from the bowl on the table.

"Yes. Poker is interesting. I play. But bridge is my passion." Luis took another sip. "My wife also plays bridge. We belong to a club in Nicoya. But here. . .I'm always searching for players. The accountant plays a fair game, but we have to hope for the occasional visitors."

"I'm afraid I'm not your man."

Luis leaned back in the chair and drummed his fingers absent-mindedly on the table. "You said that you had bad news today. Does it concern our enterprise? ICRAC will not cooperate?" Bumpy took another handful of popcorn.

"SO WE HAVE THREE WEEKS before we have to make a decision," Bumpy concluded.

"Whatever it is, be assured we are here to serve you, Bumpy."

"I appreciate that. I suspect that, in spite of the deputy director's warning, we'll be pushing ahead on the original plan. So I'll need men to clear the line and see to their protection."

"We are ready on both accounts." Luis rose and turned to the last set of shelves nearest the front wall of the house, which had a heavy set of wooden doors instead of glass. "Come." He invited his guest to join him. He drew the bundle of keys from his pocket and opened the padlock securing the doors. "There you are," he said, pointing to twelve 30-06 caliber Winchesters neatly stacked against the back of the closet. He pulled up a steel rod securing the set of drawers below and opened the top one, revealing a stash of ammunition.

Bumpy picked up one of the rifles. "I hope it doesn't come to this."

"Whatever it comes to, we are ready."

"Did you get this stuff—and I won't ask where it came from—in anticipation of this problem?"

Luis took the rifle from his guest, replaced it in the closet, and locked it up. Returning to the table, he poured them another drink and said, "My cousin, Juan Carlos, was not the man his father was and certainly not the man our grandfather was. He let that union scum walk all over him." As he spoke, his voice grew louder and harsher. "Now there's talk of building another beneficio. Owned by the growers' co-op. Can you imagine? These peasants, *owners?*" Practically shouting, he slammed his fist on the table. "My grandfather built this cafetero by the sweat of his brow. Now these ingrates are going into *competition* with us? They wouldn't know how to get out of their own way. It's those communists in ICRAC and their gringo friends—well, we will know how to take action!"

"Luis, calm yourself," Bumpy cautioned his host. The impact of any action along the lines Luis was thinking on the oil development was not lost on the Texan. "That kind of a project is a long way down the pike. These Point IV people have to have something to talk about, to account for their existence. If they had to go out and work for a living they wouldn't be any better off than your Indians." Cosgrove paused to let the comment sink in. Then he leaned over in a very confidential manner and said, "If this oil proves out, you could give *your* beneficio to the peasants."

"Never!" Luis growled.

The two men contemplated what the future held for each of them. "Yes, Bumpy," Luis finally said. "I tend to get angry at the pitiful aspirations these outside troublemakers stir up in the Indians. And we've got our home-grown troublemakers." He shook his head. "Can you imagine, one of the union scum actually thinks—agh! It's too absurd to talk about," he concluded, shaking his hand in front of his face, as if to dispel the thought from his mind. "Another before dinner?" he asked his guest.

"I think it would be a good idea," Bumpy agreed.

Luis poured the drinks. "Just remember, we are here to serve you."

"OKAY," SAID GALO, SUMMING UP. "Jorge, you and Andrés will consider proposing to your people that they become shareholders in the venture. But you'll be prepared to organize the beneficio workers and drivers according to your usual procedures."

"Being owners with them is attractive," observed Jorge, "but for now it is beyond our means. We have no money, no resources."

"That's where we come in," said Golda. "We'll pursue the international unions."

"And I'll meet with Braun next week," Sergio offered. "Those gringo unions should have something they can bring to the table."

"We're all agreed, then," said Gallo, looking up from his notes. "I think we've accomplished a lot this afternoon."

"Now the wild card," said Sergio.

"Exactly. The earthquake study."

"We must be going, compañeros," said Jorge. He moved around the table to Golda, where Andrés joined him. "When will you be leaving, ah, Compañera Golda?" he asked, taking her hand.

"Tomorrow afternoon. Padre Philippe will drive us to Nicoya."

"You will see Doctor Paco and Doña Leticia?"

"Of course. And your mother."

Jorge smiled. "I will have a letter for her, if you would be so kind." With that Jorge and Andrés took their leave, shaking hands all around. Gallo escorted them to the door.

On his way back, Gallo picked up a glass ashtray from the desk, placed it on the table in front of him, and resumed his seat. "Now for the seismic business." He took a pack of Casablancas from his pocket and offered them to the others. Golda took one. Sergio declined. Gallo lit Golda's and his own, dropped the match in the ashtray, and pushed it toward her. He began by describing the visit to the drilling camp the day before. "Chiriboga and Krueger—the ones you saw sitting under the tree—had stopped by my office earlier. They'd just had their first meeting with Cosgrove and company over the ruins." He took a drag on the cigarette. "And he was adamant that it wasn't about oil. He's furious about the rumors, and what really got him was that, before they were hardly out of the aerodrome this morning, a reporter from *El Porvenir*—you must know him, Victor Hugo Ramirez—asked him point blank if he had any comments on the oil prospecting. Of course I already knew this, since Ramirez was by here right after they gave him the boot." He took another drag on the cigarette. "I wonder where the hell he got wind of it?" Golda, leaning over to flick an ash into the ashtray, stole a glance at Sergio. "As I said before, even Margarita had suggested it, almost two weeks ago."

"So what does all this mean to the Arra'o?" asked Sergio.

"Well, sitting on an oil field is something that will affect the whole region. As you pointed out, Sergio, it's the wild card. But of more immediate import to the Arra'o is that the ruins are actually within the boundaries of the study area agreed to. To his credit, Chiriboga has taken the position that the *drillers* will have to seek alternatives."

1942

CHAPTER 13

T HAT'S WHERE WE'LL BE STAYING," says Golda as the bus rumbles
past the recently constructed Hotel Sulaco. It lurches to the
right to avoid the tree growing in the middle of the Calle Sulaco,
turns left, and goes around the block. As they approach Calle Sulaco
they get a view of the noisy commotion in the field across from the
church. The monthly parrot and monkey fair has been in full swing
since daybreak. By now most of the sales have been transacted. The
humdrum specimens and the truly exotic are the only ones left. An
Indian is holding an especially large and magnificent scarlet macaw,
the value of which he is well aware. He has been holding out for the
right price and is prepared to wait another month to get it. Vehicles
still parked at the perimeter of the field are loaded with cages containing the day's acquisitions. The bus rounds the corner and comes
to a stop across from the church and in front of a grocery store,
which also serves as the depot. It had finally stopped raining when
they left Boca del Valle two hours ago, and the skies were clearing as
they came into view of the town at the rise just north of the beneficio. "It's a bit cooler," says Golda to Antonia as they wait for their
bags to be taken down from the roof of the bus.

"Oh, my," exclaims Antonia, spying the redheaded Indian, with
the scarlet macaw perched on his arm, walking right toward them,

followed by a woman dressed in an orange skirt to mid-calf striped similarly to the man's. Her black hair comes to her shoulders, around which she clutches a shawl barely concealing her ample bosom. In her other hand she carries a basket with a few leftover mangoes. Without a word, the man holds up the bird for inspection. As if on cue, it stretches its wings and lets out a shriek, which startles the two women. As the man smoothes its feathers, a red one from the tail comes out in his hand. He offers it to Doña Antonia. She takes it from him, inspects it, and attempts to return it. The man will have none of it. He gestures at the bird and says, "Fifty pesos."

"No. I don't think so," says Antonia. The Indian woman holds up the basket. The two women shake their heads. The Indians turn to the corner and disappear up the side street.

"It's a beautiful bird," remarks Golda.

"And worth the price," someone says. They turn to see the source of the comment. "Don Carlos Palacios, to serve you, señoras," he says, removing his hat and bowing slightly. In his early sixties he wears a long-sleeved white shirt and neatly pressed dungarees, beneath which protrude pointed boots typical of the American Southwest. The two women exchange a glance. "You've heard of me?" he asks.

"You're the owner of the beneficio," says Antonia.

"My reputation precedes me. And with whom do I have the pleasure of speaking?"

"I am Doña Antonia Avellanos, and this is Señora Saenz. We are visiting an old family friend, Padre Miguel Lopez. He was secretary to my uncle for many years."

"Our esteemed pastor," mutters Don Carlos, without any hint of recognizing Antonia's name. His pleasant smile has changed to a frown. "We were expecting two men from the capital," he says, glancing at two roughnecks slouching against the wall of the depot. "Troublemakers, actually. Did you happen to notice anyone on the bus who might have gotten off outside town?"

"We saw no one," answers Golda. "And if they were trouble-makers, they made none during the trip."

"I expect not," he growls, surveying the area around the now empty bus. "I trust you will have a pleasant stay." Without another word he walks off, followed by the roughnecks. The patrón and one of the men get into the cab of a Ford Model A pickup parked behind the bus. The other, taller and slightly hunched over, climbs into the bed of the truck. They make a U-turn in front of Golda and Antonia. The man in the back stares at the two women. His malevolent smile exhibits two gold incisors. They speed off.

"If there are any troublemakers around, it's those three," remarks Golda. "I don't like it. It seems something has leaked."

"Not enough to put them onto us."

"It may not be long before they put two and two together, Antonia. In any case we'd best get over to Padre Miguel." Golda beckons to two boys standing at the entrance to the depot. They come at a run.

"Yes, Señora," they say in unison.

"We're going to the rectory," Golda says, pointing across the street. The boys pick up the bags and race toward the church, by far the largest building in the town. The upper half of the brick building is stuccoed and painted white, and pierced by eight narrow openings. The double-sloped roof, with a cupola running the full length, has eight small openings, matching the wall openings and admitting some light to the interior. The women, following the boys, come around the south façade, a massive, almost square wall ornamented with pilasters of brick and topped with a domed bell tower supported on four columns.

As they reach the front of the rectory, Padre Miguel has already answered the door and is peering around the street. He's only a few years older than Antonia but lacks her vitality. Fifteen years in a backwater parish have taken their toll. His major accomplishment since leaving his post as secretary to the first and last cardinal of Sulaco is having finished the church of San Agustín, no small achievement. It meant keeping the large landowners and the bishop in Nicoya happy and at the same time serving the least prosperous of his flock, that more noble calling, which his years with the cardinal had ingrained in him. He greets his guests, ushers them into the vestibule, and closes the door after giving each of the boys a rial.

"Doña Antonia, how wonderful to see you. How long has it been? Two years? And Doctora Lederer. A few months ago, isn't it?" He leads the way into the study. "Have the kindness," he says, motioning for them to be seated in front of his desk. "It's a wonderful work." He takes his seat and removes his glasses. "And now the day has come." He arranges the inkstand and crucifix. "I feel like I did in my early years with your sainted uncle, Doña Antonia. But a little more nervous."

"You may have reason, Padre," says Golda. "We were greeted by Carlos Palacios when we arrived."

"Oh, my," the priest responds, and rearranges the crucifix and inkstand.

"He was looking for two 'troublemakers,' who they expected were arriving on the bus."

"Oh, my," the priest says again. He picks up his glasses and puts them on.

"He didn't suspect that we were the ones he was looking for," continues Golda, "but they've gotten wind of something."

"Are we all set for tonight?" asks Antonia.

"Yes. Yes. We will meet in the parish hall."

"There will be at least ten of the organizing committee?"

"Actually, all thirteen. Oh! Thirteen. Yes. It's all arranged. At eight-thirty."

A knock on the door startles them. Padre Miguel goes to the window and announces that it's Jorge Quishpe.

A tall, muscular man of twenty-nine, clasping a straw hat in his left hand, follows the priest into the room. Golda is already on her feet to greet him. His rather severe countenance lightens as he takes her hand and smiles. "Doctora, how good to see you again. And Doña Antonia," he says, reaching over to grasp her hand. He takes a chair from against the wall, and the two women make room between them for the organizer of the beneficio workers. "And how was the trip?"

Golda describes the appearance of Carlos Palacios and his two thugs at the bus station.

"The one with the teeth is Rafael, and he *is* a trouble maker," confirms Jorge.

They go over in detail the plans for signing the charter. "I will try to get the men to the parish hall as early as possible," says Jorge. "If there's been a leak, then we will have to take all precautions."

"We should meet here in the rectory instead of the parish hall," Golda suggests. "If it's all right with you, Padre?"

"Of course." The priest seems to have been energized by the arrival of Jorge. "Or in the church." They decide to have the men arrive at the church then come through the rectory into the dining room.

"We'll sign at the table," says Antonia. "We have the documents here." Golda pats her briefcase.

"What time is it?" asks Jorge.

Antonia looks at her lapel watch. "Five-thirty."

"Then I must be going, if I am going to get the men here early." He rises to leave.

Golda pulls Gloria's letter from her briefcase. "From your mother," she says, handing the envelope to Jorge.

He smiles and thanks her for her kindness. As he reaches the door he turns and says, "I think you should stay here until the meeting." They agree.

"I've told the cook that you'll be taking dinner here," says Padre Miguel. "I'll tell her to prepare the extra room so you can spend the night."

"But we've arranged with the Hotel Sulaco," says Golda.

"I think it will be better if you stay here," Jorge says. "If they're wise to what's happening, we don't want to take any chances. And don't inform the hotel. Let them think you're still expected." With this last bit of advice, he leaves.

JUAN CALVACHE IS THE FIRST TO ARRIVE. The sanctuary lamp and the votive candles in front of the painting of Our Lady of Guadeloupe cast dancing shadows against the walls. Antonia, who has been waiting in the church, stations Juan at the entrance to the passageway that leads to the rectory with orders to direct the men inside. She returns to the dining room. Jorge is the next to arrive, with three men from his neighborhood. He sends Juan in with the three and takes up his position.

Two figures appear in the church entrance. Jorge recognizes Rafael and Hugo, the other roughneck, and steps back out of sight. The two walk halfway down the center aisle and look around. "Nobody here," grunts Rafael. "The parish hall." They retreat out the door and disappear to the left. Jorge reemerges and hurries to the entrance. He can hear the sounds from the shops around the corner in the direction of the parish house. A half moon casts enough light for him to recognize Andrés Puíg and two others at the edge of the plaza. They see him motioning for them to hurry.

"To the rectory," he whispers as they slip through the door. "Andrés, have you seen any of the others?" Andrés shakes his head. Jorge motions for him to follow the others and steps out the door to survey the street. Five to go, he thinks. They only need *two* more. Three men approach from the other side of the rectory. He recognizes Juanito Flores and is about to retreat back into the church when Juanito calls out, "Quishpe, enough praying. Come join us. We're going to warm up with a canelaso at the Salsipuedes."

Jorge, thinking of Rafael around the corner, waits until they've reached him. "I have a meeting with the padre," he says, barely above a whisper.

"Don't worry. We won't tell," Flores answers with a laugh. "Bring him along. Lord knows he needs something to warm him up." This elicits a scurrilous laugh from the others. Jorge frowns. "Well, we'll have one for you," Flores says, as they move on. "Our regards to his reverence."

Jorge watches until they turn the corner. Two figures in front of the canton administration building catch his attention. He makes out Hector Cantos and Aníbal Torres. As they approach Calle Sulaco he holds his breath and offers a silent prayer that Rafael and Hugo not see them. He steps into the street as the two reach the entrance, ushers them into the church and, with a whisper, directs them to the passageway. He goes back to the door to see if Rafael has spotted them. He is prepared to lock the entrance if the two appear at the corner. Several minutes go by. He decides that luck is in their favor and joins the others in the rectory, leaving the door ajar.

A kerosene chandelier suspended from a chain in the middle of the ceiling illuminates the dining room. Another lamp rests on the table to facilitate the task at hand. Padre Miguel is seated at the middle of the table, under the painting of *The Last Supper*. Antonia is at the end nearest the window, over which the padre has hung a blanket, with Golda to her right. To her left Aníbal Torres is gripping a pen and, with his nose about fifteen centimeters above the charter, begins laboriously to trace the letters of his name, mouthing each as he struggles to complete his signature. He finishes with a swirl under the two R's, putting a dot in the middle. He looks up with a smile of satisfaction, rises, and motions for his friend Hector Cantos to take the seat. Hector demurs.

"He cannot write, Señora," Aníbal says to Antonia with a shrug.

"Come, compañero. Take the seat," she says, and then for all to hear she adds, "The ability to write is not a requirement for demanding your rights as a citizen *and* human being." Hector takes the seat. She hands him the pen and, after staring at the paper, he makes a mark that looks vaguely like an H and a C on the line indicated by Antonia.

"Well done, compañero," says Golda. "You are making history." She turns the document around and adds her initials after Hector's mark. "There. That makes it official." She counts the signatures. "Ten. Where are the other three, Jorge?"

Jorge has been standing in the doorway with one eye on the passage where Calvache has been stationed to wait for latecomers. "They have not yet arrived, Doctora."

"Well, we have the necessary ten. Antonia and I will sign while we wait." The two women do so in the appropriate spaces: Antonia as founder of FLOC and Golda as the notary.

Jorge steps back into the hallway when he hears Calvache call out, "It's Rafael!" Golda immediately gathers up the documents as Antonia follows Andrés Puíg through the doorway. They follow Jorge to the church, where they encounter the two roughnecks. Jorge and Andrés step through, and Antonia stops in the archway. "What do you want?" she asks in the stern voice of a teacher to a recalcitrant pupil. They are momentarily taken aback.

Rafael regains his voice and with head slightly bent, says, "We have been sent——"

"Take your hats off. This is a house of God." The younger one snatches off the straw hat he is wearing. Rafael slowly raises the club he is carrying. Jorge and Andrés take a step forward as Antonia steps into the church. "I was in Los Hatos Woods with General Hernandez during the War of Separation, before you were born. You *dare* threaten me?"

Rafael looks at the three. "The patrón will hear of this," he sneers. He turns, brushes past his partner, and marches toward the back of the church. Antonia and the others watch as the two disappear through the entrance without looking back.

"Brava!" shouts Golda, standing in the archway with the padre. "My heart was in my throat."

"Brigands," Antonia mutters. They return to the dining room.

Padre Miguel excuses himself, and Calvache is dispatched to lock the church door. A few minutes later Calvache returns. "Look at this," he announces. Pedro Rivas and his brother, Jaime, follow him into the room. Pedro is bleeding from the lip and Jaime has an ugly bruise under his left eye. They tell of their run-in with Rafael and the other an hour ago in front of the parish hall. After describing how they escaped and their circuitous route back to the church, Pedro asks, "Are we too late to sign?"

"Not at all," says Golda, who has already produced the documents from her briefcase. The brothers take seats before the charter. When the priest returns, carrying a tray with a pitcher and eight cups, he announces, "Canelaso," setting the tray in the middle of the table. "To celebrate this momentous occasion."

"And the first act of the union," declares Golda, raising the cup the padre has offered her, "will be to file a grievance against those two."

1965

CHAPTER 14

GOLDA AND SERGIO MADE THEIR WAY across the plaza toward the clinic. The sun had already dipped below the coastal range. It wouldn't be long before the streetlights came on for their nightly four-hour display. Sergio was caught up in remembrances of Margarita, of those interludes with her sitting in a café during this magical moment of twilight. It was the first time all day that he had allowed himself to even picture her. He realized that in a very short time he would see the face that had graced his memory for three years in exile. He wondered if she really resembled that image. He worried that feelings of nostalgia would envelop him as they had, too frequently, in the days since his arrival in Sulaco. A certain serenity nevertheless took hold as he pondered the encounter only minutes away. But what if there'd been a change of plans, an early departure?

"This oil business is nothing but bad news for the people of the valley," Golda mused aloud. "The Arra'o will get the short end of the stick, and the coffee growers will get nothing. A few jobs *maybe*, but distracted from pursuing their own best interests, being their own bosses. I wonder how the Palacioses figure into this, Sergio?. . .Sergio?" She looked at her companion, who was ambling along, hands in his pockets and eyes straight ahead.

"Sorry, Compañera Golda, I was thinking."

"Obviously."

"What were you saying?"

"Nothing important. . . . So how well did you know this Margarita?" she asked.

Sergio took a deep breath. "We were involved in a coalition pushing for a return to a democratic, civilian government." He described their last night together.

"And you hadn't heard from each other since?"

"After I'd been three months in Argentina, I finally got some news of her whereabouts, but by that time, I thought. . . ." He shrugged, as his voice trailed off.

"Well, you must become reacquainted," Golda said, gently taking his arm. They had reached the convent as darkness descended and were walking around the side toward the clinic. Ahead of them, seated on a bench under a bare light in the colonnade of the clinic, were Margarita and Sor Marillac. The nun recognized the arriving pair. She straightened in the seat, and her hand flew to her mouth. She quickly composed herself and announced, "Here they are."

As they approached, Margarita and the nun rose to greet them. Golda released her hand from Sergio's arm. Without a word the two embraced. Margarita took Sergio's two hands. Tears came to her eyes. "I always remembered how you helped me." She embraced him again, more fervently. Sergio had never permitted himself the luxury of imagining this moment. Now that it had arrived, he was completely unprepared, but he returned the fervor of the embrace. Sor Marillac's face radiated with delight. Golda, with less invested personally, suggested that she retire to her room for a moment before dinner.

"Oh, yes. Dinner." The nun announced that Padre Phillipe had invited all four of them to dine with him, and that she would tell the cook they were ready. "Wait here," she said before rushing off to the rectory.

Margarita had put the handkerchief she used to dry her eyes into the pocket of her skirt. "Shall we sit down?" She motioned to the bench. They sat. She turned to look at him. He gazed straight ahead. They laughed after both had simultaneously begun to speak.

"Please," he said, turning toward her.

"I was thinking of the Bar Litoral and that skinny waiter. What was his name?"

"Lucho. And he's as skinny as ever. I was there just this Monday."

"And Anibal?" she asked of the owner.

"Still the same. Before I was there a minute, he said that I owed him twelve pesos from before."

"Oh, no!"

"Yes, but that he would forgive it, because I was a true patriot. Patriot. Three years in exile, because I was a true patriot."

Margarita frowned. "When did you get back?"

"It was a week ago yesterday."

"And you're already in the thick of it."

"Yes. With *three* jobs. I'm on the ORIT payroll from when I was in Argentina, The Tiger has my old job waiting, and Julio Chang Crespo—you know him, Chinito—asked me to come here with Doctora Lederer." The fourth possibility was far from his mind at that moment.

"She's the lady you're with?"

"I'm sorry—I didn't present you. She's the founder of FLOC."

"With Doña Antonia Avellanos. I've met *her*. She's quite a woman."

"Yes, she is. They both are. But what about you, Margarita? What. . .brings you to Catachoclo?"

"Well, my father managed to have the dogs called off. I joined ICRAC and completed my social work degree at the National. That's about it. It doesn't have the excitement of our days with the coalition." She paused and reflected. "It took me awhile to get over that night, Sergio. But I think I'm ready."

Before Sergio could find out what Margarita was ready for, the two others returned. He made his formal presentation, and they proceeded to the rectory, led by the obviously exuberant Sor Marillac.

"HAVE THE KINDNESS TO BE SEATED," said the housekeeper, a woman of about thirty-five years. She gestured toward the table with large bony hands from years of coffee harvesting as the guests filed through the doorway. A bowl of quinoa soup with carrots and parsnips, naranjilla juice, and an empty wine glass were set at each place; the rest of the meal was laid out in dishes and covered bowls on the sideboard opposite the entrance.

"It hasn't changed a bit since I was first here in 1942," observed Golda. "Isn't it the same '*Last Supper*,' Padre?"

"Yes," replied the priest. "A gift from a family in the parish. It goes back to the turn of the century, as does the furniture." Padre Philippe, a veteran of the worker-priest movement, had volunteered ten years before to go to Catachoclo. His order had been invited by the Costaguana hierarchy to take over the parish of San Agustín. Its extreme remoteness seemed not to agree with the local clergy, recruited by and large from the wealthy and middle class of the sierra. Padre Philippe had been looking for something that would challenge his sense of social justice and worker-priest background. The order had been glad to find an assignment that would not provoke the more conservative rural parishes it was in charge of in Provence. The priest had slipped into the role of pastor with ease. His French-accented Spanish charmed his flock, and his first-hand acquaintance with the problems of the worker had solidified the loyalty of the men. At about the time of his assignment, the nuns had taken on the operation of the clinic, which had been set up by ICRAC but lacked the trained personnel to make it a success.

"Maria, how is your son's wound healing?" asked Sor Marillac before joining Golda across from Margarita and Sergio.

"It is hardly noticeable, thank you, Sor," she responded, and then to the priest, who had moved to the seat at the end of the table nearest the street, "Will that be all, Padre?"

"Yes, Maria, I think we will manage."

"Just leave the dishes, Padre, I will take care of them in the morning." She wished them a good appetite and left.

"She usually stays to clean up, but there's some family matter." The priest said the grace and invited his guests to begin. "And to celebrate the reunion of these two compañeros," he announced, indicating Margarita, who blushed, and Sergio who took a sudden interest in his soup, "we have a bottle of Chateauneuf du Pape, 1960, a gift from my superior on his last visit."

"That was eight *months* ago," said Sor Marillac, chastising the priest for holding onto it so long.

"I've been waiting for an occasion." He rose to do the honors.

"Not for me, thank you," said Sergio. "I have a medical problem."

"A medical problem? This will cure any problem, medical or otherwise."

"I'm sorry, Padre. I'm afraid it won't cure this one." Philippe shrugged and turned to Sor Marillac.

"Nor I," said the nun.

"Agh," protested the priest. "I will not tell. My lips are sealed." The nun shook her head. "*Alors*, who is to help me with this excellent vintage?"

"I will be *happy* to join you, Padre," answered Golda, pushing her glass toward the priest.

"And a glass for me," said Margarita.

"Well, that's more like it. I was afraid that I would be drinking alone."

When they had finished the soup, Sor Marillac got up and collected the bowls. Before she could get around to the sideboard, Margarita had begun serving the others from the dishes behind her. While the plates were being passed, Philippe asked about the prospects for the workers' beneficio. Sergio filled them in on the results of the meeting earlier that afternoon. "It looks promising, but the wild card is the possibility of oil on the land of the Arra'o."

"Ah, so this earthquake study is a ruse!" the priest exclaimed.

"It's been a pretty strong rumor in the capital for over a month now," observed Margarita as she took her seat. "But no one has come right out and said it."

"There's a Texas well driller in town," Sergio said. "It's *got* to be for oil. The only question is, 'Have they found any?' Oh, and the *big* problem is that the ruins are within the study area."

"Within the area!" Margarita exclaimed. "No wonder the Arra'o are so upset."

"They don't even know *that* yet," Sergio continued. "They called a halt to further clearing because the work was getting so close, and it turns out that they *were* so close because the map of the agreement was in error."

"Of course," Margarita observed in a tone reserved for these occasions. "An error *not* in favor of the Arra'o. I suspect that my colleagues will attempt to buy them off, and if that doesn't work, then strong-arm tactics."

"I don't think either will work," said Philippe. "I have known Hugo Rigpe since I'm here. He has taken me to the ruins on two occasions." He closed his eyes. "*Incroyable! Tan mystique.* It is something very special for them. I am privileged to have been there."

"There may be some hope," Sergio offered. "Your colleague," he said, turning to Margarita, "Chiriboga. . . ?"

"Yes. Juan. Juan Chiriboga."

"Luzuriaga says that *he* said that the drillers have to come up with a solution. He apparently suggested that they adjust the survey route."

I'm afraid," began Golda, who had been silent up to then, "that if they find oil, the pressure will be relentless." She toyed with her empty wine glass, which seemed to reflect the joy that had been drained from the get-together. "We'd best think about how we'll react to the discovery and the inevitable production. And," she added with a note of foreboding, "we shouldn't feed the oil rumor until we've thought out our strategy."

AT SOR MARILLAC'S URGING, Margarita and Sergio were strolling Calle Sulaco. The breeze had shifted to the south and carried the aroma of jasmine. It was close to nine, and the streetlights were still on. The sounds of loud conversation and laughter emanated from a dimly lit café called the Salsipuedes. Four men came stumbling out. The tallest, a hunched-over brute with a dark mustache, took a moment longer than necessary to look over the strollers. Then the four continued their boisterous way toward the plaza.

"He gave me the shudders," said Margarita, taking Sergio's arm. "They reminded me of the soldiers that night." He could feel the tenseness in her grip.

"Let's check them out," he said. They walked over to the café. The waiter was righting an overturned chair. "Those guys from around here?"

"The Tres de Mayo," he answered, mopping the table. "And good riddance. Thank God, they only come in about once a month, after payday."

The two returned to the street. "I think they're the security guys Jorge mentioned earlier. Troublemakers," Sergio added. "And I don't think we've seen the last of them."

As they approached the tree they heard a voice call out from the bench on the far side, "Margarita, over here."

"It's Galo and his wife, Maruja!" exclaimed Margarita.

Maruja's red hair and blue eyes set her apart. "Margarita! How good to see you," she called out as the two approached.

Galo rose and shook Sergio's hand. "This is—"

Before he could complete the introduction Sergio said, "Maruja O'Neil."

She looked at him quizzically for a moment and then exclaimed, "Fidanza! You remembered. After all these years."

"Not so many. The philosophy class and the Young Socialists. How could I forget?"

"Of course," said Galo. "I'd forgotten you knew each other at the university."

"Yes. Fidanza was always the serious one. I remember the outing the philosophy students had." She giggled. "We were taking the introductory course, so they invited our class to join them. Fidanza spent the day trying to convince the others to join the protests against. . . . What was it anyway? There were so many." She giggled again. "Come, Margarita, sit down. I must know what miracle brought you two together here in Catachoclo."

Margarita, without reference to the night in Sulaco three years before, explained the coincidence. "How romantic!" the redhead exclaimed, much to the discomfort of Sergio.

"Maruja, you're embarrassing these poor people," Galito gently chided his wife. But her joy was infectious and would not be denied.

The conversation returned to the good times of their younger days in university. Maruja had a keen sense of the need to lighten the otherwise serious cast of their day-to-day activities. Even Sergio had to laugh at her recounting of events he had long forgotten. She was in the middle of one when the lights went out.

"Oh," said Margarita, "is it ten already?"

"Do you have to be back? Will Fidanza turn into a mouse?" Maruja asked, and burst out laughing.

"A mouse?" asked Sergio.

"It's a fairy tale. Fidanza! Cinderella? Oh, never mind." Maruja was irrepressible. "Well, Margarita?"

"No. I have a key."

"Then we'll make a night of it."

"Not too late—I don't want to jeopardize my welcome. But where can we go?"

"The Flamenco," suggested Galo. "They have their own generator, and maybe we'll run into Chiriboga and Krueger."

"I think we should avoid them, if possible," said Sergio. "I don't want to get into a discussion of ICRAC job possibilities with him tonight." Galo and Maruja looked at Margarita. "We've discussed it briefly," he added.

"He's quite amenable to meeting in the capital next week," said Galo.

"And," added Sergio, "Golda suggested that we not feed the oil rumor until we've had a chance to figure out our strategy. It can be very distracting."

"I take her point. Yes. We should make sure Jorge keeps it under his hat. The only other is Ramirez from *El Porvenir*. I don't know what we can do there. Perhaps—"

"Are we going to have a dull strategy meeting, or are we going to have a night out?" Maruja was determined.

"We could go to the Salsipuedes."

"I'm afraid those roughnecks might come back," said Margarita.

"Is that where all that noise was coming from?" asked Galo. "Well, there's El Rincón, next to the Sulaco," he suggested, pointing up the street.

They agreed. Margarita took Sergio's arm, and they made their way with the help of the light from the few establishments that were open and a flashlight that Sor Marillac had given her. "She thinks of everything," Margarita remarked.

"See," observed Maruja, "she knew you'd be late. So, Fidanza, you won't turn into a mouse."

A few minutes later they were sitting at one of the three tables in the café. The only other patrons had left as they arrived. Galo ordered four Sulacos.

"Orangina for me," said Sergio.

"Orangina? Come, Fidanza, this is a party. You're the guest of honor."

"No. I can't. It seems that I'm allergic."

"Oh, I *am* sorry." Maruja laid her hand on his arm. "You must have to do a lot of explaining."

"I'm going to get a sign to hang around my neck. 'Can't drink. Medical problem.'" They all laughed.

"Like my red hair and blue eyes. I'm always explaining: My great-great grandfather was an Irish adventurer who fought with Bolívar. Papa always said that, even after five generations, it couldn't be stamped out. He was red-headed and blue-eyed, too."

"I don't recall any of the boys at university complaining," said Sergio, and then wondered why he'd said it. They all looked at his slowly reddening face and burst out laughing.

The drinks came, and the conversation continued. Sergio felt transported to those Sulaco evenings with Margarita. When the waiter asked if they wanted another round, Margarita declined, saying that she had to get back. They prepared to leave, Maruja insisting that she and Galo treat the newly reunited. Margarita took Sergio's arm again as they made their way to the convent. The other two kept a respectful distance, with Maruja squeezing her husband's hand. When Margarita and Sergio reached the entrance, she whispered, "Thank you, Sergio." They embraced, and she kissed him warmly on the cheek. Without another word, they parted.

CHAPTER 15

T HE CUBAN, JORGE RICABARRAN, was puffing on his cigar and having an animated conversation on the phone with Pablo Menendez, the head of the Petroleum Workers Union. Sergio, sitting across the desk from him, had a view of Higuerota through the window behind the Cuban. It was a rare cloudless day. On the flight up from Sulaco, the TAMC pilot had circled the peak to provide the passengers a close look at the Sultan of the Andes. It was the first time Sergio'd seen the mountain that close from a plane. And from the ORIT office, as from any vantage in the city, it still dominated the landscape.

He thought of the upcoming week of meetings, but most of all he thought of Margarita. He could not get over his great luck. He was almost afraid to entertain the thought that she might share his feelings, and he still dared not dream of a life together. In his exile in Argentina, the disparity of their backgrounds had brought it crashing down around him. But their chance meeting in Catachoclo made it seem possible.

Ricabarran hung up the phone. "Those oil workers are a bright spot on the whole union landscape." The Cuban tapped the ashtray with the cigar and rested it on the edge. "They really know their stuff. . . . So what brings you to town?" he asked, leaning back in the chair. The office, part of CCSL—the Costaguana Confederation of Free Trade Unions—headquarters, was unadorned and reeked of smoke. The desk and chair, a three-drawer file cabinet, and three chairs for visitors were the only furnishings. There wasn't room for much more.

"Before that," said Sergio, holding up a hand, "two things. First, when you're talking to the oil workers again, find out what they know about a Bumpy Cosgrove and the Walker Tool Company. I'll write it down for you. And second, what about Nogales?"

Ricabarran stared at the ceiling. "Horrible," he answered, shaking his head. "The only thing we can do is get them a decent lawyer."

"Compañera Lederer's words, exactly," remarked Sergio.

"We have a good man in Nogales, but he's reluctant to take the case, being from the town and all. So we're sending a guy from here to front for him."

"Well, I guess it really *is* all we can do." As they sat silently, mulling the situation, the weather began to deteriorate. Clouds obscured Higuerota, and a wind stirred outside the window.

"*Compañera* Lederer?"

"Is it a problem—" Sergio smiled at the apparent discomfort the familiarity engendered in everybody— "that she's finally getting the fraternal treatment she deserves?"

Ricabarran shrugged. "I guess not." He leaned back again and eyed his visitor. "How come you're not making the rounds in Sulaco? Santa Marta is *my* territory, you know." Before Sergio could answer, a sudden downpour began, and the wind blew the rain into the room. The Cuban turned in his seat and closed the window. "You know what they say: You can't trust the skies or the chicks of Santa Marta."

As he turned back, Sergio responded. "Jorge, ORIT has been very good to me."

"Uh-oh." The Cuban guessed what was coming and reached for his cigar.

"I'm going to work for Chinito—it's temporary," Sergio quickly added. "There are other opportunities that I'm looking at."

"You could be looking at them while you're working for us," the other responded, exhaling a cloud of smoke.

"No, because I'll be in Catachoclo a good part of the time. That's where the opportunities are."

"I guess I should never've let you go there."

"Jorge, it's the best thing that's happened to me in over three years."

Ricabarran took a long puff, then waved the cigar at Sergio. "I knew there was something different about you as soon as you walked in here. You didn't have that mopey look."

"You've got that right," Sergio answered, smiling broadly. "It's the chance of a lifetime. At least *my* lifetime."

"Well, if it means that much to you, you've got my blessing. But who am I going to get to work in Sulaco, now that I've got it into the budget?"

Without a moment's hesitation, Sergio said, "Delgado."

"The Tiger'll kill me."

"For what? He's got plenty of guys. And he's so cozy with the O.S.N.—"

"Don't let *him* hear you say that."

"You're right," Sergio replied, lowering his head. "The port workers are doing *very* well." Looking up, he added, "But he can still spare Delgado, and Cantos can take over the grievance committee."

"Well, we'll see. When do you start?"

"I've started."

"What? No notice? . . . It's okay." The Cuban smiled at Sergio's discomfort. "We'll make Friday your last day. That's settled. Now, what's this about the oil workers and this guy. . .Bumpy?" he asked, looking at the piece of paper on which Sergio had written the name. "What kind of a name is that?"

"A nickname. I met him on the plane." Sergio hesitated, not wanting to reveal too much. "I was just curious. He's in the drilling business."

"Umm. Drilling." Jorge put the paper on his desk calendar. "I'll see what I can find out."

THE DOWNPOUR HAD ENDED as quickly as it started. The sun had broken through, and the temperature was rising, drying the streets. Sergio had decided to walk and was heading north toward the work-ing/middle-class neighborhood of La Floresta, where his sister lived. He was wearing a dark gray bespoke three-piece suit, his only one, as he walked up Avenida Reina Victoria, which marked La Floresta's western edge north of the old city's colonial center. He'd had the suit made just before he left Argentina.

The temperature continued to rise; he was beginning to wish

he'd worn a guayabera instead. But the shirt, popular in the coast, was not too common in the sierra. The suit, on the other hand, fit him quite well and gave him the look of a businessman. He stopped to remove the vest and, folding it neatly, tucked it into his bag. He continued on with the jacket over his arm.

A mix of row houses and apartments, with an occasional commercial establishment, made up the neighborhood. The creation of La Floresta had been part of the wave of prosperity that accompanied the arrival of the railroad to the capital from Sulaco at the turn of the century. Populated by railroad officials and merchants in that earlier era, in time it became home to bank tellers like his brother-in-law, government workers, taxi drivers, schoolteachers, and others who had managed to climb out of the working-class trap of ill-defined pay periods. Many depended upon second incomes. They rented rooms or took in boarders. Others had converted a ground floor front room into a business: small convenience stores, little dress boutiques, espresso bars, or—as in the case of his brother-in-law—a beauty salon. Giovanna had studied cosmetology at a trade school in Sulaco. When the Bank of Sulaco transferred Freddy to the capital, the house and convenience store had been available. They'd converted the store into the salon, and Freddy had taken an evening job as projectionist at the Cinema Reina Victoria, not far from the house.

The cinema was still two blocks ahead when Sergio turned up Calle Lisboa. He climbed the three-and-a-half blocks to number 357 and stopped in front of the plate glass window of the salon. Giovanna was seated on a stool at the small counter facing the door on the right side of the shop, making notes in an appointment book. He put his bag down and stood there until she looked up. Her face lighting up, she ran around the counter and through the open door, crying, "Sergio!" After a long embrace she released him and said, "You're early."

"Yes. It was a short meeting with Ricabarran, and I came directly here. You're not busy?"

"No. My first client is at one-thirty." She looked at him and exclaimed, "No! *You're* my first client. Your head needs attention." The more he protested, the more she insisted. "I have *several* men clients," she said, giving scant comfort to her brother. "I even shave an old gentleman in the neighborhood. What a tough beard *he* has!" She had picked up his bag and settled him in the chair away from the window before he could utter another word.

The shop had a black and white décor: the walls white, the curved counter tops and plumbing fixtures black. A low partition topped with shelves, on which were displayed various beauty products, separated the front counter from a sink for shampooing, behind which stood a chair with a dryer. Four chairs were lined up along the front window, facing the inside. "Shall I pull down the shade?" she asked, smiling impishly.

"No. That's all right," he answered without too much conviction.

She put on a white smock over her beige sweater and brown checked skirt. "Now, let's see," she mumbled, pulling a comb through his hair.

"Not too much off—"

"Look!" she remonstrated affectionately. "Do I tell you how to run a union?" The clipping began in earnest. "Besides, I've cut your hair many times. When I'm through, your friend Margarita won't even *recognize* you."

"Hey!"

"Hold still. I don't want to cut your ear off." She smiled at her older brother's obvious embarrassment. "It was such a coincidence you met in Catachoclo," she observed. "After Freddy wasn't able to find out anything about her at the bank, I didn't give it any more thought." Her eyes narrowed as she glanced at his reflection in the mirror. "But you said that it was union-related."

"I hadn't seen or heard from her since I deposited her with the nuns three years ago. . . . I was curious is all," he added in his defense.

"Mm," she murmured, attacking the hair above his ears with thinning shears. "Will you be seeing her while you're in town?"

"Later this afternoon, as a matter of fact."

"Well, it's a good thing you came here first. You'll want to make a good impression."

"Yes, Gigi," he responded, using her childhood nickname, "I do."

The sudden, intimate revelation stunned Giovanna.

MARGARITA'S EYES SPARKLED AS SHE SPOTTED Sergio standing in the ICRAC reception area. She had suggested that he see her before his interview with Juan Chiriboga. He *was* handsome in his new suit, and the haircut added the perfect touch. Taking his extended hand as she approached, she kissed him on the cheek. The receptionist smiled as they passed on the way to Margarita's office. "Nice haircut," she ventured to say as they walked down a long hallway. The building had housed the offices of senators and assemblymen before the legislature moved to a new location north of the center.

"My sister's a beautician," he replied.

"And knows her business," she said, taking the opportunity to look him over again.

"Yes. She said as much when I offered some advice on how to cut it." Margarita chuckled. She pointed to an open door on the left and followed him in.

"This is Daisy Rodriguez. Daisy, Sergio Fidanza." Daisy was a picture of upper class elegance: wool skirt, knitted alpaca sweater, several rings, and a filmy silk scarf held with a gold clasp. She rose from her seat, and they shook hands.

Sergio took the chair in front of Margarita's desk and was about to say something to Daisy when she excused herself. "I have to see the accountants about the prenatal pilot project." Smiling broadly, she turned as she reached the door and silently questioned Margarita about closing it.

"No. That's fine," said Margarita. Sergio, whose back had been to the door, turned in time to see the woman disappear down the hall. "She's sweet," observed Margarita. "She got her degree from the National a year before me. Great with the numbers—statistics and all that—but she isn't too keen on going into the field. I *am*, so it works out." She turned and looked out the window. "Did you get caught in that downpour?" Although the sun shone brightly, the top of Higuerota was swathed in clouds.

"No. I was in the ORIT office, and it was over by the time I left."

"How did it go?" she asked, as she gazed at him.

He felt embraced by her favor, and it filled him with an optimism that he'd long despaired of feeling again. "Fine. I think he was half expecting it. So now I'm a free agent. . . . Almost." He smiled and shook his head. "FLOC's man in Catachoclo."

"If *this* works out, you'll be *ICRAC's* man in Catachoclo." She reached for the cup on her desk. "Oh, I didn't offer you any."

"No. That's fine." She took a sip. Sergio noted that her almost austere navy blazer and gray skirt were a far cry from the flamboyant outfits she'd worn as a student in Sulaco. "I hope something can be worked out," he murmured.

"I'm sure if anything can be done, Juan'll make it happen. Oh. It's time," she added, glancing at her watch.

They both rose to leave. "I was hoping we could have dinner or something," Sergio said as they reached the door.

"Look, when you're done with Juan, we'll go for a drink and make plans."

"I'd like that."

She led him to the stairway at the end of the hall. The floors and walls were finished in mahogany, another vestige of better times. They climbed to the second floor, their steps echoing as they approached the deputy director's office. Juan Chiriboga rose as they entered. "How good to see you, Fidanza," he said, holding out his hand. He ushered Sergio into the chair before his desk. "Thank you, Margarita."

"You're quite welcome, Juan," she answered before leaving and closing the door behind her.

"She's quite an asset to the Institute. A lot like her old man," he observed as he resumed his seat. "Have you met our former president, Fidanza?"

"No, I haven't."

"I'm sure you'd enjoy his company. It was under his leadership that the Institute was created."

"Yes. As I recall, it was in the last year of his first term."

"Nineteen fifty-three," the other confirmed. "We've come a long way, and Catachoclo will play an important part in the next few years." He reached over and picked up a file folder. "I put together a resumé of your experience for the director. It's based on our conversation last week." He pushed it over for Sergio's inspection. "Needless to say the director was impressed, but he is concerned about the political aspects. We've had very little to do with trade unions, so if it's all right with you, I'll ask him to join us."

SERGIO SAT WATCHING THE EMPLOYEES of the Institute as they left, singly and in groups, at the end of the day. The receptionist was arranging her desk and the top of the counter. Her dress's understated elegance, not unlike Margarita's officemate's, and her impeccable grooming, strongly suggested an upper-middle class status. This seemed to be true of most, if not all, of the Institute's employees. As he was making a mental note to ask Margarita about it, she came into the reception area from the hallway. The receptionist looked up as he rose. She glanced at Margarita, then back at Sergio, and smiled. Margarita bid her goodnight and immediately took Sergio's arm. The door was pulled open by a uniformed guard, who touched his cap as they passed through into the cool early evening.

"No top coat?" she asked. "The nights can be chilly."

"Yes. I'd forgotten," he replied.

The former legislative office was directly behind the presidential palace. They turned left to the corner of the palace and then to the right down a moderate incline to the Plaza de Armas, the main square. Neither broached the subject of the meeting he'd just had. The charm of the hour relegated this and all other considerations to sometime in the indefinite future.

"How about El Tucán?" she suggested when they reached the square.

"The bar in the Hotel Majestic? Sounds good to me."

They headed diagonally across the plaza by one of the eight walkways that emanated from the heroic statue of Simón Bolívar, on a high pedestal with names engraved on all four sides of the Costaguana heroes and the dates and locations of the battles fought on Costaguanero soil for independence from Spain. Benches lined the walks. Frenetic shoeshine boys plied their trade at the periphery. By the time the couple reached the statue they had left the hubbub behind. One could detect the faint odor of the eucalyptus trees planted generously throughout the plaza. Royal palms defined the area at the center. She tightened her grip on his arm as she reminded him of their walks through the Alameda in Sulaco. Sergio told her that he'd been in the Bar Austral only the week before. "I was think-ing of you," he said and immediately felt like a schoolboy. He was relieved by the squeeze she gave his arm.

"I love this time of the day," she said, stealing a glance at him. The unexpectedness of her observation, and the resonance it stirred in him, left Sergio dumbfounded. He reached over and put his hand on hers where it rested on his arm. She snuggled closer to him in response as they continued toward the street, lost in the moment.

"Shine, señor?" The shoeshine boy had startled the pair.

"No," replied Sergio. The urchin quickly lost interest and joined two of his colleagues, who were enthralled by a man leading a small monkey on a leash. Across the street, shops offering a variety of services and items for the tourists lined the colonnaded block. Di-rectly opposite, a sign next to the entrance of a small theater located on the second floor advertised a production of Noel Coward's *Private Lives*, starring Arturo Hohenstein. They crossed over and stopped in front of the sign.

"I've heard it's quite funny," said Margarita. They continued strolling to the corner diagonally across from the cathedral, which occupied the entire block opposite the southern side of the square. The magnificent north portico architecturally redeemed the large hulk of a building otherwise lacking the elegance of the many large churches of the capital. "There it is." She gestured toward the hotel down the middle of the block.

The Tuesday evening crowd was light: tourists in the main. It was the only hotel of any note in the colonial center. The first-class hotels were located well to the north. The art deco chandeliers that cast a soft light on the patrons of El Tucán were part of a modestly successful revitalization of the colonial center that had been under-taken several years before, partially financed by the government.

They took seats facing each other at a small table near the window and ordered coffee.

"A little fancier than the Bar Austral," he noted.

"Yes, but at the Austral we could be sitting out on the sidewalk and enjoying the passing parade. Here the parade goes from office to home."

"Why is that?" he asked.

"I think it's the chill from Higuerota that settles on the city in the evening. *And*," she added, "the *serranos* are just not as warm and open as you *costeños*. That's why I liked Sulaco." She frowned. "But the military had other plans."

"Have you thought of going back now?"

"With you in Catachoclo, I'd need more than the Bar Austral to attract me."

Sergio's ears turned red. "Well, Catachoclo isn't forever," he managed to say, and wondered where this was going to lead. He was saved further embarrassment by the arrival of the waiter with their coffee. Margarita asked for a bottle of mineral water.

"Speaking of Catachoclo, how did it go with Juan?" she asked after stirring two cubes of sugar into her cup.

Sergio, unused to the puckish side of his companion, was happy to change the subject. "Basically they need someone to represent them in Catachoclo, and—"

"That's nothing new. Hugo Robles has been gone for six months or more."

Sergio smiled. The old firebrand was surfacing. This side wasn't as scary as the puckish one.

"As he explained it, they're having difficulty filling the position. Nobody wants to be stuck in that backwater. They think I've got the know-how, but Jaramillo is—"

"The director was there?"

"Yes. Juan called him in. He's concerned about my union work."

"But that's exactly what you have to offer." Margarita was chafing at the bit.

"Yes. And that's why it may be the best all around. They want me to represent them halftime as a consultant. Whatever that means."

"It means they can throw you to the mountain lions if things don't work out to their expectations."

"Well, I'll still be no worse off than before. This way I can help Quishpe for FLOC and look after this new beneficio. *And* the really important part is that they want me to look after the interests of the Arra'o."

Margarita's eyes lit up. "Juan really came through." Her elation quickly abated. "If it's oil, I'm afraid that there'll be trouble, and you'll be in the middle of it."

"Jaramillo all but admitted that it was oil. He said that if it is, they're not opposed to the development, but they *are* committed to defending the ruins." Margarita was listening intently. "I'm going to spend Thursday morning with that guy Krueger."

"The attorney," she confirmed. "He knows his stuff."

"And the afternoon with Chiriboga. Oh! He said that Galo would be there for the meeting and a guy from Point Four. And Maruja is coming with Galo. They're staying with her aunt."

"Wonderful! We should all go out." Margarita was warming to the occasion. "And I know just the spot. It's a new club in the north, El Candelabro."

"I'm sure Maruja will be up for it," he observed. "She was just getting started last week at El Rincón."

THEY'D HAD DINNER IN THE HOTEL dining room and taken a taxi to Margarita's home in El Placer. The narrow, winding streets of the oldest residential neighborhood in the capital made it difficult to navigate by taxi, so they got out at the Arch of San Golquí. The driver agreed to wait for Sergio, and the couple proceeded through the arch and up the cobbled lane across which a lone street lamp, thirty meters ahead at the top of the incline, was throwing a pale light. By nine-thirty a silence had enveloped the neighborhood, broken occasionally by the bark of a dog. Two-story stuccoed buildings with tiled roofs bordered the lane. The underlying brick, showing through in random patches where the stucco had flaked off, belied the wealth of the occupants. Small wooden balconies extended from most of the second story windows, with potted flowers protruding through the banisters.

As they reached the street lamp next to a low retaining wall where the lane turned to the left, Sergio asked, "Have you lived here all your life?"

"Only for the three years before we moved into the presidential palace. I left for university in Sulaco the end of my father's second term."

About five meters to the left they climbed the five steps leading to the lane above the retaining wall. There were no distinguishing signs to indicate that the Bustamante family occupied the building across from the wall: not even a number above the arched front entrance. Margarita stepped up onto the granite rise in front of the door bordered by a pair of Doric columns and put her key into the lock. She pushed the door open a crack and turned back to her escort. "It's been a wonderful evening, Sergio. Like in Sulaco."

"Yes, it has," was all he could muster. The rise put her a few inches above him. She reached out and put her hand on his cheek and kissed him on the other. "Goodnight," she said and pushed through the door. She turned and smiled before disappearing inside.

"CALLE LISBOA, THREE FIFTY-SEVEN," he said as he climbed into the back seat of the taxi. He leaned back and closed his eyes as the taxi sped east. Like in Sulaco, she'd said. He mulled the phrase. What had it been like in Sulaco? He was certain they had never kissed. They'd been good compañeros, shared their enthusiasm for the cause. But romance? No. He was *sure* that their relationship was. . .well. . .what was the term? *Platonic.* He may have harbored some feeling, but he never entertained any thoughts of—

He could still feel the warmth of her lips on his cheek.

CHAPTER 16

T HE DINING ROOM TABLE, which could seat six, was turned sideways to the window that overlooked the garden to accommodate the use of the other half of the room as a living area. A settee
occupied the wall separating the room from the beauty salon. Giovanna had just entered from the hallway. Danny was standing next
to his Uncle Sergio, seated at the head of the table.

"Uncle Sergio says that we're going to beat the Argentines in the
America's Cup next week." The boy had been delighted by the fore-
cast from the mouth of one who had actually been living in Argentina
for the past three years.

"Off to school with you, young man. It's late." The boy kissed
his uncle and sped out of the room. He was back in a flash, kissed
his mother, and was out again. "I hope you know, Uncle Sergio, that
that prediction will be all over the Escuela Fiscal Juan Carlos Vasquez
Iturralde before lunch."

"Well, they've lost Romero, and without him, we've got a *very*
good chance."

"Spoken like a diehard Costaguana. Beat the Argentines? There's
the paper." She slapped it down in front of him. "Even Salazar
doesn't think we have much of a chance." With that, his sister returned to the kitchen.

"What does he know?" Sergio shouted to be heard in the other
room. "He hasn't seen a game played outside the capital since
Vasquez's *first* unfinished term." He picked up the paper, turned to
the sports, and perused the Salazar column. "The Argentines—" he
lowered his voice as Giovanna returned, carrying a tray with two
bowls of steaming oatmeal and a pitcher of hot milk for the coffee—
"wouldn't stand for this kind of pessimism from any of *their* sports
writers."

"We'll see what happens when we play Uruguay tomorrow," she rejoined, placing the bowls on the table and taking her seat. ". . .Like on the farm," she said.

"I almost cried the first time Luz Chang Crespo fixed me a bowl of oats when I was staying with them after I got back."

Giovanna reached for her brother's hand. He gave hers a squeeze. Unlike the first few days, he seemed in control of his emotions. "They were tough times, Gigi, at the end when the Germans took over," he said, "and they came for Papa and Sabino."

"We got them back, and that's the most important thing," she said as she poured the hot milk into the cups already charged with a spoonful of powdered coffee. "Enough about those days. Tell me about your Margarita."

"*My* Margarita?"

"Is she anybody else's?"

Sergio thought a moment. "I don't think so."

"Well then, she's yours. . .for now. I'll bet you're hers, too," she added, attempting to put some backbone into her brother.

"Oh, Gigi—even if it were true, she's the daughter of *Camilo Bustamante*." Sergio pushed the empty bowl to the side.

"Oh!" she exclaimed, went into the kitchen, and returned with a plate of rolls. "Freddy got them at the bakery before he left."

"Right! The union meeting. He wanted me to go."

"He doesn't need you—Margarita does. And it's a good thing Papa isn't around to hear you talk. *He* said you could stand up to anybody."

"Yes, stand up. But marry them?"

"If she's as down to earth as you say, it won't make any difference." Giovanna had hesitated for a moment, but she got quickly back on stride. "Let's not rush it." She held the plate of rolls for him to take one. "What's next?"

"Well, we're going out tonight with Maruja O'Neil and her husband. You know her."

"The redhead from university? She's a riot. How'd you ever get together with them?"

"Her husband Galo manages a co-op in Catachoclo," he replied, buttering the roll. "We were all together last week. Do you want to join us? My treat."

"Ooh!" she exclaimed in disappointment. "Freddy has an early *and* a late show tonight. Where're you going?"

"A new place. El Candelabro?"

"In the north." She gestured toward the rear of the house. "On the road to the airport. You'll love it. The guy who owns it is the leader of the dance combo. They've made at least one record, and I've got it. Do you want to hear it?"

"No. I'll just—"

"It's no trouble." She rose and went over to a phonograph on a low table in the corner of the room. "See that? It's on the turntable." She pressed the play button and returned to her seat. "What are you doing the rest of the day?" The rhythm of a cumbia boomed out. "Too loud." She jumped up and turned it down.

"I'm going to see that American engineer I told you about. I should be leaving soon," he added, looking at the clock on the wall.

"Not before I make sure you haven't forgotten how to dance. You don't want to be disgraced at El Candelabro." Sergio did not have to be coaxed. They moved to the other end of the room and began the slow shuffle of the cumbia, accented by an undulating hip movement. After a moment or two, Giovanna exclaimed, "Yes, brother, you can still dance."

SERGIO HAD HEADED NORTH when he arrived at Avenida Reina Victoria. The capital air was invigorating, considerably cooler than the day before, and he'd decided that he had enough time to walk to the AIFLD office. He was wearing his only sport coat, a ready-made model from La Galeria in Buenos Aires. He'd decided to save the suit for Margarita. . .and ICRAC. The sidewalk was crowded with mid-morning shoppers. The Cine Reina Victoria was showing *Doctor Zhivago*.

As he continued north, the stores tended to become more up-scale. Turning west on Avenida Rio Amazonas took him past the American Embassy. Constructed only three years before, it lay fairly close to the street behind a ten-foot wrought iron fence. The gate was open, and a marine stood at ease in the shade of a small guard shed. The narrow recessed windows gave the four-story building an almost fortress-like appearance. Sergio wondered if he'd ever get inside. He suspected that it was in the cards. He'd been in the embassy in Buenos Aires with his boss to visit the labor attaché.

A small knot of people stood outside the gate of the compound, which also contained the consulate. Otherwise, the street, which was also home to the Venezuelan and Brazilian embassies, was considerably less trafficked. An Indian woman with a cart of empty bottles was negotiating the purchase of an armful of whiskey bottles from a maid at the gate of one of several large homes that shared the street with the embassies. The transaction ended, and the woman continued on her way, shouting "*Bottles*" at the top of her lungs in front of each mansion.

"SEÑOR INGENIERO'S OFFICE is at the head of the stairs." Sergio followed the receptionist's directions. Another upper-middle class young woman biding her time until marriage, he thought, then chided himself for being judgmental. Look at Maria Luisa, the FLOC secretary—the university'd had some impact on her social conscience. If only it didn't wither or get drummed out of them by their peers. He must speak to Margarita about it. The engineer was sitting behind a desk with his back to a window that overlooked the garden in the back of the large home that served as the office of AIFLD. The room was probably a bedroom. Beside the desk sat a large table with rolls of drawings and a stack of papers. The only other furniture was a sparsely filled bookcase.

"Sergio! I was hoping we'd get together, but I didn't think it'd be so soon." Braun rose from his desk and came around to shake hands. The young engineer's mustache, and the light gray knitted vest he wore, gave him the decided appearance of a Costaguana professional. "Be so kind to seat yourself," he said, pulling the chair out for his visitor.

Sergio smiled. "You've caught the Costaguana idiom quite well. I used to say it that way in Argentina. But they'd give me a strange look, so I stopped." He took the seat before asking, "How are your wife and children? It's Elizabeth, isn't it? I'm afraid I don't remember the children's names."

"Lisa and Jenny. All very well, thank you. As a matter of fact, Elizabeth asked that I invite you to lunch."

"That's very kind of you, but I don't want to impose."

"Not at all. She likes to meet the people I work with, and she's been looking forward to seeing you again. I'll call her to confirm it."

A young man in his late twenties poked his head in the doorway. "Coffee, señores?"

"Sergio, this is Pablito, our porter, messenger, and jack-of-all-trades." And then to the young man, "Sergio Fidanza is with ORIT in Sulaco." They exchanged greetings, and the porter asked again about the coffee.

"Black for me," said Sergio. Pablito retreated down the stairs. "As of this Friday, I'll be off the ORIT payroll and at least half time with FLOC. And if all goes well, the other half will be with ICRAC. *And* both halves in Catachoclo."

"Well, that *is* news. Catachoclo? How was your trip? Did you meet that Redhead, Rigpe?"

"Very briefly. But I suspect that we'll be spending a lot of time together. ICRAC are looking for me to represent their interests with the Arra'o."

"It sounds like you'll be right in the middle of it."

Margarita's exact comment, thought Sergio. "Yes. Right between Rigpe and Bumpy Cosgrove." There was a slight sigh attached to the latter name.

Pablito returned with the coffee and left. Sergio picked up his cup. "But I'm here on another matter. Did you have any discussions with Quishpe about a proposed beneficio to be owned by the co-ops?"

"Actually, that's what Wiggins was there to see Luzuriaga about. We mentioned it to Quishpe, but he seemed to think that financially, there was no way they could participate. So we dropped it."

"Have you thought of tapping the U.S. unions for help? This could be a winner for everybody." Sergio took a sip of the coffee as he waited for a reaction.

Braun looked a little perplexed. "*I* think it's a great idea, but I'm not sure how it would work. Oh, but FLOC isn't affiliated with the WCFTU."

The Cold War position, us against them, Sergio thought. He tried not to betray his reaction.

"But I don't think it'll be a problem," Braun said with some enthusiasm. "My boss doesn't let that hold him back from a good project." Sergio relaxed a little. "He was called on the carpet up in Washington over a project with the Teamsters. But he straightened them out." Sergio by then was feeling much better and looking forward to meeting John Pendleton. "John'll be in this afternoon. We can talk to him about it." He looked at his watch. "I'd better call Elizabeth."

BUMPY COSGROVE PAID THE DRIVER and headed through the gate. The marine snapped to attention. Bumpy gave him a nod and proceeded into the embassy. The sergeant at the reception desk rose and smiled at the Texan. "Good morning, Mr. Cosgrove."

"Good mornin'. Mr. Jenkins's expectin' me."

The marine glanced down at his desk then back up at Bumpy. "Yes, sir. Go right on up."

Bumpy removed his hat as he entered the elevator. Getting off at the third floor, he strode down the hall to the right, stopped at the next to last door on the left, and knocked. The tag read *Charles Jenkins*. There was no title or other identification. A moment later a man almost as tall as his visitor, but much huskier, opened the door. "Come in, Cosgrove. I'm sorry I wasn't here last week to see you."

Cosgrove took one of the two chairs in front of the desk and put his briefcase on the floor beside him. The building was even more formidable from the inside. The window behind the desk was about two feet wide and recessed from the face of the building about the same amount. The walls of the recess were angled back, providing a bit broader vista. There was another window to the right of the one behind the desk, in front of which sat a small round conference table with four chairs. Bookcases and filing cabinets lined the inside wall.

"That's all right. I've got a lot more to talk about since my trip to Catachoclo." Bumpy put his hat on the chair next to him. "We've got two problems down there. I spent yesterday afternoon with Dubois on that goddamn map. He's working on it, but I don't hold out much hope. The other is Fidanza. Did your girl find out anything?"

"We've got quite a dossier on him," Jenkins replied, taking a file folder from his inbox. "He's just returned from three years in Argentina. Apparently he got into trouble with the junta—"

"*I* knew that an hour after we got off the plane together two weeks ago." Cosgrove slapped the arm of the chair in frustration. "Then he shows up in Catachoclo. And I'm bettin' that he's the one that sicced that goddam reporter on me." Bumpy shook his head. "And I thought he was just a guest worker coming home for a visit. Hah! Sometimes this country is a little *too* small for comfort."

Jenkins put the folder back in the tray and picked up a pencil. "I'm not sure what we can do now," he said, twirling it between the thumb and forefinger of his left hand. "He's clean as far as the locals are concerned. And they're not about to do any 'rounding up of the usual suspects' with the election coming up."

"I guess I'm gonna have to do some 'rounding up' myself."

"I wouldn't do anything before we get some direction—"

"Jenkins, I'm not on your payroll," the Texan said, standing up abruptly. "This was a one-hand-washing-the-other deal. You can stick to your observin' and reportin'. I've got a business to take care of."

Jenkins put the pencil down. His eyes narrowed, and he spoke in a deliberate tone. "Cosgrove, we're doing our best to get this country in a condition where people like you can *do* business."

Cosgrove had reached the door. He grasped the handle, then turned back. "I *am* doin' business. . .with people who want to *accomplish* something for this country. And *they* have a good idea on how to get it into the *condition* to do it." He pulled open the door but turned back yet again. "But there are those like Fidanza that take their orders from Uncle Leonid and are only interested in picking our pockets. I'm bettin' with the doers." With that he left.

THE BRAUNS LIVED IN A DUPLEX on Avenida Tres de Mayo, not far from the stadium. They had just finished lunch. "Where'd you learn to make those potato pancakes, Elizabeth?" Sergio asked. A young Indian woman in her late teens, humming a popular Andean tune, was clearing the table. She wore her hair in a long braid that reached to her waist.

The dining room was at the rear of the house. Jim sat with his back to a window overlooking the garden and framing Higuerota in the distance. Lisa was to his left; Sergio sat next to her.

"Our landlady lives next door and has sort of adopted me," she answered, wiping the hands of Jenny, seated in a highchair next to her mother. "She tried to teach me how to make tamales. I still haven't gotten the hang of popping the kernels off the cob."

"Shall I serve the coffee, señora?"

"Yes, Clemencia," she said to the maid. Lifting the child out of her chair, she added, "I'm going to take this one up for a nap." The older sister was still working on a bowl of ice cream. "Lisa, when you're finished, let Clemencia wash your hands."

"You have *your* hands full," observed Sergio.

"I don't know what I'll do when we go back to the States."

"I'm sure you'll manage."

Jim got up to help Lisa, who had finished her ice cream, out of her chair. The child ran into the kitchen without a word. "Would you like a cigar, Sergio? They're Cuban. You can't get them in the States."

"Elizabeth won't mind?"

"I usually smoke them outside." Jim opened the top drawer of the breakfront, brought out a box, and opened it for his guest. They each took one of the short Montecristos. Jim led the way through the kitchen.

"The coffees, señores?"

"Oh. Right. We'll take them outside." Jim lifted a mug from the tray on the counter and proceeded through the back door followed by Sergio, who also helped himself to a cup.

"Can I come, too, Daddy?" Lisa called out as Clemencia finished drying the child's hands.

"Sure." He came back to hold the door for her.

They sat on folding lawn chairs in the shade of the unoccupied carport at the side of the house. Lisa climbed onto her father's lap. Jim handed Sergio a book of matches. After he'd lit their cigars, the child decided to play in the sandbox at the corner of the house.

"My father smoked cigars," Sergio remarked, taking a puff and blowing it out slowly, without inhaling. "But not Cubans. He smoked the short Italian stogies. The ones that look a little like dog. . . ."

Jim smiled. "I know what you mean. The Italian laborers on a highway job I worked on smoked them. Parodis. They were always offering one to me. I finally took them up on it. They aren't so bad. In fact I got to like them. But one a day is enough. And one of these," he said, waving his cigar, "is enough at this altitude."

Elizabeth came out of the back door, carrying her own cup, and joined them.

"Do you think you'll be able to meet us tonight?" Sergio asked of Elizabeth.

She looked at her husband. "We'd love to, but we'll have to leave early. Jenny still nurses in the late evening."

"Of course. Whenever you need to go," Sergio said to put her mind at ease.

"Jim has told me about Galo, and I look forward to meeting his wife *and* your friend Margarita." She smiled knowingly at her husband. "What a wonderful coincidence, running in to her in Catachoclo!"

Sergio blushed as he wondered why he had revealed so much. "Yes, it was quite a surprise. . .for both of us," he added and blushed again. "I asked my sister and her husband. But he's working tonight. She'll be disappointed when she finds out that you're coming. She enjoyed your visit to the shop."

"Uh oh," remarked Jim. "It looks like we're in for another shower. Did you want to use the car this afternoon, Liz?"

"If it's all right?"

"Sure. But we'd better get going."

"JOHN, THIS IS SERGIO FIDANZA," said Jim as they entered the office of the white-haired AIFLD country program director. Rising to shake hands, he towered over the union leader. His long bony fingers wrapped around Fidanza's hand in a firm grip.

"Jim's told me all about you. You knew Joey Ramirez down in Argentina?"

"Yes. He asked me to look you both up when I got here, so here I am."

"Sit down. Sit down," the older man said, indicating the two chairs in front of the desk. "Jim says he ran into you in Sulaco, at the port workers'. How's the Tiger doing?"

"Fine. He was hoping I was going back to work for him, but I've made other plans. And that's part of the reason I'm here."

As Sergio explained the possibility of the beneficio workers participating in the proposal for the co-op-owned beneficio, Pendleton grabbed a pipe from a rack on the desk and proceeded to scrape out the ashes and pack in fresh tobacco. Sergio described the history of the Tres de Mayo operation and the success of the union formed by Quishpe. He ended with the plan for the new beneficio and the involvement of Point IV.

John had lit his pipe and was leaning back in his chair. He quietly puffed, reflecting on the words of the newly appointed representative of FLOC in Catachoclo. Still gazing at the ceiling, he said, "I like it." He leaned forward and pointed the pipe at the two in front of him. "It has all the elements of a *winner*. Jim, I want you to write up a feasibility report for me. I want to get it off to Washington, pronto. Work with Wiggins."

Sergio felt a surge of optimism he hadn't experienced in many years.

"Fidanza, can you give us some perspective from the workers' view?"

"I'll be in Sulaco this weekend. I leave for Catachoclo Monday. Chang Crespo and I will put it together. Compañera Lederer will help us."

"Who?"

"She's the founder of FLOC. Still active. In fact she was with me when all this came up in Catachoclo last week."

John thought for a moment. "I may have met her," he said almost to himself. "Well, good! I'll be going to Washington in two months for the country program directors' annual meeting." John leaned back and took another puff. "This is going to make those guys sit up and take notice. Hah! And they said Costaguana was the end of the world." He slapped the desk. "This is great! I guess a trip to Catachoclo will soon be in the works."

"When you go we'll be happy to receive you," offered Sergio.

"John, Sergio is also going to be the ICRAC representative. He'll be looking after the interests of the Redheads," Jim informed his boss. "I'd told him what I thought about the drilling, and he says that there's a lot of talk going around about it being for oil."

"Drilling. Mmm." The older man tapped the ash of his pipe into a tray on his desk. "I just joined a poker game here in town. Point IV guys and some other Americans. One of them's a driller. Do you know a Bumpy Cosgrove?"

"Yes, I know Bumpy. He was sitting next to me on the plane when I arrived in Sulaco two weeks ago."

"WHAT TIME IS IT?" ASKED MARUJA, squeezed between Galo and Margarita in the back seat of the taxi. Galo held his watch up to the window and, as they passed a streetlight advised his wife that it was nine o'clock. "Fidanza, what time did you tell them we would be there?"

Sergio was up front next to the driver. "Eight-thirty."

"Ay. And being gringos, they're probably already there," Maruja lamented.

"My parents always told the gringos to come a half hour later than they told the Costaguanos," remarked Margarita, "and they were *still* the first to arrive. They never learn, and neither do we."

"How much farther, driver?" Maruja seemed to be the only one concerned.

"Three more blocks, señora."

In another minute the cab had turned into the driveway in front
of the club and driven past the windowless side facing the street with
a large neon sign that spelled out *El Candelabro* and depicted a can-
delabrum with three lights. He pulled up to the entrance at the side
of the building that had once been a small warehouse and was painted
completely black, with a wide patio in front of an entrance, illuminated by two ornamental street lamps, each with three lanterns. A
smaller version of the sign on the side of the building sat over the
doorway.

Inside, the Brauns were one of a half dozen couples dancing on
the ample floor to a medley of boleros by a combo made up of electric organ, drums, sax, and raspa (a ridged gourd, stroked with a
wooden stick). The inside walls were also painted black. The only
illumination came from the small candles on each table, a lamp over
the entry, and a spot on the combo.

"I was afraid of this," said Elizabeth. "You know they're always
late."

"Don't worry, Liz. We'll leave when we have to. I'm sure they'll
understand. Meanwhile, let's enjoy the music."

"It's just that I didn't want to cut short our time with—oh, *wow!*
She's a *knockout.*"

Jim turned so that he could see. "I'll say," he agreed, waving to
the new arrivals. Galo was the first to spot them. The set ended as
they met in the center of the dance floor. Introductions and apolo-
gies for lateness were offered with light-hearted comments about
gringo time and Latin time. "We're sitting over there," said Jim,
pointing to a round table off the corner of the dance floor opposite
the band.

A waiter arrived as soon as they had ensconced themselves.
"What are you drinking, Jim?" asked Galo.

"Sulaco."

"Sounds good to me. Maruja? Margarita?" They both nodded.
"Orangina for the teetotaler. Are you ready for another, Jim? Elizabeth? No? I guess that's it." The waiter left.

"Jimmy?" Maruja mused aloud. "I had a grade school classmate
we called Jimmy. That's 'Jaime' in Spanish, no?"

"Or 'Santiago,'" added Jim.

"Of course. And Elizabeth, that's Isabel. Queen Elizabeth."

"I'm glad we've got that straightened out," said Galo dryly.

"No. It's important," the petite redhead insisted. "These names sound so strange to us. It helps to know. Fidanza tells us you have two daughters, and one of them was born here."

"Yes, Jennifer," said Elizabeth. "Almost a year ago. And Lisa."

"What did your families think?" asked Margarita, who, like Sergio, had been rather quiet up to then.

"They were very nervous, but they've gotten used to it. We're trying to convince them to visit, but Jim's mother won't fly, and my father may not be able to take the altitude."

The waiter returned with the drinks as the band resumed. It was a slow bolero, and the Brauns and the Luzuriagas got up to dance. Maruja turned to the other two, who had remained seated. "Fidanza, did you forget how to dance in Argentina? Come on. Up."

The two smiled at each other and rose. The crowd had increased somewhat, and the dance floor was comfortably filled. "No, you haven't forgotten," observed Margarita after a few turns on the floor.

"That's what my sister said," he acknowledged. "She gave me a test this morning. But I don't remember that *we* ever danced before."

"You *don't?*" She gave him a playful punch on the shoulder. "What about the port workers' gala? At Sor Marillac's school?"

Sergio's brows knitted together as he strained to recall. "Oh, yes!" His eyes brightened. "Now I remember."

"I'll bet you *don't*," she said, her puckish air still disconcerting him.

"I *do*," he protested. "Delgado was making a pest of himself. I thought his wife was going to. . . . Well, *I remember*."

"I guess you do. And I remember the *last* time we were there." She put her cheek against his and held him close.

"Look at those two, Jim," said Elizabeth. "I told you he was in love. He was so melancholy when we met at the hotel, and now look. He's a changed man."

The combo segued into a cumbia. Most of the couples on the

floor separated in an exuberant response to the rhythm. Jim and Elizabeth remained together, following the steps they had learned in language school. "Turn her loose, Jimmy. Turn her loose." The instructions were coming from Maruja who, with Galo, had come up behind Jim. When he released Elizabeth the couples changed partners. "You see? Much better," exclaimed Maruja. As they passed an empty table she picked up the candle and held it above her head, continuing the shuffle and hip swing of the dance. Several other women had done the same. Inspired by his uninhibited partner and the infectious beat, Jim translated the stylized steps of the lessons into the exhilaration of the moment.

"You really caught the beat, Jim," remarked Margarita when they had all returned to the table. "You, too, Elizabeth. And if you'd had a candle and Galo for a partner, you'd've looked just like a Guajira."

"What's the candle got to do with it?" asked Elizabeth.

"It's a tradition," Margarita explained with a shrug. "The dance is from the Caribbean coast. The words are always about stars and sand and fishermen."

"And the *rhythm*," observed Maruja, "it seems to have been created to be danced on a beach, in the sand." They all agreed.

Galo picked up his glass. "Well, here's to the evening . . .*and* the beneficio." They all raised their glasses.

"Beneficio? Is this *business*?" Maruja was, as usual, on guard against the encroachment of anything that smacked of shoptalk. Her husband apologized for his indiscretion, and the conversation returned to Latin rhythms.

Jim lamented that the only ones popular in New York were from the Caribbean islands. Elizabeth described their Spanish studies, which included learning the songs and dances of the Andes.

"You probably do them better than us," said Galo. "We just follow along with what everyone else is doing."

"But isn't that more authentic?" asked Maruja, warming to the discussion. "If you've got the rhythm, that's all you need. Look at these two," she said, indicating the two Americans. "They started out trapped in their school steps, then after a little encouragement, you couldn't tell them from a native."

"Should I grab a candle next time?" asked Elizabeth.

That broke up the group. "I wouldn't advise it on a crowded floor," suggested Maruja, still laughing. "It does take a little practice."

The camaraderie among the three couples deepened as the evening passed. They seemed completely at ease with each other, dancing or talking as the mood led them. Bits of personal histories were exchanged. Maruja regaled them with more stories of university days, and especially of Fidanza's serious demeanor, then noted, "As you all can see, it's now changed for the better." Sergio took it in good humor.

The combo struck up "Flor Sabanera," a Venezuelan air.

"Jim, did you learn the joropo in your classes?" asked Margarita.

"No, but I worked in Venezuela in '57, and I learned it then. Would you like to try it?"

"I'd love to." She smiled and followed Jim to the floor.

The four watched as they began the Creole waltz. "He does very well," remarked Maruja, and then to Elizabeth, "And that was what. . .nine years ago?"

"He brought back an album of the songs," said Elizabeth. "He loves them. He taught me, though it wasn't difficult. We both like the waltz."

"Galito, show Elizabeth how they do it in the northeast." Her husband was happy to oblige. The two joined the others on the floor. "That leaves us two costeños, Fidanza. So when will you be in Catachoclo?"

"In a week or so. I go to Sulaco first for about a week."

"You mustn't be a stranger. Our house is your house. And if Margarita comes down on business, we'll make sure she's well chaperoned." Her blue eyes twinkled at her last remark.

Sergio had to laugh. "Thank you. You're very kind."

"Not at all."

The song ended, and the dancers returned. "Thank you, Jim," said Margarita, taking her seat. "I haven't danced that in a while."

Galo asked, "Are you from the northeast, Margarita?"

"No. But my uncle has a cattle ranch outside Villavieja, and I used to visit a lot."

"I'm afraid that we'll have to be leaving soon," said Elizabeth, eliciting a collective groan.

"Maybe we should all go," said Sergio. "I've got a full day tomorrow." The men settled the bill, and they made their way to the exit, with embraces and promises to do it again exchanged outside in the chill of the evening. The Brauns left in their car after the others firmly rejected Jim's offer to drive them home. "Your baby comes first," Galo had said. "We'll take one of those," he'd added, indicating a line of three taxis at the edge of the patio.

"What a sweet couple," Maruja observed as the cab pulled into the avenue.

Sergio was pondering Margarita's uncle's cattle ranch.

CHAPTER 17

THE NEWLY APPOINTED CONSULTANT to ICRAC stood in front of the unmarked door at the top of the lane from the Arch of San Golquí. The pleasant evening permitted him to wear his dark gray suit without the vest. He carried a bouquet of flowers under his arm. At about ten minutes after the appointed hour of eight, he was leaning slightly toward Latin time. He was sure that Margarita would be ready. He *hoped* that she would be ready. Maybe I should have waited at the arch, he thought. Too late, he'd already rung the bell.

"Señor Fidanza?" asked the middle-aged Indian woman who opened the door. She had on an apron over a blue woolen skirt and an elaborately embroidered white blouse with ruffled sleeves. Several gold chains hung around her neck, accenting the black hair braided to her waist. "Be so kind," she said, gesturing for him to enter. Once inside, Sergio surrendered his flowers to her outstretched hands. She led the way to the left, through the darkened foyer into the living room. The faint scent of eucalyptus issued from the fireplace on the far wall. "Be so kind as to seat yourself. The señorita will be right down." He sat in a wooden armchair with an upholstered seat, on the left side of the room away from the fireplace. A large landscape by Gangotena hung over the sofa on the opposite wall. A formal portrait of the president, seated in what appeared to be the chair Sergio was occupying and with his wife standing to his side, hung behind him. Several smaller works, including a bas relief of a cathedral apse, adorned other walls. Although not particularly small, the room had an intimate feel.

A bookcase next to the door leading to the foyer caught his attention. He went over to it and scanned the shelves. In the center of the top shelf, just above eye level sat *The History of Fifty Years of Misrule* by Don José Avellanos, and next to it the memoir by his daughter, Doña Antonia Avellanos Corbelán. He wondered if Bumpy had tried to purchase a copy. He saw three books by Jorge Luis Borges: *The Garden of Forking Paths*, *The Book of Imaginary Beings*, and *Death and Witchcraft*. He remembered seeing Borges once in a café on the Avenida 9 de Julio. Borges had been almost completely blind by then. Sergio pulled out *The Garden of Forking Paths* and opened it. On the flyleaf, in the hand of the author, an inscription read: "To Don Camilo, All success in your endeavors for Costaguana. Sincerely, Jorge Luis Borges." And *I* caught a glimpse of him in a *café*, thought Sergio. He turned at the sound of footsteps behind him.

She was dressed in a black woolen sheath to the knee and low-heeled black pumps. A single strand of pearls with matching earrings stood in dramatic contrast to her raven hair. Sergio felt for a moment that he might melt into an amorphous mass on the floor. He recovered in time to exchange a light embrace and kiss on the cheek.

"Hour *gringa*, I see," she observed with a smile. He shrugged. "One of my father's prized possessions," she added, pointing to the book.

"I saw the inscription. How did he know him?"

"He was ambassador to Argentina in the mid-forties, under Vasquez."

"Oh?"

"It was a reward for the Christian Socialists' support," she said. "But back to Borges. In those days even Buenos Aires was a lot smaller. Father used to frequent the municipal library and met Borges, who was a librarian then. On one occasion he came to dinner, and *I* met him. I couldn't have been more than five or six at the time. I probably remember it more from being told about it." The revelation was another one of those that seemed to define the differences of their worlds. He replaced the book. "By the time father left in 1947, Perón had fired Borges, who then became the poultry inspector for the municipal market." She chuckled. "Can you imagine? We certainly have a way with our artists—they're either at the top of the social heap or inspecting chickens."

The maid entered with Sergio's flowers arranged in a vase. "They're beautiful, Sergio. You're going to make a big hit with my mother. Orchids are her favorite. Would you like something to drink?" Before he could ask for his usual, she said, "Oh. I know just the thing. Iced maté. Consuelo makes the best." He nodded. "Three, Consuelo. Doña Elena will be down shortly."

She sat on the sofa and patted the cushion next to her. "Come. Sit down." He obliged. "Mother is very eager to meet you. And you mustn't be deferential." She turned to look directly at him, crossing her knees and resting her arm on the back of the sofa. Sergio's heart skipped a beat. "She's quite down to earth and likes being challenged. We're at it all the time." Consuelo returned with the drinks. After distributing straw coasters on the coffee table, she placed the drinks on them, went to the fireplace, stirred the embers, and put two more pieces of eucalyptus on the grate.

Margarita picked up two of the glasses and handed one to her guest. "Health." They both took sips. "Well?"

"Quite good," he acknowledged. "I've never had it iced before." He took another, longer sip. "Yes. I like it."

They returned the glasses to the table. "I'm sorry father's in Caracas. Party business. But there'll be other opportunities. And here's Mamá." They both rose.

"Señor Fidanza. At last I have the pleasure of meeting you. Welcome to our home." She grasped Sergio's hand in both of hers. In her mid-fifties, she exuded the charm of a stateswoman. "Orchids!" she exclaimed upon seeing the vase. "My favorite. They *are* lovely."

She bent over to take in the faint aroma. Margarita seemed to feel that the biggest hurdle was over.

Her mother was smartly dressed in a dark gray woolen wrap-around skirt and green alpaca sweater, buttoned down the front. A gold chain and cross were her only jewelry. A hairdresser obviously attended to her on a regular basis. She picked up her glass and sat in the armchair opposite the two young people. "Our Argentine friends would recoil at the thought of iced maté," she remarked, taking a sip, "but they don't know what they're missing. Don't you agree, Señor Fidanza?"

"It's quite good, Doña Elena."

THE DINING ROOM WINDOW OPPOSITE SERGIO overlooked the colonial center of town: a lovely view, day or night. The vase of orchids occupied the center of a table that could seat ten. Doña Elena sat at the head with her back to the fireplace, and Margarita and Sergio on either side of the hostess. Consuelo, who had been standing at the doorway to the kitchen, at a nod of Doña Elena approached the table and cleared away the soup bowls.

"Yes, Señor Fidanza, the establishment of ICRAC satisfied my husband more than any of his other accomplishments. In the Sierra Morena Province, he led the way by distributing his holdings according to the new law. Needless to say, he was very pleased that Margarita has taken a position with the institute." She reached out and squeezed her daughter's arm. Margarita accepted the gesture but rebelled inwardly against the maternal condescension, even knowing that it had been done innocently. She was still her mother's child. "And you have also joined the institute, Señor Fidanza?"

"On a part-time basis, Doña Elena, in Catachoclo—where, by the way, land reform was instituted over fifty years ago during the brief existence of the Occidental Republic."

"That long? I wasn't aware of it."

Consuelo had wheeled in a cart with four large serving dishes. She uncovered the first, revealing pieces of baked chicken basted in a honey mustard sauce and held it with gloved hands so that Sergio could help himself. He picked out a leg. "Please, Señor Fidanza.

Here!" his hostess said, taking the spoon and adding a thigh to his plate. Consuelo then offered the dish to Margarita. Her mother insisted she also take another piece. "It's like eating with monks," she admonished while serving herself a thigh. The maid then offered glazed yams, French-fried cassava, and lima beans. When the plates had been filled to Doña Elena's satisfaction, she wished them a good appetite then asked Consuelo for more iced maté for her guest.

"It's nice having chicken," Sergio said. "The Argentines eat nothing but steak."

"Yes. And bad for your health. It clogs the arteries."

"Mamá is an expert on nutrition, Sergio. She reads everything she can get her hands on. I've been hearing about—what is it?—cholesterol, for years now."

"You'll thank me for it when you're older," Doña Elena insisted. "Of course it's more important for you men, Señor Fidanza. But I don't want to bore you. What *were* we talking about?"

"Land reform in Catachoclo," said her daughter. "I believe that Papá used the Occidental Republic's system as a model."

"Unfortunately it was of little benefit to the peasants," observed Sergio. "Even Alfonso Palacios, the founder of the beneficio, at first resisted the land reform, but he soon realized that it really didn't make any difference. Although they were given the land and the coffee growing on it, the peasants had no outlet for their crop except the beneficio, which is *still* in the hands of the Palacioses and, therefore, at their mercy."

"The Palacioses," mused Doña Elena. "They have powerful friends in the legislature. I'm sorry Don Camilo isn't here. He could have advised you."

"There'll be other opportunities," said Margarita.

"Of course," her mother replied.

Sergio thought he detected a note of apprehension but went on to describe developments in favor of the peasants. He told of FLOC unionizing the beneficio in 1942 and the development of the cooperative movement in Catachoclo when ICRAC became law.

"Whenever I think of unions, I think of the Peronistas running amok during the end of our stay in Argentina."

"Mamá," cautioned Margarita, "you can hardly compare Argentina with Costaguana. The country is much more advanced, and they were being manipulated by Perón and his crowd."

"It's still happening," interjected Sergio. "When *I* left Argentina, there was a lot of politically motivated labor strife. There were even rumors that Perón might return from Spain."

"That's my point," insisted Doña Elena. "They are so easily seduced by some politician."

"But unions provide the *only* way to defend the rights of the workers," said Sergio with as much emphasis as he could permit himself under the circumstances.

"I'm sure," opined his hostess, "that the majority of employers would do the right thing by their workers."

"*Mamá*, even if that were true, and I doubt it, it would still be paternalism. We *cannot* continue to treat these people like children."

"It wasn't children that lynched that man in Nogales," observed Doña Elena with a shiver. "His poor family!"

"A heinous crime by desperate men, Doña Elena," Sergio said. "My friend and colleague Doctora Lederer had it right when she said, 'He didn't deserve it, no matter how ill-used those men were. But the bloody system grinds the humanity out of people.'"

"I suppose," she said, raising her eyebrows in vain expectation. But rather than reflect on the event, the consummate hostess brightened and said, "Let's not let it darken our spirits. Would you like more chicken, Señor Fidanza, or cassava?"

"No, thank you. Everything was quite delicious, Doña Elena."

Consuelo appeared and cleared the table. "I hope you left room for flan, Señor Fidanza."

DOÑA ELENA HAD BID THE YOUNG PEOPLE an early good-night, and Margarita suggested a walk to El Pozo, a small park at the top of the lane that had once been the site of a water supply for the neighborhood. Though the evening was warm, she had wrapped herself in a black ruana. The glow of the streetlamps, suspended from the eaves of the houses, provided the only light in an otherwise moonless night. She slipped her hand under his arm as they made their way up the cobbled pavement. At the top of the lane the last lamp, mounted on a pole, illuminated the grassy area of the little park. The center of town lay behind them, the eerie presence of the snow-capped Higuerota to the left. Above them glittered a dome of incredible beauty.

"Father loves the stars," she said as they approached a pergola in the middle of the green. "He has a telescope and brings it up here when it isn't windy. Like tonight." They mounted the wooden platform, crossed to the opposite side, and leaned against the railing. "Look! There's the North Star just above the horizon." Sergio's hand slipped around her waist. "And the Little Dipper," she added, drawing an arc with her right hand.

He turned her gently toward him and kissed her. He could feel the warmth of her lips—those wonderful lips he had dared not think about during those years in Argentina. Her arms went around his shoulders. Cradling his head in her hands, she responded equally to his ardor. How long was it before they parted, breathless, from their passion? She hugged him and whispered, "Oh, Sergio, I thought this day would never come."

It was too dark for him to see the tears streaming down her cheeks. They kissed again and then stood for what seemed to be an interminable time, pressed together. When his embrace relaxed, she looked up. He asked, "What will your parents say?"

She put her head on his shoulder. Realizing she was crying, he reached into his pocket for the handkerchief that Giovanna had insisted he take. "You never know," she had said. How did *she* know? Sergio wondered. Margarita took the handkerchief, dried the tears, and dabbed at her nose. When he drew up the ruana that had slipped from her shoulder, she took his hand and placed it against her cheek.

"There's nothing they can say, my darling." The endearment startled him. "I've waited too long." She put her arms around his shoulders. "If you feel the way I do, there's no turning back."

"I do. . . ." I do: It was all he could muster. Thoughts of an indignant ex-president spun through his head. "You can stand up to anybody," Giovanna had said. But marry his *daughter*? he thought, then surrendered to the moment. He leaned back against the railing of the pergola and drew her against him. The rail yielded with an ominous crack, which caused them to jolt upright to regain their balance. Sergio was flustered, but Margarita burst into laughter.

She finally managed to say, "I guess we'd better find a safer spot." She sat on the bench at the entrance to the pergola and drew him down next to her. She used the handkerchief again, and then tucked it into her sleeve. They kissed.

Drawing away, he asked, "Now what?" still trying to make some order of what seemed to be a flight of fancy.

"Yes. We must give that some thought," she teased. Sergio had to smile. He put his arm around her and, turning her head toward him, kissed her again. "Sergio, time for planning," she insisted. She leaned forward and outlined the possibilities of trips between Catachoclo and the capital. He would have to report to ICRAC on occasion, and she had her inspections of the clinic to complete. He marveled at her ability to make it seem so simple. "And next time you'll meet Papá." An indignant ex-president loomed large again in his mind. "And we even have the new telephone line for chitchat," she said with an air of triumph. "But I think we should go." They rose to leave, but not before Sergio managed to steal another kiss.

As they reached the top of the lane they heard the moan of the night watch's horn and saw the man and his dog disappear into the lane that led to the arch. The neighborhood dogs had long since stopped barking. The only sound was the footsteps of two people in love.

THE SUN HAD BARELY BROKEN over the Eastern Cordillera as Sergio, sitting at his sister's dining room table, perused *El Semenario*, the capital's daily newspaper. The front-page headlines trumpeted the win over Uruguay the night before. He looked up smiling as Giovanna entered with a tray of oatmeal and hot milk for the coffee. "Uruguay is not Argentina," she stated flatly as she put a bowl in front of his place and the other at hers. "But I must say it does bode well." She took a spoonful of the cereal and frowned, shaking her head. "I don't think so. Even without Romero, it would be a miracle."

"Miracles happen," her brother observed.

"Yes, and you're proof of that. And speaking of miracles, how was dinner last night?"

"Roasted chicken, cassava, and glazed yams."

"Do tell. And what was for dessert?"

"Flan."

"*Sergio!* She pounded the table. *What happened?*"

He smiled and then turned serious. "Gigi, I'm a very happy man. Happier than I could ever expect."

Giovanna jumped up and embraced her brother. She not only embraced him but also rocked him sideways in his chair.

"Hey. Take it easy."

She stopped and looked at the clock. "What time's your flight?"

"Nine o'clock."

"Oh!" She rushed to the doorway. "*Danny*," she called.

"Coming!"

"Where's your father?"

"Shaving," the lad answered, bursting into the room. "Uncle Sergio! We beat Uruguay!" he shouted. "The cup is ours!"

"Not so fast. It isn't over yet," the boy's uncle cautioned. Giovanna gave Sergio that I-told-you-so look. "But we'll take Argentina, and *then* it'll be ours," he added unequivocally.

"Dreamers," commented Giovanna as she set out a bowl of oats for her son. "But I hope you're right."

"Three-two, Sergio. Would you believe it?" Freddy Arpe had entered the dining room, rubbing his hands together, relishing the news of the victory. He pushed dark-rimmed glasses back on his nose. Giovanna's husband was slightly built, wore dark trousers and a white shirt, and looked like the bank teller that he was. "Argentina, watch out!"

"Another one," observed Giovanna. She gave her husband a good-morning kiss. "I guess I have no choice but to join the wishful thinkers. Oats, Freddy?"

"Yes," he answered, taking the chair next to his brother-in-law. "Who made the winning goal?"

"Gomez. He headed it in," Danny replied, "Their goalie never saw it."

"What does Salazar have to say?" asked Freddy, spotting the paper in front of Sergio opened to the sports page.

"He claims he saw it coming but has nothing to say about our possibilities with Argentina." The banter continued. Giovanna brought a bowl of oatmeal for her husband and joined in the discussion, in which teams were picked apart and put back together.

Giovanna glanced up at the clock. "Look at the time. We've got to go."

Ten minutes later they were all squeezed into the Toyota, heading to the airport to see Uncle Sergio off to Sulaco.

CHAPTER 18

THERE HE IS," SAID SEGUNDO, the black chauffeur, pointing to Sergio, who had just appeared at the arrivals gate of the TAMC terminal, and who, spotting him and Chinito, wove through the crowd toward them.

"Thanks for picking me up," he said.

"You have any luggage?" Chinito asked.

"Just this." Sergio indicated his carry-on bag.

"You look different," remarked the chauffeur. Taking charge of the bag, he started moving toward the main entrance.

"I'm the same guy you dropped off here on Tuesday."

"You look happier," insisted Segundo. "The capital must agree with you. But you gotta be careful—the altitude is bad for the liver." He pushed through the doorway.

"I never heard of such a thing," said Chinito.

"Oh? I had an uncle who moved to the capital. In a few months he turned yellow."

"Yellow? How could you tell?" the incredulous secretary general exclaimed.

"Oh, he was my uncle by marriage. On the other hand, he was a heavy drinker. Maybe it was the combination." Segundo installed the bag in the trunk. They boarded the taxi. "Back to headquarters?" he asked as he started the engine.

"Chinito, could we stop at the Tiger's? I want to settle my employment status once and for all."

"Fine by me."

Ten minutes later they were at the Port Workers' Union. Segundo had offered to drop the bag at Chinito's office after going to the main terminal to try for a fare from the international flight. "Don't let some gringo run off with my stuff," warned Sergio. "It's got my only suit!" he shouted as the chauffeur sped off.

On the way in, they waved to Paco Fuentes behind the counter of the commissary, and Sergio couldn't escape another over-the-counter embrace with Magda Ponce.

Hector Rivera, opening mail at his desk, looked up as the two entered. "I thought you'd be at your old job by now. . . . Did the Tiger know you were coming?" he asked, eying the desk in the corner.

"No," answered Sergio. "We'll only take a minute."

Hector reached for the phone on the wall and dialed the boss. "It's compañero Fidanza and compañero Chang Crespo. . . . Right. He says to go right in." He stood up to replace the phone and, in a nod to formality, shook hands with the two. "It'll be good to have you back," he said with half a smile.

As they entered the room with the ten small desks, the door to the Tiger's office opened and Matilda Estevez, clutching her steno pad and ever the delight in a sleeveless shift, appeared followed by René Andrade. She smiled and bid them good morning. They returned the greeting and exchanged handshakes with the boss of the port workers. "It's still waiting for you," he said, pointing to the desk just outside his door. "When the hell are you going to start?"

"That's what I'm here about."

They followed Andrade into the office. "What happened to the air conditioner?" Sergio asked, noting the clear view of the port through the open window.

"The goddamn thing stopped working after it blew another fuse, so I junked it." Andrade sat down in the squeaky chair. "Actually I gave it to the girl," he muttered, "but she got rid of it. She couldn't get it fixed either." The two visitors took the seats opposite the Tiger. "Well, when *are* you going to start?" he asked, leaning forward, elbows on the desk.

"I'm going to work in Catachoclo, René." Sergio felt his heart drop at the look of dismay on the Tiger's face. "René, just think about it," he went on without a pause. "You've gotten along without me for over three years. Delgado is doing just fine. Now admit it," he added, holding up his hand, as the Tiger was about to object.

"What does Ricabarran expect you to be doing in Catachoclo?"

"I'm not going to be working for him."

"Who then?" the other asked, glaring at Chinito.

"He'll be working half time for me," Chinito admitted, trying to deflect some of the Tiger's unhappiness from Sergio.

"And half time for ICRAC," Sergio added.

"*ICRAC?* I can't believe it!" Andrade practically shouted. "What the hell are you going to be doing for *them?*"

Sergio waited a moment before leaning back in his chair and proceeding to give René a brief description of the proposed beneficio and the dispute between the Arra'o and the drillers. . . ."René, it's right where I want to be."

The Tiger sat, nodding. "I guess I can't argue with that. Though why you want to bury yourself in that backwater, I'll never understand." He looked at his watch. "After all this, I need a drink." He pushed himself out of his chair. "How about I buy you guys lunch at the Litoral?" As they left the room, he asked rather offhandedly, "Who's Ricabarran going to get to take your place?"

Without looking directly at his old boss, Sergio mumbled, "I suggested he try to get Delgado."

"Oh, my God!"

"I THOUGHT RENÉ WAS GOING TO CROAK when you said that," Chinito remarked as he and Sergio climbed the stairs to the FLOC office.

"I think he got over it," said Sergio. "By the time we left the Litoral, he was talking how shuffling around the committee heads would be good for morale."

From the top of the stairs they saw Golda Lederer talking with Maria Luisa. "Doctora Lederer," Chinito called out, "I'm so sorry we're late."

"Not at all, Julio, I'm early," Golda replied. "Luis dropped me off on his way to the clinic. We've been chatting. Fidanza, good to see you again. I trust your trip to the capital was fruitful. And it appears that it was very enjoyable, too."

Sergio blushed. "It was *very*. . .enjoyable, compañera Golda. Thank you."

Julio's eyes widened at Sergio's familiarity, but he recovered and invited them to his office. "Would you like some coffee, ah. . .Doctora?"

"That would be nice," she replied. Sergio asked for an Orangina.

"I'll bring them right down," said Maria Luisa. "Oh, compañero Fidanza, Segundo left your bag here," she added, pointing to the suitcase next to her desk.

They proceeded to the office and had hardly arranged themselves when Maria Luisa entered. She set the two cups of coffee, a sugar bowl, and the soda on the desk. Julio pushed the bowl to Golda, who took two spoonfuls. Julio had three. Golda took out her cigarettes and, confirming that the others didn't smoke, lit one for herself. "Well, tell us about your adventures in the capital, Fidanza," she said, taking a drag.

"On Tuesday I had a meeting with Chiriboga. I guess they were serious, because he called in the director. He was concerned about my union connections. Apparently this is something new to them. But as Margarita said—"

"Bustamante?" Julio exclaimed.

Golda asked, "She was at the meeting?"

The flurry of interest in Margarita changed the direction of the conversation.

"Oh, so your sister had some news about her?"

"Hasn't he told you?" Golda announced, smiling at the reddening Sergio. "They met in Catachoclo."

"So *that* explains the good humor."

"I was going to tell you this evening."

"Well, I look forward to hearing all about it. So, where were we? Oh, yes. *Was* she at the meeting?"

"No. But we discussed it after. Anyway, she said that my union experience was exactly what I had to offer. I guess they were happy. They mulled it over for a day while I met with that AIFLD guy—Julio, you know Braun—and his boss. And on Thursday ICRAC offered me a half time 'consulting' job to be their representative to the Arra'o."

"Consulting?" Julio asked.

"Margarita says it's so they can throw me to the mountain lions if things don't work out." He shrugged and took a sip of the Orangina. "What can I lose?"

The other two didn't comment.

"They're also interested in the beneficio," Sergio went on. "It seems the Valley of the Redheads is one of ICRAC's major areas of interest. It's just that they can't seem to recruit anyone willing to work there." Sergio rolled his eyes in self-deprecation. "I spent practically the whole day with Chiriboga and their lawyer Krueger. You remember him, compañera Golda. The thin blond guy."

Julio sat silently as Fidanza explained the so-called earthquake study, the problem with the erroneous location of the ruins, and Bumpy's involvement in the whole affair. "Imagine—sitting next to him on the plane. Will *he* be surprised when I show up in Catachoclo!"

"That's what worries me, little brother," Julio said. "It's one thing being thrown to the mountain lions, but it looks like we're marching you right into their den." He was worried and instinctively turned to Golda. Sergio followed her gaze to the photograph of Doña Antonia.

"What's the difference from that time you and Doña Antonia marched into Catachoclo to organize the beneficio union?"

"The stakes are much higher now, Fidanza," Golda observed.

"They probably are, but relative to the times, there isn't much difference. It took some courage for two women to take on the Palacioses."

"Antonia was fearless. Imagine her in the woods around Los Hatos, with her uncle and General Hernandez, after the siege of Sulaco. After that, there was nothing that could intimidate her." Golda fell silent. She watched the smoke curling up from her cigarette, caught up in the memory of Catachoclo twenty-some years before. "Yes, the stakes are *higher*," she finally said, stubbing out her cigarette, "but as remote as it is, Catachoclo is getting a lot of attention these days, and we must be part of whatever happens. *Making* it happen."

"And it's coming to a head," said Sergio. "The way Chiriboga explained it, in three weeks the die will be cast for the Arra'o. That doesn't give us much time."

"Let's not forget Quishpe and the beneficio workers," Julio reminded them.

"We have to keep after AIFLD," Sergio said. "Braun and his boss, Pendleton, are very enthusiastic. They asked me to put something together on the proposed new beneficio from the workers' view."

"Doctora Leder—" Julio started to say, then blurted out, "Compañera Golda will help us."

"See? That wasn't so hard," Sergio kidded his new boss.

"Fidanza, you have done me a great service. And Julio, I will be happy to write it up for you."

Julio was obviously relieved. In the taxi from the Litoral they'd discussed Sergio's sudden use of the term of address, but he wasn't sure if he could bring it off himself after all the years. "She will be very happy to hear it, especially from you," Sergio had assured him.

Golda reflected on her promise to Luzuriaga. "I had said that I'd write some of the international unions, but I'm not sure which one right now and how much interest I can stir up. Oh, and I spoke to Mario Puentes about his guys pressuring the beneficio drivers. He'll see that it stops." She glanced at her watch. "I guess we're finished, at least for the time being. Fidanza have you ever met Doña Antonia?"

"I think we were introduced at a meeting many years ago."

"If you have time, we can look for her at the cathedral. She usually goes there in the afternoon."

"I'd like that very much."

"Will you join us, Julio?" she asked as they all rose.

"I'm sorry. I have a meeting now with Gomez of the Textiles de La Sierra. There've been some repercussions from the affair in Nogales."

"I *must* write the ILGWU about it. Dreadful," she said, shaking her head in disbelief.

Julio followed them out to the reception. "Sergio, I'll see you then for dinner?"

"I'll be there," Sergio agreed as he grabbed his suitcase.

A FAINT SCENT OF INCENSE hung in the cool air of the cathedral as Golda and her younger companion made their way down the side aisle. A few of the "beatified"—as Segundo referred to the old women dressed and veiled in black—knelt at various locations in the great space, each exercising her claim to a particular seat, which, if inadvertently intruded upon, would result in a withering look. Just past the north portico, they stopped in front of the bust of Don José Avellanos. "See there, Fidanza? 'Patriot and Statesman,'" Golda read from the inscription. "'. . .died in the woods of Los Hatos, worn out from his life-long struggle for Right and Justice, at the dawn of the New Era.' Now you see where Antonia gets it."

She drew his attention to a marble medallion in the wall a few meters from the bust. In an antique style, it portrayed a veiled, seated woman with her hands clasped loosely over her knees. The inscription read: *To the memory of Martin Decoud, his betrothed, Antonia Avellanos.* "He died while saving a shipment of silver from the hands of the Pedrito Montero gang. But Antonia never despaired." Golda looked about. "I don't see her. But I'm sure she'll be here." She looked up again at the medallion. "Do you know, Fidanza, it was Martin Decoud's sister, Leticia, who put me in contact with Antonia? Yes, we met in Paris. I'd been working in Prague with the Socialists as a staff attorney and member of the executive committee. But when Von Hindenburg died in '34 and Hitler declared himself Führer, I became very apprehensive, as did most of the Jews I worked with, and decided to continue my efforts with the socialists in France." They took seats in a pew near to the medallion. "I was most concerned for my family in Karlovy Vary. My father was a secondary school teacher of Romance languages, and my brother managed one of the spas in the city. But I *could not* convince them to leave with me." She paused, shaking her head. "Because of my father, I was fluent in Spanish as well as French, so within a month of my arrival in Paris I began to move in Latin American expatriate circles and became good friends with Leticia Decoud. She was convinced that even France would not prove a safe haven for Jews. She told me about a girlhood friend who lived in Costaguana. This friend, a newspaper publisher, was trying to form a labor federation. She proposed that I emigrate and join that friend in her work. With a letter of introduction to Doña Antonia Avellanos, I left for South America on November 24, 1934." She mentioned the date with some finality.

"It's interesting," Sergio remarked. "I arrived in Italy a year before you left for Costaguana. But I was only three at the time. . . . What became of your family?"

"I never heard from them again."

"I'm so sorry," he said, and thought for a moment. "Our biggest problem was the Nazis confiscating our crops during their retreat in '44. But they confiscated your whole family."

Golda shrugged. "Antonia was my saving. We threw ourselves into the work. There are others in Sulaco who have lost family. We keep in touch." Sergio reflected on the grief of his companion. She seemed to have gained some solace in the telling. "We don't dwell on it, but it helps to relate it on occasion. Thank you for asking. . .and listening," she whispered, placing her hand on his arm.

"Oh. There she is." Golda indicated a tall, white-haired woman on the far side of the nave. As she passed ramrod straight through the south portico into the sunlight, she opened a white parasol. They got out of the pew and followed. By the time they reached the doorway, Doña Antonia had seated herself on a bench on the side of the building facing the sun. She was wearing a loose-fitting cotton print dress with wide, elbow-length sleeves.

"Antonia!" Golda called out as they approached.

The older woman turned. "Golda! How nice to see you." The

beauty and strength of character that had once so captivated Martin Decoud was still apparent.

"I'd like you to meet a friend of mine, compañero Sergio Fidanza. He's recently returned from three years in Argentina."

The woman looked directly at Sergio, who extended his hand. She took it in a firm grip. "Fidanza?" She looked down, considering the name for a moment, before her piercing blue eyes returned to him. "I once knew a sea captain named Fidanza. A most remarkable man." She released her grasp. "He played a crucial role in the War of Separation that has gone singularly unnoted in the history books. But do sit down." She waved the two to seats on either side of her.

"My father used to tell of a cousin once removed who would fit that description."

"Gian' Batista Fidanza." She said the name with a sense of awe. "Most remarkable," she repeated, peering straight ahead as if the man were standing there before her. "But he met a most cruel and undeserved end." She shook her head as if to rid herself of the memory, then looked back at Sergio. He, unnerved by the comment, glanced at Golda, who distracted him by telling Antonia that they had just returned from Catachoclo.

"Did you meet with the beneficio workers, Golda?"

"Of course. We saw Jorge Quishpe and Andrés Puíg and the others. They send their regards."

"And Gloria? Did you see her?"

"Yes, I stopped at my brother-in-law's on the return."

"A remarkable woman. Have you met her, Fidanza?"

"No, Doña Antonia, I haven't."

"There are people, Fidanza, who lead simple lives but go about their daily tasks of survival with an immense grace. Gloria Quishpe is one of them." She turned again to look directly at him. "They have an intuitive grasp of the world that surpasses our understanding. Among our indigenous people are poets, philosophers, statesmen who go unrecognized, because they are illiterate. Did you know that the Incas had no written language?. . .But I *am* going on," she said turning to Golda.

"No! No!" they both replied.

"It's most interesting," insisted Sergio. "Especially since I'll be representing ICRAC to the Arra'o in Catachoclo."

"The Arra'o," repeated the older woman. "In our enthusiasm for the rights of the workers of the beneficio, we didn't realize that those people were being slowly pushed off their land." Turning again to Golda, she said, "I know. We've discussed this, Golda, and you're right. We don't have the resources or the know how, but it is an issue that will overtake us if we don't do something."

"Perhaps ICRAC should take more initiative," said Sergio. "My friend is a social worker for the Institute, and when she was in Catachoclo two weeks ago she spent a day at a clinic that had been set up for the Arra'o. She voiced some of the same concerns."

"The initiative is for the Arra'o to take, Fidanza. What we must do is not *obstruct* it but make it *possible*." An urgency was evident in her tone. "If I were twenty years younger I would pursue this, but Doctor Quiroga insists that I not exert myself." The tone had become resigned. "And he is right." She sat up straight. "But I can write. I shall write an essay for *El Porvenir*. I shall write a series of essays," she added with some excitement. "Ah, here is my guardian angel now." A young costeña not unlike Matilda Estevez had been observing the conversation from beneath a tree at the corner of the cathedral nearest the Alameda.

"Good afternoon, Maria." The young woman returned Golda's greeting with broad smile. Sergio had risen at her approach.

"This is compañero Fidanza," said Antonia. "He is a colleague of Doctora Golda. Fidanza, Maria Gomez, my companion. She always manages to discern when I am exceeding Doctor Quiroga's instructions. I'm afraid we must be going."

"Antonia, we are expecting you this Saturday."

"Of course. Luis's birthday. Another decade. Well, we all get there," she observed, rising and extending her hand to Sergio. "I have enjoyed our talk, Fidanza. I look forward to more news of Catachoclo."

As she crossed to the Alameda, with her upright carriage and her hand resting lightly on the arm of Maria, she seemed to be relishing the dawn of a 'New Era,' the coming of more revolutions.

"My dearest friend, Fidanza."

"I can see why," he answered. "May I offer you a coffee?"

"I'd be delighted." They strode off in the direction of the Bar Austral.

CHAPTER 19

T wo suitcases?" Segundo asked as Sergio loaded them into the trunk.

"I'm staying a while." Sergio jumped into the front seat beside the driver.

"Not flying this time?" Segundo started the cab and took off toward the Alameda.

"I have to be there as soon as I can."

"I prefer the train, too," the chauffeur remarked. "I flew to the capital many years ago when they were still using those small planes. It had a load of groceries in the front part. I didn't think we were going to make it over the cordillera. No. Like you, I'll take the train anytime." Segundo's monologue petered out by the time they reached Plaza Rembrandt, but only after settling the finer points of air versus rail travel. His passenger was happy with the silence. At the terminal Sergio offered him a coffee. He declined, claiming that after all the years he'd finally concluded that coffee was making him break wind and, having to pick up some gringos at the hotel later, he didn't want to risk offending them.

The spacious waiting room was finished in the dark wood and brass common to the major stations on the line. The British did things first class. It had a high ceiling with four inoperative fans. Only one of the three ticket windows on the right was attended. The man behind the bar on the left was sitting on a stool, waiting for his first customer of the day. Six passengers were scattered on the four pews facing the doors leading to the platforms straight ahead. There was no line at the open window, so Sergio went there first. The agent produced the ticket, took the money, and gave change without uttering a word. Sergio started for the bar on the opposite side. He'd decided to get a few rolls to have with the coffee that was available on the train. The barman wrapped the rolls in a napkin. Sergio tucked them into a pocket on the smaller of his two bags and headed through the door to the platform.

The Capital Express consisted of two modern, diesel-driven cars. It made the round trip to the capital three times a week: up one day, and back the next. It was four hours to Tonoro, where he would change for a steam locomotive, and another four hours to Nicoya. Golda had insisted that he stay with her brother-in-law. "You'll have the opportunity to meet Gloria Quishpe," she had said.

The former secretary of the grievance committee, at that moment a consultant for ICRAC, found a seat in the forward car. He stowed his baggage in the overhead rack and settled in for the trip. By the time the train left, ten minutes late, most of the seats were filled.

Here comes the coffee, he thought, eyeing the young man in a bellhop's uniform making his way down the aisle with four thermoses strapped to his chest. The young man filled a cup at Sergio's request and set it on the tray that folded down from the back of the seat in front of him. Sergio had taken out the two rolls and smiled as he thought of the two large ones cut in half, generously slathered with Camembert cheese, and wrapped in wax paper, that Golda had produced from her briefcase on their flight to Catachoclo two weeks before. He leaned back and gazed out the window.

The cane shacks of the suburbs at the edge of the city soon changed to lush countryside. Farmhouses and little villages dotted the still, flat coastal plain. At the speed they were traveling, the conditions in which some of the villagers were living could not be discerned, but Sergio knew that even in wartime Italy he'd had it better. The express sped by the small town stations served by the slower, steam-powered trains. Between the smaller villages, passengers rode in buses mounted on rail car carriages. It was an efficient system in spite of the varied use of the single track. Safety was maintained by a telegraph system. The express train they rode had the right-of-way. The steamers were scheduled to be on sidings when the express passed, and the buses had to check in at each station for clearance to proceed to the next.

Sergio took out the reports Chiriboga had given him to review and settled in for the long ride. It would be mid-afternoon before he reached Nicoya.

THE INDIAN WOMAN SITS on the low wall bordering the small paved area at the bottom of the front steps of Doctor Francisco Saenz's home in the Nogales section of Nicoya. A rooster crows. The day has broken, but the sun has not yet risen. A folded woolen poncho, a brown fedora, and a double-ended cloth sack, not unlike a small saddlebag that can be thrown over the shoulder, lie at her side. A tall youth of about twelve years ambles around the entrance drive, kicking stones. He wears heavy duck trousers and a white cotton shirt with long sleeves. The woman fingers the travel bag as she watches him. A sound from the road catches the lad's attention. He runs to the edge of the drive as a wagon, drawn by four mules, approaches. After waving to the driver, he starts back to where the woman was seated to get his belongings. She has already picked them up. The boy turns back to the approaching wagon. The driver, a man in his late-forties with the weather-beaten face of a muleteer, waves *his* brown fedora at the two, who are waiting for him. He is wearing a red woolen poncho, similar to the one the woman is carrying, over white duck trousers and a white shirt. The wagon comes to a halt in front of the entrance. The driver sets the brake and gets down from the seat. He extends his hand, then embraces the lad, who is almost as tall as the older man. The woman approaches, still holding the boy's belongings. The three stand together. It's an awkward moment. The man finally takes the things from the woman and motions for the boy to mount the driver's seat. He hands them up to the youth. The woman suddenly returns to the wall on which she has been sitting and retrieves a second cloth bag. She gives it to the boy in the seat. The man puts his hand on the shoulder of the woman, the only display of affection he deeply feels, then climbs into the wagon next to the boy. They wave, and taking the reins, the driver calls to the mules. The animals strain at the traces, and they are off. The woman steps into the roadway and watches the wagon retreating from view. Just before it disappears the boy rises in the seat and waves. She returns to her place on the wall. She sits for a moment, then buries her face in her hands.

GLORIA QUISHPE LOOKED UP from the bench where she was sitting, reading a magazine, as Paco Saenz turned into the driveway in his 1956 Chevrolet sedan. She carried her soon-to-be-fifty-three years with grace. In addition to the natural effects of the years there were marked changes in her appearance. Her wavy hair, by then quite gray, had been trimmed to an attractive length above the shoulders. Her skirt and blouse were decidedly European in style. As he pulled up to the entrance, a woman, awaiting their arrival, came out of the house. Still agile in his late-seventies, Paco got out of the car and was opening the trunk as Sergio joined him. He retrieved only one of his suitcases. The woman smiled, took it from him, and retreated into the house. Meanwhile Gloria had left her seat on the bench and approached the two.

"Gloria, this is Sergio Fidanza. Sergio, Gloria Quishpe."

"You know my son Jorge," she said, taking his hand.

"Yes. We'll be working together for a while." She nodded in agreement, apparently aware of the arrangement.

"The señora is waiting in the parlor," she said and looked after the two as they entered the house.

The frail wife of Paco was seated in a sofa under the window that faced the street, with a crocheted afghan covering her legs. Her well-groomed gray hair framed a pretty face accented by dark brown eyes. She put down the book she'd been reading and welcomed her guest. "You are in your house, Señor Fidanza. Be so kind as to seat yourself."

"It's very kind of you to have me," Sergio said as he took a seat in an armchair facing his hostess. Paco sat on the sofa next to Leticia. The parlor reflected the charm of the provincial doctor and his wife. Eucalyptus logs were stacked in the fireplace, ready to ward off the occasional chill of an inter-Andean valley evening. Although the house was large, the furnishings were modest: a rugged colonial style reminiscent of the haciendas in the sierra.

"And what news of my sister-in-law?"

"We were together yesterday, as a matter of fact. She introduced me to her friend, Doña Antonia Avellanos."

"Ah, yes, and how is she?"

"Quite fine. The doctor has told her that she mustn't excite herself, but she's irrepressible. When she left us she was promising to write a series of essays on the rights of the indigenous."

"That would be her," commented Paco. "Sergio, can I offer you a drink?"

"I can't drink alcohol."

"A cup of Maté, then?"

"That would be fine."

"And you, my dear?"

"Maté sounds good."

"Now I hope we have some. I'll see." Paco retreated to the kitchen.

"We are so happy to have you, Señor Fidanza."

"Please. Sergio."

"Of course. And please, call me Leticia. We are too formal. Not like the North Americans." She paused to adjust the afghan. "But as I was saying, we don't get as many visitors as we used to. It's feast or famine. It was only the week before last that Golda was here with a young woman, Margarita Bustamonte—oh, but you know her!" she added, her face lighting up. "Golda was describing your chance meeting. How sweet. Bustamante. I didn't think to ask. I wonder if she's related to the former president."

"He's her father," Sergio said without expression.

Paco returned to announce that Gloria had bought the herb the day before.

"Did you hear, Paco, Margarita is the daughter of Camilo Bustamonte."

"Really? She *is* charming—and so dedicated to her work. She had a long chat with Gloria."

The woman who had taken Sergio's suitcase entered from the

kitchen, carrying a tray with a teapot, three cups, and a plate of pastries. She set the tray on the low table between the sofa and the chairs and asked if there was anything else.

"That'll be fine, Maria. Oh, by the way," Paco added, "This is Sergio Fidanza. He will be working with your cousin Jorge." The woman smiled, slightly embarrassed at having been included in the conversation. "We'll be going to Catachoclo tomorrow." She smiled again and beat a hasty retreat.

"We?" asked the surprised visitor.

"Yes. I've decided that a visit to the clinic is overdue." Paco poured the maté and handed cups to his wife and visitor. "Leticia and I used to go every month for a few days. The trip is much easier now, but retirement takes its toll."

"Oh, my dear, you are as spry as ever," Leticia protested. "I can't make the trip, Sergio. But I'm satisfied with my little projects here in Nicoya."

"My Leticia is too modest. She and Gloria are counselors at the women's center."

"Gloria?" Sergio was surprised.

"Yes. They make a good team. After Gloria learned to read and write Spanish, she taught Leticia Quechua. She never ceases to astound the women they serve at the center."

"*I'm* astounded," Sergio exclaimed.

"Yes," agreed Leticia. "Your Margarita was also astounded. She spoke to Gloria about it. And imagine, she wants to visit our center *and* send observers."

My Margarita, thought Sergio. "I'm sure she'll put the experience to good use," he said, wondering if the whole world was witness to his budding romance.

"Try one of these, Sergio," said Paco, offering his guest the plate of pastries. "They're a specialty of Boca del Valle."

"Of course. Allullas. I remember years ago taking the bus to Catachoclo. When we arrived in the village, women would descend on us with trays of them."

"They still do," Paco responded.

"They're quite good," said Sergio, taking two.

It had been getting darker, and Paco reached over and switched on the bridge lamp at the end of the sofa. He refilled the cups of maté. "Shall I light the fire?" he asked. Leticia thought the sweater that Paco helped her into would be fine. Sergio said that he was quite comfortable.

"Allullas have become a minor industry," Leticia explained. "Gloria gets them in town. We are all retired, even Gloria, but she insists on doing the shopping."

"Retired." Sergio sipped the tea and mulled the idea. "I've never really thought about it. I mean, with respect to household servants. They're like an invisible class. My mother always had a girl to help with the laundry. They didn't live with us. If they left to get married or a better job, there was always another one." He was warming to the subject. He thought of his recent dinners with Margarita and her mother and the Brauns. The Brauns' maid was barely out of her teens and appeared to be just another set of hands for Elizabeth. The two he'd observed in the Bustamonte household, however, seemed to be well trained in their duties. Sergio described the two cases to his hosts.

"I think most of our friends would fall into the Bustamonte situation. Wouldn't you agree, Leticia?"

"Yes, I think so. And I believe the maids all have families either in town or in one of the nearby villages. Some have their own children who live with extended families." Leticia shrugged. "If they're well treated, it becomes a way of life. In most cases the employer doesn't get involved." She paused, placing her cup on the table. "But Gloria is different. She was a gift from God." Leticia took her husband's hand. He gave it a loving squeeze. "Her father brought her here under the most distressing circumstances," she began, her face growing somber.

Hoping to spare her pain, Sergio said that Golda had told him of her being taken advantage of by the founder of the beneficio, and that Jorge himself had confided this in him.

"Yes, but for us, we were married only a few years and were still childless. Here was a girl—girl indeed, only about ten years younger than I—who needed help. It was a distraction from our concerns about children, but when I learned she was pregnant, I think I became a little jealous. In the end it has been a blessing for us. When her child, Jorge, was born, they became almost part of the family."

"We would have sent him to university," said Paco, "but it was not to be. Once he started riding with his grandfather, the struggle of the workers at the beneficio became his calling." He raised his eyebrows in resignation. "And maybe in the end this work is the greater good."

"But Gloria!" Leticia exclaimed. "I had decided to teach her to read and write. We would sit at the kitchen table and go through the lessons. She was like a sponge. In just two years she could read and discuss *anything* in the newspaper."

"She's five years younger than my brother Luis," Paco put in. "Had she been born into *our* family, she would be a doctor or lawyer."

"She could have been anything," Leticia agreed.

"Does she go to Catachoclo often?" asked Sergio.

"Never!" they answered in unison.

"The trauma of the experience has left its mark," offered Paco. "But I think there's another reason." He rose and said, "I'm a little chilly." He went over to the fireplace and stuffed some sheets of newspaper up the flue. He crumpled other sheets and set them in the middle of a stack of split eucalyptus, lit the paper in the chimney, then the others. Before he got back to his seat the wood was ablaze. Meanwhile, Sergio had accepted Leticia's offer of another pastry. Paco continued, "Her father had brought her mother and her for a visit only a week or so before she came to stay. Her father's sister was our maid at the time. It was the first time she'd ever been out of Catachoclo. I think she realized that life in that backwater was not for her. Even if the whole sordid affair had not happened, she would have come to the city sooner or later."

"She has many friends among the servants and the merchants," observed Leticia. "As you can see, she even cut her hair. That was a bit traumatic. She wouldn't leave the house for a week or more after she'd had it done. But now it's as if it had been that way forever." She thought for a moment. "It *has* been many years now, come to think of it."

"It's a wonderful story," said Sergio, "and a case in point. Only yesterday Doña Antonia was saying that among our indigenous people are poets, philosophers, and statesmen, but that we don't recognize them because they are illiterate. And here is an example."

"Yes, it is. And you may glean more from her own lips, if we can persuade her to join us at table," said Leticia. "It's only on rare occasions," she added.

"Two weeks ago with Golda and Margarita was one of them," said Paco. "That you're going to be working with Jorge may make the difference."

CHAPTER 20

ALLULLAS!" THE ANCIENT INDIAN WOMAN SHOUTED as the 1956 Chevrolet pulled off the road onto a crude parking area in front of a long one-story building nestled under three Ceiba trees at the edge of Boca del Valle. Paco stopped next to a huge truck with *Cafetero Tres de Mayo* emblazoned on the door. "Allullas!" she called again as Sergio emerged from the car.

"Four," he said. ". . .Make that eight. I'm going to bring some to the people in Catachoclo," he added to Paco as he came around to where Sergio was making the purchase. The woman had set her tray on the hood of the car and was wrapping the pastries in a sheet of newsprint. Sergio handed her the money; tucking the coins into a gray-and-white-striped bag hanging around her neck, she picked up her tray to look for another customer. A *mixta* pulled in from the other direction. "Allullas!" she shouted, joined in chorus by another saleswoman. "Allullas!"

Paco looked at his watch. "We should be in Catachoclo before noon." They climbed the two steps onto the thatch-covered deck in front of the building and took seats at a rough-hewn wooden table. "Two coffees with milk," Paco asked of the waiter who had emerged from the building. "We usually break up the trip here. They say it's always been a stopping place for the truckers and the teamsters before them. I remember Gloria's father mentioning it. They used to change teams here. The owner stabled the mules for the beneficio."

"Had you been going to the clinic for a long time?" Sergio asked.

The doctor thought back. "There was a local doctor there in the late thirties. He was getting on, and four of us in Nicoya took it upon ourselves that one of us would go each week for two days. The government supported the effort to the extent that they expanded Doctor Sanchez's—that was his name—clinic. He died in. . .1943? Yes, 1943. The year after Golda and Antonia formed the union." The waiter returned with the cups, a cruet of the dark coffee liquor, and a pitcher of hot milk. Sergio opened the package of pastries. He and Paco helped themselves. Paco continued as Sergio poured the coffees, "If I recall correctly, the existing clinic was built in the late fifties. Fifty-eight. I retired the next year. The other three are also retired. There's a young doctor assigned to the clinic. Did you meet him?"

"No. He was in the capital at the time." Sergio took a bite of the allulla. "They *are* good. I'd better get a few more. Did you ever treat any Redheads?"

"None in the early days," the other recalled, sipping coffee. "They have their own shamans. More recently we've treated broken bones and other injuries. But no diseases. They were—still are— very robust. You'll see as you get to know them." They watched a man, who had been having coffee at one of the tables, pay his bill, get into the truck next to the Chevy, and roar off, heading north. "Should I say anything about the oil?"

"Certainly," Sergio assured him. "The more the rumor spreads, the better. Just don't mention where you heard it. I'm going to have my hands full with the drillers' boss as it is."

"You're not concerned for your safety?"

Sergio shrugged. "The word'll be out soon regardless of their denials. When the time comes, my job will be to help the Arra'o get what they deserve, which won't be easy. At least there's some support in ICRAC for their cause." Sergio finished off his allulla.

"And everybody from the presidential candidates on down will have a say. It'll be interesting."

Paco looked around. "I wonder what happened to our waiter. I'll go inside and pay."

"I'm going to buy some more allullas," said Sergio as the two got up. He found the old woman sitting on a crate, waiting for the arrival of the next truck or bus, and bought eight more. The woman quickly wrapped them and took the money.

"All set?" asked Paco, opening the door on the driver's side. Sergio deposited the pastries on the back seat. "They are *good.*"

PACO MADE A U-TURN and stopped in front of the Hotel Sulaco. Both men got out. Sergio retrieved his suitcases. "The allullas?" said the doctor.

Sergio opened the rear door. "Here. Take these for the nuns," he said, handing Paco the larger of the two packets. "I'll keep this one for later."

"You won't be coming to the clinic?"

"I have to meet Jorge at the union hall. Tell Sor Marillac I'll stop by later. Will you be going back today?"

"No. I'm staying with the doctor. Tell Jorge I'm here and to come by."

"We'll be there."

They shook hands, and Sergio entered the hotel. He put his bags on the bench in the lobby opposite the counter and entered the dining patio. "Hello?" he called out.

The bald manager appeared from the kitchen at the opposite end. "Ah, Señor Fidanza. We have you in room six. The same as last time."

"That'll be fine." The two returned to the lobby. Sergio filled out the registration card and took his key. "Carlos, isn't it?"

"Yes," the other responded with a smile. "Will you be staying long?"

"It's indefinite. I may be getting an apartment."

Sergio mounted the stairs. There were four rooms on each side of the dark hallway. His was the next to last one on the left, facing the street. The last room on the right had been refitted as a bathroom. His room was painted dark gray, as was the rest of the building, inside and out. The head of the bed abutted the wall on the left, about a meter from the window. The washstand was at the foot of the bed, a table with a kerosene lamp and chair occupied the right corner just inside the door, and an armoire of sorts sat in the other corner. All the comforts of home, he thought. He opened the suitcases he'd put on the bed and arranged his clothes in the armoire, which had a set of shelves on the left and a pole with two distorted wire hangers on the right. Just enough, he thought, straightening them as best he could, and hanging up the two pair of pants he'd brought with him. He'd left his warmer clothes with Chinito. The armoire had a hasp. He would get a padlock.

Five minutes later he was at the Beneficio Workers' Union. Andrés Puíg, the secretary of the finance committee, was seated at the table in the middle of the room. "Compañero Fidanza!" He came around to greet the visitor. "We were expecting you later. You will be with us for a while?"

"Yes. Compañero Chang Crespo has hired me half time, and ICRAC has taken me on as a consultant half time." He placed the package of allullas on the table. "I suspect that each will be looking for me to work full time on its behalf."

"You must organize a union." The voice was that of Jorge, who had just come through the doorway. "Welcome! Compañero Fidanza." They shook hands. "We expected you later. On the bus."

"I stayed with the Saenzes last night. And I met your mother. She's quite remarkable."

"Thank you."

"Paco hadn't been to the clinic in a long time so he drove me. He said he'd see you later."

They all took seats at the table. The two beneficio workers, with their decidedly European aspect, looked oddly out of place in the rustic circumstances of the union hall. "Where are you staying?" asked Jorge.

"At the Sulaco, for the time being. The American drillers are staying there. It'll give me chance to get to know them on an informal basis."

"The ICRAC assignment?" Andrés asked.

"Yes." Sergio was seated facing the kitchen. A pair of brown eyes peered from the doorway. "Olgita," he called. "See what I have for you." The eyes disappeared. A moment later the child came into the room, holding the hand of her mother.

"Good afternoon, Señores. Come, Olga. See what the señor has for you."

Sergio opened the package of pastries. The child's eyes widened. She looked up at her mother. "Allullas," exclaimed Magda. The two men were also attracted. Sergio held the package for the child to take one. She carefully picked the one on the top. He offered them to the mother, who took one, then to each of the men, who were also glad to have the treat. After taking one for himself, Sergio gave the remaining one to the woman. She thanked him profusely. "Coffee, señores?" she asked. "The water is boiling." They all nodded. "Now, what do you say"? the mother asked the child.

"Thank you," she replied. The two returned to the kitchen. The men sampled the pastry.

"They're always a treat," remarked Andrés. Jorge remembered that they had been sold at that spot in Boca del Valle at least since he started riding with his grandfather. Magda returned with the coffee and a glass arranged with paper napkin squares. They each took one to wipe their fingers, sticky from the pastry and the heat of the day.

"So you'll be looking into the drilling?" remembered Jorge.

"It's a lot more complicated than that," Sergio began. "They're prospecting for oil, though they don't admit it. If they find it, you can imagine the push to cheat the Arra'o, let alone the havoc that will be wreaked on the valley. I suspect that the oil business will run the coffee into the ground." He finished off the allulla and took a sip. "I wonder where the Palacioses sit in all this? They could probably make more in oil."

"It's hard to see them getting out of the beneficio," observed Jorge.

"Three generations is a long time," Andrés said. "Don Luis will probably keep the cafetero going and fight the new beneficio just to spite us. He's just like his grandfather." He shook his head. "The only halfway decent one was Luis's cousin, Juan Carlos. Too bad he got run off the road by one of his own coffee trucks. The driver disappeared. Thought the family would kill him. They probably would've."

"We've got to be thinking about the possibility of oil," Sergio said. "There'll be jobs, which is not bad, but it'll be short term. Permanent work will probably go to workers from the oil fields in the Oriente."

"There's *already* been some talk about work," said Jorge. "Teeth was asking around about clearing jungle for the earthquake drilling."

"Teeth?" Sergio asked.

"That's what we call the boss of the guards. The big guy."

"A good name for him," Sergio agreed. "He was the one raising a ruckus with two others in the Salsipuedes, when I was here last."

"Yeah, they tend to get a little out of hand on payday. But the work. He was asking right about the time you were here. But it stopped as soon as it started."

"That fits in," Sergio suggested. "Chiriboga—you know him, the ICRAC guy, who's also my boss—*one* of them—he told me that he'd thought that they were going to strong arm the Arra'o, but that their tune changed. We actually have a little time before they decide if they'll "dogleg" around the ruins or not," he added, using the English term.

"Dogleg?" It was Jorge and Andrés's turn to be perplexed.

"In English it means to take a detour. Make a crooked line of a straight one. Like a dog's hind leg." There were smiles and nods of comprehension. "It also means that I'll have to devote some time to this, but I did want to lay out the groundwork for our beneficio project."

"Before we start," said Jorge, "have you had lunch, compañero?"

"As a matter of fact, no."

"Well, let's go over to the Rincón for some rice and beans."

"Sounds good to me."

THE WAITER, LOOKING RATHER DISHEVELED with a three-day growth of beard, picked up their empty plates. "Coffee, señores?" he asked.

There were no takers, so he produced the bill. Sergio insisted.

"Let's see if they're serious about expenses." He paid the waiter and stuck the bill into the pocket of his guayabera. "So we're set for the time being. When Wiggins and Braun get the plan for the new beneficio together, they'll come down for a big kickoff with the co-ops. Luzuriaga and I will coordinate this end for them, getting ready for the big meeting. The beneficio workers will be invited as observers. In the meantime we'll have to talk it up with them." They all got up from the table and started for the door. "Will you be stopping at the clinic now?" Sergio asked.

"As a matter of fact, we've got to be getting back," said Jorge, glancing up at the clock on the wall.

"We may be union officers, but we have jobs, too," said Andrés. "And the patrón is making it harder to get time off for union business. Is that clock right?" he asked the waiter, who just shrugged in response.

"It's fifteen minutes fast," offered the owner from behind the bar. "It helps when you're trying to close up."

The three moved to the street. When they reached the plaza, Sergio said, "I'll see you later at the clinic." They parted company, and Sergio headed to what was soon to become his office.

"Señor Fidanza!" exclaimed Gloria Manzano from behind the desk in the foyer. "I was so happy to hear the news. Imagine, you were here only two weeks ago, and now you are back as the chief. And look, telephones!" she exclaimed again, as if the modern convenience were the result of his arrival. Sergio was taken aback by the welcome. "Pedro," she said at the appearance of the porter in the doorway to the kitchen, "Señor Fidanza has arrived."

Pedro came over and shook hands. "Welcome, Señor Fidanza. We have a case of Orangina, should you want one."

"Thank you both very much. Is Galo around?"

"The licenciado is in his office. You can go right up." She called after him as he mounted the stairs, "Everything is in order in your office, Señor Fidanza, including your telephone."

He knocked at Galo's open door. "Let me add my welcome," said the co-op manager. "I must say we're all a bit relieved by your arrival." He motioned his visitor to the chair opposite him. "It won't be easy, but be assured we're here to help in any way we can."

"That's good to hear. I think I'm going to enjoy this."

"Maruja expects that you won't be a stranger to our house. In fact she's invited you to dinner this evening."

Sergio thought for a moment. "I should stop by the clinic first. Paco Saenz drove me here from Nicoya. I stayed with them last night."

"That's no problem," the other confirmed. "Now, why don't we get you settled in your office?" He led the way across the hall. "Have a seat," Galo said, pointing to the chair behind the desk.

"As the secretary of the grievance committee I usually sat on the other side of the desk."

"You'll get used to it."

"I'm sure I will," Sergio replied, unconvinced. He rocked back and forth, testing the chair. It squeaked like the one in the Tiger's office.

They discussed in some detail the proposed new beneficio, Wiggins and Braun, and the planned kickoff. Galo had suggested they spend the rest of the afternoon visiting the offices of the Canton Prefecture and the Carabineers of the Campo. "They're the ones in charge. The prefect is mostly concerned with the roads and streets. He's also in charge of the electric plant." Pedro appeared at the door and made a gesture with his hand, suggesting a cup of coffee. They both declined with a shake of the head, murmuring their thanks. "The Carabineers," Galo went on, "have a barracks, and a jail with two cells on the other side of the landing strip, but the captain also has a small office across the courtyard. They patrol the canton on horseback, usually in pairs. Mostly concerned with thievery and disturbing the peace. Drunkenness or domestic violence, or both as is usually the case, and which they deal with very poorly, if at all." They were both startled by the unexpected sound of the telephone. It rang again before Galo gestured for Sergio to answer it. He picked up the receiver and very tentatively said, "Hello? . . . Yes, Juan. . . . Uneventful. . . ." He covered the mouthpiece. "It's Chiriboga. He's asking about Rigpe."

"Tell him it's set up for tomorrow morning."

"Luzuriaga has it set up for tomorrow morning. . . . Yes, I'll tell him. . . . Thank you. Goodbye." Sergio hung up the phone and raised his eyebrows in the realization that the remoteness of Catachoclo had been considerably reduced. "Tomorrow morning?"

"I was going to suggest it anyway. I'll send a message to Rigpe that you will be attendant upon his concerns, or something to that effect." The other laughed at Galo's diplomacy. "Why don't you check out the connection to your boss in Sulaco? In the meantime, I've got some things to do." He rose and added, "When you're ready, we'll make those visits."

After two failed attempts and a quick tutorial by Gloria, Sergio finally reached Chinito. They spoke for about five minutes. After hanging up, he withdrew a piece of paper from his wallet and smoothed it before him on the desk.

DAISY REACHED OVER AND PICKED UP the phone from the credenza between the two desks. "Hello? . . . Yes it is. . . . Of course. Just a moment." She rose and, handing the phone to Margarita, stepped out of the office, closing the door behind her.

"Hello? . . . Sergio!" She turned her chair and looked out at cloud-capped Higuerota, cradling the phone in both hands as if it were the face of the one on the other end of the line.

PACO WAS SITTING WITH SOR MARILLAC at the conference room table, filling out the examination form for the last patient of the day. Sor Beatrice poked her head in the door and announced that the two gentlemen they were expecting had arrived. "Just in time," said Paco, signing the form with a flourish.

The two rose to greet Jorge and Sergio as they came through the doorway. The doctor and his former charge embraced with great affection and launched into an exchange of family news. The labor leader and the nun shook hands. She could hardly contain herself but managed to refrain from asking about his trip to the capital. "Doctor Saenz tells us that you are going to be with us for a while. What wonderful news! But then," she added, casting restraint to the winds, "perhaps you would have rather been assigned to the capital." Her eyes widened, and her hand flew to her mouth, too late to have stopped the words.

Sergio smiled at her lack of guile. To save her—and himself—further embarrassment, he commented on his meetings with Margarita, including the dinner with her mother. He was actually pleased that he had a confidante of sorts, *and* an ally. It balanced the pessimism he felt whenever he thought of Margarita's father; her assurances notwithstanding, marrying the daughter of an ex-president remained an impossible dream.

While Sor Marillac was enthusing vicariously over the budding romance of her friends, Paco finished the latest news of the Saenz household. "I'll be dining with Jorge," he said, turning to the other two.

"Will you join us, Sergio?" asked Jorge.

"Thank you, but I've been invited to the Luzuriagas."

"We must then take our leave," said the doctor, shaking hands with the nun.

"Will you be leaving directly in the morning?" she asked.

"Yes. I don't want to leave my Leticia for too long."

"Of course, Doctor. Please give her my regards. I hope she will be able to make the trip to Catachoclo on the next occasion."

"I'm sure she would like that." The doctor picked up his medical bag and left the clinic with Jorge.

"And, Fidanza, we will be seeing more of you?" Sor Marillac walked to the entrance with the ICRAC representative.

"It will be my pleasure."

CHAPTER 21

S ERGIO GROPED FOR THE ALARM CLOCK on the floor beside the bed, found it, and shut it off. He lay back on the pillow, staring straight ahead, trying to orient himself. The pitch-dark of the night had been relieved by faint daybreak coming in through the shutters. He sat up and threw off the sheet and thin blanket. His feet hit the floor. He opened the shutters, illuminating the room, as a rooster crowed in the distance. He wondered if there was anyone in Costaguana not within earshot of a rooster. Another crowed. It seemed to have come from below. He looked down. The buildings across the street were plainly visible. It was six-thirty. He went to the washstand, lifted the pitcher out of the basin, and poured the contents into it. He splashed the cool water on his face and neck, ran his wet hands through his hair several times, and dried himself off. He pulled on his clothes and made his way downstairs.

"How did you wake up?" asked Carlos, the manager, emerging from the other end of the dining patio.

"Well, thank you."

"Wherever you wish," Carlos offered, waving his hand over a half dozen tables at the edge of the garden, where a variety of flowering plants and vines grew in haphazard vigor. Sergio recognized the back of the only other patron.

"Good morning," he said in English. George Fuller, the geologist for the drilling company, turned to see who was speaking.

"Oh! Señor. . . ?"

"Fidanza. Sergio Fidanza."

"Oh, yes. Are you staying here, Señor Fidanza?"

"Yes, I am, and please—call me Sergio. It's George, isn't it?"

"Yes. Won't you join us? Walter'll be right down."

"Thank you," Sergio replied, drawing back the plastic chair next to him. Two birds jabbered their objection to the noise and fled from the tree nearest the table. Walter arrived, and reintroductions were being made as Carlos approached to take the breakfast orders. The menu, printed on heavy white paper, soiled and dog-eared from use, was not complicated: coffee, naranjilla juice, rolls, and eggs, any style. The two Americans conferred, and Walter ordered for both. Sergio and Walter would have coffee, juice, and rolls. As Carlos asked George how he wanted his eggs, he held out his hand with his thumb up, turned it over with the thumb down, and then waved his index finger in a circular pattern. George, having learned the drill, made the circular pattern with his index finger. Carlos retreated to the kitchen.

"I didn't expect to see you again, at least not so soon," Walter remarked. "When Luzuriaga brought you out to the drill camp, I thought you were just sort of sightseeing. You did say that you were connected with that union federation. . . ?"

"FLOC," offered Sergio. "I'll be working with the beneficio workers. But I've also been hired by ICRAC to represent the interests of the Arra'o."

Walter's eyes widened.

"Arra'o?" asked the perplexed geologist.

"The Redheads," said Walter. "That's the real name of the tribe." Turning to Sergio, he added, "Does that put us on opposite sides of the table?"

"Well, we're on opposite sides of the table all right, but whether we'll be at odds depends on how the drilling proceeds."

Carlos returned with the juice and rolls, a jar of quince jelly, and a ramekin of butter. He set the dishes down and, waving his index finger in a circle, said the eggs would be right out.

"Look," Sergio began, "to avoid any awkwardness, let me tell you what I know." He took a sip of the juice before continuing. "First, Bumpy Cosgrove and I, quite coincidentally, were sitting next to each other on the plane when we both arrived in Sulaco a month ago. Neither of us had any idea at that time that I would be working here in Catachoclo. I'm not sure if he even knows I was here in town when you guys had that meeting with ICRAC. In any case, feel free to tell him. Not that you wouldn't," he added, taking another sip of the juice. "Secondly, I know all about the problem with the location of the ruins, and that you'll be making a decision about whether to dogleg around them or not in a week or so."

The roar of the weekly arrival of the TAMC flight interrupted the conversation. Carlos returned with a pitcher of hot milk, a cruet of coffee liqueur, and George's butter-laden scrambled eggs. They each helped themselves to the coffee, and George started in on the eggs.

"Well," observed Walter, "that's all very interesting."

SERGIO SPOTTED GALO STANDING next to a green Jeep station wagon parked in front of the office shared by ICRAC and the co-ops. After shaking hands, he remarked the vehicle. "I thought you drove a pickup."

"I do. As a matter of fact, this belongs to ICRAC, so I guess it's yours."

Sergio ran his hand through his hair. He looked away for a moment, then said, "The problem is, I don't know how to drive." The look on Galo's face spoke volumes. "I did try it in the port," Sergio hastened to add. "I had a compañero who was teaching me, but it was rather haphazard. We couldn't seem to set a schedule."

"Well, we'll have to remedy that. *I'll* give you some lessons. We can start when we visit Rigpe."

"Good morning, señores." Juanita was at her desk. The radio behind her was still squawking in spite of the newly installed telephones. "I've sent Pedro to pick up the mail from the weekly flight. He should be back any minute."

"There's some advantages to having the airport across the street," remarked Galo as the two ascended the stairs and entered the ICRAC office. Sergio sat on his squeaky chair. "But the only thing in the mail you can be sure of is a week's worth of *El Porvenir* and *El Semenario*. We get the weekly, *El Tiempo*, from Nicoya by bus just a day late. Nothing older than yesterday's news, but in this backwater it's the best we've got." The co-op manager took the chair opposite. "Except for the radio. And speaking of the radio, El Dedo made it official. He's entering the race for interim president. *And* he'll be making a grand tour of the country to promote his candidacy."

"Is Catachoclo on his itinerary?" Sergio asked dryly.

"It's probably not at the top, but if he gets wind of what's going on, he'll be here. Especially if he gets an offer to come by private plane." Galo got up and retrieved the ashtray from the conference table.

"You know we arrived in Sulaco on the same plane?"

"I didn't! Imagine—you, Cosgrove, and Vasquez Iturralde. I wonder what that portends." He pulled out a pack of Casablancas from his pocket and lit up.

Sergio shrugged. "We should probably think about whether it's in our interest to promote his coming here."

"Yes." Galo took a drag on the cigarette. "After we've met with Rigpe, we'll know better about his intentions. They aren't kidding, you know," Galo reflected. "If the drillers make a move in the direction of the ruins, *something* is going to happen."

Pedro arrived with the stack of newspapers. "Here you are," he said, laying it on the end of the desk. "And two letters," he added, placing them with a flourish in front of Sergio. "I put yours on your desk, Señor Galo. Coffee, señores?" The two nodded. Galo recognized the hand on one of the envelopes.

"Margarita," murmured Sergio. He put the letters to one side.

"I guess we should get a plan together," offered Galo. "The best way, I find, is to work from a schedule. Then the rest seems to fall into place. Wait," he said, rising from his chair. "I have one of those large planning calendars I'm not using." Pedro was returning with the coffees as Galo went to his office.

"Over there, Pedro," said Sergio, indicating the conference table at the far end of the office.

Galo returned with the calendar and a pad of foolscap. "The tools of a manager," he remarked. "Now, let's see. We have the new beneficio and the earthquake investigation," he said drawing a vertical line down the pad. Sergio felt considerably relieved. Management was not his forte.

SERGIO RELEASED HIS FOOT from the clutch, and the Jeep lurched forward. He hit the brake, and the vehicle stalled. "That's all right.

Everyone has the same problem," Galo said, trying to keep Sergio's spirits up. This was the third attempt. They were out on the road to the old ferry, and Sergio was having second thoughts about learning to drive, but he dutifully put the shift into neutral and turned the key. The engine kicked over. He depressed the clutch and shifted into first. "Now release it easy and give it a little gas." The engine revved and they started to move ahead. The learner seemed a little relieved. "Now shift into second." Sergio completed the maneuver and also shifted into third without incident. He managed a smile as they moved briskly down the road.

His joy was short-lived. A coffee truck, bearing down on them, appeared to the new driver to be in the middle of the road. He edged to the side. The right wheels hit the rough shoulder. The car continued to bounce along as the truck hurtled by. Sergio brought the Jeep to a halt but forgot to depress the clutch, and stalled again. Galo turned to his student. "This probably wasn't the best place to start lessons. But just to make sure you don't lose your nerve, I think you should drive it a little farther. There won't be another truck along for at least fifteen minutes." This was scant consolation to Sergio, but he tried it again. In another few minutes they were moving along at a good pace. "See? You're doing fine." Sergio stared ahead at another truck. This time he retreated to the shoulder and stopped without stalling.

"I think you'd better take it from here," he said, slightly rattled.

"You're right. This road is not for beginners." They switched places, and ten minutes later they were at the ferry.

Galo parked the Jeep in a graveled area next to the market—a collection of thatch-roofed stands similar to the ones along Avenida del Valle in Catachoclo. The merchants were mostly Indians from the sierra. The customers were a mixture of sierra Indians and Redheads.

"Galito!" The voice had come from a stand piled high with watermelons. It was Germán Estevez. "Galito, I wanted to thank you for your help. But they only gave me three-quarters of what I asked for."

"Germán," Galo replied with all the patience he could muster, "the committee reviewed your application, and they figured that that was all you needed."

"With a little more I could have improved this shack," the other complained, waving his hand towards the watermelon-laden stand.

"You did quite well with what you got," Galo observed. "Just be sure you make the payments." He headed back to where he'd left Sergio. "He'd try the patience of a saint, really."

Sergio smiled. "Is he good for it?"

"Yes, if we keep after him. At least he doesn't drink—now, let's see." Galo scanned the area around the huge acacia tree. "He said that he'd meet us at his brother's stand. I think it's that one, over where they beach the ferry." They started in the direction he'd indicated. "There he is," said Galo, waving at the Arra'o chief, who had just emerged from behind the substantial structure, further differentiated from the others by a huge scarlet macaw sitting on a perch at the right-hand end of the counter. As if on cue, when the two approached, it stretched its wings and let out a shriek that startled them. When the brother smoothed its feathers, one from the tail came out in his hand. He offered it to Sergio, who took it from him, looked it over, and tucked it into the pocket of his guayabera. An eclectic mix of merchandise filled the stand: candles, soap, the red dye they used on their hair, strange stuff in jars and open sacks, coriander, and other spices.

Hugo stepped forward, and Galo made the introduction. "This is Sergio Fidanza, Hugo. He is ICRAC's new representative. He speaks for Señor Chiriboga. Sergio, Hugo Rigpe."

"Please to meet you." Hugo thrust out his hand, and then, turning to the man behind the counter, added, "My brother, Tito." They all shook hands. Tito was a bit taller than his brother but dressed the same: striped wrap-around skirt and bone necklace with matching strands tied below each knee. His hair was also dyed red and plastered down, forming a conical cap. As the introductions were being made, a younger replica, down to the plastered red hair, entered the stand from the rear. "This Tito, Pablo son. He Christian like mother." The boy, about twelve years old, shook hands with the two newcomers before taking a seat on a stool in the corner.

"That's a beautiful bird," remarked Sergio.

"He belong to our father," Tito said, gesturing to Hugo. "He try to sell for many year at market in town. But I think he ask too much. *After ,* he make price even higher. He not *want* to sell."

"How old is it?" asked Galo.

Tito thought for a moment, consulted his brother in Arra'o, and then finally said, "Maybe twenty-seven year."

"Amazing," observed Galo.

Hugo motioned for the visitors to follow him. He went behind the stand, where four wooden chairs had been set up around a small table. "*My* office," he said. A broad smile revealed his missing teeth. They all took seats. Tito arrived followed by Pablo, carrying a tray with four mugs of coffee. He set the tray on the table and left. Tito took the remaining chair. "Please," the host said, pointing to the mugs. They each took a cup. The brothers continued to sip the coffee until it was finished. The other two took sips and put the mugs down on the table. "Not like coffee?" Hugo asked.

"No. No," said Galo. "It's just that it's so very hot." This seemed to satisfy the host, who, like his brother, hadn't had any problem with the temperature. He leaned back in the chair in expectation of some word from his visitors. Galo looked at Sergio, who began his prepared speech.

"Hugo, Señor Chiriboga has spoken with the chief of the earthquake study. He has *told* him that they are *not* to go any closer to ChiriYacu." He went on to describe how the drillers were considering alternative plans that could keep the work away from the ruins by 'going around' them. The concept of 'going around' the ruins was taking considerable effort to explain. At one point Sergio got the map from the Jeep.

"He doesn't get it," said Galo. The concept of something on paper representing the location of ChiriYacu did not work any better than the arm waving they'd been engaged in. In the end Sergio and Galo decided to take Hugo out to the drilling camp and try to explain it on the ground at the end of the drilling road. *If* they were permitted to enter.

GALO SPOKE TO THE COOK, who, with his helper, was loading a pickup with the lunch he had just prepared for the drilling crew.

Stacks of steaming metal plates with lids, held together by a wire frame, had been wrapped in towels. Utensils, cups, and other paraphernalia went in a plastic crate, and rolls, condiments, mangoes, and bananas in another. A large portable urn of coffee completed the mess assembly. Galo returned to the Jeep and announced that Walter and George were out at the drill rig. "I was hoping to get their permission to go onto the site," he said to Hugo, seated in the back with his nephew Pablo.

Hugo wrinkled his nose. "Earthquake men on Arra'o land. Arra'o no need permission."

Galo glanced at Sergio, who thought for a moment and said, "It sounds right to me. Let's go." Galo nodded in agreement and came around to the driver's seat. As he climbed in, the cook emerged from the kitchen with what looked like two more wrapped sets of plates. He put them in the back and climbed into the driver's seat.

"I'll let him lead the way," said Galo, who followed the pickup down the embankment and over the bridge. "You've been here before, Hugo?"

"Yes. Many time," the chief confirmed.

The road climbed out of the river channel and continued up a gentle grade. As they left the river, the jungle on either side closed in so that it formed a canopy over the road. Every two to four hundred meters a partially overgrown clearing, probably a drill site, appeared, and provided a place where two vehicles could pass. They forded a stream; after fifteen minutes, the cook blew his horn and pulled into what appeared to be the end of the road. There were two picnic tables with benches on the right set up under an open-sided tent to accommodate a dozen diners. It wasn't until they reached the clearing that the drill rig loomed ahead in the forest, a hundred meters down a road at right angles to the one they had driven in on. George and Walter had been examining a rock core but set it aside at the sound of the horn and started toward the newly arrived vehicles.

"Just in time for lunch," Walter called out as they approached. Sergio looked at the provisions being unloaded. "We'll have plenty," Walter assured them. "José radioed us that you were in the camp and were coming out."

Hugo and Pablo had climbed out of the back seat and were conversing in Arra'o. The boy then took off toward the drill rig. "He tell Arra'o workers we here," Hugo explained. "I go see them." Without another word he strode off, following his nephew.

"What brings you out to the site?" asked the drilling boss.

"We were having difficulty explaining the concept of 'going around the ruins' to Hugo, so we thought we'd try it on the ground," Sergio explained. "You know who he is, don't you?" He pointed to the figure marching toward the rig. As he spoke, the drilling crew, walking towards the clearing, was about to encounter the Arra'o chief. They parted to permit him to pass, which he did, looking neither to the left nor right.

"Yes. We've met on several occasions. Actually, he's the one who provided the men who are working for us. And as to 'going around' the ruins, *that* decision hasn't been made." The drillers had arrived at the clearing and were taking places around the tables, where the cook had arranged the meals. There were four seats available at the end of the nearest table. Walter invited Sergio and Galo to join them. Walter introduced them to the men in the immediate vicinity. Sergio was seated next to Enrique, the crew foreman and lead driller. Sergio made it known that he had worked with Pablo Menendez, the head of the petroleum workers union. Walter expressed his surprise at the revelation and made a mental note to tell his boss, to whom it would be no revelation.

Getting back to the going around, Sergio asked what it would entail in the event that they decide to do it.

"This is a transect," Walter explained, waving his hand in the direction of the rig. If we go around, we would continue in that direction for another three and a half kilometers and then resume a westerly course—a turn to the left."

"What do you base that on?" asked Sergio.

"The main line, the road you drove in on, heads almost due west. The ruins are five and a half kilometers in that direction." Walter pointed west-southwest.

"How do you know all this?"

"We took our own aerial photo right after they refused to continue cutting."

"I WONDER WHERE HUGO GOT OFF TO?" Sergio remarked as he and Galo were preparing to accompany the drillers to the rig. They had started down the transect with the two Americans when Hugo and Pablo appeared at the edge of the clearing.

"We'll be at the rig if you need us," said Walter. They all shook hands and parted. Sergio and Galo started toward the two Arra'o. They met in the middle of the clearing.

"Hugo, if the drillers decide to go around the ruins," Sergio began, stressing the *if*, "they will go three and a half kilometers farther." He emphasized the direction and the distance by waving his hands. The chief wrinkled his nose and grunted.

"Sergio, let me try," said Galo, picking up a stick about a half-meter long. "Hugo, look." Facing him and with his back to the main road, Galo twisted around and pointed down the road, turned back to Hugo, and drew a line in the dirt. "This is the road. We are here," he added making a circle at the end of the line. "The drill rig is here." He made another mark in the direction of the rig about ten centimeters from the first.

"Please," said Hugo, taking the stick from Galo. "Chiri Yacu is here," he said, making a mark in the dirt about a half-meter from the one indicating where they stood and in the direction Walter had pointed at lunch. The other two looked at each other in astonishment.

"How far?" asked Sergio.

The chief thought for a moment and said, "More than five kilometers. Less than six."

"Amazing!" said Sergio.

"Please," said Galo, taking back the stick. "*If* the drillers go around the ruins, they will go like this." Using the stick and the distance to the mark Hugo made to indicate Chiri Yacu as his scale, Galo drew in the ground the route the drillers would take to avoid the ruins.

The chief eyes narrowed. He was noncommittal.

CHAPTER 22

S EÑOR FIDANZA!" GLORIA MANZANO was standing at the street door of the ICRAC office as Sergio and Galo got out of the Jeep. "Señor Quishpe has just sent for you. He would like you to come to the headquarters right away. You too, Licenciado." The secretary, obviously agitated, entered the street and stood there wringing her hands. "It's awful. The carabineers ordered the families living in the South Forest off the land. They were given twenty-four hours. *It's awful.*"

"We'd better get over there," said Sergio. Galo resumed his place behind the wheel just as the streetlights came on. They left Gloria explaining the event to Pedro, who had just appeared at the doorway.

"Where is the South Forest?" asked Sergio as they proceeded up Calle Sulaco.

"It's the area that extends from the limits of the old plantation, ten kilometers south of here, to about where the army barracks is."

"Army? I've got a lot to learn."

"There're not many soldiers, twenty at the most, including the officers. They monitor movement through the area to Cayta. It used to be a smugglers' route, but there's little of that now." Galo slowed down to negotiate around the tree, blowing his horn at a feral pig that had wandered into the street. "It's located just before the road—if you can call it that—climbs over the steep hills that separate us from the south."

"Whose land is it they're being thrown off?"

"It belongs to Palacios. It was pretty much uninhabited at the time of the land reform and was never included in it." Galo made a right turn just past the Hotel Sulaco. "It remained that way until just a few years ago, when some of the younger sons, who didn't inherit and hadn't migrated to the city, took to squatting there.

There're about five or six families, maybe more. But they've never had trouble from the Palacios. . .until now." He turned into Calle San Martin. Rubén Castro, the carrier of the message, was just entering the union hall ahead. As the Jeep came to a stop, he welcomed the arrivals.

Jorge rose as the three entered. "I'm glad you could make it so soon." They shook hands, and Jorge introduced them to Jacobo Vidal, a slight man with a wispy moustache. "Compañero Vidal, tell our friends here what happened." They all took seats around the table. The lone bulb hanging from the ceiling heightened the somber atmosphere.

Vidal, his straw hat clutched in his hands and wearing the long-sleeved white shirt and duck trousers of the field laborers, began the story of the events of earlier that day. The look in his eyes told more than the words from his mouth. At about noon, four of Palacios's security men arrived on horseback with two carabineers. They had rounded up all of the families into the yard of Vidal. The only one missing was Raúl Estevez, who lived alone. "The big one with the teeth did all the talking," the peasant said, his hands grasping the straw hat even more tightly.

"Rafael," noted Quishpe. "Go ahead, compañero."

He continued describing the nightmare. At the end they were told that they had to be out of their houses and off the land by sundown the next day or face the consequences.

"And what were they?" asked Sergio, placing his hand on the shoulder of the man, who had started to tremble.

"They burned Estevez's place to the ground." Jorge made the statement, his face reflecting thirty-seven years of Palacios brutality.

"We rescued his goat, but the big guy shot her."

"My god!" exclaimed Sergio. "They were armed? What did the carabineers do?"

"Nothing," answered Vidal. "They just sat on their horses."

"The first thing we have to do is to see to the safety of the eight families," said Jorge. "Vidal says that they've all fled and they're with relatives or friends. It's too dark to do anything more tonight, but at daybreak we'll go back with wagons to get the household effects and the animals."

"Could we not all go out and stand by our compañeros?" The proposal had come from Castro, who seemed eager for a confrontation. The alternatives, temporary retreat or standing their ground, were discussed, complicated by the fact that there were three cows that needed to be milked, and Estevez had not returned.

Sergio, still shocked by the viciousness of the act, said, "We've got to get on the offensive, Jorge. Let's pay a call on Señor Palacios. It's about time I presented my credentials. And then the chief of the carabineers."

"When do you suggest?" asked Jorge.

"Right now."

Galo, obviously not familiar with the rough and tumble ways of the unions, had been rather quiet up until then. He declared, "I'm with you. We've got to let them know we're united in this."

They decided to be ready for either plan depending on the outcome of meeting with Don Luis. Galo would get his assistant, Arturo Morales, to drive four of the men out in his pickup to milk the cows that night.

"YOU BURNED DOWN THE *SHACK?* " Don Luis had no sooner returned from Nicoya than he'd heard the news. He'd summoned his chief of security to his office, and the fellow was standing in front of him.

"You said to put the fear of God in them," answered Rafael, stone-faced.

"Yes. I did say that. That's why I issued the rifles to you. And one of them was fired." He had noted it when he returned the arms to the cabinet in his living room.

"I shot Estevez's goat." Again, the answer was dispassionate.

Don Luis mulled over the situation. "They were squatting on my land," he finally said. "If one doesn't protect what's his, the world will take advantage. I'd have a whole village of peasants living there." He decided not to issue a reprimand or ask for prior notice of the steps his security chief might take in the future. Some things were best left vague.

His thoughts were interrupted by a disturbance in the patio. A Jeep had stopped in front of his house, and the guard was running up from the gate, shouting.

"You stay right here," Palacios ordered Rafael. "*I'll* see what the problem is." He hurried toward the patio. Three men were descending from the Jeep. He recognized Quishpe and Luzuriaga in the dim light from the lanterns on either side of the entrance to the residence. The third he didn't know.

As the beneficio owner approached, Sergio handed him a business card:

SERGIO FIDANZA

ICRAC

Catachoclo Regional Manager

Palacios read it and grunted. "You should ask permission before entering another's property."

"Did your men ask permission to burn down that shack?"

"It was on my *property*," the owner retorted, reddening perceptibly and glowering at Jorge.

"The *shack* wasn't your property."

Palacios, a head taller than Sergio, raised his hand as if to strike. Quishpe stepped forward, and the beneficio owner lowered the hand.

"Well," said Sergio, "if we're not to be invited in, we'll state our case here." Without a pause, he continued. "Our people are not moving until the law decides who owns the land. Until then, they are to be left in peace. I've reported this incident to my office in the capital, and they will start an investigation tomorrow regarding the status of the South Forest." Without waiting for an answer, Sergio went around the vehicle and got into the front passenger seat. The other two followed. With Palacios standing rooted to the patio, Galo spun the Jeep around and sped down the driveway.

"There's Rafael," said Jorge, looking back over his shoulder. "He must have been in the office all the while." Turning back, he added, "Palacios's probably having a fit with that thug." He clapped Sergio on the back. "I don't remember *when* I've felt so good. Don Luis was speechless. Ha!"

"It ought to hold them for a while. But we can't let up," Sergio cautioned as they passed through the gate of the cafetero and turned toward the town.

Galo, ever the manager, asked, "Do you want to stop at the office to call Chiriboga?"

"A good thought, but first to what's-his-name, the carabineer's chief."

"Barrios," offered Jorge. "Capitán Vicente Barrios. He's a neighbor of mine."

THE BARRIOS RESIDENCE WAS A TIDY cinderblock house on a concrete slab. A small verandah, illuminated by the light from a kerosene lamp in the window of the living room, occupied the front left corner. The capitán was taking the mild night air in a hammock slung between the corner column and the front wall. As the three approached he swung his feet down and sat in the middle of the hammock, rocking slightly as he peered at the newcomers.

"Oh, neighbor. I didn't recognize you at first. And Licenciado Luzuriaga. What brings you around on this soft night?"

"I'm afraid it's serious business," said Galo. "But first, you remember Señor Sergio Fidanza, ICRAC's new representative?" Sergio handed the capitán a card, which he put into the breast pocket of his guayabera without reading. The man, rather chunky with an almost completely bald head, was barefoot. He got out of the hammock and offered his guests seats in three plastic chairs lining the wall, but they did not avail themselves.

"We're here about the terrible act of arson in the South Forest this afternoon," reported Sergio matter-of-factly. "The more egregious because it occurred as two of your officers were looking on."

The capitán was obviously not surprised by the news but was temporarily taken aback by the delivery. "Those people," Barrios retorted, "were squatters on land belonging to Don Luis Palacios."

"The *house* did not belong to Palacios. And the goat that was shot did not belong to Palacios. And as for the land, *on which these people have been living for over four years*, my office is looking into the status of ownership." Sergio let his remarks sink in. The capitán looked very uneasy. He was not used to having the activities of his force questioned, especially in such an overbearing manner.

"We'll await to see what ICRAC comes up with," he finally managed to say. The mention of the agrarian reform institute had obviously tempered his response.

"Good. In the meantime we would appreciate your officers keeping an eye on the area to see that no other criminal acts are carried out."

"*I'll* decide what my men will do. . .or not do. If that's all you have to say, I'll be retiring." The capitán, who seemed to have recovered somewhat from the verbal assault, shuffled into the house without another word.

SERGIO, SEATED AT HIS DESK, hung up the phone. "He's already heard. Apparently Palacios got to someone by phone, and it wasn't long before Juan was informed. . . . It's incredible. News that would have taken a day or two to circulate gets around in hours." Sergio thought for a moment and added, "They're going to follow through on my request to investigate the ownership. But he believes that Palacios does have the title. He says that it goes back to a grant to the family before the turn of the century."

"That'd be about right," Galo observed. "The grandfather of Don Luis started the cafetero in the mid-nineties."

"My grandfather was one of his first muleteers," Jorge murmured without elaboration. The other two glanced at each other. "One thing worries me," Jorge added. "Estevez still hadn't been seen when we were together in the hall earlier. He's a bit of a hothead."

"And having his house burned down is liable to really set him off," Galo put in. "I hope we can get to him before he does something reckless. He's the younger brother of that guy with the watermelon stand out at the ferry, Sergio. The one I spoke to about the loan?" Sergio nodded. "Raúl's got a lot more going for him then Germán, but the first born gets the farm."

"He worked in the beneficio for a while but kept getting into trouble," said Jorge. "When Rafael and the others came on the scene, it was all Raúl could take. He quit. He'd been working that farm for three years while he was still at the beneficio. That Rafael had it in for him." Jorge brooded over it for a bit. "Bad business," he finally decided.

They discussed the plan for the following day and agreed that Castro's idea now seemed the best: take a stand with their compañeros. As they were working out the details, their attention was drawn to the door by the sound of footsteps on the stairs. "So, burning the midnight oil?" It was the prefect, Licenciado Jean Kattah. His wavy black hair and olive complexion set the first generation Lebanese apart from the other citizens of the area.

"We were discussing South Forest," said Galo.

"Oh, that," the political chief replied. "That's best left in the hands of the carabineers."

"They didn't do a very good job of it this morning," said Sergio. "Two officers witnessed the whole sorry affair."

"Those people are on land belonging to Palacios."

"*That* point of law doesn't excuse the arson and the killing of the goat," Sergio responded. The lights went out as he was speaking. Galo struck a match and lit the candle that Sergio had retrieved from the credenza behind him.

"Well, I'll have a report from capitán Barrios tomorrow," the prefect said. "We can discuss it further then."

"I'll be happy to," rejoined Sergio. There was an awkward silence before he added, "I guess it's time we all got some rest."

They all shook hands in the street, and Galo offered to take Sergio and Jorge to their respective residences. They both declined. Sergio said he'd get something at El Rincón. They agreed to meet at six at the hotel. Kattah excused himself, saying he had to get something from his office.

IT WAS CLOSE TO ELEVEN WHEN SERGIO returned to his room. He went immediately to the table in the corner, lit the kerosene lamp, sat down, and took Margarita's letter from the pocket of his guayabera. He tore the corner off the envelope, carefully inserted his index finger, and ripped open the end. He flattened the letter on the tabletop. Pulling the lamp over, he began to read: *"My dearest Sergio. . . ."*

CHAPTER 23

I T'S THE FIELD CALLING." DALE COSGROVE, hung up the phone in the Santa Marta office of the Walker Tool Company. "Terrible patch. Gotta take it on the radio," he explained, leaving George Mitchell, Senior Geologist, alone in the office. The room was small but comfortable. A map of Costaguana hung behind the hand-carved wooden desk. The geologist sat in one of the two visitor chairs. The two windows in the wall on either side of the map did *not* afford a view of Higuerota. A conference table, with a map depicting the true *and* erroneous locations of the ruins lying on top, and four chairs, occupied the other half of the room. A bookcase, on the inside wall of the office, was stuffed with equipment catalogs, exploration reports, maps, and an eclectic collection of books on drilling and geology, with two recent additions, *The History of Fifty Years of Misrule,* by Don José Avellanos, and next to it, the memoir of his daughter, Doña Antonia Avellanos Corbelán.

The geologist picked up the copy of *El Semenario* lying on the desk and absent-mindedly scanned the front page. His limited Spanish permitted only a minimal comprehension of the contents. He readily understood that it was Thursday, July 29. The headline said something about a raucous debate in the constituent assembly the night before. Had he a better knowledge of Spanish, he would have noted in the lower right corner an article reporting the proposed campaign tour of the country by Juan Vasquez Iturralde, which might, if time permitted, include the Province of Entre Monte's coffee region. He turned the paper over and perused the comics on the back page. He recognized "Blondie," but the dialog escaped him.

Putting the paper back on the desk, he rose to look out the window. The office was in a former residence set back from a narrow street not far from the Legislative Palace. He spun around when Bumpy burst into the room.

"The rig's broke down!" he exclaimed, taking his seat behind the desk. "It's major." George returned to his chair. "They jerked the winch right off the front of the rig, trying to pull out of that creek, and *then* they dropped the drive shaft, trying to back out. And the *worst*—they could fix the drive shaft—the rotary table's about had it!" He reached forward and picked up the phone. "Get me Hector," he ordered, and slammed it back in its cradle. "Damn!" A moment later he picked up the ringing phone. "Hector? The rig's broke down. . . . You knew? . . . That other one hasn't *left* yet?" There was a long pause as Bumpy absorbed the lengthy lament of Hector on the vagaries of rig repair, his face reflecting the despair of anything happening on schedule. "Make *damn* sure it does!" he finally concluded, slamming down the receiver again. "Damn! Wagner radioed him earlier this morning about the replacement. Hector wanted to be sure it was in number-one shape. Says it'll be ready to go on Monday. Damn! It'll be at least a week from when it leaves before it gets there."

A knock on the door broke Bumpy's tirade. "Coffee, Mr. Cosgrove? Mr. Mitchell?" asked the blonde secretary, carrying a tray with two steaming mugs and a sugar bowl.

Bumpy was about to refuse but changed his mind. "Maybe that's what I need. George?" The geologist nodded. "Fine, Madelyn." The very attractive older woman placed the tray on the desk and retreated. As the door closed Bumpy opened the right bottom drawer of his desk and extracted a bottle of Johnny Walker Black. "Sometimes, George, it takes a belt to get over the unacceptable." He poured a generous portion in each mug. Adding a spoonful of sugar, he sat back and took a sip. George followed suit.

"Where do you get this stuff, Bumpy?"

"A poker buddy from Point IV gets it for me from their commissary." Bumpy took another sip and set the mug down on the blotter on his desk. "Wanna get into the game? We play in pesos. Makes some of the guys feel like high rollers. They lose big and don't realize it right away." He smiled at his observation. A different side of the wildcatter was emerging.

"Sounds good. When do you play?"

"It's tonight, as a matter of fact. We're playing at a new guy named Pendleton's place. I'll pick you up at the hotel at seven." He took another swig of the coffee and leaned back in his chair. The old Bumpy returned. "George, you ready to take it to the bank?"

George set his mug down. "I looked at the latest from the transect. It's very good." He hit the arm of his chair with the palm of his hand before saying, "I'm ready, but I think you'll need the rest of the line to convince the syndicate."

"That's the trouble. Investors sit up in Houston. Don't want to get their hands dirty. 'Spect us to put everything in a neat package." Bumpy added another generous shot to his cup and offered the bottle to George, who declined. "Townsend nixed using the coffee growers for line clearing. At the same time he wants results, and fast. Says the syndicate is getting nervous. Hah! What do they know about bein' down here? *They* should be sitting in Catachoclo." He leaned forward with his elbows on the desk and spoke deliberately. "George, I've made up my mind. I told Wagner to pay off the Redheads. When we get to drillin' again, we're heading west on the main line. And with a different crew clearing the brush." George's raised eyebrows were his only comment. "When we get to the *real* drilling, those ruins, *wherever* they are, will be finished anyway. Redheads might just as well get used to it." He picked up the phone again. "Get me Palacios."

"YES, BUMPY. WE WILL USE utmost discretion. . . . Yes, of course." Don Luis hung up the phone, strode out of his study, and headed for the office. He was proud of the fact that he'd been one of the first to be hooked up with the new telephone service but annoyed that they had not yet extended the line to the office building. As he crossed the patio he spotted his chief of security and motioned to him. Rafael followed his boss into the building.

"The co-op manager and the ICRAC guy were out at the South Forest with a gang of the squatters at daybreak," announced Rafael as the patrón took the seat behind his desk.

"They didn't see you?"

"No."

"Good. We've got an important assignment. We'll take care of those goddamn squatters later." He paused, glaring fiercely. "We're going to recruit men to clear the brush for the drillers. And this time we'll go up towards Boca del Valle," he added, alluding to the previously aborted attempt. "This way the word won't get around so fast."

"When do they start?" asked Rafael.

"In two weeks."

"THIS ROAD'S A LOT BETTER for beginners than the one out to the ferry," remarked Galo, seated in the passenger seat of the ICRAC jeep. Sergio was tight-lipped as he negotiated around the gullies in the road from the South Forest, eroded by the occasional downpours. He'd finally caught onto down gearing during those maneuvers. "I think you're probably right about the carabineers," Galo continued. "I was sure glad to see them there this morning. And according to Jacobo, they aren't the same two that were there yesterday."

"Yeah. The families weren't too keen on staying before we had our talk with the new guys," observed Sergio, considerably more relaxed with a smooth road before him for as far as he could see. "Barrios, it seems, got the word through Kattah. Chiriboga'd said that he was going to alert Barrios's boss in Nicoya."

"I'll bet that's why Kattah went back to his office when we parted last night," recalled Galo. "Probably called the provincial prefecture."

"I feel a little better with your guy, Arturo Morales, staying out there, but this isn't just going to blow over. Palacios was ready to sic his *dogs* on me last night," Sergio said, slowing down as the road ahead turned to the left and disappeared from view. "Did you see the look in his eyes when I told him that I was reporting him to the ICRAC office in the capital? I wonder how long before—?" The student stopped talking as they turned into the streambed they'd successfully forded on the way out. Sergio brought the vehicle to a halt without stalling just before entering the water.

"Good job," remarked his instructor. "Although you probably don't have to, you can shift into four-wheel drive just to get the hang of it." He reached over and pulled back the shorter of the two levers in front of the gearshift. "Now you're in four-wheel. We'll put it into the low gear range," he added, pushing the other lever forward. "O.K. Just start up like normal. You'll feel the extra power." The vehicle lurched ahead as Sergio released the clutch, but it didn't stall. They crept over the rocky streambed until they reached the far side. "See? Now give it a little gas and we'll climb up out of here." They were soon on the road again. "O.K. Now stop and take it out of four-wheel and the low range. It's bad for the transmission if you keep it in on hard ground." Sergio performed the maneuver with a satisfied smile.

"I think I'm getting the hang of it," he said, shifting smoothly through the gears as they resumed driving. The road was fairly straight.

"This is where the Esperanza co-op starts. It extends from the creek we just crossed almost to the edge of town," Galo explained with a wave of his hand. They began to pass peasants seated on the side of the road next to crates of produce: tomatoes, onions, peppers, watermelons, corn. Galo exchanged a wave with each as they passed. "They're waiting for the co-op truck to take the stuff to the market in town. They used to be at the mercy of the middlemen and really got a screwing. Next to a fair price for their coffee beans, it's our greatest achievement."

"The union is the strength," said Sergio, quoting an old maxim.

"There *were* a few slashed tires before the dust settled."

About 100 meters ahead they spotted a peasant who had risen and hailed them upon hearing the vehicle's approach.

"It's Estevez," said Galo. Sergio stopped alongside the man, and Galo leaned out the window. "What's up, Germán?"

"It's my brother Raúl, Galito. He hasn't turned up, and nobody knows where Miguel Huerta has gone off to either."

"Another hothead," muttered Galo to Sergio. "I wonder what this will lead to." Turning back to the peasant, he said, "If you hear anything, let me know. I'll ask around town."

"Please, Galito, anything you can do," Estevez called after the retreating Jeep.

"We will," the co-op manager shouted out the window. "He'd have us here all day with his laments," he added to Sergio as they sped off. "But I *am* worried about this." He mulled the predicament. Sergio pulled off the road at the approach of a rack truck. The driver honked and waved as he sped by. "It's the co-op truck," said Galo. "Say, do you want me to drive?"

"If you don't mind. I think I've had enough of a lesson for today."

The men switched seats. After a couple of silent kilometers Galo asked, "Sergio, do you know anything of a Gustavo Escobár?"

"Tavo Escobár? Oh, yes. He was one of the bad company I was keeping before I took that freighter for Santiago. Chairman of the International Workers' Party in Sulaco. A stand-in for the Communists," Sergio added with a shake of his head. "What about him?"

"Well, about a year or so ago, he and another—"

"Anibal Tobár?"

"That's the one," Galo added.

"I don't doubt it. They were a team. So?"

"The two of them were nosing around Catachoclo without much success. Though they did manage to get the attention of Miguel Huerta, Raúl Estevez, and few of the other *younger brothers*. They'd buy them beers at the Salsipuedes and give them the party pitch. They didn't get too far. I'd heard that they were roughed up by some of Palacios's goons and left town." Galo thought about the possibilities. "I hope they aren't thinking of going that route," he concluded with a touch of apprehension.

"Well, Sulaco isn't that far,. . .if your house's been torched," observed the ICRAC representative.

"Leaving? No!" Jacobo Vidal still wore the worried look he'd had when he first reported the torching incident at the union headquarters the day before. "Stay! We'll help you rebuild." He was standing in the doorway of his thatched-roofed shack in the South Forest. A lean-to extended three meters from the door to a crude fire pit. A faint breeze carried the smoke to where he was standing and into the house. The plume rose and clung to the exposed thatch.

"Rebuild? And have Palacios throw us off the land just when we get the roof on?" Raúl Estevez and Miguel Huerta were sitting on the dirt floor of the shack, leaning against the platform that served as the family bed. They were keeping themselves from being seen through the only window, which faced the road, sipping coffee their host had provided. "We're leaving as soon as the carabineers take off."

"Where will you go?" asked Jacobo, slumping into one of the two chairs at the table in the middle of the room, the only room in the house. He cradled his forehead in his hand.

The two looked at each other. "We're going to Sulaco," answered Raúl. "There's nothing for us here anymore."

"How will you get there?" Jacobo still could not believe that his neighbor was leaving them.

"I got the pesos I buried behind the house. It's enough to get us there by bus." He patted the pocket that held the money. "We'll stay with Miguel's family for a couple of days."

Miguel, who'd had little to say, got up and placed his cup on the table. He peered out the doorway and muttered, "If I never see this pest hole and that bastard Rafael again, it'll be too soon."

"What about Germán?" Jacobo was still trying to dissuade his neighbor.

"Just tell my brother you saw me, and that I'll let him know how I'm doing as soon as I can. But don't say *anything* about where we're going," Raúl added, shaking his head. "He's such a blabbermouth. And, Jacobo, you mustn't say anything to *anyone else* about this."

Miguel turned from the doorway. "It's the carabineers," he announced, resuming his place next to Raúl. Jacobo walked out the door and over to edge of the yard. The other two sat in silence.

A few minutes later he returned. "They're going to town. They said they'd be back tomorrow."

"Good riddance," observed Miguel. "Now we can leave." The two rose.

"Whatever you can salvage from my place is yours, Jacobo."

"I'll store it for you," the older man offered.

"No. It's *yours*."

Jacobo pondered his generosity. "We had to cook your goat,

Raúl," he announced, averting his gaze from his young neighbor.

The full impact of the loss finally hit Raúl. He sat on the platform and covered his face. Jacobo put a tentative hand on his shaking shoulders. When the young man finally got control of himself, he got up and strode to the door. "When I get the chance," he snarled, "I'll *kill* him!" Miguel picked up their packs from the bed and followed the other out. Jacobo watched them march down the road toward town.

As the Jeep approached the town plaza, Galo spotted Hugo Rigpe striding across the sandy expanse towards the ICRAC office. He tooted the horn to no avail. The leader of the Arra'o was on a mission. Galo reached the door of the office as the Redhead was crossing Calle Sulaco. He smiled when he identified the passengers of the vehicle. "Good morning," he said. They shook hands at the curb.

"Let's go inside," suggested Galo, gesturing for Rigpe to proceed.

"Good morning, señores," Juanita called out. "How did it go at the South Forest?" she asked with a bit of apprehension.

"As good as could be expected," Sergio told her. "Things have calmed down considerably."

As they proceeded up the stairs, Pedro appeared from the kitchen. "Coffee, señores?"

That sounds like a good idea." Galo turned to the others, who nodded. When they reached the top, he ushered them into Sergio's office. "He's your man now," he murmured as he passed Sergio, who smiled and directed his visitors to the conference table. They were seating themselves when Pedro appeared with the coffee, set a steaming cup before each, and waited until Rigpe picked up his and took a sip.

"Good!" The Redhead reinforced his approval with a smile and proceeded to consume the rest of the hot liquid. When he set the empty cup on Pedro's tray, his aspect became quite serious. "Truck-with-tall-house-on-back broken. Arra'o men sent away," he announced.

"When did this happen?" Sergio asked.

"Djero."

Sergio looked at Galo.

"Yesterday," the other interpreted.

"Yes-ter-day." The Indian struggled with the word.

"Did the men say how long it would be broken?" Sergio asked.

"Arra'o get pay today. Not know how long before start again."

"If I see the drillers at the hotel tonight, I'll ask them," offered Sergio. "In the meantime, you will tell me what you hear, and I will tell you what I hear."

Satisfied that his message had been received, the Indian prepared to leave. The other two rose and shook hands with him. His machete clanged against the chair when he turned abruptly toward the door. Seated again at the table Sergio picked up his cup and took a sip. "Ooo! How can he drink it so hot?"

"And almost without stopping," observed Galo.

Sergio took another sip. "He didn't bring up the ruins."

"As far as he's concerned, it's not an issue unless the drillers start to encroach on them." Galo was the manager again. "Nothing will happen before they start back to work. When you see those guys, see if you can find that out. In the meantime we can do some planning for the new beneficio project." He extracted a pack of Casablancas from his pocket and offered one to Sergio, who declined. After lighting up, Galo asked, "Just when exactly is Wiggins coming down?"

CHAPTER 24

THE AIFLD PROGRAM OFFICER was particularly exuberant as he walked into Charles Wiggins's office at Point IV. He shared the small windowless quarters with Manuel de Cardenez, a Puerto Rican agronomist, who was in the field. "You know, I think I was riding in the elevator with Pavo what'shisname," he exclaimed, "that air force colonel who was part of the junta."

Wiggins rose to greet Jim Braun. "That was him. Ernesto Picornell."

Braun took one of the visitor seats opposite the co-op expert and laid his briefcase on the other. "Yes. El Pavo. He supposedly lives a couple of blocks from me, but I've only ever seen him in person once before."

"He has an office on the top floor," Wiggins said, raising his head. "Does consulting for the American business community. It's really lobbying the constituent assembly," he added, rolling his eyes. "Probably makes a good buck at it, too. Better than his junta days, I'll wager."

"Pavo." Jim smiled at the reference to a turkey. "The political cartoonists had a heyday with his pointy chin and wattles. Some of them were particularly unflattering *and* incisive the weeks before the junta got dumped. But that's history."

"Yep. Except for Pavo, they've all gone back to their haciendas," Wiggins concluded. "The big worry now is El Dedo. The money is on a return of the military if he gets elected again."

"How many times *has* he been elected?"

Wiggins leaned back in his chair. "Four, I think. But he's only finished one term. And the last one wasn't it. I'd just arrived when his vice-president, Irrizary, took over. And *he* only lasted four months. A drinking problem, among others."

"Do you think the old man'll make it?"

"Over the years he's managed to get a lot of his people into the civil service, including the fire chief, who *still* has the job. So there's support there. And from all reports he's an absolute demagogue. Can charm the votes out of the masses just by lifting his famous finger." Charles imitated the popular pose with finger raised in remonstration. "*Mis adversarios son mierdas!*"

Jim laughed at the imitation. "Would he really say something like that?"

"I don't know. Whatever it takes, I guess."

"The election's in November. It's going to be an interesting few months." Jim reflected. "I wonder how it'll affect our project."

"Another wild card," remarked Charles. "Meanwhile, what do we have from the unions?"

"My secretary's been working on the English translation since we received the stuff from FLOC yesterday." Braun reached for his briefcase and pulled out a file. "Here's your copy of the original and a draft of the translation. She's still going over it, though it reads pretty good to me. I have a copy of the original for Juan." Charles leafed through the material while Braun continued. "I think it'll fit well between your introduction and description of the project and the cost estimate."

"Yeah. Our local engineering staff can crunch the numbers when they have to. And in such detail, it makes you wonder if they really know what they're doing. But they were very close on that textile mill we got involved with in Nogales."

"God," exclaimed Jim. "And look at it now. And we were there only five days before it happened."

"Pretty dismal scene," Charles agreed, "but I never thought it would end that way."

"One of our staff's been up there," the other reported, shaking his head. "There's not much to do except to see that they have a good lawyer. I've never even mentioned it to Elizabeth."

The two fell silent. Charles glanced at his watch. "We'd better get going. Those restaurants in the Center can fill up for lunch." He put the folder on the credenza behind him. "I'll go over it and give you my comments."

JIM SPOTTED THE ATTRACTIVE BRUNETTE among the ICRAC staff leaving the office for lunch. "Margarita," he called. She smiled as she recognized him. "This is Charles Wiggins. He's with Point IV. Charles, Margarita Bustamonte." The two shook hands. After an exchange of pleasantries, Charles excused himself to let Chiriboga know that they'd arrived.

"You're seeing Juan?" she asked.

"Yes. We're going to discuss the new beneficio. ICRAC is prepared to provide some of the infrastructure. A water well. Stuff like that.."

"I'd heard. That's wonderful." Then her eyes brightened. "I'm going to Catachoclo next week," she revealed.

"You'll be seeing Sergio?"

"Yes." She added quickly, "The clinic has asked me to help them plan a new program for social services. The nuns' order in France is providing the money. It was in answer to a request that I'd helped Sor Marillac prepare."

"We should all get together there sometime soon. I'd love to have Elizabeth see the area. We could go out dancing," he added, thinking of that evening when they first met.

"Yes. We'll do that," she answered, smiling to herself at the rather remote possibility of replicating the night at El Candelabro. She reflected for a moment before confiding in her new friend. "Sergio is arranging for us to visit the ruins."

"That's great!" he enthused. "Ever since I heard of them, I've wanted to see them."

"I'll mention it to Sergio and Galo," she offered. "When will you be going down?"

"Not until the kickoff for the new beneficio."

"Oh, there's Juan now," she said, waving at her coworker, who had appeared at the top of the stairs with Wiggins. "I must go, or I'll miss my bus." She turned and hurried across the street.

After greeting each other, Juan suggested El Tucán in the Hotel Majestic. "It doesn't get the crowds like the others."

THE WAITER HAD SET DOWN THREE Sulaco beers and had his pencil poised to take the orders. "I'll have the grilled ham and cheese," said Jim. The two others ordered the same. The waiter picked up the menus and retreated to the kitchen. Their table in the bar next to the window afforded a view of the street and a glimpse of the corner of the plaza. A lottery salesman stood before the window for a full minute, holding a sheet of tickets for them to examine, and then, deciding that the prospects for a sale were remote, moved on. Jim reached for his beer. "How is Fidanza doing down in Catachoclo?" he asked.

"As a matter of fact, I was on the phone with him earlier this morning," reported Juan, picking up his glass. "He said that the drill rig broke down, and they've laid off the Arra'o brush cutters."

"I wonder what that means?" mused Wiggins.

Juan leaned forward and, putting his glass on the table, nodded in the direction of the dining room. "*Those* gentlemen know exactly what it means." The two turned to see the back of Dale Cosgrove, retreating into the inner room followed closely by Licenciado Alfredo Ribadeneira.

"Bumpy Cosgrove," announced Jim.

"You know him?" Juan asked.

"We met when I was staying at the Humboldt with my family three weeks ago. Do you think he saw us?"

"I didn't notice him until he turned into the dining room. I suspect that he would have come over had he seen us," Juan suggested. "He's not one to shrink from confrontations."

"Uh-oh," said Charles, who was facing the dining room entrance. "I guess he *did* see us." Bumpy was striding toward them.

"No. Please don't get up," the driller said as the three moved in their chairs. "Señor Chiriboga," he continued, nodding to Juan. "Braun, I was playing poker with your boss last night." He seemed to be reveling in the encounter.

"So he told me," Jim responded. "And this is Charles Wiggins of Point IV."

"Pleased to meet ya," Bumpy said, taking Charles's outstretched hand. "I know what they mean when they say that Santa Marta is just like a small town. Like a game of poker with all the people you know sitting at the table." Without pause he turned to the ICRAC deputy director and asked, "Have you heard from your Redheads?" Juan leaned forward with a puzzled look, as if he hadn't heard. Bumpy repeated the question in Spanish.

"I think, as you Americans say," he replied, leaning back, "the ball is in your court, Señor Cosgrove."

Bumpy's eyes narrowed ever so slightly. "Ah was hoping they might want to avoid a standoff."

"Again, Señor Cosgrove, the standoff is yours to avoid. We've heard the rig is broke down. So it seems that there is time for both sides to reconsider."

Cosgrove stared directly at Juan, who stood his ground, then finally said, "Time is very short." He turned to Braun. "Your boss is a fine poker player." With that the driller nodded to Wiggins and returned to the dining room.

"I'm not sure that bodes well for the Arra'o," Juan concluded.

The waiter returned with the sandwiches. The baguettes had been heated between two hot plates to the melting point of the cheese. As the three turned their attention to lunch, Charles posed the question, "What does it bode for the beneficio?"

Juan spoke first. "It's hard to imagine the coffee industry surviving a large oil discovery," he said matter-of-factly. "But then again, it may amount to nothing."

"Not from the way Bumpy is acting," offered Jim. "It seems he can almost see the wells pumping the crude."

"It's probably true," agreed Juan. "But we must press on. I understand you have information from the unions?"

"Yes. In fact we've got the draft of their write-up with us," said Charles, looking at Jim.

Juan took another bite of his sandwich as he leafed through the material. "A good beginning. I'm sure the project will move ahead," he said, injecting a note of optimism he did not feel.

"PAPÁ!" EXCLAIMED MARGARITA, upon entering the living room. "When did you get back?" Don Camilo, seated in the chair beneath his portrait, rose and warmly embraced his daughter. The ten years since the portrait was painted had been good to the former president. He stood erect and, brown hair only slightly gray, looked the part of the elder statesman. The trip to Venezuela to consult with Don Rafael Caldera, head of the Christian Socialists, on the progress of the agrarian reform program under the then-president Raúl Leoni attested to the international respect he enjoyed for instituting the program in Costaguana. Margarita turned to greet her mother. "Mamá, how wonderful to have Papá back. . . . We weren't expecting you until tomorrow," she told him.

"They finished a day earlier than planned," Doña Elena explained, answering for her husband, "and all those Venezuelans wanted to do then was to talk and play dominos. Is that not so, my dear?"

"I'm sure Papá is equal to the Venezuelans in talking *and* dominos," Margarita said in his defense.

"Yes, but they speak so fast one can hardly understand them, and they play dominos so slowly," observed Doña Elena. "Is that not so, my dear?"

"Yes, Papá, I can well imagine your impatience. I remember you complaining to Aunt Clara about her deliberateness in playing bridge."

"But your aunt Clara was an excellent player, Margarita. Her patience was legend except when it came to teaching the game."

"I guess that's why I never learned. But I can give you a game of dominos, right, Papá?"

Don Camilo, who had been smiling at the banter on his behalf, said, "If I am permitted a word, I think lunch is ready." Consuelo had been standing in the doorway, awaiting the opportunity to announce the meal. "And as for your prowess at dominos, we shall see about that this evening." Doña Elena led the way to the dining room. Margarita took the arm of her father. "It's good to have you back," she said, leaning her head against his shoulder.

Don Camilo took his place at the head of the table with his daughter on his left and his wife in the seat that Sergio had occupied just over a week before. The view of the city center was as spectacular in the daylight as in the evening. A bowl of *seviche*—raw shrimp, marinated in lemon juice with onions, cilantro, and *ají*, and garnished with roasted corn kernels—and a glass of Chilean white wine had been set at each place. "Welcome back, my dear," said Doña Elena, picking up her glass. The other two joined in the informal toast.

"The Venezuelans don't know what they're missing," Don Camilo remarked, picking up his fork to taste the shrimp. "Delicious." They all followed his lead. "Tell me of your trip to Catachoclo," he inquired. "You were going to leave the day after I left for Venezuela." Margarita, expecting a discourse on her father's trip, was taken aback by his interest. "*And* your mother tells me that you met the young man who assisted you that night." *That night* and *those days* had become the family code words for Margarita's adventures of three years before, culminating in the now famous escape from the soldiers through the Bar Litoral. Her father, in spite of his concern for her safety, was rather proud of her political savvy and self-assurance. Her mother, on the other hand, attributed it all to the mistaken decision to allow the girl to attend university in the coast.

"It was quite a remarkable coincidence," she replied. The vision of Sergio walking toward her in the courtyard of the clinic evoked a feeling of pure happiness. She thought she might cry.

"I'm sure it was a moment you won't soon forget," Don Camilo said, sensing his daughter's emotion. "And the young man has graced our table, I hear?"

Before her daughter could reply, Doña Elena said, "I told Papá that it was just last week Señor Fidanza joined us for dinner. A most pleasant gentleman," she added, smiling at Margarita. "*And* I've told Papá of his work with the Institute."

Margarita wondered what else had been discussed before her arrival. Her father, astute diplomat, reminded them that he had looked into the whole affair at that time, hoping to provide whatever aid the young man might need, but that his flight to Venezuela had precluded any support he might lend. "His work with the unions was, *is*, most commendable, and I'm delighted to hear that he is working for ICRAC, and in Catachoclo."

Margarita was considerably relieved by her father's admiration of Sergio's record. "Papá, Sergio's main responsibility is to the Arra'o."

"A most interesting group," her father reflected. "I remember when we instituted the agrarian reform, we patterned our law after the one that had been created in that area during the Occidental Republic. Scant attention had been given the Arra'o, and we, unfortunately, gave them little more. We tend to avoid dealing with our more exotic citizens."

"Exactly, Papá!" Her exclamation startled Consuelo, who had started to clear the empty seviche bowls. Margarita waited until she withdrew into the kitchen. "But now we will have to deal with these poor people. There's a drilling company who are supposedly doing an earthquake study on the Arra'o land, or what they've been left with west of the Chaco. They've all but admitted that it's oil exploration."

Consuelo wheeled in a serving cart with the main course: baked haddock, boiled cassava, and sautéed string beans. Doña Elena busied herself with directing the serving with her usual remonstrations on the size of the helpings. She had listened to the exchange with mixed emotions. She knew that affairs of state were an inextricable part of her husband's, and by extension her own, life. But she feared that her daughter's interest would only, in the long run, work to her detriment. The prospects of a marriage to one of her many suitors, and for grandchildren, retreated with each passing day. She wouldn't allow herself to even consider the consequences of a future with the young man under discussion.

"That's very interesting," observed Don Camilo. "As I mentioned to you some time ago, I'd heard the rumors. But at a conference I attended while in Caracas, the minister of petroleum asked me straight out if there was any truth to the rumor *he'd* heard." He extracted a small notebook from his inside jacket pocket. He flipped through the pages. "The Walker Tool Company," he finally said, and then added, "Dale Cosgrove?"

"That's him!" Margarita elicited another start from Consuelo. "He's the one heading up the operation." She briefed her father on all that had transpired in Catachoclo in the past month, up to and including the rig breakdown of the day before.

"That settles it," he concluded. "It's oil. And I'm afraid our friend Sergio has his hands full."

For a moment *our friend Sergio* was all that Margarita heard.

CHAPTER 25

S ERGIO ACTUALLY ENJOYED HIS BREAKFASTS with the two Americans. They gave him a chance to practice his English and glean whatever tidbits of information came out about the drilling operation and its effect on the Arra'o. Walter's Spanish was quite good, but George Fuller, only recently arrived in Costaguana, struggled mightily with the language. He had just finished his morning egg-ordering ritual with the waiter Carlos. "What he needs is a long-haired dictionary," said Walter, chuckling at his own joke. "Tell you what," he went on to his partner, "I have a date with Ofelia tonight for the movies. I'll tell her you're coming along. She's always got her girl friend in tow," he informed Sergio. "This way it'll be a four-some." He leaned back in his chair, contemplating the brilliance of his plan.

"Good luck," Sergio offered, thinking it was more than likely a third girl would show up. Carlos returned with three glasses of guava juice, a basket of rolls, and the makings for the coffee—a pitcher of hot milk, sugar, and a cruet of extract. "I haven't been, but I understand they show the movies at the soccer field on the other side of the strip," said Sergio, helping himself to the extract.

"Every Wednesday," replied George. "They usually have Spanish movies, but tonight it's *Goldfinger*, which makes it easy for me."

"What do they do if it rains?" asked Sergio.

"It's only happened once since we've been here," Walter observed. "They show it free the next night. I guess they can't return the money. They kind of lose control, since a lot of people show up after it starts, when it's dark."

Sergio mulled over the idea of attending with Margarita, who was arriving on the morning flight. Maruja had invited them to dinner. The four of them could attend the movie. It would be a pleasant diversion. "What time does it start?" he asked.

"At seven," George replied. And they're pretty prompt, not like everything else around here."

Carlos returned with a plate for each—scrambled eggs and home fries all around. Sergio spooned a generous amount of chili onto the eggs and potatoes from the bowl on the table. Walter used it more sparingly, and George passed.

"When is the new rig showing up?" Sergio asked Walter, without looking up.

"It was supposed to be here this coming Monday, but they lost two days with some heavy rain and flooding in the Oriente. Barring any more trouble, they should be up by the end of next week."

"When will you be hiring back the Redheads?" Sergio had learned from Chiriboga that a decision on the direction of the drilling should have been made, so he got right to the point, hoping the directness might reveal something. He thought he detected an awkward moment. If there was any, Walter recovered.

"We'll see." And without missing a beat, he added, "It'll take a day to get it set up on site, and we've at least two days' work with what's cleared already." That was that. Sergio didn't pursue it further. They concluded breakfast with Walter lamenting that they were all caught up with the paperwork and had really nothing to do. He thought they might go to Nicoya, get some R and R, and meet the rig there.

SERGIO HAD JUST LEFT THE HOTEL and was heading toward his office when the siren sounded, warning of the imminent arrival of the flight from Sulaco and providing the populace the opportunity to clear their livestock and themselves from the strip. As an extra precaution the airport manager rode the length of the runway in a pickup truck. It would be another fifteen minutes before touchdown. Approaching the tree in the middle of the road, Sergio remembered walking from the other direction with Margarita just two weeks before. How could one's life take such a turn? The specter of Don Camilo appeared in spite of Margarita's assurances that her father was not the ogre Sergio made him out to be. The clinic was just ahead. She was staying with the nuns. Just as well. The thought of being alone with her made him nervous. What had Maruja said that night at El Candelabro? "If Margarita comes down on business, we'll make sure she's well chaperoned." His head was spinning when the siren sounded again, announcing that the plane was on final approach. He looked up to see it just over the end of the runway. In the middle of the plaza, waiting for him to catch up, was Victor Hugo Ramirez, the Nicoya stringer for *El Porvenir*, easily recognized in his jipijapa.

"Good morning, Señor Fidanza," he called. "Are you receiving someone on the flight?"

"An ICRAC colleague," Sergio answered, hoping that he would

not have to elaborate further. "And what brings you to Catachoclo?"

"I guess I'll be here on a weekly basis. My editor is sure some-thing is about to break on the drilling operation. I hope you'll con-tinue to keep me informed."

"I'll be happy to," Sergio replied. He picked up the pace as the plane approached the terminal. Ramirez kept up in spite of his limp. "The rig's been broke down now for a week," He went on. "They're expecting the replacement the end of next week." He thought about how much he should divulge. "I don't think there'll be much to re-port until they start up again. You may want to be around for that." He thought that that should do it. The reporter lingered with him as they reached the building. A moment later the passengers began to enter from the other side. "Oh, there she is. Excuse me."

Margarita smiled. Sergio put out his hand. She took it with a slight frown. "A reporter," he murmured, turning his head slightly to the left. The smile came back. He turned to find Ramirez right behind him.

"Margarita, this is Victor Hugo Ramirez of *El Porvenir*. Ramirez, Margarita Bustamante." He said her last name with some trepida-tion.

"My pleasure," murmured Ramirez. "Any relation to Don Camilo?"

"By marriage," Margarita answered without hesitation. Sergio smiled.

"I see that fellow from the beneficio," Ramirez said. The object of his observation was Don Luis Palacios. The reporter bowed slightly and excused himself.

"I think the baggage is at the door," said Sergio, taking Margarita by the arm. "So you were traveling with Luis Palacios." He kept Margarita between himself and the owner of the beneficio, who was being occupied by the reporter. "I'd rather he not see us together." They were the first to reach the cart. Sergio moved around to the back, and as soon as they were partially obscured by the luggage, he kissed the young woman passionately on the lips.

"That's better than a handshake," she whispered as her fellow passengers started to crowd around the cart. They picked up her baggage, and in five minutes they had reached the clinic. Sor Marillac's eyes lit up when she spied the young couple entering the clinic.

"*Bienvenue!*" she exclaimed from the entrance to the office. Striding across the courtyard, she met them halfway. Embracing Margarita, she said, "It's good you've been able to return so soon!" She smiled broadly at Sergio as she made the comment. "And Fidanza, I'm so happy you could receive Margarita at the terminal," she added, vigorously shaking his hand.

"It was my pleasure, Sor Marillac. But I must be going."

"Sor Marillac," said Margarita, "we've been invited to dinner by the Luzuriagas. I hope it won't be a problem."

"Of course not."

"And we may go the movies after," Margarita added, hoping that she would not be imposing on the hospitality of her host.

"I can lend you the flashlight," the nun offered without hesitation. She could hardly contain herself.

"I'll be back about five then." Sergio turned to Margarita who thrust out her hand. He hesitated for a split second before taking it. He smiled, never ceasing to be surprised by her puckish side. But he *did* kiss her on the cheek. "Until five."

The nun picked up Margarita's bag and, with the other hand, took her arm. They walked over to the office. "*Ça va*, Margarita?"

"*Ça va bien.*" The nun gave her arm a squeeze.

"MARGARITA, FIDANZA, WELCOME!" THE PETITE REDHEAD called out to her guests from the doorway as they reached the gate. She met them at the edge of the verandah and embraced them both. "You came in the Jeep. Good. It will save us some time getting to the movie."

"He's turning into an accomplished chauffeur," Margarita teased.

"Galo is a good instructor," Maruja replied. "He taught me how to drive." Sergio shrugged.

The Luzuriagas lived in the section of Catachoclo just behind the Flamenco, where the houses were a touch more substantial, with established gardens. Theirs was one of the smaller ones: one bedroom, a dining room/living room area, a large kitchen, a bath with a water closet (only available on the east side of the air strip), and separate maid's quarters, which they used for guests. In the garden grew a towering mango tree that bore a bumper crop every year. Galo would hire La Esperanza co-op members to harvest the fruit with Raúl as foreman. Galo hadn't thought about how he was going to get the job done without him.

"He's in the garden, putting the finishing touches on dinner." She led them along the side of the house, to where her husband was turning a rabbit on a spit. "Galito, our guests have arrived."

He waved from his station at the small barbeque pit. "You are in your house. I hope rabbit is to your taste." He pulled off a glove as Margarita approached, and took her hand.

"It smells great!" she exclaimed, leaning over to catch the aroma.

"It's all in the marinade, which is Maruja's department. Sergio, I'm afraid we'll bore you with our limited menu." He shook hands with his friend, and then replaced the glove to attend to his roasting.

"Not at all," Sergio replied. "Besides oatmeal, it's what I ate the most of on the farm. It was practically the only meat we got to eat during the war. That and chicken. The pigs we sold to the government. And later the Germans," he added, shaking his head. "They took what they wanted and paid what they wanted."

"And you, Margarita—I don't suppose you have our rustic fare very often."

"Not since before university. But in those days my uncle would roast a whole calf for a big family get together."

Sergio winced inwardly at the thought of the uncle with the ranch in the northeast. At that moment Margarita slipped her hand in his as they stood watching their host baste the rabbit, and both uncle and ranch retreated from Sergio's thoughts.

"I must see if the cassavas are ready," said Maruja.

"I'll come, too," Margarita offered. She gave Sergio's hand a squeeze before following the redhead toward the kitchen.

"So it's arranged with Rigpe to visit the ruins?" Galo asked as he cranked the spit and applied the marinade.

"Yes, we're going Saturday."

"Is Margarita all set?"

"I guess. I told her last week. She's quite excited about it. You know her. I think she's taken on the Arra'o as her cause."

"Sergio, I don't need to tell you that if they discover oil, the Arra'o cause will be the most serious and dangerous one in the country."

Maruja meanwhile was thrusting the pressure cooker under the water faucet. A loud hiss issued from the pot. She peered out the window. "Look at those two. It looks like the conversation is already getting serious." She was, as ever, vigilant. Galo shouted something. "What's he saying?" she asked.

Margarita stepped outside. "He said, 'The rabbit's done.'"

"Good. We're all set here."

The furnishings in the Luzuriaga home were not atypical of a provincial cottage: sofa and chair arranged at right angles, with an electric bridge lamp between, in the corner adjacent to the front door; a kerosene lamp stood on a small end table between a plain wooden armchair and a bookcase on the opposite side of the room. A gate-leg table, moved from against the wall on the right side of the house to a spot near the kitchen, would accommodate four comfortably. Unframed oil paintings filled every available space on the plastered-over cinderblock walls.

The men took their seats as the women brought in the food already arranged on individual plates. Galo poured the drinks, Orangina for Sergio and a red wine for the others. The host picked up his glass and proposed a toast, "To our *happily* reacquainted friends."

"Hear, hear!" responded Maruja. The other two smiled at each other and said nothing. The conversation centered on the recent developments in the town. Maruja dropped her vigilance and joined in. She had a considered opinion on all aspects of the life around them.

"So you like living here?" asked Margarita of her hosts as they were finishing.

Maruja answered, "For me it does have its drawbacks, but I always have my painting." She gestured to the walls.

"They're yours?" Margarita exclaimed. "How lovely!" She

turned in her chair to see them all. "And there's the tree where we met that night," she enthused, pointing to a canvas prominently displayed on the wall where the table had stood.

"I *did* major in fine arts, and it's paid off."

"I never knew," said Margarita. "Did you know, Sergio?" she asked.

"Yes, I did. As a matter of fact, Maruja used to paint signs for FLOC."

"Yes. I became quite inventive at different ways to say, 'Down with the boss!'" That got a laugh from the others.

"The best," recalled Sergio, "was that caricature of Fabiano Ortíz, the owner of the textile mill in Los Hatos? It depicted a woman machine operator sticking a needle in his bum." There was a moment's pause before the table erupted in laughter, partly because of the obvious embarrassment of the relater.

Galo glanced at his watch. "We'd better think about leaving. We've got about twenty minutes." Margarita started to clear the table. "No, no," protested Maruja. "There's not enough time. I can get it later." It was Margarita's turn to protest, to no avail. In a minute they were out the door. Sergio handed the keys to Galo.

"Capitán Ulloa," shouted Don Luis Palacios from the doorway of his office. "Welcome to Tres de Mayo." The light was fading as he hurried down the path to the main house. His guest was just getting out of the Jeep he had parked at the edge of the patio. "I'm so glad you could join me for dinner. How long has it been since your last visit here? Too long, I'm sure," Palacios concluded, slightly out of breath.

"I believe it was March and before that in the holidays." Capitán Bertrand Ulloa was of medium height and slender. Dressed in brown tunic, jodhpurs, and visor cap, the uniform of the cavalry officer, he had the black hair, dark brown eyes, hawklike features, and severe demeanor to command instant obedience from his subordinates, officers and men alike. His boots clicked on the stone patio as he came around the Jeep to greet his host.

"Well, then. There have been changes."

"Yes. I see the—how do the gringos call it? —*bunkhouse* has been finished. And your office, you have moved in?"

"Yes, we have. Can I show you the new facilities?" Without waiting for a response, Palacios called to the teenager standing at the far edge of the patio and tilted his head in the direction of the bunkhouse. Without another word, the youth ran off. "We have our *own* army, as you will see," he added, gesturing toward the newly completed buildings.

Fifteen minutes later they were seated in Don Luis's study, having completed the tour he had given to Bumpy three weeks before, concluding with an examination of the cache of arms stored in the last section of the bookcases that lined the studio. "Those gringos and their gin. Like you, I'll take rum any day," he remarked, pouring a generous glass for his guest. "What will you have with it?" he asked, pointing to an array of mixers.

"Coca-Cola, please."

"Ah, Cuba Libre." The patrón smiled; as quickly, the smile turned to a glare. "That communist bastard is going to infect the whole continent if we don't watch out." The capitán did not respond immediately. Don Luis took his drink and, still glowering, sat down in the leather-upholstered chair in front of the empty bookshelves. A smile returned to his face. "Well, what do you think of our garrison?"

"I'll have to keep a close eye on my men so that they don't desert me for *your* army." The officer raised his glass. "Here's to our respective forces."

Don Luis acknowledged the toast, and then asked, "Tell me. How is it going in your camp?"

"When was the last time you were there, Don Luis?"

"It must be over a year."

"Well, you will be surprised at the changes *we've* made. The camp has doubled in size. I expect a promotion soon."

"A major! Congratulations!" exclaimed the host. "But I hadn't been aware of any activity out there."

"It's all been done out of Cayta," the capitán explained, lowering his voice. "We don't want to call too much attention to the work."

"Cayta? Over that awful road?"

"It's been improved enough for our purposes."

The beneficio owner's eyebrows rose. "And what might those be?"

Ulloa drained his Cuba Libre and leaned back in his chair. "About the time of your visit I had just returned from a year's special training in the United States. In Fort Benning, Georgia." The other shrugged at the mention of the name. "They have a school there for Latin American military. A counterinsurgency course." Ulloa looked around.

"We are quite alone, Capitán."

"It was my second tour. An advanced curriculum. As a result I have been assigned to train our people in the methodology, and because of the camp's remoteness, the training will be given there. It's a rather small operation. I don't think the former junta was even aware of it. I report directly to General Aníbal Espinosa."

"You need say no more." Don Luis smiled broadly. "Well, this calls for another drink. I guess there's more than one way to inoculate against Cuban contamination."

THE RATHER PRIMITIVE BLEACHERS of the soccer field offered preferred seating for the performance at a cost of five pesos. Entry there was more easily controlled than on the open field, where patrons sat on folding chairs, spread cloths, or the bare ground for one peso. The two couples had just taken their seats in the top row, the women between the two men, when Walter and George arrived with three young women in tow. Walter spotted Sergio in the fast-fading light and waved. He gestured at the three and shouted, "You can't win."

"What did he say?" asked Maruja. Sergio explained the plan Walter had come up with at breakfast. "Of course. That's why *we're* here," she observed, winking at Sergio. Before there could be any more elucidation of the intricate mores of Costaguana courtship, the movie started. The projector was housed in a large panel truck, parked at the far right end of the bleachers. The screen, mounted at a forty-five degree angle to the stands, required the five-peso patrons to look slightly to their left. Those seated on the field looked straight ahead. Power came from a line run to the field for just that purpose. A generator supplied emergency power in case of a failure at the town facility. As the credits rolled, Margarita put her hand under Sergio's arm and snuggled a bit closer. He felt like a schoolboy on his first date—and he liked it.

"SERGIO, HOW'D YOU LIKE TO GET behind the wheel of Double-O-7's Aston Martin?" Galo asked. They had left the Jeep in front of the ICRAC office on the plaza and were seated at a table in El Rincón, across from the Sulaco. Even with seven reel changes, the movie had ended at a quarter past nine, so the lights in town were still on.

"I've got my hands full with the Jeep," he sighed. "And Pussy Galore would be a distraction."

"Oh?" Margarita gave a look of mock surprise.

Without pause, Sergio said to the others, "You see? Now I've *really* got my hands full."

This prompted another "Oh" from Margarita accompanied by a playful punch in the arm.

Sergio spied a platter of pastries on the counter. "I could go for an allulla and coffee. Are they fresh, Pepe?"

The waiter, the same taciturn fellow with the perennial three-day growth of beard, had been standing there, waiting for the order. "They bring them in every day from Boca del Valle," he grumbled. "I'm surprised there're any left."

Maruja nodded. "That sounds good—we didn't have time for dessert." The other two went along.

"We *did* leave in a hurry," said Margarita. "I didn't really have a chance to look at your paintings, either. From what I saw, you've really captured the feel of the place."

"She exhibited in the conference room of the Canton Building about six months ago," Galo said proudly. "Luis Palacios purchased two and commissioned another."

"I hope you soaked him," Sergio put in.

"Don't worry. He paid a premium," the artist replied. "The commission was a large one of the house, with the beneficio in the background."

"I'd love to get one of your paintings for my mother," said Margarita. "But no reduction for friends!" she added, holding up a finger.

"What are friends for, if not to treat them better?" Maruja protested. "They're not all for sale, but I'm sure you'll find one you like."

Pepe returned with the order. They passed the coffee makings around and helped themselves to the pastries. Maruja looked at Galo. "We have an announcement to make." The seriousness of the statement caught the others' attention. "We're going to have a baby."

"That's *wonderful!*" Margarita enthused, reaching over to grasp the hand of the mother-to-be.

Sergio, standing up and embracing Galo, added, "This *is* a surprise. When's the event?"

"March. You're the first ones we've told," said Maruja, breaking into happy tears. Her husband put his arm around her and gave her a squeeze. She buried her head in his shoulder.

THEY HAD MADE THEIR GOODNIGHTS at El Rincón, repeating their well wishes with embraces. Maruja had dissolved in tears again. The expectant couple, also equipped with a flashlight, had convinced Sergio that it would take just as long to retrieve the Jeep as it would to go straight home.

Calle Sulaco seemed quieter than it had three weeks before. Margarita and Sergio strolled arm in arm toward the clinic. "You're very quiet," she commented as they reached the tree.

It was a moment before he answered. "I was thinking about them moving to Nicoya in November. They're going to be missed here."

"He *did* say that Arturo Morales was quite capable of taking over management of the co-op," she reminded him.

"I guess. But there's the new beneficio."

"Which he'll still be involved in from Nicoya." She gave his arm a tug. "What we have to think about, Sergio, is *us*."

Us was a new dimension in Sergio's life. He had appeared in Costaguana a month before, a returned exile without any idea of what he wanted to do. Now an employer he had never dreamed of working for had assigned him to Catachoclo, and the woman he'd had no prospect of ever seeing again was tugging on his arm.

"Yes, Sergio, *us*," she repeated.

"But Catachoclo?"

"Darling, when I saw you waiting for me in the airport this morning, I thought if I never left Catachoclo, I could die happy."

"Living in Catacholco?"

"I know a nice cottage that will be available in three months." They had reached the entrance to the clinic. "We both have our work. And it won't be forever." She turned to him and asked, "Don't you feel as I do?"

"Yes! I do!" The next moment they were in each other's arms, the beam of the flashlight shining absurdly up into the trees. A bird let out a squawk; they parted when another light appeared through the gate.

"It's the watchman," she whispered, giving him a parting kiss. "We'll talk tomorrow."

CHAPTER 26

THE ICRAC REPRESENTATIVE WAS MAKING his first solo drive in the Jeep. An early appointment with Arturo Morales had gotten him up well before breakfast at the Sulaco. He'd left at daybreak and was nearing the South Forest settler village. The trip had been uneventful; fording the river so easy his full attention was not on the road but instead on his conversation with Margarita the night before. *Us*. That summed it up. She'd tied up all of the loose ends by invoking that one word. It seemed too easy. But what were the complications? Her father for one, and her mother. Assurances to the contrary, he dreaded the time when he had to confront them with his proposal of marriage. On the other hand he had the full support of Julio and Giovanna. In a letter he'd just received, his sister had repeated her admonition that he could stand up to anyone. He de-

cided to call and surprise her. Maybe it would give him the courage
to—

He slammed on the brakes about fifty meters before reaching
the first thatch-roofed settler shack when a dark brown dog of mixed
ancestry darted from the side of the road and began chasing his vehicle. He stalled, and the dog broke off its pursuit and fell panting
in the ditch. After starting the engine and continuing on his way,
Sergio was disconcerted when the dog resumed the chase. His relief
was short-lived when it again gave up its pursuit, only to be replaced
by another, larger mongrel. He passed a second shack and waved at
the owner, who took time out from milking his cow to call after the
dog, to no avail. Since leaving Catachoclo, Sergio had put aside any
thought of the return trip, which might have included an encounter
with the co-op's produce truck. Then he spied that *bête noire* parked
on the side of the road about two hundred meters ahead. As Sergio
approached, the second dog gave up, but a third took up the task.
When he pulled up in front of the truck, the third dog lost interest,
so Sergio was able to descend from the Jeep unmolested. Arturo,
standing next to the firepit, on which the promised breakfast was
being prepared, waved and called out, "Sergio, back here." When
the newcomer reached the fire Arturo remarked, "We could follow
your progress down the road by whose dog was barking."

Maria Cunshi de Vidál was deep-frying slivered cassavas, and
what appeared to be shredded meat, in a cast-iron skillet. A pot of
mountain coffee rested on the wall of the pit, ready to be transferred
to the grill. The infant strapped to Maria's back yawned but did not
awaken. Jacobo appeared at the door. "Good morning, Señor Fidanza. Please, have the kindness to be seated." He motioned to the
table in the center of the room. Sergio shook the proffered forearm
as he and Galo's assistant passed into the room. A dozen rolls, courtesy of Arturo, lay on the center of the table next to a bowl of chili.
Before each chair sat a knife, a fork, and a cup. "Please," the host repeated, indicating the two chairs at the table.

"Aren't you joining us?" asked Sergio.

"We have breakfasted already," Jacobo answered, motioning
again to the chairs.

Maria arrived with two plates heaped with the cassava and shredded meat. "The coffee is almost ready," she said. The baby began to stir and let out a cry. The mother went over to the bed and sat down. She whisked the child from her back, opened her blouse, and began to nurse it. "Jacobo, the coffee," she said in a low, hardly discernible voice. Jacobo left, and Sergio reached for the chili. This will make anything taste good, he thought, ladling on a generous portion. Arturo did likewise. Jacobo returned with the coffee and a pitcher of milk, filled the two cups, and offered the milk. They both nodded. Sergio dug into the cassava. He reluctantly tried the shredded meat, which tasted surprisingly good. It turned out to be the remains of Raúl's goat.

"Has he returned yet?" Sergio asked of his host.

"No."

"Do you know where he went?" Jacobo exchanged a glance with his wife but said nothing. The two guests turned to look at their host. The worried look he'd had when he described the affair with Rafael came over his face. "He said I shouldn't tell anyone." Without waiting to be asked again he blurted, "They went to Sulaco." He seemed almost relieved that the secret was out, as if it might hasten the return of his neighbor. Arturo looked at Sergio.

"It's all right, Jacobo," Sergio assured the crestfallen man. "There's nothing we can do about it anyway. But if he returns, let Arturo know. We don't want him to get into any trouble."

"Trouble?" Jacobo wasn't sure what that could be.

"Not trouble, Jacobo," said Arturo to allay any fears the man might have. "We want to help him get started again. We want to help *all* of our members." The revelation about Raúl had surprised them. The purpose of the visit had been to assure the settlers that they would not be disturbed. Sergio had not heard anything about the ownership of the land, but it wouldn't do any good to leave them without hope.

SERGIO AND ARTURO WERE STANDING in the road next to the Jeep when the settlers disbursed to their homes. The nine heads of household and three teenaged sons had gathered at Vidál's neighbor's yard, the one milking the cow when Sergio arrived. They had listened attentively to what he had to say about their land tenancy and the threat of expulsion. He spoke with authority without betraying his shaky conviction that their plight was not real. They had already arranged for a night watch and had a plan for warning the people of any danger. Sergio prayed it would never come to that. The meeting ended with a report, by the man who'd stood watch the previous night, of the return of the army Jeep driven toward Catachoclo by a capitán earlier that afternoon.

"How far's the camp?" Sergio asked. Arturo estimated about twelve kilometers. "How's the road?"

"About the same as from here to the river. Maybe a little worse. There're two streams to ford, but they're quite shallow most of the year."

"Shall we pay them a visit?"

Arturo thought for a moment. "Why not?" He was warming to the prospect. "I know the capitán. He used to come into town regularly. But neither he nor his men have been around for the best part of this year, come to think of it."

"Do you mind driving?" Sergio asked.

"Not at all."

"WELL, THIS IS QUITE A CHANGE!" Arturo exclaimed. They were waiting in the Jeep just beyond the sentry post next to the road. "It looks at least twice the size I remember. It's hard for me to even recall just what it used to be." Fifteen meters along the road had been cleared, leveled, and covered with gravel back twenty meters to a rectangular space, about the size of a soccer field, that stretched to the surrounding woods. And a soccer game was in progress. The flag of Costaguana was flying from a pole. One net stood in front of the pole, its mate at the far end of the field, where the play was.

The guard on duty had disappeared into a wooden building at the corner of the field nearest the guard shack. A Jeep was parked in front of it. The building, with a double-pitched roof, about six meters square and painted gray, sat on a cinderblock foundation. Next to it stood another building double the size of the first. Barrack tents, with wooden platform and sides and a canvas roof, lined the right side of the field and the farther half of the left, the nearer half occupied by four double-pitched wooden buildings. Soldiers were gathered in front listening to an officer. A dining hall and other support facilities stood at the far end of the field.

"Here he comes," said Sergio.

The guard approached the driver's side. "The capitán can see you now. You can leave your vehicle here."

The two got out and walked over to where the corporal had indicated. Two steps led up to the door in the center of the front wall. Hinged shutters on the windows on either side of the door had been propped open.

"Welcome, Señor Morales." The capitán stepped around his desk and held out his hand.

Arturo shook it and turned to Sergio. "Capitán, this is Sergio Fidanza, ICRAC's newly appointed representative in Catachoclo." They shook hands, and Sergio offered his card to the officer, whose lips tightened as he glanced at it. It was the same as the one Don Luis had shown him the night before.

"Pleased to meet you," he said perfunctorily, looking again at the card. He wheeled the chair from the desk in the front corner of the room and placed it next to the one in front of his. "Teniente Calderón is on leave," he said, motioning for the two to be seated. "And to what do we owe this visit?" he asked as he took his own. His desk, larger than the other, faced the door. Behind it, the standard of the Costaguana cavalry hung on the wall between two windows next to a framed photograph of the capitán receiving a diploma from a United States Army general. The framed diploma was also on view. Sergio noted *School of the Americas*, lettered in old English text across the top of the certificate.

"Señor Fidanza wanted to acquaint himself with the area, Capitán," Arturo explained.

"We were just this morning meeting with your neighbors to the north," Sergio said.

"Those squatters on the land of the Palacios?" There was a definite edge to the capitán's voice. "But of course, that's a civil matter," he allowed. "Under the junta it would have come under our purview, but now it's a civil matter," he repeated.

"Yes. A civil matter," Sergio agreed. "As a matter of fact, Capitán, my office in the capital is at this moment looking into the matter of their tenancy."

At this the officer rose and announced that he had some urgent business to attend to. "Had we notice of your visit, I would have had you join us for lunch. Perhaps another time." He moved around the desk and held the door for his visitors.

Halfway back to their vehicle, Sergio observed, "'Perhaps another time.' Did you get the feeling that he wasn't very happy with our being here?"

"Yes. Especially after he examined your card." Arturo chuckled as they climbed into the Jeep. "Shall we take a look at the road to Cayta?"

"I think it would be a *splendid* idea," Sergio replied.

"Hard to believe they brought all of the material for this new construction over it," remarked Arturo, "but it certainly didn't come through Catachoclo." As they pulled out into the road a tank truck slowed down before turning into the camp. "I guess that proves it," he observed.

In five minutes they were at the point where the road began its steep climb over the hill. Arturo, looking in the rear-view mirror, announced that they were being followed. He pulled over. The Jeep came alongside, and the corporal jumped out. Saluting, he said, "Corporal Mora, señores. Sorry—but no one is allowed beyond the post without a permit."

"And who gives the permits?" asked Sergio.

"Capitán Ulloa," the corporal replied. Arturo nodded, turned the Jeep around, and headed back. The corporal followed at a distance.

"From what I could see there's been a lot of work done on that road," observed Arturo.

Sergio agreed. "That's how they got it in, all right."

"Shall we apply for a permit?" Arturo asked.

Sergio laughed as he pondered the possibilities. "Perhaps another time."

"Señorita Bustamante—"

"Sor Lourdes, please, call me Margarita. The other nuns do."

"Yes. But you're older than I am."

"Nonsense," Margarita objected. "I'll bet we're the same age." She turned to look at her traveling companion. "When were you born?"

"April 12, 1935."

"See? You have two months on me. *I'm* the younger!" Margarita delighted in the surprised look on the nun's face. "I'll call you Lourdes, if it makes you feel better."

"I'd like that. But not in the convent."

"Of course," Margarita agreed. "But I'm sorry. I interrupted you."

Sor Lourdes and Margarita were driving out to the first aid station in San Miguel. Margarita was behind the wheel. "I was going to say, 'You're a very good driver.'"

"Thank you. I learned to drive on my uncle's ranch. I've even driven a tractor."

"A tractor? Oh, my! Well, it's fortunate that you do drive—else, with Don Lorenzo ill with the fever, we wouldn't have been able to make this visit." Margarita slowed as she overtook a hayrick being pulled by a burro. The man walking alongside the animal tipped his straw hat when he recognized the nun's habit. "You went to the movie last night?"

"Yes. With the Luzuriagas. You know them?"

"Yes. Señora Luzuriaga is a painter. We saw her work in the Canton Hall last year. And Señor Fidanza also?"

"Yes." Margarita blushed and quickly added, "We were all friends at university. Do you ever go to the movies?"

"Oh, yes. When Sor Therese gives permission. We saw *Mary Poppins* in June. What did you see?"

"*Goldfinger*. One of those action thrillers." Margarita had a passing mental picture of Pussy Galore. "I've seen better," she observed dryly.

Margarita's instinctive graciousness invariably succeeded in drawing out even casual acquaintances. She learned that her companion's ancestors had been farmers in the valley of San Tomé. At the turn of the century the English mine owner, Don Carlos Gould, had recruited her grandfather, because of his mechanical skills, to work in the San Tomé mine. He'd worked there until it closed and then gotten a job at the port in Sulaco, moving his young family to the city.

"My father and uncle worked with him. That's how I came to go to the Escuela San Tomé." Two cows ambled into the road ahead, followed by the cowherd brandishing a stick. Margarita slowed as the cowherd, with shouts and whistles, got them onto a path on the other side.

"Did you know Sor Marillac from the school?"

"No. She came after I left. But it's why I joined the order. I was the first professed Costaguanera." The nun's face brightened as she described her entry into the order. "I spent my novitiate in the capital. There were four of us, but I'm the only one to become a nurse. I trained at the university hospital."

"And you like it here in Catachoclo?"

"I love it, Señ—Margarita."

About a hundred meters ahead the road widened. A bit farther, on the right side, stood a two-story building that served as a general store and housed the first-aid station in a room on the far side. Columns supporting the roof and second floor balcony formed a crude colonnade on the sides of the ground floor facing the main road; a narrow gravel road led off to the right. Peppers, strung on a line between two of the columns on the second floor, were drying in the sun. Above the entrance to the store, flowers in a large earthen pot were protruding through the railing. Across the road a crude sign advertised a mechanic's shop, tire repair, and gasoline for the imprudent driver who hadn't filled up at Boca del Valle or Catachoclo. The gasoline was dispensed from a fifty-five-gallon drum elevated on a stand about a meter high, located well back from the road.

As they got closer, a man who had just left the store mounted one of the horses hitched to a rail on the side. He turned the horse and proceeded toward them at a fast walk. As they passed the horseman, Sor Lourdes bowed her head slightly and cast her eyes down. Margarita glanced briefly at him and immediately recognized the leering face of one of those who had caused the disturbance at the Salsipuedes the night of her reunion with Sergio. She slowed down to park the vehicle in front of the building and, before turning, glanced into the mirror. Rafael had stopped his horse and turned back to observe the two. Margarita pulled in alongside the building. She looked back to see him coming toward them, staring at their car. Then, apparently thinking better of it, he turned again toward Catachoclo.

"Do you know that man, Lourdes?"

"I've seen him in town. He is not a nice person."

"That's an understatement. He gives me the shivers."

The two got out and collected their things from the back seat: Sor Lourdes a medical bag, Margarita a small briefcase. They made their way up wide concrete steps to the colonnade. Two men lounging on a bench between the entrances to the store and the first-aid station and carrying on an excited conversation in Quechua, paused to salute the nun and her companion before returning to their conversation. Margarita proceeded into the clinic. Sor Lourdes paused outside and took a moment to inspect the contents of her bag before joining her.

"LOURDES, I'M STILL AMAZED at how well you were able to treat that machete wound on that poor man's leg. You even stitched it up."

"It's thanks to Doctor Saenz and Doctor de Vaca. When we assist them at operations in the clinic, they always have us do the closing and other procedures. But it isn't often we have the opportunity to do it on our own, thank God. It's good when injured people are able to get to the station. Many are self-treated, which can lead to a worse condition."

"I can imagine."

Margarita and Lourdes were returning to Catachoclo after spending the day. They discussed the qualifications of the three women candidates Margarita had interviewed for the social services training program. It was getting late and would be dark before they reached their destination. Margarita was thinking of the encounter with Rafael and did not look forward to driving past the Cafetero Tres de Mayo.

"Before I forget, Margarita—I want to tell you what those two sitting on the bench when we arrived were talking about."

"They were speaking Quechua. You could understand them?"

"I spoke it at home as a child. My mother is Otlaco."

"I wish I'd learned Quechua," mused Margarita. "Maybe I'll take lessons. . . . So what was it about?"

"The work they'd just been offered by that man who left on horseback."

"What kind of work?"

"Clearing the forest across the river from us, on the land of the Redheads. It must be for that earthquake drilling that's going on."

"Earthquake," Margarita commented with disdain. "It's more likely, Lourdes, that they're exploring for oil."

"Oil?"

"That's the very strong rumor making the rounds in the capital."

Margarita had had to drive considerably slower. More than once they'd encountered a steer lying in the road. "They do it for the warmth and to avoid the bugs," Lourdes had remarked. It was dark as they passed the entrance to the cafetero marked by the lights from the beneficio. Rafael's leering face kept looming in Margarita's imagination. She breathed a sigh of relief at seeing the last of the beneficio workers walking toward town.

"We're going to be a little late for dinner," remarked Lourdes, holding her watch up to the light of the dashboard. "Should I say anything about the oil?"

"We should be thinking about the possibility. If it happens, this area will be changed beyond recognition."

How was she going to get the word to Sergio about Rafael's offer of work?

"THIS IS CALLE DOCTOR FLEMING," observed Miguel, squinting up at the sign on the building at the corner where they'd gotten off the bus.

"Tavo said Calle Muguruza would be two blocks from where the bus let us off," said Raúl. He peered anxiously at Tavo Escobár's card in the light of the corner street lamp.

"Ask the girl in the doorway there," Miguel said.

"You ask her," replied Raúl, thrusting the card at his companion. Miguel took it reluctantly. As he approached, the girl stepped out of the doorway, revealing heavily rouged lips and a tight skirt.

"We're looking for Calle Muguruza."

"Right down the street," she said, motioning in the direction they were heading. "How about buying me a drink for the information?" she added without hesitation, nodding toward the doorway she had just stepped out of. Miguel Looked at Raúl.

"We have to meet a friend," said Raúl, pushing Miguel along. "What are we going to buy drinks with?" he whispered.

"I wasn't going to buy her any drinks," protested Miguel. A similarly dressed girl stepped out of another doorway not twenty meters from the previous encounter.

"Looking for some fun, guys?" she asked.

"We have to meet a friend," said Raúl. They picked up the pace. "Bring him along," the second girl called after the two retreating figures. Two men engaged in a conversation with a third girl in a doorway across the street turned to see what the shouting was about. "Bumpkins," explained the second girl. By that time Raúl and Miguel had turned into Calle Muguruza.

"He *did* say that he'd wait for us?" Miguel was getting nervous. Having slept in an empty shed near the bus station the previous night, he was looking forward to Tavo's promise of better accommodations. There was no one loitering about on Calle Muguruza, but the absence of streetlights made the numbers on the buildings impossible to see without lighting a match. Raúl would soon have been out of matches, if Miguel hadn't spied a light in the next block.

"It must be there," he said without much conviction. A minute later they were knocking at the door, which had no number, only their last hope for a bed.

Gustavo Escobár, a short bull of a man with curly brown hair over a round face, welcomed them in a reedy voice, which belied his otherwise formidable appearance. "Come in. I thought maybe you got detained up on Fleming." The comment was greeted with perplexed looks. "Never mind," he said, motioning them into the next room and up a flight of stairs. "You've come at just the right time. From what you told me on the phone, I think you'll be interested in what this guy has to say." They entered the room at the top. "You know compañero Tobár," he said, gesturing to the shorter of the two men who rose from the table at the end of the room. "And this is compañero Ricardo Mendez. He just got in from Cuba." This news elicited no response from the two arrivals.

They appeared to be in a meeting room of sorts; about fifteen chairs were arranged in front of the table, at which Mendez and Tobár had been seated. The only decorations were a poster proclaiming that the fifth conference of the World Federation of Trade Unions had been held the previous year, and a diploma certifying the membership of the International Workers' Party of Costaguana in the WFTU. Two more chairs were drawn up to the table; a bottle of Pistola and five glasses were produced. Tobár poured the drinks. Tavo proposed a toast. The visitors stared at their glasses. What's the problem?" asked Tavo.

The two looked at each other. Finally Miguel spoke up. "We haven't eaten all day."

"Well, we can do something about that," said Tavo. "Aníbal, see what the porter can give us." Aníbal disappeared down the stairs. "In the meantime, tell Ricardo here what you told me over the phone."

Raúl was at the point in the story where Rafael shot his goat when Aníbal returned with Ramón, the porter, each carrying a plate of rice and beans and a bottle of Orangina. The two dug in with gusto. About halfway through, Raúl took a breather.

"Feeling better?" asked Tavo.

"Much better," said Raúl. Between slower mouthfuls he completed his story.

"Does anybody know you're here?" asked the Cuban.

"We told my neighbor, but we didn't mention who we were going to see. I told him to keep his mouth shut," he added, looking at his friend for support.

"Will he do it?"

Raúl looked again at Miguel and shrugged.

"He'll think they're just looking for work,"Tavo observed.

"Yeah," agreed Raúl. He hadn't mentioned his threat to kill Rafael.

CHAPTER 27

F RESHLY SHAVED AND SITTING by the window, Sergio was rereading the letter he'd received the night before.

My dearest Sergio, it began. He still could not believe being addressed in such terms. *We've just returned from San Miguel (7pm). If
you're serious about starting at the crack of dawn tomorrow, then I will have
to get to bed right after dinner.* Is eight o'clock the crack of dawn? he
wondered. *But I must tell you of what we heard in San Miguel*, it went
on. *That creep causing all the commotion in the bar the night we first met—
oh, Sergio, what a miracle!—was in San Miguel, hiring men to clear the forest for the drilling work. That's all I know. See you at 8, my love. Margarita.*

He folded the letter and replaced in its envelope. It was six-
thirty, *really* the crack of dawn. He wondered if his breakfast mates
would be up. With the absence of activity they were getting to the
dining room later than usual. He decided to wait until seven. He
took out the letter and again reread it.

When he went down, the dining room was empty. Taking his
usual seat, he ordered guava juice, rolls, and coffee from the waiting
Carlos. His breakfast arrived at the same time the drillers appeared.
They seemed a little reluctant to join him. Sergio waved them over.
"Good morning," he called out. "I thought you'd be on your way to
Nicoya by now."

"We're leaving right after lunch," answered Walter as the two
took their places. Carlos had waited to take the orders. The usual
mime show ensued between George and the waiter. That being set-

tled, Sergio offered them coffee from the ample supply.

"Still expecting the rig here next Friday?" he asked. Walter nodded. "That's a long time in Nicoya."

"We're going on to the capital for some meetings." Walter looked a little uncomfortable, fearing he'd already said too much. Sergio let him squirm a bit. "The head geologist wants to go over the results so far."

"Should we expect a big one soon?" asked Sergio.

The two were momentarily dumbfounded by the remark. It was George who recovered first. "You really can't tell until it's compared with the data from the rest of the country, and even into the surrounding countries." He was in his element and enjoying the moment, even though it was a compete fabrication. "It'll be a while before any conclusions can be reached. Even then any predictions of earthquakes are out of the scope of our work."

The eggs arrived with a pitcher of hot milk for the coffee. Sergio mixed another cup while the others dug in. He had decided to hold off any confrontation on the replacement of the Redheads. It would probably only succeed in ruining their breakfasts, which George as usual, was making short work of. He'd gotten eggs over easy. While he was mopping up with a piece of a roll secured with his fork, the conversation turned to the vagaries of Costaguana courtship. Walter decided that it would be home leave before he got to do any serious snuggling, and that couldn't come soon enough. "As soon as this job is over," he said in answer to Sergio's question.

Sergio looked at his watch: seven thirty-five. It was now or never. "I hear that security guy from Tres de Mayo was up in San Miguel hiring peasants to cut brush for your operation."

It was an anguished driller who replied. "I don't make those decisions, Sergio. If the boss in the capital tells us to use those guys, then that's what we'll do. I feel badly that the Redheads'll lose their jobs. They were good at it, but. . . ." He shrugged.

"The jobs aren't the big issue," counseled Sergio. "This means you're not going to make the dogleg."

"To be very honest, Sergio, we haven't been told one way or the other. But I see your point." Sergio looked at his watch again and rose from his seat. "You're going out to see the ruins? We'd love to see them, but I guess it isn't in the cards."

"I'm afraid not." They shook hands, and Sergio started for the door. He took a few steps and turned back. "Listen, Walter. I think there's going to be trouble," he warned. "For everybody, and especially the Redheads, we've got to try to work it out. So keep me informed to the extent you feel comfortable."

"Right now, you know as much as we do, maybe even more."

MARIA LUISA CISNEROS SET THE TRAY down on Julio's desk and placed a cup of coffee before her boss and his visitor, compañera Lederer, as he had finally gotten used to addressing her.

"Thank you, Maria Luisa." Golda turned to face the young woman. "How is the widow of Sebastian Perez doing?"

"She's taking the family back to Spain. They'll be leaving next week."

"I'm sure it's the best thing. What does she have here?" Golda shrugged. "Only bitter memories."

"Yes," Maria Luisa said. "It's the best." She withdrew without further comment.

"Her parents knew the Spanish factory manager and his wife," observed Julio. "She met them once." The two discussed the situation and agreed again that it was out of their hands.

"So, you've heard from the New York textile workers?" Julio asked, getting down to the business at hand. "I hope the Nogales incident isn't going to affect this."

"No, it won't. They've had their share of violence," she assured him. "They recommended the Amalgamated Dress Makers Union, and you know, they're *quite* interested in the beneficio. *And* AIFLD has *already* contacted them."

"I guess Sergio's meeting with them in the capital paid off. What do we do now?" he asked, pushing an ashtray over to Golda as she lit up a Casablanca.

She took a drag on the cigarette, set it in the ashtray, and picked up her cup. "Fidanza has to keep up the interest of the beneficio workers. Get them to realize they can be *owners* as well as workers.

That's the main interest of the New York union. They've gotten onto some worker-owner movement—Basque, I think—and they see this as a great pilot project. They're even going to send someone down to look into it." She took a sip and leaned back in her chair. "My Luis keeps after me," she remarked, looking at the smoke curling from the cigarette. "I don't smoke as much as I used to." She shrugged. "What do you hear from Fidanza?"

"He calls a couple of times a week. But the connection isn't always that good."

"We must fill him in on the developments. But Point IV and AIFLD have the ball, so he'll have to keep on top of them." She thought for a moment. "Has he mentioned Margarita Bustamonte?"

"As a matter of fact, she's *in* Catachoclo on a short assignment. And they're supposed to visit the ruins today." Golda smiled at the news. The FLOC secretary general shook his head. "His involvement with the Redheads worries me. If it's oil, nothing is going to stop them. They'll brush the Redheads aside. I just hope Sergio doesn't get brushed with them." He got up and walked over to the window.

"It's always the danger," Golda observed. "I hope we get enough warning."

"Everything appears so peaceful," Julio said, gesturing out the window to the scene below. "The generals go back to their farms without a shot being fired. People going about their business. You'd never know we had a military dictatorship just months ago. Even the oligarchs were glad to see them go."

"That's what worries me, Julio." Golda had joined the younger man at the window. "It's as if they're expecting big things from the next government, or they have other plans."

"Well, Compañera Golda, the junta weren't the ogres they are in our neighboring country. But I get the feeling that there's a festering just under the surface."

"Nogales testifies to that," observed the doctora.

"*Exactly.*" They gazed out of the window, each mulling the consequences of these observations. "I'm going to Catachoclo," Julio said with a sudden resolve, pounding his fist into his palm.

"Good idea."

He strode back to his desk and picked up the phone. "Maria Luisa, please get me a ticket to Catachoclo. . . . By plane. Yes. On Wednesday. I feel better already," he said to Golda, replacing the receiver.

"So do I," agreed his boss.

SERGIO TURNED INTO THE ENTRANCE of the clinic and immediately spied Margarita and Sor Marillac, sitting where he'd first seen Margarita with the nun four weeks earlier. The clinic was already abuzz with activity. The postulant was interviewing the patients, mostly women with one or two children, seated on the benches along the outside corridor. The two rose and started toward Sergio. He was mildly surprised to see Margarita in blue jeans and a long-sleeved denim shirt worn outside the trousers. Rugged hiking boots, a red cotton neckerchief, and her hair combed up under a wide-brimmed straw hat, typical of the cowboys of the northeast, completed the outfit.

"Margarita is ready for the adventure," exclaimed the nun in response to what she perceived as Sergio's more than passing interest in the attire. He was similarly prepared: jeans, a long-sleeved cotton shirt, and a straw hat of the local variety, which he removed before kissing Margarita on the cheek. "*Et voilá, sandwiches à la Américain.*" Sor Marillac held up a canvas bag with a shoulder strap.

"She thinks of everything," said Margarita, taking it by the strap.

"Of course! We don't want you coming back on your hands and knees, weak from hunger. Some day *I* hope to go to the ruins," the nun added.

"But you will have to find yourself a pair of jeans," Margarita observed.

"Agh, I've been in the forest dressed like this," the nun assured her with a wave of the hand. "Besides, we are in discussion already on modifying the habit. Maybe even giving it up altogether. But go, go! Or you'll be caught in the dark."

They started across the plaza. Galo, standing next to the Jeep parked in front of the office, waved as they approached. He held up a knapsack. "Maruja prepared a lunch," he said, opening the rear door.

Margarita held up the canvas bag. "Compliments of the convent cook."

"Well, we won't starve," Galo remarked, taking the bag and putting it next to the knapsack and a canteen on the front seat "Shall I drive?"

"If you don't mind."

"THERE HE IS." GALO POINTED to the Arra'o chief next to his brother's stand. Tito, the brother, was behind the counter, and the twenty-seven-year-old cockatoo at its place at the end. They all descended from the Jeep to greet the chief. Galo began to introduce Margarita.

"We've met," she said. "It was at the first-aid station the last time I was here." Hugo smiled in acknowledgment.

"We'd better get started," said Galo. "We don't want to get back in the dark." Hugo agreed. They all mounted the Jeep: Galo and Hugo in the front, and Margarita and Sergio in the back, joined by Hugo's nephew, Pablo, who squeezed in next to Sergio. Galo drove off in the direction of the new bridge.

"It used to be an all-day trip from the other side of the ferry," observed Galo. "But with the bridge and the line cut into the forest, it should only be a few hours to get to the ruins. What do you think, Hugo?"

"One hour. Maybe one hour and half."

The Arra'o were already using the cleared path of the survey line. They encountered several Indians when they crossed the bridge. One was leading a burro, not a common sight for a Redhead. Ten minutes later, Galo stopped the vehicle at the point where the line turned to the right for the transect. If all had gone well it would have been the beginning of the dogleg. It appeared at the moment that was not to be. As they descended from the Jeep, three Redheads emerged from the edge of the forest. Hugo made introductions. The names were hardly distinguishable, and none of them spoke Spanish. But they smiled, displaying missing front teeth. Hugo said that two of them would lead and clear whatever was necessary, and the third would take up the rear, keeping an eye out for animals. Sergio and Galo looked at Margarita.

"Don't worry about me," she remarked. "It can't be any worse than the bulls on the ranch." They didn't pursue it further but grabbed the provisions from the front seat. A few words from Hugo, and the rear guard took charge of the knapsack and Pablo the convent pack. Before there could be any other discussion, Galo slung the canteen over his shoulder.

The two cutters had already disappeared into the forest. Hugo led them to the point where they had entered. They had obviously been working for some time before the arrival of the others, perhaps even a day or two and were still out of sight. The path was relatively clear. They turned abruptly to the left; in a minute, there was no sign of the drilling road. They were on a moderate descent. The sound of machetes hacking vines and low branches rose from up ahead. Otherwise the stillness was interrupted only by the occasional screech of monkeys making their way from treetop to treetop. The path dodged around the larger trees, and they had to step over some low branches. In twenty minutes they had caught up with the cutters who were standing in a path about two meters at its widest and surprisingly clear of underbrush and low branches. It was the main access to the ruins. They all stopped for a rest. The cutters, who had disappeared into the forest, reappeared with four papayas, which they quartered and offered to the others.

Refreshed, they continued the trek. The going was considerably easier. Although the ground was relatively clear, the forest enclosed the path overhead so that they never had a clear view of the sky. The way continued downhill until they reached a swiftly flowing stream about seven meters wide, crossed by a crude bridge: a tree trunk about twelve meters long supported on abutments, consisting of cribs of logs. A railing of sorts provided a measure of security. The path continued on a gradual ascent.

Then, without warning, they found themselves at the edge of a clearing.

A logic-defying scene unfolded before them. The foreground

was in shadow, but the intact arch in the far wall of the main structure dazzled in the late morning sun. The low ruins of the remaining walls, and those extending out from them had been
meticulously cleared of all growth. The lower branches of the
trees had been trimmed to about ten meters, permitting an unobstructed view. They stood at the edge of the clearing, the newcomers gazing in silent awe at the sight. No one spoke. After a
minute or two Hugo motioned them forward. They walked down
a slight decline to the wall of the main structure across from the
arch. Hugo invited them to accommodate themselves on the wall.
The three found a relatively even area, and the others sat on the
ground with their backs against it. It seemed for a moment that
even the animals were quiet. After a few more minutes of silence,
Hugo started a chant that was picked up by the others. Sergio
and Margarita looked at each other. The Indians were singing in
Arra'o, but the melody was vaguely familiar. The song lasted a
minute or two. When it ended, Pablo rose and walked to the arch.
He genuflected and made the sign of the cross. Hugo arose and
turned to the three. "Thank you," he said. He put his arm around
his nephew, who had returned to his side, and added, "Pablo
Christian like mother." And then looking at the bags of food, he
asked, "You want to eat?"

Two fallen tree trunks were found at the edge of the clearing.
They sat on the makeshift benches and laid out the provisions. The
Redheads produced a sackful of tamales. By coincidence Maruja had
also prepared tamales. The convent cook's contribution was four
baguettes stuffed with cheese, and a half dozen pineapple slices. The
two cutters disappeared into the forest. The Redheads peeled back
the cornhusks from the tamales and began eating with gusto. Sergio
and Margarita chose baguettes. "I'm going to try one of *those*
tamales," said Galo, indicating the Redheads'. "I've had them before.
They're *very* spicy." After his first swallow, he breathed in quickly
and reached for the canteen.

"Here," said Sergio, handing him a baguette. "It's better than
water." Without a word Galo bit into the sandwich. A few minutes
later he was finally able to speak.

"Ooo-*ooh*! That was hotter than *I've* ever had!" he exclaimed.

Hugo had been watching. Pablo and the rear guard could hardly contain themselves. "Spanish have soft mouth. Not like Arra'o," Hugo remarked, sticking out his tongue. The chastened Galo contented himself with his wife's tamales. He offered one to Hugo, who politely took a bite. "Good," he observed, "for soft mouth."

The cutters returned. One of them, who was carrying a stalk of bananas balanced on his head, placed it on the ground, trimmed off several hands of the short fruit, and offered them to the others. Galo was the first to peel one and take a bite. "That'll help put out the fire," observed Sergio, finishing his baguette. Galo offered the canteen to Hugo and the other Arra'o. They declined. They had drunk liberally from the stream they'd crossed earlier.

Galo looked at his watch. "I guess we'd better get going." Hugo agreed. They threw the remains of the meal into the brush behind the logs and prepared for the trip back. Returning to the wall opposite the arch, they stood silently. After a minute or two, Pablo walked up to the arch and again genuflected and made the sign of the cross. Then they left.

"I LOVE THIS TIME OF DAY." He said it almost to himself. Not in the habit of expressing feelings, he lived in a world of issues: wages, working conditions, grievances—things he felt strongly about, things he could articulate at a union meeting or at a confrontation with the bosses. But this feeling was stronger than the union issues, when he thought about it. Why had he never said it before? The one to whom he *had* said it was holding tightly to his arm as they walked up Calle Sulaco. She pulled him even closer.

"I love it, too," she replied. "Whenever I was out in the early evening, I would think of you."

They had reached the tree and taken seats on the bench. She was still holding his arm. He thought about what she had just revealed. "I think we should get married," he blurted.

She sat straight up and turned toward him. Her eyes narrowed slightly, and with that puckish smile she asked, "You do? Is that a proposal?"

"Margarita will you marry me?" The words came tumbling out. He had said it. No looming specter of Don Camilo: He saw only Margarita.

Tears came to her eyes. She buried her head in his chest. She could feel the beating of his heart. "Oh, yes, yes," she murmured. "I'm so happy."

He put his arm around her shoulders and, lifting her chin, kissed her. It was a gentle kiss. There were tears in his eyes, too. She sat up at the sound of voices on the sidewalk behind them, took a handkerchief from the pocket of the jeans she was still wearing, and daubed her eyes. "Sergio, we will have to elope." The stark statement brought back the specter and the reality of marrying the daughter of the ex-president. "Mamá will make it the capital's biggest party of the year." He hadn't thought of that.

"But elope? To *where*?"

"Here. In Catachoclo."

"Catachoclo?" He was confused.

"Remember? Maruja and Galo will be moving to Nicoya in three months."

He nodded as the plan began to make sense. "But elope?" No. It still was not clear.

"We have so much to think about, my darling. Besides our wedding *not* being the social event of the year."

He looked at his watch. "Maruja and Galo! We're expected for dinner." They started up the street.

"Shall we tell them the news?" asked Margarita.

Sergio thought before exclaiming in a burst of abandon, "Let's tell everybody!" A couple about to enter the Rincón turned to see the source of the outburst. "We're going to be *married*!" he shouted. The woman smiled, and the man shook his head.

"Sergio!" She laughed and squeezed his arm. "You're crazy."

"Yes! Crazy in love."

"But I must tell Mamá and Papá before we announce it to the whole world."

"Ohhh," he murmured, covering his eyes to again avoid the specter of his future father-in-law.

AFTER RICE AND BEANS and an avocado salad, the women cleared the plates and beer and Orangina bottles. Maruja brought out a coffee service. Margarita placed a heaping bowl of sweetened popcorn in the middle of the table. Two electric lights cast an intimate aura over the room. Maruja reached for a handful of popcorn. "Galo, my dear, it seems that our guests have been a little distracted this evening. I wonder—have they been completely awed by the ruins?"

"It's better than that, Maruja."

Maruja broke the silence that followed Sergio's comment. "That's it?" she asked. Sergio looked at Margarita.

"We have an announcement," she confided. "We're to be married."

"*Married?*" Maruja shrieked. "How wonderful!" She jumped up to embrace Margarita, who, rising to receive the hug, was crying. The two men embraced.

"Congratulations, Sergio. We wish you long life and happiness."

Maruja embraced Sergio. "See? I knew something was afoot."

They found their seats again. "When? And where will you live?" asked Maruja.

"If we wait three months we could live here." Margarita winked at Sergio.

"Of course. When we move to Nicoya." It had taken just a moment before the reasoning dawned on the redhead. "Except for the paintings and our personal things, the place is yours. But one painting will stay," she added, pointing to the one depicting the tree in Calle Sulaco. "That will be our wedding gift."

PADRE PHILLIPE DISMISSED THE WORSHIPERS at the ten-thirty service. "The Mass is ended," he called out, raising his arms. "You may go in peace."

"Thanks be to God," came the response from the congregation. He came around the altar where the young server, Hugo Rigpe's nephew, joined him. They bowed and processed into the sacristy. The incongruity of Pablo's red head protruding from the white acolyte's surplice was unremarkable. The congregants, who had risen at the final blessing, began to move to the main entrance. The low murmur of conversing neighbors filled the church. Several women all in black remained kneeling at the rail, where they had been since receiving communion. Others, having purchased long white tapers from the older man who had set up shop just inside the entrance, were streaming toward the painting of *Our Lady of Guadeloupe*, now ensconced in a broad, ornate recess above the newly constructed side altar. After taking a light from one already burning, heating the bottom, and affixing the candle to the large round steel plate that already contained several dozen, the supplicant would either continue to stare at the flame or kneel at the communion rail and gaze fervently at the image of the Virgin. The candle man was Juan Calvache, a charter member of the Union of Beneficio Workers. Since he had been stricken with diabetes and was no longer able to work in the mill, Padre Philippe had arranged for him to have the candle monopoly.

After the dismissal, Margarita and Sergio had moved to the side of the church. They continued down the aisle and took seats near the passage to the rectory. "It's still strange to hear the Mass in Spanish," she whispered.

"They started in Argentina just before I left," he replied, "and seemed to be quite enthusiastic about it."

"I wonder, are the marriage vows in Spanish now?" she asked. "*Then* you'll know what you're getting into."

He looked back quizzically. "When was the last wedding you were at? They're always in Spanish."

"Just testing."

They rose as Padre Philippe appeared at the sacristy door, followed by Pablo. The Redhead stopped only long enough to greet Sergio and Margarita, and was on his way.

"So, my friends, what is the important business we must discuss?" the priest asked, shaking hands. "But not here. Come into my study." They followed him through the passage. He turned and asked, "Do you want coffee?" They nodded, and he relayed the request to Maria, who had stepped into the kitchen doorway to greet the visitors. In his office he gestured to the chairs in front of his desk. "Please," he said. "Now, how may I help you?" he asked, after settling into *his* chair.

The two looked at each other. The priest waited patiently. Margarita nodded at Sergio, who finally got up the courage. "We—we want to get married," he stammered.

"Wonderful! I'm happy for the two of you." He leaned back in his chair.

Sergio turned to Margarita, whose eyes widened slightly as she inclined her head toward the priest. Sergio went on, "We want you to. . .to. . . ."

"Preside?" offered the priest.

"Yes. Yes," Sergio blurted. "That's it. Preside."

"Well, I'm honored. But neither of you is from Catachoclo. Will your family be content with such an arrangement, Margarita?"

"That's just it, Padre," she answered, and launched into a detailed account of her dilemma. The priest listened with gentle attention. When she had finished, she grasped Sergio's hand, and they waited for a response.

Padre Philippe leaned forward and toyed with the inkwell on the desk before speaking. "Sergio, what of *your* family?"

"My parents are dead for some time now, Padre, and my only sister lives in the capital. I'm sure she could not be happier."

They were interrupted by a knock at the door. Maria entered with the coffee. After setting a cup before each, she asked, "Will there be guests for lunch, Padre?"

"It will be my pleasure," responded the priest. He stretched his hands toward the visitors.

"I'm afraid," said Margarita, "that I have a mountain of work to finish here before leaving tomorrow for Nicoya. I'm going to visit a women's center there."

"I am disappointed, but I'm sure there will be other opportunities." Maria left, and they resumed their discussion.

"I understand your concerns, Margarita. I also know from what you have told me, *and* from what Sor Marillac, an ardent admirer of you both, has added, that you have known each other for some time, and that your affection for each other has been forged in a prolonged separation. I would be delighted to officiate at your wedding. For the ceremony to occur is only a matter of formalities." He waved his hand in dismissal of the issue. "What is more important is how you resolve the dilemma of your family. It may be, Margarita, that you exaggerate this problem. Yes, I know," he added at her reaction. "A woman in your mother's position would have certain fixed images of her only daughter's wedding. But what you're proposing would not be a source of scandal."

"It depends on what you mean by scandal, Padre. I'm sure my mother's circle of friends has a list of candidates for my hand. But *I* have chosen the best!" The fire in her eyes and the pressure of her hand on Sergio's said more than the words.

"Ah, yes. To be sure." The priest nodded and pondered her response. "A country wedding may be the solution," he enthused. "It will be a gala affair. The more so for the grace you will bring our humble church." He smiled at the effect the occasion would have on the community before he returned to the immediate concern. "From what you say, your father may be more open and possibly a negotiator for you. You should think about this." In conclusion, he added, "We are always ready to serve you. I hope I have been of some help."

"You have!" they both said in unison.

"I guess I have, then." They rose to leave.

"Oh, one thing, Padre," said Sergio. "Do we say the vows in Spanish?"

"Of course."

"Don't listen to him, Padre. He's getting to be such a tease."

The priest, smiling but not quite understanding the exchange, escorted them to the door. "Go with God," he said as he closed it behind them.

They stood in the entrance. Sergio turned to Margarita and asked, "Are you sure?"

She threw her arms around him and kissed him.

CHAPTER 28

Don Luis Palacios was livid. "Bumpy, there's to be a *meeting* tonight!" he shouted into the phone. "Two gringos and the secretary general of FLOC arrived on the morning flight. . . . I have my sources. They're going to present the plans for that goddamn beneficio. . . . Yes, the one I told you the gringos are building for the co-op. And they are getting that shitty union involved. I won't *have it*, Bumpy!" He emphasized the last by slamming his fist on the table. ". . . How can I be calm, when they're threatening my life's work? *And* my family's work. My grandfather built this by the sweat of his brow! . . . No. I haven't forgotten. We are ready to serve you. The men are lined up to do the clearing. It's all arranged. . . . Friday? Fine. We'll be ready."

Bumpy Cosgrove was sitting in his office at the other end of the conversation. "Luis, you should try to keep this in perspective." He winced as the response was shouted into his ear. "Yes. Yes, Luis. I *do* understand. . . . Fidanza? I know who he is. . . . Yes, I will." Bumpy hung up the phone, his face still contorted. "Oo *ooh*! Is he *pissed*. I hope he doesn't do anything—Walter, I want you to keep me informed about this business." Walter Wagner was sitting across from him. "I know it's not our business, but at the same time, with Fidanza running around, it could have a big impact on us." He looked down and shook his head. "I still can't get over him sitting next to me on that plane." He leaned back in his chair. "How's the rig?" he asked in an exasperated tone.

"I looked it over last night," Walter replied. "It's really in good shape. It was worth the extra time to do it right."

"Well, I hope so," drawled the boss. "Is it on the way?"

"Yes. They left bright and early this morning. They should be in Nicoya tomorrow night. We'll catch up with them there."

"Good. If I can arrange things here, I'll try to get down there myself."

"That'd be great," answered the young man, relieved that the next part of the operation might not fall completely on his shoulders.

THE BENCHES AGAINST THE WALL of the Beneficio Workers' Union hall had been rearranged in rows. The chairs had been moved behind a table, forming a dais of sorts. Jim Braun, Charles Wiggins, Sergio, Jorge Quishpe, Julio Chang Crespo, Andrés Puíg, and Galo Luzuriaga occupied the chairs. The union members filled the benches. The overflow lined the walls; a few spilled out into the street. The play of shadows on the stoic participants, cast by the electric light and two kerosene lanterns was worthy of a Daumier.

After Quishpe introduced the others, Galo led off the program by describing the project from the perspective of the Cooperative La Esperanza, which would be the major stakeholder. Wiggins, who described the involvement of Point IV, followed him. As Braun, in creditable Spanish, finished his description of the proposed involvement of AIFLD and the New York union, Sergio was getting more than a little uncomfortable. Except for Galo, the dry recitation of facts was not inspiring. Determined to not lose the moment, he raised his hand and was recognized by Jorge. He pulled his chair back from the table and, to even Jorge's surprise, climbed onto it.

"Compañeros!" he shouted from the elevated position. Every eye was riveted on the former secretary of the grievance committee. "As I stand before you, I see we have with us five charter members of the Beneficio Workers' Union. We have compañeros Quishpe and Puíg." He gestured to the men, sitting to his right. "And there's Compañero Juan Calvache in the first row. Juan, raise your hand." The old man raised his hand and turned partway around. "Compañero Aníbal Torres over by the door. Aníbal?" Aníbal responded by raising *his* hand. "And compañero Jaime Rivas. Jaime? Twenty-three years ago these men and seven other compañeros risked *life and limb* to meet in the rectory of San Augustin and sign the charter. Jaime and his brother, Pedro, arrived late after being severely beaten by Palacios's thugs, bent on destroying *your* union before it was *organized!*" Sergio paused for a moment. A murmur rose from the audience as the facts took hold. Galo marveled at this newly revealed dimension of his friend. Braun, seated at the end of the table, got up and moved around to the doorway.

"Compañeros!" Sergio shouted again to regain their attention. "Tonight we are beginning a process no less important than the one begun twenty-three years ago. It is the next step in the worker movement—becoming our own bosses!" Another murmur passed through them. Sergio explained very briefly the experience of the worker-controlled Mondragon Cooperative Federation in the Basque region of Spain. He managed it without losing the excitement for the cause. "We will have time to discuss and understand the details of this undertaking. What is most important for the moment is that you see yourselves as part of a worldwide movement." He raised his fist and concluded by shouting, "In the union is the strength!" A cheer erupted from the audience, captivated by the urgency of the speaker.

At that moment, Braun snapped a photo. "I hope it comes out," he remarked to the man next to him.

Before Sergio could get down from the chair, an automobile horn blared in the street. Someone shouted, "Go to the shit, Communist scum!" The vehicle roared down the dark street, stopped abruptly at the corner, and sped out of sight.

"It was the beneficio pickup," reported a member standing in the doorway. A hubbub ensued.

"Compañeros!" shouted Sergio, still standing on the chair. "Compañeros!" They quieted down and resumed their seats. "They're showing their hand, and it's *empty*. These night-time bully tactics won't work in the light of day." He reminded them again of the incident of twenty-three years before. "We know our goal is worthwhile from this reaction of the bosses. We're hitting them where it hurts, in their *pocketbooks!*" He ended by shouting again, "In the union is the strength!" He hoped the cheer he received was as fervent as the first.

Jorge rose, reiterated Sergio's sentiments, and announced that the presentation would conclude with a few words from the secretary general of FLOC. Julio rose and asked Jorge if he could make them from the floor. "I'm a little afraid of heights," he said, and then turning to Sergio, he added, "Well, little brother, I see your time in Argentina was well spent." He congratulated the members on their acceptance of the challenge, especially in light of the disturbance, and promised to make the success of the project his main goal for the foreseeable future.

Braun had returned to the dais and whispered something to Sergio. As Julio concluded his remarks, Sergio rose and announced that compañero Braun would record the moment for history. The benches were hastily rearranged and Braun took the photo. "Now everybody hold still. I don't have a flash," he said, taking the shot. "Hold it! I have to take another to fit everybody in." At that moment Rubén Castro and his wife appeared from the kitchen. She was carrying a tray with an assortment of shot glasses filled with Pistola. Her husband carried a bottle of the liquor. She passed among the participants, offering a glass to the eager members, who obviously appreciated the reinforcement. Waiting until each had downed his shot and replaced the glass on the tray, Rubén refilled them for those who had not been served in the first round.

The meeting ended at eight-thirty. In fifteen minutes most of the attendees had left. Galo, who had been discussing the next steps with Wiggins, excused himself. "I'm going to make it an early night, Charles." Jorge, Andrés, and Julio were discussing the attempt on the part of the National Chauffeurs to organize the beneficio truck drivers.

"Yes, compañera Golda informed us, Jorge. We straightened them out. They won't be trying *that* any more," Julio assured them.

"I got it about, let's see, fifteen years ago," said Jim to Sergio, who was admiring the camera. "With the bellows, it folds up, and I can carry it unobtrusively under my jacket—when I'm wearing one, that is."

"I hope that photo comes out. It's important to record these events."

"I've been pretty successful under these conditions. You just have to brace yourself. That's why I leaned against the wall. I'll send you enlargements. But tell me, Sergio." The young engineer had a worried look. "What do you make of that racket in the street before?"

"I'm sure it was Palacios's goons. It's not so much the competition, it's that the competition is from their workers. I'll bet Don Luis is steamed."

"Don Luis?"

"He's the current Palacios in charge of the business. I met him just a few days ago." Sergio turned as Jorge and Andrés started for the door. "Are you leaving?" Sergio asked. "Won't you join us for a cup?"

"No," answered Jorge. "We have to be up early." They shook hands all around and left.

"Well, Rubén, I guess the party's over," said Sergio to the beneficio grievance committee chairman. "We'd better let you close up."

"We can prepare some coffee, if you'd like."

"No, thank you. We'll be going." The four remaining took their leave. They were all staying at the Sulaco and started down the street. Braun stopped for a moment and gazed at the stars, glittering in the black, clear, moonless sky. The street lighting had not yet been extended to the sector. Sergio said he would see if Rubén had a flashlight.

"*I* have one," said Braun, pulling a pencil light from his pocket.

"You must have been a pioneer," remarked Julio.

"Pioneer?"

"I think it means *boy scout*," offered Charles.

Fifteen minutes later Sergio and Julio were sitting by themselves at a table in the candle-lit dining room of the hotel, sipping coffee that Carlos had managed to produce. Wiggins and Braun had turned in. "Braun was disappointed that he couldn't visit the ruins," observed Sergio. "I told him that he should leave more time on the next trip."

"Well, that's all well and good, little brother, but I want a report on the developments in the romance department."

"We went to see Padre Philippe on Sunday. He's very happy for us and would be delighted to. . .preside. And I'm depending on you being my best man."

"Luz and I wouldn't miss it. It sounds like you're set."

"I guess."

"You guess?"

"Well, he strongly advised that Margarita resolve the issue with her family. He wouldn't let it stand in the way, but, in the long term, he thinks she should try at least."

"So. . . ?"

"She's going to speak to her father first. I haven't heard anything so I guess it hasn't happened yet." He chuckled. "You know, Julio, I've proposed, we're making plans, but I haven't asked her father for permission, and. . . . It's crazy."

"You've certainly got your hands full. And we haven't even gotten to the Arra'o yet."

"Yes. The Arra'o."

EARLIER THAT SAME CLEAR, MOONLESS NIGHT, Don Camilo and Margarita were climbing the cobbled lane from the Bustamante residence to El Pozo. Margarita wore her black ruana, her father a tan cable-knit sweater, against a lower but not uncomfortable temperature. Don Camilo had a case in his left hand and a collapsed tripod in his right. As they approached the grassy area of the little park, Margarita used a flashlight to augment the glow from the last street lamp. They made their way to the far side of the pergola. Don Camilo proceeded to remove the telescope from the case as Margarita recalled her first embrace with Sergio. "Shine it over here, Margarita. Margarita?"

"Oh. Sorry, Papá." He continued to attach various appurtenances to the barrel of the scope. Since her childhood, she had enjoyed these excursions to the park with him. In the early days he would set the tripod low so she could look without him having to hold her. But her encounter with Sergio seemed to have relegated stargazing to a faint memory.

"There," he said, finally. "Now, let's see what Jupiter has to offer tonight." He swung the instrument to the bright planet about forty degrees above the eastern horizon. Locating his quarry in the finder scope, he went to the eyepiece and adjusted the azimuth and elevation until he had Jupiter in view. "Ah. What a beauty!" He stood very still, hovering over the eyepiece. "Come, Margarita, see what Galileo saw. The view that changed the world." She came over, handed her father the flashlight, and gently adjusted the eyepiece to her vision. "See? The shadow of Ganymede." She had seen the moon before and shared her father's enthusiasm, but this time. . . . She stepped away from the scope, covered her eyes with her hands, and began to cry.

"My darling! What is it?" He took her in his arms. She buried her head in his heavy sweater. The tears streamed from her eyes. "Come," he said and led her to the pergola. They climbed the two steps to the platform and sat on the bench. She drew a handkerchief from her pocket and daubed her eyes. He waited.

"Papá, it was right here. I've never been happier in my life." He said nothing. She recounted the story of the reunion. She recalled the earlier days in Sulaco. They became entwined with Catachoclo and the capital; dinner with Mamá and the visit to the ruins seemed inseparable. She ended by saying, "And then we saw Padre Philippe." As disjointed as it was, he knew his daughter was desperately in love with Sergio Fidanza, and he with her, and that they would get married, and that she was sure her mother would not approve.

"CAMILO, YOU *ALWAYS* SIDE WITH HER. Do my feelings not count for *anything?*" Doña Elena Aguirre de Bustamante was sitting at the dressing table, vigorously brushing her hair; her husband was watching from a loveseat near the window of their bedroom. Both were in robes, ready to retire. He knew that the long discussion the three had had in the living room had not settled the matter in his wife's eyes. He did sympathize with her and would have been equally pleased with a wedding in the cathedral and an elegant reception in the newly completed Hotel Santa Marta. But he did not share her feelings about their prospective son-in-law. He had checked into Sergio's background soon after the incident three years before. What he learned pleased him. He would not have chosen the secretary of the grievance committee for a son-in-law, but he admired everything about him. He searched his mind for the right words. He almost found himself praying.

Doña Elena put down the brush and looked directly at the reflection of her husband in the mirror. "I *knew*, when you permitted her to attend university in the coast, it would lead to no good." She got up, strode to the bed, and sat down.

"Leny, come. Sit by me," he said gesturing to the seat next to him. "Come now. We can't go to bed with this on our minds." She reluctantly did as he wished. He took her hand as she sat next to him. She stared straight ahead. "Leny, we can be very proud of our daughter. She has become a self-assured woman who will have the world on her terms."

"I would be happier if her terms were more in keeping with—"

"Leny," he said, gently interrupting, "then they wouldn't be *her* terms."

"We don't even *know* this man," she protested.

"You've had dinner with him, and from *your* report he was quite respectable."

"That was before. . . ." She smiled weakly.

"You see. We can't have two measures of the man. On the other hand, as you know, I checked on him after the incident. He has impeccable credentials. Even Monseñor Torres had the highest praise."

"The red priest! Oh, Camilo! What are we to do?" She threw her head back.

"Leny, my darling, I want you to think back thirty-two years," he said, sitting up and looking into her eyes. "Two young people in love. Do you remember when I asked your father for your hand?" She smiled. "Yes, you remember. He was *not* thrilled to have a leader of the Christian Socialists as a prospective son-in-law. Remember? I was having dinner with your family, much the same as the night Fidanza dined with you and Margarita. After I'd made the proposal, he left the room without saying a word. And didn't return."

"But you were a lawyer. You had *position*," she countered.

"Her young man has position. He's been to university. And

most important, they're deeply in love." He paused. Elena turned away. "She's had ample opportunity to be married," he went on. "Lord knows there's been a parade of suitors. Now we know why they were all rejected."

She looked back again and shrugged. For the second time that evening Don Camilo had a woman weeping in his arms.

"Come, my darling," he said finally. "We'll go downstairs and have a maté with honey, like the old days."

JULIO PUT DOWN HIS CUP and, leaning his elbows on the table, looked directly at his good friend. Only the two candles between them relieved the surrounding dark. "Little brother, your business with the Arra'o really has me worried."

"Well, Chinito, it's probably the dicier of my two assignments."

Carlos appeared in the doorway. "Señor Fidanza, a phone call for you." He jerked his head toward the recently installed telephone on the front desk. "I think it's the driller boss." Sergio watched as he retreated down the hall to his quarters. "Be sure the lights are out," he said before disappearing into his room.

Wagner was standing at the reception desk in the darkened lobby of the Hotel Gertrudis in Tonoro. "Sergio, I really shouldn't be doing this, but you said to keep you informed if I felt comfortable. I *don't* feel comfortable, but I don't know what else to do. . . . In Tonoro. We'll be there Friday with the rig. And we won't be doing the dogleg. . . . I can't talk long—George'll be wondering where I am." He pulled a bandana from his pocket and wiped his brow. "Yes, but *please*, Sergio, don't tell anyone *I* told you. . . . Not before Monday." He hung up.

Sergio returned to the table. "The dice have been thrown." Chinito looked up. "It *was* the driller. The new rig'll be here Friday, and they're not going to do the dogleg."

Julio shook his head. "Now what?" Unions he knew. But he was out of his element, working with the indigenous.

"I feel sorry for the guy," observed Sergio. "He sees the problem but finds himself on the wrong side."

"Sorry for *him*? What about *you*?"

Sergio shrugged. "For whatever reason, Chinito, I feel like a by-stander, observing and reporting."

"You didn't sound like a bystander at the meeting. You really impressed me with that speech."

"Yeah, but *that* was union business. These Arra'o are something else." Sergio sat down. "I appreciate your being here, Chinito. I think it was a shot in the arm for the union. *And* for me. I knew Jorge was feeling a lot better about them getting involved." He drained the last of his coffee. "But getting back to the Arra'o. Now we know Cosgrove's plan, but we can't do anything with the information."

"Shouldn't—what's his name, the Redhead—"

"Rigpe."

"Shouldn't he know?"

"We can't tell anybody until we have a plan. If this were a union problem, we'd know exactly what to do, but—what time is it?"

Julio looked at his watch. "Ten-thirty."

"It's not too late to call Chiriboga." Sergio got up from his chair, started toward the reception desk and, as abruptly, returned to the table. "I know Wagner didn't tell me just to keep me awake tonight. I'm sure he expects me to act on it," he said, sinking into the chair. "Else, why would he tell me? He just doesn't want it to get back to *him*, and I don't want to get him in trouble." He leaned on the table and cradled his head in his hands. "We need to talk about this, Chinito."

"You had a meeting with Rigpe set up tomorrow to introduce me," offered Julio, getting his union juices roiling. "We can sound him out. You *can* tell him that the rig's due back Friday."

"Right. And we can tell him that they are planning to hire other cutters. Margarita heard that last week. We've got to get a handle on what the Arra'o are prepared to do. Right now we don't have a clue. They've done all right up to now because Cosgrove had to placate them. But now, when push comes to shove, I don't know how they'll behave." They both mulled the situation.

"You can call Chiriboga after we've talked to Rigpe," said Julio.

"Yes. We have until at least Monday before they start to drill again," said Sergio. "I guess we've got a plan. . .of sorts." He thought for a moment. "Let's turn in. We've got a long day ahead of us."

"I *am* tired," said Julio. "It must be the altitude." They each grabbed a candle from the table. The chairs scraped across the concrete as they rose. A bird let out a squawk. As the two climbed the stairs total blackness enveloped the dining room.

CHAPTER 29

WHEN SERGIO AND JULIO REACHED Hugo's brother's stand near the ferry terminal, expecting to meet the Arra'o leader, his nephew Pablo was there instead with the message that he would take them to his uncle's home.

Ten minutes later they were climbing over the transom of an eight-meter boat attached with a cable and pulley to another cable stretched across the river. Four Redheads, each carrying sacks of various kinds of produce, had preceded them and were seated in the bow. The ferryman, standing in the water, pulled the stern free of the land and proceeded to guide the boat as he waded across the river only thirty meters wide and a half-meter deep in the middle. Julio gripped the gunwale with his right hand and the seat with the other.

"Relax, Chinito. Why are you so nervous?" asked Sergio.

"I can't swim," Julio muttered, disturbed by the depth of water. In less than three minutes they were on the other side. By the time the two union men had climbed out of the boat, Pablo was waiting at the top of the embankment. They took the path cut into the slope to accommodate those, like their fellow passengers, carrying sacks of produce.

"How far is it?" asked Sergio.

"About half a kilometer," the lad answered.

"Through the jungle?" Julio looked at the loafers he was wearing.

"If the path is as good as the one out to the ruins, there won't be a problem," Sergio assured him. And there wasn't. A mat of lashed-together logs bridged the one wet area. In fifteen minutes they had reached a third clearing, this of about three hectares. The predominant crop was corn. A line of cassava plants bordered the near edge, onions and other crops unrecognizable to a former Italian farmer grew in neat sections. Two women were harvesting corn in the middle of the field. A collection of thatched-roof dwellings, each with a round wall enclosing one room about five meters in diameter, bordered the far end of the field. The path skirted the left side of it. Unlike the dwellers in the South Forest, the Arra'o had no livestock and therefore no need for fences around their homes.

Hugo was awaiting them at the first dwelling off the far corner. "Welcome," he said, reaching out for Sergio's hand.

"This is my boss, Julio."

"ICRAC?" Hugo's eyes narrowed as they shook hands.

"No. I'm with the beneficio union." The Redhead leader seemed not to make a connection but didn't pursue it further.

Pablo joined two men on a crude log bench. Sergio recognized them from the visit to the ruins. Hugo motioned for them to take seats on another log, facing the three, who then made room for Hugo. They all listened patiently as Sergio recounted what he knew about the resumption of the drilling work. He completed his report, which did not include the decision regarding the dogleg, stating only that the drillers were not going to rehire the Arra'o. He looked directly at Hugo.

"Arra'o know," Hugo said matter-of-factly. The others grunted in agreement.

"You know?" But Sergio quickly realized that, if Margarita had found out, it wasn't a well-kept secret.

"Many Arra'o still live near San Miguel," Hugo explained.

"That's where Margarita heard it," Sergio muttered to Julio. "What will you do?" Sergio asked, not with any enthusiasm.

"Earthquake men agree to hire Arra'o, if we agree to build bridge upstream, not at ferry. *ICRAC* also agree."

Sergio had wanted Galo to accompany them and was regretting

that he'd decided to come without him. "What will you do?" Sergio asked again; he had to report to Chiriboga.

"Earthquake men not cross bridge." The finality of Hugo's response alarmed Sergio, but then what alternative had they? he thought.

"Hugo, I will call Chiriboga immediately," Sergio declared, rising to confirm the urgency.

"Good," said Hugo, also standing. "You and Señor Julio my guest. First eat, then go." He shouted something at two women who were working at a communal cooking area in the center of the collection of houses. The women waved. "Please to sit." Sergio obliged, retaking his seat next to Julio.

The women carried over two large trays. One had an assortment of fruit, the other a bowl of roasted corn on the cob and a bowl of the tamales that had caused Galo the distress on the trip to the ruins. Sergio reached for the corn. Julio picked a tamale. Hugo, Pablo, and the rear guard watched Julio peel back the husk and bite into the ground corn. "Very good," he remarked, taking a second mouthful.

"Señor Julio has hard mouth like Arra'o," observed Hugo. Julio looked at Sergio.

"He's surprised at your tolerance for spicy food. It was one of *those* that nearly choked Galo on our visit to the ruins."

"Oh. Well, my father is from Szechwan, in China," Julio said by way of explanation. Hugo smiled.

"Julio, I don't think he'll ever understand."

"AND REMEMBER, JUAN, THE ARRA'O already knew they weren't going to be rehired. . . . Right." Sergio hung up the phone. "I feel a little better," he said to Julio, sitting across from him in the ICRAC office. "He's going to call Cosgrove right away, and he thinks he can bring some pressure from the Vasquistas."

"Vasquistas? What the hell are they going to do?"

"I don't know but Juan's got a lot more experience than we do in this business. He'll let me know what comes of it."

"Maybe it'll work," mused Julio. "There was never any love lost between El Dedo and the Palacioses as I recall."

"But if he gets wind that it's oil," Sergio observed, "it'll be over for the Arra'o. . . . And how could he not know? . . . Chinito, I hope this doesn't blow up in our faces."

Julio thought about that for a while. "How about Margarita?"

"Margarita?"

"I mean her father. He's got a stake in this. ICRAC is his creation, and Galo's co-op is one of the leading projects."

"You're right."

DAISY HANDED MARGARITA THE PHONE, rose from her desk, and left the office, closing the door behind her.

"My darling, I have such good news. Mamá has relented, sort of. We had a long talk last night. But at breakfast she was suggesting that the wedding could be in Nicoya. You know, Sergio, *that* would only be a *little* smaller than if it were here in the capital. But Papá came to my rescue." She paused, expecting a reply. There was only silence. She suspected that he was not alone. "Is there someone with you?" At his answer she could almost feel the heat from his red face. Sergio launched into a description of the encounter with Hugo and his conversation with Chiriboga. She listened intently, trying not to be distracted by the truncated discussion of their wedding plans. He concluded with a proposal that she see if her father had any advice or could do anything. She wrote down the number of the Hotel Sulaco and then said, "I love you, darling," before hanging up.

She sat looking at the pad with the number. A knock at the door was followed by Daisy discreetly peeking in. Seeing her officemate off the phone, she entered. Margarita buried her face in her hands. "Margarita, is there bad news?"

"Not really. . . . Daisy, I'm so worried."

SERGIO HUNG UP THE PHONE. "Chinito, I'm a very lucky guy." He thought for a long moment, staring at the empty cup on the desk, before he said, "I guess we've done all we can."

"What are you going to tell the driller?"

"Yeah, Wagner. They'll be here tomorrow." He paused. "The

only news we have for him is that Rigpe isn't going to let them over the bridge. What do you think?"

"I think telling him will only get the bullies prepared. Better not," Julio advised. "But then," he added, "they'll find out anyway from Cosgrove after Chiriboga speaks to him."

"We'll just have to see how it plays out on Monday," Sergio said, vaguely gesturing toward the phone. "I'll be there, for all the good it'll do."

"Ready to go?" The question had come from Galo Luzuriaga, standing in the doorway.

"Just about," Julio answered. The two rose to greet the visitor.

Galo came over to the desk. "I'm sorry I couldn't make it this morning. How'd it go?"

They resumed their seats and Sergio summarized the events, ending with the calls to Chiriboga and Margarita. "We've decided not to tell Wagner what Rigpe has in mind."

"There's not much else you can do."

"Well, I guess you want to get going?" Julio asked.

"Yes," answered Galo. "If we leave now, we can be in Nicoya before dark."

"Little brother, I feel like a rat deserting the ship," Julio said, embracing his friend.

"Hey. What can you do now? It's just wait and see. Like I said, 'Observe and report.' Where's Maruja, Galo?"

"She's chatting with Juanita. Getting practical advice from a mother of three. We'll get the professional advice in Nicoya. We're seeing an obstetrician Dr. Saenz has recommended."

"Good. Give my regards to Señora Saenz and Gloria, if you see them."

"We're planning on it. I have a letter for Gloria."

"Of course. And Julio, on to the capital?"

"I'm meeting with Braun's boss. Gotta keep the heat on those gringos."

They descended the stairs to the reception area. Galo introduced Julio to his wife. After shaking hands with him, the irrepressible redhead turned her complete attention to Sergio. "And what news from Margarita?"

"It's all good, Maruja. I'll fill you in when you return."

"Ooo! Must I wait till then?"

"If we wait for the news now, we won't get to Nicoya until midnight," her husband chided. They moved outside, and after loading Julio's bag into the back of the pickup, they all squeezed into the front and took off.

Sergio returned to his office followed by Pedro with a fresh cup of coffee for him. He felt strangely alone.

AT FIVE IN THE AFTERNOON JUAN CHIRIBOGA, ICRAC's deputy director for colonization, and the attorney Felipe Krueger, were sitting at the conference table in Bumpy Cosgrove's office. "I'm glad you could meet with us on such short notice, Señor Cosgrove," Chiriboga said as the Texan took a seat across from them.

"Always glad to oblige. . . . When I can," Cosgrove replied with all the graciousness he could muster. "I've asked Licenciado Ribadeneira to join us. He should be here any minute." Juan glanced at his watch. "But you can get started. If there's any matter requiring his input, we'll just hold off until he arrives."

"Señor Cosgrove," Juan began, "it has come to our attention that the Arra'o *themselves* have heard that they are not to be rehired to clear the survey paths."

Having been assured by Palacios that they were going to be more discreet this time around, the revelation caught Bumpy off guard. Without waiting for additional comment, he launched into a response that was uncharacteristically off target. "Señor Chiriboga, the people who are paying for this survey are anxious to see it completed. As I mentioned the last time we spoke, we've been delayed by a rig breakdown. We have to make up the time lost. *And* I still haven't been given an explanation for the error in—"

"Señor Cosgrove," Krueger interrupted, "there are two issues here. *Regardless* of where the ruins are located, the contract with the Arra'o specifically states that, in return for permission to build the bridge at its present location instead of at the ferry, the Arra'o would be hired to clear the survey paths." The attorney waited for a response. Bumpy's icy stare was all he was going to get, so he continued. "Since the performance of the Arra'o is not a factor, we can only conclude that you are not going to make the—how you say '*dog-leg*'?—but rather proceed on your original plan."

"Which brings us back to the other issue," Bumpy snapped. "We're going on the agreed-to boundaries."

"You'll be encroaching on the—"

"The ruins be damned! We're movin' ahead."

"Señor Cosgrove, as the representatives of the Arra'o, we cannot accept your position," Chiriboga said flatly, hoping to salvage some concession.

"You may represent them Redheads, but we're here by agreement with your bosses, the Ministry of the Interior." Bumpy pressed his hands down on the table, his anger palpable. "In my conversations with the minister, he's made it very *clear* that this is a *most* important project, and that we are to let *nothing* stand in our way."

"The minister of the interior is *not* our boss, Señor Cosgrove. We report directly to the president." Bumpy glowered but did not comment.

"Señor Cosgrove," Krueger observed dispassionately, "I don't understand how a. . .*seismic study* can be permitted to trample on the rights of our people."

Bumpy, jaw set and eyes straight ahead, rose, and said, "I don't think we have anything else to discuss."

The two ICRAC men rose and strode to the door. When they opened it, Alfredo Ribadeneira was standing there ready to knock. The two nodded to the licenciado and proceeded through the reception area and out of the office. Bumpy waved the lawyer in, motioned him to the chair in front of his desk, and closed the door. Without a word he took two glasses from the credenza. He sat down, opened the desk drawer, and extracted the bottle of Johnny Walker Black. He poured himself three fingers and held the bottle up to his guest. Ribadeneira nodded. After pouring a generous shot for the lawyer, Bumpy took a long pull on the whiskey. "We're going ahead as planned, Alfredo. Just you make sure our friends at the Ministry of Hydrocarbons are informed."

"MINISTRY OF THE INTERIOR INDEED," snorted Krueger. "You can see Hugo Puentes over at Hydrocarbon's hands all over this."

"Taxi!" shouted Juan. The cab screeched to a halt in the middle of the street, and the two got in. "Avenida Bolivar, Twelve."

"A popular destination these days," remarked the driver.

"I'm sure," responded Juan, and then to Felipe, "Yes. Interior is just a front. It's amazing how much we've put together in the past month, but still no—how do the gringos say it?—*smoking gun*."

"You think El Dedo will want to do anything? For my part Don Camilo would be a better possibility."

"I strongly suspect that that route is being pursued by his daughter."

The two descended from the taxi in front of an elegant home of post-reunification vintage surrounded by a two-and-a-half-meter, plastered adobe wall topped with embedded shards of glass and towered over by four eucalyptus trees. At the entrance gate, Juan proffered his business card to the police officer, who waved them in. A functionary, dressed in a dark suit and somber tie, received them at the door and ushered them past groups of hangers-on to a study at the rear of the house. "El Presidente will be with you shortly," he announced, and left, closing the door. The honorific was a lifetime accoutrement, as was the cabal of Vasquistas ever ready for political mischief. Whether the cabal used El Dedo or El Dedo used the cabal was a question for future historians. For the present, Costaguana was bracing itself for another ride on the political merry-go-round, to which the group they had just passed bore ample witness. Conspicuously absent was the military, whose lack of respect for El Dedo was said by some to be the country's saving grace, having delivered him from office in three of his four presidencies.

A desk, slightly large for its surroundings, dominated the study. The bookshelves were filled, attesting to the man's earlier pursuit of a doctorate in political philosophy at the Javeriana University in Bogotá. His full-length portrait in presidential sash hung on the wall opposite the desk. Juan and Felipe were still standing when the door opened and the twenty-fourth, twenty-sixth, twenty-ninth, thirty-second, and candidate for thirty-fourth president of Costaguana entered. He strode over and vigorously shook their hands. He seemed even taller in person. "Please, be seated." His gaunt visage betrayed no feeling. "Señor Chiriboga, we have met, have we not?"

"Several times, Señor Presidente. This is my colleague, Licenciado Krueger."

"And this is my secretary, Aníbal Robles," said the former president, presenting the person who had accompanied him into the study. He gestured again to the chairs in front of the desk and took his seat. The secretary remained standing to his right. "Well, Robles tells us there is some trouble with our friends the Arra'o in Catachoclo. Wonderful people," he observed, and went on to extol the virtues of the tribe and their industry in developing the parrot and monkey trade now these many years. "We were thinking that ICRAC should promote the singularity of these people to the visitors to our country. Who else of our neighbors can boast of such exotic indigenous? As we were saying to the Minister of the Interior, it would be a boon to the valley. What do you think?"

"An excellent idea, Señor Presidente, but I'm afraid it won't help their current crisis," responded Juan, bringing the conversation back to the problem at hand.

"Oh?" The president glanced at his secretary. "And what might that be?"

Juan briefed the former president on the history of the seismic study, the arrangements that had been agreed to between the driller and the Arra'o, the error in the location of the ruins, and the decision by the driller to hire others to clear the lines for the study. He ended by stating, "The Arra'o have made it clear to us that they will refuse to let the drillers on their land."

The old man turned to his secretary, who bent over and murmured something to him. "To be sure," he began, "this is a delicate matter. On the one hand, our indigenous are simple folk and deserve our protection, but—"

"Excuse me, Señor Presidente," Juan interrupted. He was determined not to let the candidate off the hook. "The Arra'o are quite aware of their rights and their predicament. They are looking to ICRAC to represent them, but they are determined not to let the study proceed except on their terms, or better put, on the terms to which they have agreed."

Again the secretary mentioned something, at which the candidate said, "Robles tells us that we have a trip planned to Entre Montes Province week after next. It will be an opportunity for us to see first hand the situation."

"I hope, Señor Presidente, that the problem will not have been settled by that time to the detriment of the Arra'o."

"To be sure, Señor Chiriboga. If there are any developments, do let us know. You can speak to Robles here. He will see that we are kept informed." At that he rose, indicating the end of the interview.

"A waste of time," growled Krueger as the front door closed behind them. "I'm sure he knows about the oil."

"Maybe," said Juan. "But he also knows that he can't be *too* cavalier about this. . . . However," he added after some reflection, "the prospect of oil *will* carry the day. We can only hope to get the best deal for the Arra'o."

THE DAUGHTER OF THE THIRTY-FIRST PRESIDENT of the republic had just entered the house in El Placer. "In here," came the voice of her mother from the living room. Doña Elena was seated on the sofa. Don Camilo had just added a piece of eucalyptus to the fire. Margarita bent over and kissed her mother on the cheek. She turned to her father. He immediately sensed the tension in her embrace. "Margarita, dear, your father and I have just been discussing the wedding and—"

"Mamá," she interrupted, "there've been some developments in Catachoclo that are even more important."

". . .Oh?"

"Yes. I spoke to Sergio earlier this afternoon. The drillers are not going to respect the ruins. There's going to be a confrontation." Don Camilo led his daughter to the sofa and seated her next to her mother. "I'm so *furious* at our treatment of these people," she finally exclaimed, pounding her fist into the seat cushion. "Like trees in the forest. Cut down and burned when it suits our needs." She threw her head back against the sofa. "Papá, what can we do?" Anger momentarily distracted her from her concern for Sergio.

He stroked his forehead. "The army will be of no help," he said. "It's better they stay out of it. The Carabineers. I'll call Comandante Soto."

"The Carabineers?" Margarita exclaimed. "They didn't even interfere when Palacios's thugs burned that peasant's house in the South Forest last month. What will they do when he has his little army leading the charge? Oh, Papá, it looks hopeless."

"It's not hopeless, my dear, only a little dark." Don Camilo, not one to mull a situation in which possibilities of action were limited, chose what to him was the obvious. "Perhaps I should have a talk with your Sergio. Do you know how we can contact him?"

The simple declaration energized Margarita. She looked at her watch. "He may still be in his office."

"Good. Let's go into my study." He rose and turned to his wife. "Will you join us, Elena?"

"I think not, Camilo. I'm not too helpful in these matters. But please give Señor. . .give Sergio my fondest regards."

Margarita hugged her mother. "Thank you," she whispered and hurried to join her father.

"Señora?" Consuelo had appeared at the door as the two left.

"We will have to wait dinner, Consuelo. But please, bring me a maté. . .with honey."

"I WILL, SEÑOR PRESIDENTE. Thank you very much for calling. . . . Margarita? . . ." Sergio turned in his seat to face the dark street below the window. "Thank you for arranging the call," he said softly. "It's always good to have the benefit of experience. . . . I will, darling. I love you, too."

Sergio hung up the phone and turned back to Jorge and Andrés, who had come about the new beneficio just before the call from the capital. "Don Camilo has always been supportive of our efforts," commented Jorge. "I'm sure he was of help in this affair."

"Well, he points out that I have the authority but, unfortunately, not the power. He also thinks that no one will be running down to

Catachoclo on *anyone's* behalf. They'll let it run its course." The chair squeaked as he leaned back. "Only if there's some head knocking or bloodshed will somebody put in an appearance."

"The Arra'o know how to take care of themselves," remarked Andrés. "And they outnumber those Palacios henchmen."

"That's the trouble," observed Sergio. "It will take brute force to dislodge the Arra'o."

"Will they expect them to block the bridge?" asked Jorge.

"I'm not sure. Chiriboga told Vasquez, and Don Camilo was going to call the comandante of the carabineers. So one way or the other, it will probably get back to Cosgrove. I'm not so much worried about what happens Monday," Sergio said. "It's Tuesday that will be trouble. And I suspect Luis Palacios will be giving the orders."

"Not the driller?" asked Andrés.

"Wagner doesn't have the experience. Besides, Palacios is supplying the cutters. He's in it up to his ears. *And* probably knows it's oil."

"Anybody home?" The voice had come from the reception below.

"We're up here," Sergio called back. "Who the devil can that be?"

Victor Hugo Ramirez, *El Porvenir* stringer, appeared at the door. He removed his jipijapa and crossed the room to join the group.

CHAPTER 30

WELCOME. DO COME IN." Padre Philippe's broad smile gave a needed lift to Sergio's spirits. The priest showed his guest into the study and took his seat behind the desk. "To what do we owe this visit? Good news, I hope."

"Well, yes. There is very good news, Padre. At your suggestion, Margarita spoke to her parents. Her father first," he quickly added. "He was quite supportive. Doña Elena needed more convincing, as

Margarita made clear in our meeting with you."

The priest thought of her original concerns, which seemed to have considerably abated. "Of course," he observed. "A mother always has a greater investment in her daughter's well being, at least as she perceives it. So, have you set a date?"

Sergio leaned forward; his demeanor turned somber. "Padre, Catachoclo is not going to be a pleasant place for a while. There's going to be a confrontation between the Arra'o and the drillers."

"They're ready to resume drilling?"

"The replacement rig is expected to arrive later today. The Arra'o will not be rehired to clear the lines. And the driller is under orders to proceed as originally planned."

"That *is* bad news. Does Rigpe know this?" the priest inquired.

"He knows they're being replaced by peasants from San Miguel, so they intend to prevent the drillers from crossing the bridge."

The priest exhaled through puffed cheeks. "I don't know what I can do, but I *am* at your service."

"Thank you, Padre. You don't happen to have any influence with Don Luis?" Sergio asked, smiling at the unlikely prospect.

"Except for calling down fire and brimstone, which isn't my style, and he wouldn't care anyway, I'm afraid not. The last time we spoke was when he attempted to bring in non-union workers about three years ago, just after the military took over. He thought he was going to get their support. But it turned out that the junta didn't want any trouble in some backwater to get out of hand."

"That's what we're likely to get now," said Sergio. "And this time it's oil, not coffee."

"Yes. That will make all the difference." The former worker-priest was feeling the call to the barricades. "Listen, Sergio, I'll go wherever you want me."

"Thanks, Padre. Perhaps you could put in an appearance at the bridge on Monday morning. I think it will be important to have witnesses."

"I'll be there."

"I feel a lot better now," Sergio said as he rose to leave. When he got to the door, he asked, "Can I get to the clinic through the back? I want to see Sor Marillac."

"Of course. I'll show you the way," the padre replied, leading his guest to the rear of the rectory. "And I anticipate with great pleasure presiding at your wedding."

The nun had just finished instructing a mother on administering aspirin to a feverish child when she spotted Sergio. She admonished the woman on the dangers of giving too many pills, stroked the child's cheek, and promised to remember them in her prayers. The mother grasped the nun's hand and kissed it before taking leave. "Fidanza," she called out. "Over here." She took Sergio's hand and ushered him into the office. "What news of Margarita?" she asked, clearing a chair of file folders, which she put on the already-overcrowded desk. "Please, sit down."

Sergio regarded the nun. After Margarita, his sister, and Chinito, he felt the strongest connection to her. He had admired her work with the porters on the wharves in Sulaco and the work at the clinic, but what clicked with him most was her joyousness. He and Margarita had each remarked upon it. And though she hadn't actually brought them together, she certainly was a strong link between them. She enthused as Sergio described Don Camilo's support and the resolution of the mother's concerns. She was ecstatic when Sergio told of their plans to have the wedding in Catachoclo. "*Ici? Magnifique!*" she exclaimed. "My sisters will sing for the liturgy."

Sergio thanked her for her thoughtfulness. "But, Sor," he cautioned, "there is a problem. The situation with the Arra'o is not going well. There will be a confrontation with the drillers and Palacios," he explained.

"*Alors*, what can we do?" she asked, crestfallen.

"Nothing, I'm afraid. Padre Philippe will be at the bridge, but only as a witness."

"But we can pray!" she declared, not to be left without recourse.

YES, PRAY, HE THOUGHT. The irrepressible Sor Marillac had once again lifted his spirits. He was sitting under the tree in Calle Sulaco, reminiscing about the precious moments he'd spent in that very spot over the previous month. He could finally admit to himself that the three years in Buenos Aires had been the loneliest of his life. Although he'd thrown himself into his ORIT assignment, which even included a trip to New York City, the truth of the matter was that after a day's work, be it the endless meetings with the local union leadership, the occasional embassy cocktail party, or one of the more exciting labor demonstrations, he'd still end up in his lonely studio apartment. That chance meeting in this Costaguana backwater had all but erased these thoughts from his memory.

The street had been deserted in the noonday sun when two peasants, trotting by on horseback, brought him back to Catachoclo, Redheads, and the Palacioses. He'd exhausted all possible plans of action. He did not like the position that he found himself in. There was really nothing to do but wait: wait for the drillers to arrive, wait until they attempted to cross the bridge on Monday morning, wait for the reaction of Palacios, then, and only then, might he be able to take some action. The worst was that there was no one to wait with.

COMPAÑERO CHANG CRESPO! It's good to see you." Jim Braun rose to greet his visitor. "Be so kind as to seat yourself."

"Sergio sends his regards," said the FLOC secretary general, taking a chair facing his host.

"How's it going with the Redheads?" asked Braun, taking his seat behind the desk. He'd developed a fascination with the Arra'o ever since he met Hugo Rigpe.

"Not good."

"Oh?"

Julio explained. "So, you see, it's likely that *everyone* knows that the Redheads are going to try to prevent the drillers from crossing the bridge."

"Now what?"

"We wait and see." Julio paused as the import of what he'd just described sank in and then added, "Nobody's going to come to the aid of the Redheads." He shook his head. "When you think of it, it's rather depressing. And Sergio's in the middle of it. I should've stayed with him," he added, suddenly rising from his chair as if he were going to leave immediately for Catachoclo.

Sensing the concern, Braun pointed to the telephone. "Do you want to call him?"

Julio fished his wallet out of his pocket and read the number of Sergio's office from a piece of paper. After dialing, Braun handed over the receiver. "Juanita? . . . It's Chang Crespo. Is Sergio there? . . . Would you please tell him to call me at. . . ." He read off the number Braun pointed to on the telephone. "Yes, thank you." He hung up. "He hasn't returned from lunch."

"Lucha our secretary will let us know as soon as he calls. Meanwhile let's see if John's here yet." Julio followed Braun downstairs and into the office of his boss, who had just arrived from a meeting with the labor attaché. Introductions were made, coffee ordered.

"I'm glad we've finally met, Julio. I've heard a lot about the work of FLOC, and we're looking forward to collaborating on the new beneficio. Has Jim told you of the interest in Washington?"

"I thought I'd wait until we could discuss it together. Meanwhile, Julio was bringing me up to date on Catachoclo. There's going to be a confrontation between the Redheads and the drillers," Braun added. Before Julio could comment, Lucha Pallares was at the door, announcing a call from compañero Fidanza.

"Put it in here, Lucha," said John. A moment later the phone rang. John handed the receiver to Julio. After inquiring about the situation, he listened as Sergio brought him up to date.

". . .Okay, little brother," Julio finally said. "It looks like you've got the pieces in place. Let me know what the drillers have to say. . . . I'm staying with Ricabarran. You can reach me there. . . . Yes, I will. Chao." Julio handed the phone to John and added, "He sends his regards."

"How does it look?" asked Braun.

"Well, he's heard from Presidente Ponce. Not too helpful. *He* believes that *no* one will come running down to Catachoclo unless blood is spilled. Padre Philippe will be with him but just as a witness to the affair and maybe to keep Palacios on good behavior." He smiled wryly at the thought of Palacios backing down because his pastor was in attendance. "There's nothing much either can do. There's nothing *anyone* can do." They all silently contemplated the situation.

"How will this affect the proposed beneficio?" asked John.

"Directly, it won't," replied Julio. "It will probably make Palacios a little meaner, but he's already—let's say the man is not going to take it lying down. And *we* should continue like it's our top priority, which it is."

"Good! We're ready," John observed and added, "Jim, what can we tell our compañero here?"

CHAPTER 31

A T FIVE-FIFTEEN SERGIO ENTERED the street and headed toward the plaza. "Good morning, sir. The tomales'll be ready in a minute." The voice had come from a woman fanning the coals under her grill as she readied herself for the breakfast crowd.

"I have an appointment at five-thirty," Sergio answered.

"What a pity." She smiled as she increased the speed of her fan.

The Salsipuedes was still shuttered as he passed. But at the plaza the bus terminal was already a focus of activity. Passengers were handing suitcases, crates, baskets, and all manner of containers to the man on the roof. A skinny dog had been working the crowd for breakfast, to no avail. Sergio rounded the corner, passed the church, and mounted the steps of the rectory.

"Come in! Come in!" Padre Philippe beckoned. He passed the priest, who glanced up and down the street before closing the door and ushering his visitor into the dining room. A breakfast had been laid.

"We shouldn't delay too long," Sergio observed.

"Agh! A cup of coffee? We must fortify ourselves."

"Yes. I'm sure the drillers will have theirs." They helped themselves to coffee and rolls.

"Any new developments, Sergio?"

"No. Walter was tight-lipped when he showed up Friday evening. I haven't pressed him." Sergio absentmindedly buttered a roll. "He's in over his head," he observed. "But I guess we all are." He took a sip of coffee. "The only one with a clear idea of what he's going to do is Rigpe. Everything else will be in reaction to what he does." He took a bite of the roll.

The priest took a long swallow of coffee. "Do you intend to intercede for him?"

"Chiriboga said I shouldn't, but how can I just sit by? Besides, they—I think we'd better get going, Padre."

"By all means." The priest took a last bite of roll and another long swallow of coffee before rising. They left by the front door and headed across the plaza to the alley next to Sergio's office, where the ICRAC Jeep was parked.

At ten of six the road west to the ferry was deserted. The absence of traffic permitted Sergio to drive considerably faster than was his custom. Halfway to the ferry, a car sped by in the opposite direction. The priest wheeled around. "I think it was Pedro Nuñez," he remarked, turning back in his seat.

"What could he have been doing out there?" Sergio wondered.

"He hires his car out. Sort of a taxi service."

"I'll bet it was Ramirez."

"Ramirez?"

"Victor Hugo Ramirez. He's a stringer for *El Porvenir*. He's been spending a lot of time here recently. As a matter of fact, he was in my office Thursday evening."

At the ferry Sergio pulled off the road and down the slope to Hugo's brother's stand. He got out of the vehicle and called out. There was no response. "No one," he remarked, climbing into the vehicle. As he maneuvered the Jeep back onto the road, Walter's pickup sped by.

"It's Sergio," observed George, looking back over his shoulder. "Shouldn't we talk to him?"

"There's nothing to say at this point, and I want to get to the camp." Walter kept his eyes riveted on the road, not slowing down until he approached a washout about a kilometer from the bridge. The truck lurched through it. "We've got to get that filled in, George. Bring the dozer back there while we get the rig in place," he ordered, jerking his thumb over his shoulder. Bent over the wheel with eyes straight ahead, he couldn't see the man in the jipijapa hidden behind a giant ceiba tree at the edge of the road that towered over its neighbors and was festooned with trailing vines.

"Jeez, they're there already." A dozen or so peasants were milling around a rack truck and pickup parked next to the large storage van. Walter drove the pickup over to the end of the bridge. He'd never thought of the bridge in terms of a confrontation with the Redheads. He never thought he'd be confronting his jungle clearers. Now the possibility loomed large. The bridge was a simple affair, consisting of two parallel trusses about a meter and a half deep with a four-meter wide, wooden-decked roadway attached to the lower edges. Walter had been there when five prefabricated sections were assembled and the fifteen-meter span lowered onto compacted soil abutments at each embankment. Boulders had been dumped previously at the abutments to prevent erosion.

He looked over the area on the other side. Except where his work road entered, thick growth prevented him from seeing beyond the fifteen-meter expanse sloping up from the river. The area was empty. He took no solace in the fact. He would have rather confronted them there than in the jungle. He wheeled around and parked next to the tent that served as the office.

As the two men installed their briefcases under the drafting table, Rafael shambled over from his pickup. "Good morning, señores. We are ready." The brief announcement was accompanied by an even briefer smile. He stood there with his hands shoved into the back pockets of his Levis.

"Yes. I see," Walter observed. "George, I'd better go speak to these guys." As he started off toward the group of new cutters, he called over to his own crew, who were finishing breakfast. "Nestor. Over here." Then to Rafael, "Nestor is in charge of the clearing. Your men have their own machetes?"

"Yes, Señor."

"And you know we can't feed them? Not even coffee."

"We are prepared, señor."

"WHY DIDN'T YOU SAY SOMETHING?" asked Sergio as the third man climbed into the back seat of the Jeep. "Padre, this is Victor Hugo Ramirez, the *El Porvenir* reporter I mentioned." The two shook hands and the Jeep sped off.

"I thought you might not want me around."

"Nonsense. We need all the help we can get. Actually, I should have asked you to come along when you were in my office. No matter. You're here."

"What's the plan?" asked the reporter.

"You'll have to ask Rigpe. He's the one with a plan." They had come within sight of the camp. "Palacios's cutters are here," Sergio added, pointing to the group paying close attention to what Walter was saying. He repeated Walter's maneuver, stopping at the end of the bridge. "No one."

"I suspect they're just out of sight," Padre Philippe observed. Sergio parked at the edge of the clearing near the road to town. The three got out and walked over to the tent.

Walter had already returned. "Sergio, I'm glad you're here," he said, extending his hand.

"You know Padre Philippe. And this is Victor Hugo Ramirez. . .an associate," Sergio added, and asked the by-then familiar question, "What's the plan?"

"*I'm* going to work." Walter shrugged and looked around. "And it looks like we're ready, if you'll excuse me." He strode over to his pickup, got in, backed it into the clearing, and headed toward the bridge. The rig fell into line, followed by the water truck carrying the drillers and the rack truck with the new clearing gang. Rafael moved his vehicle up alongside the drill rig. Sergio and the other two began walking toward the bridge.

When Walter's rear wheels were on the bridge, about a hundred Redheads appeared at the edge of the jungle and began running to the bridge. They assembled in a mass on the far end, extending fifteen meters on either side with Hugo Rigpe standing in the center, arms folded across his chest. Rafael jumped from his truck, opened the tool box behind the cab, withdrew a Winchester rifle, and fired a round over the heads of the Indians. Without flinching, the Redheads drew their machetes. The new cutters cowered in the back of the rack truck. Walter jumped from his Jeep and started running toward the Palacios foreman. "What the hell are you doing?" he shouted. "*Put that goddamn gun away!*"

Rafael lowered the rifle but stood his ground. "I've got orders to—"

"*I'm* giving the goddamn orders!" Walter shouted, shaking his fist in the foreman's face. Rafael looked at Sergio and the priest who had reached the two just as Walter gritted, "Put that goddamn gun *away!*" The brute stepped back to his truck, replaced the rifle in the toolbox, and slammed the lid. He turned and leaned against the door, not taking his eyes off Walter.

"I'll go talk to Rigpe," said Sergio. "Padre. . .?" He seemed to indicate that the priest keep an eye on things.

As he stepped onto the bridge he was struck by how vulnerable the Arra'o looked, armed only with machetes. As he got closer he realized how fruitless it would be to resist, but the Arra'o chief stood impassively as Sergio approached, convinced that they would stop the driller from crossing. More of the tribe appeared at the edge of the jungle. Before Sergio could say anything, Rigpe declared clearly and unconditionally, "Driller not cross bridge." Sergio glanced back over his shoulder. Padre Philippe had taken Walter aside and appeared to be helping him sort through his position. Confident the priest could keep a lid on the situation on that end, he turned his attention back to Rigpe.

"Hugo, ICRAC supports the Arra'o. You are right to demand that the drillers keep their bargain. But, please, they're armed."

"One rifle, nothing," declared the chief. "We are many," he said, brandishing his machete. "We not let driller cross."

"What shall I tell them, Hugo?"

"Tell them what we agree. Arra'o clear jungle, and driller not go to ruins." The two shook hands. Sergio started back. The vehicles had already begun withdrawing. By the time he reached Padre Philippe they were all in the positions they'd occupied before the move began.

"I convinced Walter that he shouldn't take this on himself,"

reported the priest. "He's going to radio his boss in the capital."
They walked toward the office tent. Ramirez, who had been
scribbling notes the whole while, followed behind. A generator
started up. Walter began to tune the radio stored on top of the
filing cabinet.

MADELYN, BUMPY'S SECRETARY, was at the radio in the outer office.
"He's not in, Walter. . . . I see." She seated herself at her desk and
began transcribing Walter's description of the morning's events in
shorthand. "Yes, I'll tell him you can be reached on the radio or by
phone at the hotel in the evening. . . . I will." She rose, walked over
to her boss's door, knocked, and entered. "It was Walter, Mr. Cosgrove. I told him you were out. There's a problem at the site." She
read the details from her notes.

 "Thanks, Madelyn. That'll be all. Oh, and get me Palacios at
the Cafetero Tres de Mayo."

TERESITA, THE HOUSEKEEPER at the Cafetero Tres de Mayo, ran up
the path to the office, shouting, "Don Luis! Don Luis! The telephone!" The door of the office flew open, and Don Luis rushed past
her.

 "Shit!" he shouted at no one in particular. He tripped up the
step before the entrance. "Shit!" he screamed, lurching through the
open front door. He dashed to the still-ringing telephone in his
study. "Hello!" he wheezed as he flopped into his chair, gasping for
breath. . . . "Oh, Bumpy, I'm so sorry for the delay. . . . Those goddamn phone people still haven't given me a goddamn extension in
my office. . . . Yes. Yes. I'm all right. . . . No! That communist
trouble maker and the priest?" . . . For the next minute Don Luis
Palacios listened attentively, nodding in agreement. "I understand
perfectly, Bumpy. We are always at your service. . . . I will. Be assured."

 He sat in the chair a few minutes longer, catching his breath and
contemplating his next move. "But first," he said, getting up and
striding to the kitchen and over to the sink, where the cowering
Teresita was standing. He smacked her across the head. "I've told

you a thousand times, 'Just pick up the phone and say, "Don Luis will be right with you."' Is that so goddamn hard to understand?"

General Aníbal Espinosa, Comandante of Special Forces, was sitting at the conference table in his office, poring over a map of the Valley of the Redheads, when, after knocking, a staff sergeant entered. "Don Luis Palacios on the first line, sir."

The general picked up the extension on the table. "Don Luis, a pleasure to hear from you. . . . Fine, thank you. And Doña Evalina? . . . Glad to hear it. And how is your bridge game? . . . Well, we must remedy that the next time you are in the capital. Now, what can I do for you?"

Sergio, back in his office, was describing the events of the early morning to Juan Chiriboga. "Yes. Walter is waiting for instructions from his boss. Palacios's gang left. Actually some of the cutters took off as soon as the shooting started. That thug is dangerous." Pedro arrived and set three cups of coffee before Sergio, Padre Philippe, and Ramirez. He waved his hand toward his mouth. The three nodded. "Yes, I will. Right away." Sergio hung up the phone. "He's going to call Vasquez's office." After reporting that fact, Sergio stopped to reflect on it. "I wonder what that's all about."

"Well," offered the reporter, looking up from his notes, "with the election coming up, maybe he thought that Vasquez would rather not have any unrest to distract from the issues he can stoke the masses with."

Pedro returned with a platter of rolls and chunks of cheese. Padre Philippe's eyes lit up. "Just what I need. I'm afraid these early morning adventures are better accomplished on a full stomach."

"He suggested I call Margarita and try to get her father involved," Sergio said, picking up a roll and piece of cheese.

"Margarita?" the reporter asked. "Is she the one I met at the airport a while back?"

Sergio hesitated. He had forgotten about the encounter. "Ah, yes," he replied. "She's actually Camilo Bustamante's daughter."

"Oh? Related by marriage, as I recall." He chuckled at the deception. "Well, at this point I don't think it would hurt," he said, flipping through his notebook. "I'd like to get this story to my paper. Is there a phone I could use?"

"I'll make this call, and then you can use this one. But nothing about Bustamante. Vasquez is okay, but please don't say anything about Bustamante."

"Vasquez will do splendidly," the reporter remarked, thinking of the scoop he had.

Sergio picked up the phone and dialed Margarita's number.

EX-PRESIDENT CAMILO BUSTAMANTE sat facing his predecessor *and* successor in office, José Maria Vasquez Iturralde. "It was good of you to see me on such short notice, Don José."

"Not at all, Don Camilo. It was most opportune. Not an hour ago, just before you called as a matter of fact, Robles here reported a phone call from Señor Chiriboga over at ICRAC." The old man gestured to his secretary, standing to his right. "Most disturbing news. It seems that this dispute over the location of some. . .ruins? " He furrowed his brow. "And a seismic study? Hardly an issue for a confrontation."

"If I may offer some detail. Don José, I think the importance of both has been significantly understated."

"Oh?"

"Yes. On the one hand, the ruins are most sacred to the Arra'o. The spiritual center of the tribe, if you will. Akin to our cathedrals." Don Camilo paused to let the point register. "On the other hand," he said with total conviction, "the drilling is oil exploration."

Vasquez and Robles exchanged a glance. "To be sure, Don Camilo. Only yesterday the minister of hydrocarbons, Doctor Puentes, met with us here," he announced, wanting to assure his visitor that he was quite aware of the prospects in the Valley of the Redheads. "He most generously shared the news that the latest results of the exploration are most promising. It is quite certain that we have another source of petroleum for our poor nation." The candidate for the presidency leaned forward, placing his hands flat on the desk. "Of course, any announcement must be couched in terms that

will not unduly excite the masses, and the timing is of great importance."

"I understand the delicacy of the matter, Don José. *And*, if I may
add, a confrontation at this time with the Arra'o should be avoided
at all costs."

"To be sure, Don Camilo. My very thought."

Don Camilo reflected only a second on his next move. "Time
is short," he said. "The drillers are intent on moving ahead. A call
to Doctor Puentes might be in order. I'm sure he can persuade the
drillers to honor their agreement with the Arra'o."

"To be sure, Don Camilo. Robles, be so kind as to get the minister on the phone." The secretary nodded and left the room.
"There. That should do it." The old man leaned back with a satisfied
look. "We'll deal with our Arra'o friends under more favorable circumstances." In a moment of uncharacteristic candor, he added, "A
most productive meeting."

"GOD *DAMN* IT!" BUMPY COSGROVE slammed the receiver down,
causing the bell in the apparatus to jingle. "God *damn* it!" he repeated, this time pounding the desk.

George Mitchell, seated at the conference table, looking over a
map of the Valley of the Redheads, jumped in his seat. "What was
that all about?"

"Some sonabitch's jerked the rug right out from under us. That
was Puentes over at Hydrocarbons. He says we gotta honor the
agreement with those Indians. I can't believe it!" Bumpy pounded
the desk again. "Went on about how it bein' the election campaign,
they don't want to ruffle any feathers. He jumped up from his chair
and strode over to the door. "Madelyn, get me Wagner in the field.
And then Palacios."

"THIS WILL BE CONFIDENTIAL," said the newly minted Major Bertrand
Ulloa. The staff sergeant and corporal left him alone in the day room
of the special services camp. He sat in the chair the sergeant had
placed before the radio, switched off the speaker, and put on a set
of earphones. "Present, my general. . . . Yes. Completely." Ulloa

leaned back and with eyes closed, listened without taking notes. "I know him, my general," he finally put in. "As matter of fact he was nosing around here about a week and a half ago."

Shortly thereafter, at the officers' noon mess, Lieutenants Espinoza and Torres were listening to Major Ulloa holding forth on the importance to Costaguana of the drilling on the outskirts of Catachoclo. He reported on how he'd only just heard of a confrontation that morning between the Redheads and the drillers and their team of brush cutters. "These indigenous have been persuaded by a newly arrived troublemaker that they have some intrinsic right to the land. I can only imagine what ideology inspires these types. They have nothing better to do than to create mischief." The conversation then drifted from local politics, to troop morale, to the opportunities for R and R in Cayta, to the performance of the national soccer team. But the thought of promotion to capitán was uppermost in both the young officers' minds. Both had been to Fort Benning, Georgia. Each was eager for the opportunity to impress the new major.

SERGIO AND RAMIREZ HAD JUST COME down from the ICRAC office to the reception. Spotting the porter in the kitchen, Sergio called out, "Pedro, tell Juanita that we've gone to lunch." He glanced at his watch. "I'll be back around two," he added.

"Yes, señor," came the reply. Pedro was having his own lunch with his wife and two young daughters.

Sergio and the reporter were stepping out the door when Walter Wagner rushed up from his pickup. "Sergio, am I glad I caught you. I got a call from Cosgrove," he said, shaking hands with the two men. "We're rehiring the Redheads and doing the dogleg." His relief was evident.

"That *is* good news. Come on up to the office."

"I don't have time. I've got to get a hold of Rigpe," the drill boss said, motioning toward his vehicle. "I was hoping you could help me."

"We can start at his brother's stand."

"I stopped there on the way in. There was only a kid, keeping an eye on things."

"His nephew. *He* could have helped you," Sergio added.

"Yeah. I guess," Wagner replied, looking down and shaking his head. "But I was so concerned about finding him, I came straight here."

"Well, we'll just have to go back. Ramirez, you want to come?"

"If you don't mind, I'd like to use your phone again."

"Help yourself. But we can wait."

"This may take some time."

LIEUTENANT ESPINOZA, SEATED AT HIS DESK, had been lecturing Master Sergeant Emil Rodriguez, dressed in jungle fatigues, standing rigidly at attention before him, on recent political developments. "It seems that, notwithstanding our efforts to bring some order to our country since the recent political events," he concluded, "there are some who find it in their interests to continue to spread the long-discredited Communist ideology. We want you to be aware of this and to be prepared to take action if required. And, Sergeant, we have an important assignment for you. You will lead a daily patrol in Catachoclo—starting tomorrow."

"SEÑOR FIDANZA, UNLESS THERE IS something you need, I'll be leaving," announced Juanita, standing in the doorway of Sergio's office.

"No, everything's fine. I guess we've had enough activity for one day."

"Yes, we have. And Licenciado Luzuriaga and his wife will be back tomorrow." She paused for a moment, before adding, "But it all ended well, thank God. Goodnight, then."

Sergio drained the bottle of Orangina and placed it on the desk. He had filled in Chiriboga on the events of the afternoon, including tracking down Hugo Rigpe with Wagner and giving him the news of the change in the driller's plans. Chiriboga in turn reported on his activities. The director of colonization finished by expressing his admiration for the way Sergio had handled the affair and warning him that he should exercise extreme caution. They didn't want any martyrs.

Martyrs, thought Sergio. No, he had too much to live for now. He picked up the phone and dialed the Bustamante residence. "Good evening, Consuelo. Is the señorita in?" She had just then arrived, he was advised, and would be right on. "Light of my life, how are you?" he asked when he heard her voice, blushing though he was alone.

CHAPTER 32

SERGIO AND PADRE PHILIPPE HAD DESCENDED from the Jeep and were talking at the entrance of the ICRAC office. "I appreciate your going out with me again, Padre," said Sergio. "I didn't think there'd be any trouble. *Especially* after talking to Hugo yesterday."

"Not at all, Sergio. One must be vigilant," he replied. "Situations like this can change almost without reason. But all's well that ends well."

"It hasn't ended yet, Padre. . . . What's this all about?" Sergio was looking over the priest's shoulder at the airstrip. The priest turned to see a Jeep heading in their direction followed by a personnel carrier.

Sergeant Rodriguez, neatly turned out in pressed fatigues and wearing his Special Forces black beret, sat in the passenger seat of the Jeep. Corporal Mora was driving. The second vehicle carried two men in the front and eight on benches on either side of the truck bed. The two men in the Jeep sat erect and surveyed the plaza. Mora brought the vehicle to a stop as Sergio and the priest stepped into the street. The personnel carrier squeaked to a halt.

"Good morning, Sergeant," Sergio said, leaning against the windshield frame and looking directly at him. "To what do we owe your visit?"

"Sergeant Emil Rodriguez to serve you," he replied, snapping a salute. "My squad has been ordered to make a daily patrol of the area."

"Interesting, isn't it, Padre?" remarked Sergio without taking his eyes off Rodriguez. "I've just found out that the camp exists, and now we're to get a daily visit."

"It has been reported to my commander," the sergeant went on, taken aback by the other's contentious stand, "that there was a confrontation yesterday between the company doing the drilling for the earthquake study and those Redheads." The last word had a derogatory edge.

"There *was* some misunderstanding," said Sergio, "but it's been straightened out. Padre Philippe and I have just come from the drill site. Work is proceeding."

"Glad to hear it. But we will check it out for ourselves." Rodriguez had regained some of his mandate. "With your permission," he concluded and motioned to the corporal to proceed. As the truck passed, Sergio and Philippe noted that each soldier was holding a rifle between his knees.

"He's the one," said Mora once the Jeep was underway. "I saw him at the camp a week and a half ago." Rodriguez frowned but said nothing.

"Armed to the teeth," the padre was meanwhile observing. "Should we follow?"

Sergio thought for a moment. "I don't think so. I'm sure whoever gave the orders to get the Arra'o back on board has told their commander not to cause any trouble. I suspect it's just a show of force."

"Yes, but I don't like it. It's so heavy-handed." The priest shook his head. "We've always managed our affairs without *their* help."

"I guess we've done too good a job of it."

The priest nodded. "Well, I must go," he said as they shook hands. "I've Mass at eleven. A funeral. But if you need me, Sergio, just let me know."

"YOU *TOLD* THEM WHAT I *SAID*?" Don Luis Palacios was standing at the entrance to his house, staring at a knot of campesinos gathered at the gate of the Cafetero Tres de Mayo.

"I told them, 'You didn't work, so you don't get paid.'" Rafael, next to his boss, was also looking at the group.

"Then why are they here? Who put them up to this?"

The majordomo, head of security, work gang boss, and anything else Don Luis needed, shrugged. "They've got nothing better to do. I guess they want to hear it from you."

"They'll hear it from me." Don Luis stalked over to the pickup that Rafael had been driving the day before. "Get in!" Rafael climbed in the back and was barely seated when Don Luis tore off. He blasted the horn as he slammed on the brakes at the gate. It's likely he would have run down one or two of them had it been open. He jumped out of the vehicle and immediately began to shout, "No work, no *pay*! Now get out of here, or I'll sic the dogs on you." He wheeled around, got into the pickup, and roared back up the road toward the house. He stopped at the office, got out, and motioned for Rafael to follow him. In the office he sat at his desk, and pounded it with his fist. "It's that bastard from ICRAC, meddling where he doesn't belong."

Elbows on the desk he leaned forward and covered his face with his hands for a full minute. Rafael stood motionless, looking at him. The boss finally took both hands from his face, slammed the desk again, and leaned back in the chair. "My grandfather would have known how to deal with these Communists. My uncle, Carlos— you knew him, didn't you?"

"Yes, Señor."

"He wasn't the man his father was. Nor was my cousin, Juan Carlos. We're in the predicament we're in because of *those* two." He rose from his seat and stared at his majordomo, who did not blink. "But I'm changing things. The stick is the only thing these people understand. But with some it will take more than the stick."

Rafael's brief sneer exposed the gold teeth.

SERGIO HAD TURNED TO GO into his office when he spied Galo's pickup rounding the same corner the patrol had rounded just min-utes earlier. The truck stopped in front of Sergio. Maruja's bright face peered from the passenger seat. "We're back," she exclaimed. The irrepressible redhead opened the door and greeted Sergio with a hug. "And now the news of Margarita."

"She's had nothing else on her mind since we left Nicoya, Sergio," said Galo, getting down from the vehicle and embracing his friend. "She didn't even want to stop for allullas."

"I hope you *did*," said Sergio. Maruja displayed the bag she was carrying. "Good. Well, let's get settled upstairs. Then I'll give you the news of Margarita and the drilling, which has been resolved."

"Resolved? I'm so glad to hear that. It certainly was a worry for us *and* Chang Crespo. But Margarita first," she insisted with a frown.

"Of course. I'm only teasing."

"Welcome back," Juanita called out, coming around her desk to embrace the travelers. "And how was the trip?"

"Uneventful," Galo said.

Maruja reached into the bag, extracted a package of the cookies, and handed them to the delighted receptionist. "But none for *you* until we hear all about Margarita." Sergio acquiesced. Pedro appeared from the kitchen, greeted them, and made the usual offer of coffee.

Seated around Sergio's desk, each with a cup of coffee and a package of the cookies open in the middle, the Luzuriagas listened as Sergio described the phone call from Margarita, in which she had revealed her discussion with her father at El Pozo, his defense of her interest in Sergio, and her mother's final acceptance. "*Oo!*" cried Maruja. "I'm so *happy* for you!" There was more probing into the details and enthusiastic responses to the revelations.

Finally Galo asked, "Have you heard enough, my dear?"

"No! But I will just have to write Margarita a long letter. You *men* are not very. . .very revealing."

That provoked a laugh from her husband. "Can we hear about the drilling now?"

"Of course, Galo," she said with a rare look of hurt in her eyes. "I really *am* concerned about those poor people."

"I know that, my darling." He squeezed her hand.

She quickly regained her spirit. "And Chang Crespo—by the time we got to Nicoya, he was ready to return to Catachoclo." She turned to look at her husband. "But Galo convinced him to go on to the capital."

"I thought he could be of more service there."

"Well, whatever turned it around happened in the capital," Sergio remarked and proceeded to describe events since they had left five days before. He concluded with the visit he and the padre made to the drill site earlier that morning. "Everything seemed to be back to normal: the Arra'o clearing the jungle, and the crew starting the dogleg."

"It'll probably keep a lid on the controversy until they finish the drilling," observed Galo. "But if they find what they're after. . . ."

"I know," Sergio agreed. "And there's a new complication. Only minutes before your arrival we were visited by an army patrol from that camp out past the South Forest."

"What's *that* all about?" Galo was annoyed. "They've *never* shown their faces around here."

"The sergeant said they were responding to a report of a controversy between the Redheads and the drilling crew. *And* would be making daily visits."

Maruja, who'd not had much to say during Sergio's report, turned to her husband. "Galo, I think we should be going." The joy had been drained from her.

"Of course, my darling. I haven't been thinking. You must get some rest after that trip."

They rose to leave. Sergio escorted them to the door. Maruja turned to embrace him. "I'll write Margarita." She managed a weak smile and hugged her friend again. "Take care of yourself, Fidanza." Sergio nodded.

"I'll stop back after lunch," said Galo as they descended the stairs. "I've some news of the new beneficio."

"YOU'VE REALLY GOT THE HANG OF IT, SERGIO. It was only, let me see. . .three weeks ago that you had your first lesson?" Sergio and Galo were heading south down the road through the Cooperative La Esperanza.

"Well, I've had a lot of practice. Now, it's only the coffee trucks that give me problems."

"It's just a matter of time. Speaking of which, you'll have to be thinking of getting your license. Next time you're in Nicoya, stop by the prefecture. You shouldn't have any trouble." Galo consulted the plans unrolled on his lap. "The property we have in mind is just ahead on the right." Sergio eased the vehicle off the road into a cleared area.

"I can't get it here?" Sergio asked, turning to get out of the Jeep.

"Get what?" asked Galo as he spread the plans on the hood.

"The license."

"Oh. No. You've got to go to the provincial capital. We're here." He pointed to the map. "The main buildings will be here," he said, indicating an area outlined on the map and vaguely waving in a direction south and west of where they were standing. "ICRAC made these drawings with the help of Point IV. They did a pretty good job, considering the old maps and aerial photos they had to work with."

"I hope they did a better job than the ones who drew the earthquake study map," Sergio remarked with a grin.

"I take your point. But to make sure, there'll be a survey crew here next week to lay out the property lines and general building areas."

"The Hotel Sulaco's going to be crowded," remarked Sergio. "I guess Carlos can handle it. Who owns the land?"

"The co-op. Actually, we had a community center in mind for this area from the beginning. It'll still be a community center of sorts, only much bigger." Galo rolled up the plans. "Let's take a look over the rise there," he said, pointing to the west. They started out in the direction he had indicated. The area beyond the edge of the clearing was planted in coffee. The eight-foot evergreen shrubs had recently been harvested so it was clear of brush, making the walking easy. In a few minutes they had reached the top of the low ridge and could see for several hundred meters beyond. "There. See, Sergio? That's the stream you ford farther south. We're planning a small dam and reservoir. With an elevated tank we can put in a distribution system for the members. Most of them live close to the road." The co-op manager was obviously pleased with the prospect of improving the lives of his members. The two stood there, each contemplating the future of the La Esperanza and the town of Catachoclo.

"I think you're going to miss your work here, Galo."

"You've got that right," he answered. "But I'm resigned to it. No. I think, deep down, it's time. There're a lot of reasons that make this the right time for a move. First and foremost is Maruja."

"I thought you said that the report was very good."

"It was, but she's thirty-three. We've been trying for a long time and don't want to take any chances. As you know, we'd already planned to move to Nicoya in November."

"Look!" interrupted Sergio. "A deer." The animal had appeared at the edge of the creek and waded into the water as they watched. Reaching the other side, it disappeared into the brush. "Sorry, Galo."

"That's all right. You're just a city boy at heart." They turned back to the road. "The move," he continued, "will give Maruja more exposure for her painting. There's not a big market here in Catachoclo, *and* it's going to be a new job for me. ICRAC wants me to— uh-oh! We've got company." The Special Forces patrol had just stopped next to the Jeep, and Sergeant Rodriguez was out inspecting the vehicle. Sergio put his fingers to his lips and let out an ear-piercing whistle. They both waved as the soldier turned in response. A minute later they were face to face.

Rodriguez rendered a snappy salute. "Corporal Mora, here," he said, motioning toward the driver of the Jeep, "thought he recognized your vehicle."

"Well, it *was* only this morning, sergeant," Sergio pointed out. "And this, by the way, is Galo Luzuriaga."

"At your service," the sergeant replied. "You're the manager of the cooperative?" he asked, eyes narrowing.

"Yes, I am." Galo and Sergio stood there, not saying any more.

After a moment Rodriguez said, "We'll be on our way then." Without further ado, he climbed into the Jeep, and they moved on.

"Another good reason to leave Catachoclo," said Sergio, looking at the eight armed soldiers in the back of the truck.

"If it wasn't for Arturo, I'd've felt like I was leaving you in the lurch. But he's a good man. Really knows the business."

"I know. We've spent some time together. In fact he was with me when we visited their camp." Sergio nodded toward the patrol that was almost out of sight.

A minute later the two were heading back to Catachoclo. "So we're going to be colleagues," observed Sergio. "What does ICRAC have in mind?"

"I'm going to be Chiriboga's assistant in Nicoya." Sergio turned to look at him. "I know. I wasn't too keen on ICRAC when we talked about it last month. But as I said before, it's really in our best interests. . . . But enough about me. What about you and Margarita?"

Sergio instinctively slowed down. "We spoke yesterday," he began. "I called after the dust settled to let her know that everything went well. She finally had to remind me that there were *other* important things we had to discuss. I think she was a little—"

A coffee truck had overtaken them, roared past, and sped on down the road. "Maybe we'd better wait until we get to town. I get a little distracted."

"Probably a good idea," Galo agreed.

IT WAS NOON BY THE TIME THEY HAD REACHED the building that housed their offices, parked the Jeep, and headed to El Rincón for lunch. Except at the eating establishments along Calle Sulaco, street activity was at low ebb. El Rincón was filled. Rather than walk up to El Flamenco, they took Pepe's suggestion to return in twenty minutes and walked over to the tree to wait. All the benches were shaded from the noonday sun.

"So," Galo began, easing onto the bench facing El Rincón, "Margarita was a bit annoyed at your lack of attention to the more important things. Can't say that I blame her." Sergio winced. "Hey, don't take it so seriously."

"It *is* serious, Galo."

"Of course."

Sergio leaned forward, hands clasped, elbows resting on his knees. "We talk on the phone almost every day. She writes at least once a week. I'm afraid I'm not as good a writer. But our conversations are. . .well, you know. . .friendly." Galo had decided to let it come out without any prompting, which so far hadn't been helpful. "My problem," Sergio continued, "is that when we're not talking I don't think about it. I just go on about my business."

"I know," said Galo, and added, hoping to be helpful, "I get pretty wrapped up in *my* work."

"Yes, but you have Maruja right there when you're finished for the day. When I get back the hotel, I see the drillers or I meet with Jorge, or something comes up that needs my attention, and I'm off— without a thought of Margarita."

"That happens to everybody. What *you* need is a *plan*. Now, let's review where you are." Galo swung around on the bench to face him. "One," he said, holding up his thumb. "Margarita's parents have approved. Two." The forefinger joined the thumb. "Her mother is resigned to it not being a big affair in the capital. . . . Right?" Galo asked, looking for some sign of agreement. Sergio nodded. "Okay. Three, Padre Philippe is ready."

"And Sor Marillac will have the nuns sing for us," added Sergio.

"Now you're getting it!"

Sergio rolled his eyes.

"No, no. I'm serious. *Now* you can set the *date*. There should be a lull in activities after we have the kickoff for the beneficio. Once it's set, Margarita is in charge of getting them down here, and we make the plans to receive them, have the wedding and the party, after which everyone is on their own. And you go on your honeymoon."

"How are we going to house everyone?" asked Sergio, finally taking him seriously.

"They come and go the same day. Without the big wedding in the capital, your father-in-law-to-be can afford to hire a plane." Galo was on his feet. "Let's go. Pepe's waving at us." Sergio got up, and, as the two headed for the restaurant, Galo put his arm around him. "There's nothing like setting a wedding date to get people focused. Propose this to Margarita, and your phone calls won't be just friendly chitchat."

They took their places at the table Pepe had cleared and was wiping with a cloth. "Two beers, Pepe. My friend here is celebrating. Oh, make that a beer and an Orangina."

"Thank you, Galo."

Sergio had been reflecting. "The problem is the Arra'o and the drilling."

"Sergio," Galo responded, "unless the drilling plan changes *again*, nothing is going to happen until the results are reviewed and they decide whether or not they're going to drill for oil. That's got to take enough time for you to have your honeymoon. You can check with the drillers on how long it will be before they finish the exploration."

"Set the date," Sergio murmured, staring into space. After pondering the idea for a time, he declared, "I'll do it. I'll call Margarita this evening."

"Good. That's settled." Pepe returned with the drinks and took the order for lunch. Galo lifted his glass. "Here's to the wedding!" He took a long swallow and set the glass down. "Sergio, I'm not worried about the Arra'o right now. It's that goddamn Palacios. There's no telling what he's liable to do."

MARGARITA WAS SITTING AT THE DESK in her father's study on the second floor of the Ponce residence in El Placer. She had been writing notes on a pad of white foolscap resting on an ornate blotter. Returning the pen to its holder, she leaned back in the sumptuous black leather chair, pressing the phone to her ear. "Oh, my darling," she murmured, "I am so happy. Monday. I can't wait. . . . I love you, too, my dearest. . . . I will. Goodnight." She replaced the phone on the hook and leaned back again. Her eyes reflected the joy she felt. It had been frustrating trying to settle a date for the wedding. At every turn, the tenuous situation in Catachoclo seemed to insinuate itself into their planning. Now, almost without warning, all of the obstacles had been cleared. She would be together with the light of her life in six days, and it was less than six weeks to the wedding. She finally let the tears of happiness flow.

CHAPTER 33

T HE FIRST FLIGHT FROM SULACO that Monday morning had been
crowded. It was ten o'clock before Sergio descended from the
taxi at Calle Lisboa, 357. He was wearing a brand-new tan tweed
sport coat and brown trousers. Julio's wife, Luz, had had them made
to measure based on his gray suit, which he had left with them when
he moved to Catachoclo. "He can't marry the daughter of Camilo
Bustamante with only one suit to his name," she'd declared to Julio
when he announced the news. When Sergio passed through Sulaco
on his way to the capital, the outfit had been ready, together with
two new dress shirts and two ties. The trip had included lunch with
the Tiger, after which he found out that his long-dormant credit
union account had grown to 25,000 pesos, a tidy sum for a soon-
to-be newlywed. He handed the driver the fare and, feeling quite
prosperous, a generous tip.

His sister Giovanna wasn't in the shop. He rang the bell at the
residence. A moment later she appeared at the door and, without a
word, threw her arms around her brother. "Sergio. Oh, my Sergio,"
she finally murmured, still in his embrace. She relaxed her hold and
invited him in. "Come. We have so much to talk about." She attempted to pick up his new two-suiter.

"I've got it," he insisted. She preceded him into the dining room.
He set the bag inside the door and took the chair she had pulled out
for him.

Sitting next to him, she exclaimed, "You've set the date!"

"Yes, Gigi, September 25."

"That's just a month away!" she observed. "There's so much to *do*."

"Yes and no," he replied. He explained the plan to take over the
Luzuriaga house, the small wedding in Catachoclo, the Bustamantes
and their guests, which would include Giovanna, Freddy, and Danny

arriving by plane, and the honeymoon in San Andrés.

Giovanna's excitement grew with each revelation. "I'm so happy for you, Sergio. San Andrés! How wonderful!"

"Doña Elena thought we should go to New York, or at least to Miami. But we think San Andrés will be just fine." *We*, he thought. He still couldn't get over his using the word. "And *tonight* I meet Don Camilo *and* ask for his daughter's hand in marriage."

"See? A month ago it was an impossible dream. Now it's all coming true. Remember what Papa said, 'You can stand up to anybody.' And," she added, giving her brother a professional once-over, "you need a haircut."

Sergio looked at his watch. "I have to meet my boss—one of my bosses—in an hour."

"In the center? You'll make it. Come on." She led the way out of the front door and into the shop and fetched her smock from behind a partition topped with shelves, on which were displayed various beauty products, while he settled himself in the chair. "Let's see," she mused, tucking the apron under his chin. "It was a month ago that I cut it last." She pulled the comb through his hair. "You're lucky. With your thick, curly hair you can get away with it. But you'll need another one before the wedding." She started to trim the sideburns. "I'll bring my tools—"

"That morning?" Sergio was getting nervous at the thought of a haircut an hour before his wedding.

"It'll only take me fifteen minutes," she insisted.

"We'll see."

"YOU STOPPED BY YOUR SISTER'S," said Margarita as they walked down the hall to her office. Sergio blushed at the once-over he was getting. "I love the haircut. And the tie. Very nice."

"Chinito's wife, Luz, picked it out for me."

"Well, I hope I do as well. Here we are." She ushered him into her office and closed the door behind them. "Daisy's over at the university, collecting some data." The next moment they were in each other's arms, exchanging a passionate kiss. She pressed her cheek to his. "I never thought I would be this happy." He cupped her chin in his hand and kissed her again. "You've got to see Juan," she said, disengaging herself. She pulled a handkerchief from the pocket of her skirt and daubed her eyes. "I think I'd better stay here. Can you find your way?"

"Yes. And I have to meet with AIFLD right after." He looked at his watch. "When will we get back together?"

"Pick me up here at six. We can have a coffee at the Majestic and then go home. Are you nervous?"

"Why should I be?" He shrugged. "I'm just asking the former president for his daughter's hand in marriage."

"Sergio! He's just my father."

"I know." He thought about that for a moment and said, "I think I'd rather ask the former president."

"Sergio!" she exclaimed, giving him a playful punch. "You'd better get going." After another long embrace he turned to leave.

"Just a minute," she said, turning him back toward her. She took the handkerchief from her pocket a second time and rubbed his lip. "There. Now you won't scandalize Juan."

THE TALL, WHITE-HAIRED COUNTRY PROGRAM DIRECTOR for AIFLD extended his hand. "Good to see you again, Sergio. Have a seat. Jim should be back in a minute. He went to pick up Wiggins over at Point IV."

"Thank you, Mr. Pendleton—"

"Please, call me John."

"Of course. I'm looking forward to hearing their plans for the inauguration of the new beneficio. I've just been discussing ICRAC's participation with my boss and their attorney."

"Attorney?"

"In addition to my FLOC union responsibilities, I look after ICRAC's interests in Catachoclo. That's how I'm involved with the Arra'o. As for the attorney, we have a group of peasants who have occupied land that the owner of the Tres de Mayo thinks is *his* property. But then he thinks he owns everything in the canton. And it's not like he was *pushed* off the property. It's never been worked, so these families moved on it about three or four years ago. Kruger—

that's the attorney—researched it and found that the property does indeed fall under the agrarian reform laws. Previously unused property that is occupied for at least two years becomes the property of the occupier. I have five copies of the finding," Sergio said, holding up the folders in his lap, "signed by a judge, which I will hand-deliver to Don Luis Palacios."

"You'd better not go alone," suggested John.

"I take your point. Actually the copy for the local prefect has a cover letter from the ministry of the interior charging him with the responsibility to deliver the finding to Don Luis *and* the capitán of the carabineers. And I want to be there when he delivers it to the capitán, if for no other reason than to rub *his* nose in it."

"Oh?"

"Two of his men witnessed one of Palacios's thugs torch a peasant's house and shoot his goat, without lifting a finger. So I want *him* to see where the law stands on the issue."

"Rough folk," John observed.

Braun and Wiggins entered the office, followed by Pablito, who took the coffee orders. Sergio rose to greet the newcomers, and they arranged themselves around John's desk. They discussed the beneficio in detail. Wiggins confirmed that the official laying of the cornerstone would take place on Thursday, September 16, less than a month away. John expected to be in Washington for the AIFLD directors meeting and hoped to confirm the participation of the New York union. Sergio was feeling a surge of optimism.

Wiggins excused himself; his wife was picking him up for an early movie, *The Sound of Music*. "We saw it Friday. Loved it," Jim reported.

Sergio glanced at his watch. "Are you heading to the center?" he asked Wiggins.

"No. Sorry. It's playing at Cine Norte."

"I can give you a lift," offered Braun.

"I guess we've got it under control," commented Sergio, summarizing the results of the meeting. "At least as well as can be expected anyway." They all rose to leave. "Well, John, best of luck in Washington. I hope we can get you to Catachoclo soon."

"That's a promise," the man said, clapping him on the shoulders as they left the office.

A few minutes later, Braun and Sergio were heading downtown in Braun's 1964 Chevrolet sedan. "The ICRAC office?" Braun asked as he navigated the narrow streets.

"Yes. I'm going to pick up Margarita. We're having dinner with her parents."

"Oh? Any special occasion?"

"Well, it's to formalize our engagement."

"Wow! Congratulations! Elizabeth will be delighted. She said that you were in love when we first met in Sulaco."

"Was it so obvious?"

"It was to her. She has a sense for stuff like that. And when you showed up with Margarita at El Candelabro, that confirmed it."

"We'd like you to attend the wedding. It'll be in Catachoclo next month. But you'd be on your own getting there, unless we can fit you on the plane Don Camilo is chartering."

"A chartered plane?"

"Yes. It seems the only way to get the families there and back the same day. I'll let you know how it's working out."

"Maybe we could drive down with the kids," the engineer mused. "I'm due for an in-country vacation. I'll talk to Elizabeth about it." When they reached the office of the agrarian reform institute, Braun extended his hand. "Please give Margarita our regards. Maybe we'll have a dance at your wedding."

"Thank you. That would be great."

GEORGE MITCHELL POKED HIS HEAD IN THE DOOR. "Bumpy, ya'got a minute?"

Dale Cosgrove was sitting with his feet up on the desk, reading *The History of Fifty Years of Misrule(Un Historial de Cinquenta Años de Mal Gobierno)*, by Don José Avellanos." C'mon in," he replied, pulling his feet off the desk. He laid the book down. "My Spanish ain't good enough for this."

"Better'n mine," allowed George. "I can't even get through the comics."

"Listen. *They* can be tougher," Cosgrove observed. "Sometimes I can understand all the words and still don't get it. . . . You come to any conclusions on the review we got from Clinton?"

The senior geologist took a seat and started leafing through pages in a ring binder. "Well, he says right up front that he agrees with my overall conclusions."

"Good. But will he take it to the bank?"

"He'll take it to the bank," confirmed George.

"Yah!" exclaimed Bumpy, hammering the arm of his chair.

"He thinks we might want to consider running the line back across the river. Just to tie it all together. But he's ready to take it to the bank. Yes, *sir*." George was pleased with the review they'd gotten from the head of the geology department of the Colorado School of Mines.

"Damn! That's good news," declared Bumpy, hammering the arm of the chair again. "Does he agree with your pick for the exploratory well?"

"He does." George put the ring binder down on the desk for his boss's perusal. "What're you thinking on doin'?"

"I'm thinking you and I should be goin' up to the States to make a presentation to Townsend and the syndicate."

"I'm ready. I've been hankering for a juicy, rare California burger. Now I can almost taste it."

Bumpy reached into his bottom drawer and pulled out the bottle of Johnny Walker. "This calls for a celebration." He got glasses from the credenza behind him and poured two fingers of the scotch into each. "Maybe hiring those Redheads back was the right way to go, but if the syndicate gives us the green light, they're *gone*." He lifted his glass.

"We'll still be drilling the exploratory well on their land," observed the geologist, raising his glass.

"I think when Puentes over at Hydrocarbons hears from the syndicate, whose land it is is gonna be up for grabs."

SERGIO HAD HIS ARM AROUND MARGARITA. They were sitting on a bench in the center of the plaza facing the statue of Bolivar. The lamps cast the glow that made that time of day special to them both. She leaned her head against his shoulder. He had suggested they stop for a while in the plaza instead of having coffee in El Tucán. "I have something for you," he said. She turned and smiled. He reached into his pocket, produced a small box, and handed it to her. She opened it.

"Oh, Sergio, it's beautiful."

"Here. Let me," he said, taking the European-cut, triple diamond, set in gold, from the box and placing it on her finger. "Does it fit all right?"

"Oh, Sergio, it's beautiful," she repeated.

"It was my mother's," he announced.

"Oh. It's beautiful," she said again, stunned by the recognition that their engagement was almost official.

"My father always said that he wanted to show his rival that he meant business."

"Your mother must have been very happy."

"She was," he replied. "She gave it to me, after my father died, so that I would have it for my intended."

"I wish I could have known your parents."

"You would have enjoyed them."

She gazed at the ring on her finger for a long moment then turned to Sergio and kissed him. "Thank you, my love." They kissed again. "I think we'd better get going." After another embrace they rose and went to the taxi stand at the corner of the plaza.

Ten minutes later they were walking through the Arch of San Golquí. The Bustamante residence was visible above the low retaining wall at the end of the lane. The moment of truth had arrived, and Sergio felt ill prepared. "I don't think you have to worry," she said, reading his mind. "My father will probably come directly to the point. In a cordial way," she added. "I suspect they're still upstairs. It'll give him the opportunity to meet you first, alone." Sergio took a deep breath.

Margarita mounted the step, put her key into the lock, and opened the door. A minute later he was standing alone in the living room, looking up at the portrait of his future in-laws. Eucalyptus logs blazed in the fireplace. The unnerving silence of the house was broken by the sound of steps on the stairs. He turned to face Camilo Bustamante Aragón, thirty-first president of the republic, striding toward him, hand outstretched. "Sergio, at last we meet in person," he exclaimed.

"Don Camilo," Sergio replied in a barely audible voice.

The other, a half head taller, was dressed informally, a dark blue sport jacket and gray trousers. He gestured to the sofa opposite the portrait. "Have the kindness," he said, seating himself in the chair under the picture. "I'm afraid the womenfolk will be a while. I left them admiring the lovely ring you presented to our daughter."

Sergio was feeling better already. "Thank you, Don Camilo," he responded more robustly. "Things are happening so fast. I had wanted to formally ask for your daughter's hand. Perhaps I should formalize it now." He surprised himself with *that* proposal.

"Consider it done," said the older man. He seemed genuinely pleased with the prospect of Sergio becoming his son-in-law.

Consuelo appeared at the doorway, bearing a tray with three glasses of iced maté, a pitcher of the iced herb tea, a glass of what appeared to be scotch and soda, a plate of miniature tamales, and a bowl of roasted corn, which she arranged on the low table between them.

Thanking Consuelo, Bustamante turned to his guest and said, "Please," gesturing to the drinks. Sergio took a glass of the iced tea and Don Camilo the scotch and soda. "Your health," he said, lifting his glass. "We'll save the formal toasts for dinner." Don Camilo asked for and received the latest news of Catachoclo, ending with the proposed delivery of the judgment to Don Luis Palacios. The former president expressed his pleasure at the resolution, if only temporary, of the Arra'o crisis, and also suggested that Sergio not go alone to deliver the judgment. "I'm afraid that Don Luis, like too many of the old families, is living in the past. Ah, here they are," he said, rising to greet his wife and daughter.

Doña Elena came directly to Sergio and embraced him. "Sergio, we are delighted. And the ring is beautiful." She linked her arm in his and turned to Margarita, who was radiant with joy. "As you can see, you have made our daughter the happiest woman on earth."

CHAPTER 34

S ERGIO HAD AWAKENED BEFORE the alarm went off. He lay there reflecting on the events of earlier that week. Could it have been only five days before that he'd given Margarita the ring? The family dinner that night had been followed by a small, hurriedly arranged engagement party the next evening. Small? There'd been at least thirty guests, including Giovanna and Freddy. His sister had been a bundle of nerves in anticipation but, at the affair, acted like it was a common occurrence in her life, and in Freddy's, who enjoyed a long chat with the rancher, Doña Elena's brother, who attended with his wife and son. That whole week had been filled with meetings; the time he'd had alone with Margarita that Wednesday evening, when they walked up to El Pozo, he savored the most.

The alarm rang. Thoughts of El Pozo would have to wait. He remonstrated with himself. Wasn't that exactly what he'd complained to Galo about, putting Margarita on the back burner? He sat on the edge of the bed for a moment, shrugged, and went over to the wash basin.

Twenty minutes later, he was approaching the drillers in the dining room. "Welcome back, stranger," said Walter as Sergio took a seat. "How are things in the capital?"

"Couldn't be better," responded Sergio, "in *all* respects." Carlos arrived with the menus, and George managed to order his eggs in credible Spanish. "Well done," remarked Sergio. "Are you taking lessons?"

"If you're spending an evening with three *seenyoritas*, you have to have *something* to say," explained Walter.

"So you haven't found the solution to the chaperone dilemma."

"Not yet," lamented Walter. "And speaking of *seenyoritas*, did you see your lady friend in the capital?"

Before Sergio could answer, eight men dressed in work clothes entered and occupied two tables pushed together for their benefit. "They're surveyors," offered Walter. "Working south of town. I'm not sure exactly where. Your friend Galo knows them."

"They're mapping out the new beneficio," offered Sergio. "I'm going to introduce myself," he added, rising from his chair and striding over. "Good morning, gentlemen, I'm Sergio Fidanza of ICRAC, to serve you."

"Oh. Luzuriaga told us about you," said the man sitting opposite. "I'm Patricio Tapia, party chief. We're working out at the beneficio site," he added, gesturing to the others at the table.

Carlos had brought the first table's coffee and was approaching to take the orders of the survey crew. "I'll come by later today," said Sergio.

"We'll be there," replied the other.

"Well, it's moving along," observed Sergio, resuming his seat. "They'll be laying the cornerstone on the sixteenth of next month. We expect that the director of ICRAC and his deputy will be coming down for the festivities. There may even be a candidate or two."

"Is *this* place going to be crowded!" put in George.

"I suspect that they'll be heading back to the capital as soon as the party is over," said Sergio.

"Speaking of the capital," said Walter, "you didn't say if you saw your lady friend."

Sergio poured some coffee extract into his cup from the cruet. "I did," he said. Following up with the hot milk, he added, "And we're going to be married."

There was a stunned moment of silence. "Congratulations!" exclaimed Walter, so vociferously that it turned the heads of the survey crew.

"Congratulations," said George, extending his hand to the red-faced Sergio, sitting next to him.

Walter got up, came around the table, and gave him an embrace. When's it going to happen?"

"In a month. The week after the beneficio inauguration. Right here in Catachoclo."

"Here?"

"Yes. And you're both invited, if you're still in town. *And* your señoritas. . .all three of them."

"Well, I'll be damned," Walter managed to say.

SERGIO RETURNED TO HIS ROOM TO WRITE Margarita a letter, determined not to put her on the back burner. It took a while to gather his sentiments and compose them in coherent words. It was ten o'clock when he reached the mail drop at the bus station. With luck she'll have it by. . .Tuesday? he thought. Oh, well. I'll phone later.

He headed to the church.

"Fidanza!" called Sor Marillac from the clinic. He diverted from his path to the rectory. She was obviously bursting with curiosity. The clinic only opened in the morning on Saturday. There were just three patients in the courtyard. "Come. Let us sit," she said, motioning to the bench she and Margarita had been sitting on that day a month and a half before. "What's the news from the capital?"

He hesitated before answering, knowing the suspense was killing. Her eyes grew large in anticipation. "We've set the date," he announced. "September 25th."

She pressed her hands against her cheeks, seemingly to cool the flush of excitement. "I am so. . .*happy*!" she exclaimed. "The 25th?" The nun rose from the bench. "That's less than a month!" she added, and as quickly sat down. "There is so much to *do*. We must prepare." She could barely contain her enthusiasm. Sergio quickly summarized the plan for the guests to fly in and out the same day. "Yes. But the reception. We must speak to the prefect and arrange for the canton hall. Yes, the canton hall." She rose again and, with one hand on her hip and the other pressed to her lips, gazed around the courtyard. "We will host the bride's family here prior to the ceremony," she decided, pointing to the ground. "Margarita can use our guest room to prepare. *Oui*." The wheels were turning. Sergio felt relieved. He hadn't thought about the arrangements. And now that she was enumerating them *and* making plans, he was grateful. "And dancing! I will speak to Luis Junquera. He and his brothers are quite talented. Guitar, trumpet, and drum." She went on about the food, serving, the choir, a host of other things.

"Sor, I must see Padre Philippe," he finally interjected.

"Yes, of course. By all means. I will make a list of the things we must do."

Sergio rose to take his leave. "And Maruja Luzuriaga will want to help us."

Oh, *mais oui*. Will you be seeing her? Yes? Tell her to stop by the clinic. We will make plans. I am so happy!" she repeated. They shook hands. As he made his way toward the rectory, she called out, "See if he has any more of that Chateauneuf du Pape."

"CHATEAUNEUF DU PAPE? WHY, YES," the priest assured him. "I have a case, less the bottle we consumed the day you and Margarita were reunited. It will be a wonderful occasion to use it."

Sergio had given him all the wedding news from the capital and a rundown of Sor Marillac's preliminary plans. The priest had duly noted the date of the marriage in the calendar of the church and re-placed the book in the drawer of the desk. "It seems that our friend has it under control," the priest observed. "She loves to do these things. I remember a year ago she planned the centenary of the parish." He rummaged around a side drawer in the desk and pulled out a program and three photos. "It was a huge success," he said, showing his visitor the memorabilia. "We're overdue for a party." The padre reflected for a moment; his demeanor grew serious. "And what of. . .our other concerns?" he asked, inclining his head in the general direction of the drilling site.

Sergio returned the photos to the priest. "It's all good news, Padre. At least for us. . .and for now. The plans for the new beneficio are moving ahead. In fact, there is a survey crew working at the site right now, locating the major structures. We expect to have the lay-ing of the cornerstone on the sixteenth of next month."

"Just before your wedding?"

"Yes. And, like the wedding, we would like your blessing on the enterprise."

"It will be my pleasure."

"Thank you, Padre. You'll get a formal invitation from Luzuriaga. It's really his project. There is nothing new on the drilling. I suspect that it will proceed peacefully to its conclusion. . . . The situation with the campesinos who occupied the land in the South Forest is a different story."

"Yes. That disgraceful affair where the man's house was burned down."

"Exactly. Kruger—that's the ICRAC attorney—has researched it. According to the agrarian reform laws, the fact that they've homesteaded for more than two years, the property is theirs. I have four copies of the finding, signed by a judge, which I intend to hand-deliver to Don Luis Palacios *and* Captain Barrios on Monday and another copy for the prefect."

The padre frowned. "I don't think you should go alone," he advised. "Why don't you deliver Kattah his copy first, maybe even today, and ask him to invite Palacios to the prefecture for a discussion. You can give it to him then. Kattah can get the word to Barrios, too."

"You're a mind reader, Padre. The cover letter of his copy *does* charge him with the responsibility for delivering the finding."

"There you are. I think it's the better way."

JEAN KATTAH, PREFECT OF CANTON CAJAMARCA, was standing at the window of his office above the assembly hall, facing the interior courtyard of the canton administration building, wondering how the peaceful backwater of Catachoclo had suddenly become such a center of turmoil that it required a daily patrol of the Special Forces. He'd barely known of their existence the month before and had never met the commandante until he paid a courtesy call the day the patrols began.

Kattah's parents, fresh from Lebanon, had settled in Nicoya in 1930, and Jean had been born a year and a half later. The family had adapted well to the provincial life, and Jean had gravitated to politics, becoming the president of the Young Vasquistas in Nicoya while still in secondary school. He'd been named prefect in the last Vasquez presidency and survived the military takeover. To him the assignment would have served as a stepping stone to greater things in Nicoya and eventually the capital. But it looked like success was coming to him in Cata-choclo. The promised arrival of the railroad, the gringos' proposal to build a new beneficio, and now the prospect of oil—with luck, the con-fluence of these events might just catapult him into the national political scene. He would just have to keep the volatile Don Luis Palacios under control, a task that would tax his political skills and Middle Eastern temperament. But what about *this* fellow? he thought, as he watched Sergio Fidanza stride across the courtyard below.

The prefect returned to his desk. The office was smaller than the ICRAC office across the way but more elegantly decorated. A group of framed photos hung on the wall behind the desk, which faced the entrance. Most had been taken on the stage in the court-yard or in the assembly hall. The largest and most prominent de-picted the prefect shaking the hand of the then-president José Maria Vasquez Iturralde. The desk itself was brass-bound polished ma-hogany. The recently installed phone sat on a matching credenza below the photos. A similarly styled conference table, seating eight, stood to the right near the window. A large map of the valley hung on the opposite wall flanked by the Costaguana flag to the left and the provincial standard to the right.

The prefect rose to greet his guest. "Please," he said, gesturing to one of the two chairs in front of the desk, "be so kind." He hadn't thought much about Fidanza since their encounter the day the campesino's house was burned down, but realized the part-time rep-resentative of ICRAC and FLOC was someone an aspiring national politician had to reckon with, perhaps cultivate. "I understand you've been to the capital."

"Yes. But I stopped in Sulaco first."

"Sulaco?"

"I went to see my FLOC boss. Besides my work with the insti-tute I look after the interests of the beneficio workers."

"Yes, I know," the other replied. He mulled the revelation for a moment. "Speaking of the beneficio, there's a survey crew already working at the site."

"They're locating the major structures," Sergio offered.

The conversation continued, each contributing bits of information.

The prefect, less than candid, was trying to ascertain exactly what his guest's position was in the enterprise. "I can understand ICRAC's interest," he said, "but what, if anything, is FLOC's involvement?"

Sergio had smelled it coming. "None." To forestall further inquiry, he added, "My purpose for this visit, Don Jean, concerns ICRAC's responsibility to the settlers in the South Forest."

The prefect reached into his pocket, extracted a pack of Casablancas, and offered one to Sergio, who declined. "It seems that the issue has not attracted much attention since the confrontation between the Redheads and the drillers," he observed. He lit the cigarette and leaned back in his chair. Taking a long drag, he added, "As I recall, you—that is to say ICRAC—was going to look into the matter of who owned the land. Have you come to any conclusions?" he asked, exhaling a column of smoke into the air above him.

"As a matter of fact, we have, and I have the findings right here, signed by a judge on the institute's judicial bench." Sergio extracted a copy of the report from an elegant, hand-tooled leather writing case, an engagement gift from Margarita, and handed it to the prefect. "This is *your* copy. It says," Sergio summarized, "that, according to the agrarian reform laws, unused land, regardless of any previous claim, that's homesteaded for at least two years becomes the property of the occupier." The prefect, putting the cigarette in an ashtray on the desk, accepted the spiral-bound document, flipped through the pages, and stopped at the last to inspect the signature and authenticating seal. He laid the report on the desk and picked up his cigarette. "What's the next step?" he asked, taking another deep drag.

"I have copies here for Don Luis and Capitán Barrios," Sergio said, tapping the writing case. "I'm prepared to deliver them myself on Monday, but you'll notice in the cover letter of your copy that *you're* responsible for delivering the documents." The prefect picked up the report and turned to the letter. He took his time reading it. His raised eyebrows were the only sign that he was the least bit concerned. After giving him what he thought was enough time to digest the situation, Sergio offered to accompany him. "But perhaps," he suggested, "it would be more appropriate if you asked him to come here to receive it. I could be here when he arrives."

Kattah leaned back in his chair and took another drag on the cigarette. It looked like keeping the volatile Don Luis Palacios under control was taking on another dimension. Having the ICRAC representative present would go a long way toward deflecting the wrath of the beneficio owner. "Yes, that would provide an ICRAC presence. . . . Yes, I believe that it would be most appropriate."

"I DON'T ENVY KATTAH OR YOU. Palacios will be fit to be tied," said Galo when Sergio finished summarizing the meeting. They were sitting in the co-op manager's office with Arturo Morales, Galo's assistant.

"Will Major Ulloa be informed?" asked Arturo.

Galo turned to Sergio, who promptly replied, "Yes. The finding is also on the way to the camp."

"You've done all you can, Sergio. Now we'll see what Palacios does," said Galo. The other two nodded in agreement. "I'm not sure I'd want to be in Kattah's office on Monday morning. And I'm *sure* I don't want to show up for lunch today without you. I have strict orders from Maruja."

"*YOU'VE SET THE DATE?*" THE REDHEAD threw her arms around her guest. "I'm so happy, Sergio! And here in Catachoclo." She pulled away. "We must make plans," she said. A frown creased her brow. "There's only four weeks."

"Sor Marillac is already making a list," Sergio reported. "She asked that you stop by the clinic when you have a chance."

"I will. This very afternoon. There is no time to lose. But come—before the soup gets cold." She took Sergio's arm and walked him through the kitchen into the dining room. "Galo," she said to her husband, "please bring the pitcher of maté. It's in the refrigerator." She sat her guest in the chair facing the painting of the tree in Calle Sulaco.

"You've had it framed," he observed.

"Yes. Since it is to be a wedding gift, I had the frame made when we were in Nicoya," she said, "and it will stay right there for when you and your bride move in."

My bride, thought Sergio.

CHAPTER 35

T HE BLACK PICKUP ROARED THROUGH the gate of the Cafetero Tres de Mayo and up the road to the house. Workers loading a truck with bags of coffee turned to see it screech to a halt at the front door, and the patrón jump out and rush up to the entrance. He stopped and returned to the truck. They could almost hear the string of curses as he opened the door and withdrew something from the cab. The door slammed, and in two seconds he was in the house.

The housekeeper, who had seen the arrival from the kitchen window, retreated to the pantry. Her patrón stormed into his study, flung himself into his chair, slammed his copy of the ICRAC finding on the desk, and picked up the telephone. He consulted a pad on the desk before dialing a number. "General Espinoza!" he shouted. "...What? ... The Reinosa residence? Aagh!" He slammed the receiver down and grabbed the pad. He ran his finger down the page, but the numbers seemed to be moving in circles. He dropped the pad. He hadn't gotten so fired up since his peasants let a prize fighting bull fall into a pit on the hacienda five years before. He'd fainted, and the doctor'd warned him at the time that he risked an attack if he didn't control his temper. He wasn't going to let those lousy squatters get the best of him. He leaned back in the chair and began to take deep breaths as the doctor recommended.

A few minutes went by. He heard muffled voices from the kitchen. "Rafael?" he called out.

The door opened, and Rafael stuck his head in. "Yes, patrón?"

"Tell her to bring me a maté."

"Yes, patrón."

Don Luis continued the deep breathing. He tried to keep his mind clear of thoughts of squatters and beneficios. It was almost impossible. Seventy years of toil, and now, when the railroad was becoming a reality, he would have to share the rewards with those ignorant peasants, and the goddamn ICRAC was giving his land away. The last straw. But he wasn't through fighting. He shook his head as if to remove these thoughts from his mind. He concentrated on the breathing. It helped. Following a knock on the door, Teresita entered, carrying a tray with a pot of boiling water, a metal cradle holding a gourd filled with the herb, and a silver straw with a perforated bulb at the base. "What took you so long?" The frightened housekeeper set the tray in front of the patrón and managed to ask if he wanted anything else. A wave of the hand was his answer. She beat a hasty retreat. Don Luis picked up the pot and filled the gourd slowly until the water appeared at the surface. He leaned back again and continued the breathing. He sat up, topped up the gourd with more water, inserted the straw, and took a long sip of the maté. "Ahh," he sighed. He leaned back, taking occasional sips until it was empty. He withdrew the straw, reinserted it at a quarter turn of the gourd, replaced it in the cradle, and refilled it with water. He picked up the pad. His vision had cleared.

"DON LUIS PALACIOS ON LINE ONE, my general." The sergeant withdrew, and General Aníbal Espinoza picked up the phone.

"Good morning, Don Luis." The general rolled his eyes as the events of the morning were described to him. He listened patiently for five minutes. "Don Luis. . .Don Luis, you must face certain facts. . . . With respect to the ICRAC finding, you should seek legal counsel. . . . Yes, but there is nothing that needs or should be done at this moment. The situation will not change. You will lose no advantage." The last' comment seemed to have struck a responsive chord. "Licenciado Alfredo Ribadeneira? An excellent choice, Don Luis. And do keep us informed." Espinoza picked up a cup from his desk and took a log sip before pressing the intercom button. "Sergeant, will you please get me Major Ulloa."

"I'M SURPRISED YOU COULDN'T HEAR HIM from here," remarked Sergio, seated in Galo Luzuriaga's office along with Arturo Morales, the assistant co-op manager.

"It sounds like the meeting lived up to expectations," said Arturo.

"That's an understatement. He didn't even look at the document after I'd summed it up. He went into a tirade about how his family was responsible for all of the progress here in the valley, and that he wasn't going to let a band of shiftless peasants take it away from him. When I suggested that the peasants had made some contribution, he jumped up and stormed out, shouting almost incoherently."

"What did Capitán Barrios have to say?" asked Galo.

"Nothing, while Palacios was there. After he stormed out, he did say he'd keep an eye on things." Sergio shook his head. "Of course that's what he was doing when that thug burned the house down and shot the goat." They all thought about that for a moment. "Well, we'll see."

"What's next?" asked Arturo.

"I spoke to Chiriboga before the meeting," Sergio replied. "He said for me to get the survey crew started on the South Forest settlements. I'm going out to see them now. Then," he added, holding up a copy of the finding, "I'm going to give the good news to our friends in the South Forest."

"We must arrange a formal presentation of the deeds," said Arturo.

"We can do it when we have the cornerstone laying," said Galo, warming to the possibilities. "I have an idea we'll be attracting a candidate or two."

"If that happens, Palacios will really have a fit."

"I'd better be going," Sergio concluded. "Do either of you want to go along?"

"I can't," said Galo.

"I'll go," offered Arturo. "It's about time I made another visit."

"Good," said Sergio, rising.

"Speaking of making plans, Sergio," said Galo, "Maruja and Sor Marillac are well under way. They're going to see Kattah this afternoon. And Maruja wants to use your phone later to consult with Margarita."

"IT'LL PROBABLY TAKE US THE BETTER PART of a week to run a line down to the settlement," reckoned the party chief, Patricio Tapia. "But it won't take the whole party. The others can start locating the individual property markers."

Sergio looked at Arturo. "Do they have markers?"

Arturo shrugged. "I think they have an idea where their property lines are," he offered, "but we may have to check with the dogs."

Patricio laughed. "I know what you mean. The last property survey we did in the sierra, the damn dogs knew exactly where their responsibility began, *and* ended. It's pretty uncanny," he observed. "Meanwhile, you can start them thinking about it."

"We'll do it," Sergio said. They shook hands, and the two got into their Jeep. In thirty minutes the first dog started chasing the vehicle. Five minutes and two dogs later they were at the house of Jacobo Vidál. The owner, in an adjacent field tending a stand of cassava, saw the vehicle as it pulled up, being chased by his dog. He waved, stopped what he was doing, and hurried over.

"Welcome, señores. Be so kind as to enter my home," he said, gesturing to the thatch-roofed building as he proffered his forearm in greeting. He ran ahead, shouting, "Maria, Maria! We have guests!" Before disappearing behind the building, he turned to wave on the newcomers.

As Sergio and Arturo reached the back of the house, they saw Maria tending a pot on the firepit. "I thought they'd be finished eating," whispered Sergio. Arturo shrugged. The two had had an early lunch before leaving town.

"Please, take a seat. Have something to eat," the settler offered, pulling out the two chairs.

"We have eaten, Jacobo," Arturo insisted. "You mustn't let us take you away from your own dinner. We'll have a cup of coffee." The request seemed to satisfy the other's duty as host. A bench was secured from the patio and places arranged at the table. Of course the visitors were given the chairs, and the hosts occupied the bench. The coffee was hastily prepared, and two bananas were produced for the guests. Jacobo and Maria each had a plate of rice and cassava. They began eating in silence. The baby, who had been sleeping on the bed, stirred. Maria rose to tend to its needs. Sitting on the edge of the bed, she picked up the little one and began to nurse it.

"Jacobo," Sergio began, "we have good news. The ICRAC judge has found that, because you and the other dwellers have occupied the land here in the South Forest for more than two years, it belongs to you."

Jacobo was stunned. The spoon stopped in midair, then sank slowly to the plate. "Maria, did you hear? The land belongs to us!" He repeated it in Quechua to be sure she understood. The woman put her one hand over her eyes and, continuing to nurse her baby, wept for joy. Jacobo went over to comfort his wife. He whispered something to which she nodded in agreement. "It is very, very good news, indeed," he said, his own eyes filled with tears. He wiped them on his sleeve as he returned to the table.

"I have the finding signed by the ICRAC judge," Sergio announced, holding up the copy he had carried in from the Jeep. He opened it to the signature page, suspecting that his host probably could not read. Jacobo looked at the writing and rubbed his hand over the embossed seal. They discussed getting the dwellers together and making an announcement later in the week. They asked about property markers. Jacobo allowed as how there were some, but that each had a good idea of the extent of the individual land holding. When he was told of the work the surveyors would be undertaking in the next day or two, he said that they would be ready.

Sergio and Arturo took their leave, and their host accompanied them to the vehicle. "By the way, Jacobo," asked Sergio, climbing into the vehicle, "have you heard from Raúl?"

The same look came over the campesino's face as when he had informed them that Raúl had left for Sulaco. The two waited for an answer. It wasn't long in coming. "It was my turn on watch the night before last," he started. "Just before dawn I was walking down the road toward my home near Raúl's place when I saw him." He stopped talking and looked down at the ground.

"Who?" asked Sergio. "Raúl?" The campesino turned away. "Jacobo, we must know. It's for his own good as well as for the rest of you."

"He said I should tell *no one*."

"Well, you have. Now you must tell us every thing. Don't worry. We won't give you away," Sergio added, trying to reassure the man. "What was he doing here?"

"He came for some of his tools. He thanked me for keeping them together and not taking any. I *told* him that I would do that."

"What tools?" asked Arturo.

"A pick, a shovel." He rubbed his forehead, trying to picture what else his former neighbor took. "He was wearing good boots," he added, almost in astonishment.

"How was he traveling?" asked Sergio. "Was he riding?"

"I didn't see a horse. He just put the tools over his shoulder and walked into the woods. He warned me again, 'Don't tell anyone!'"

At the north edge of the settlement, when they had left the last of the barking dogs behind, the driver relaxed. "What do you make of this business with Raúl?" Arturo asked. The now-returned, former squatter was uppermost in their thoughts.

"It has the odor of *trouble*," observed the driver.

"Maybe he's just found another place to squat," said Arturo.

"I'd like to believe that," said the other, "but going to Sulaco then coming back. . . ."

"Maybe they didn't find work," opined Arturo, looking straight ahead.

"No. There's always work to do in Sulaco." Sergio shook his head. "I'm afraid, if they hooked up with Tavo Escobár, they're back on some other business, and trouble making will be a major part of it."

"But why the tools?"

"Well, if they're in the trouble making business, they'll have to stay out of sight. Set up a camp of sorts." Sergio ran his hand through is hair. "Arturo, what's the area deeper inside the forest like?"

"It's almost impenetrable. Years ago there was talk of logging it. But the lack of access to the valley stalled the scheme. With the new railroad though, it will probably come up again. Wow, with the coffee, now oil, then logging, this is going to be a busy place."

"A place where my former comrades will want a presence," observed Sergio.

"I don't get it."

"I don't, either, Arturo. We'll just have to keep it under advisement." They both fell silent, each in his own struggle with the sparse facts.

Fifteen minutes later Sergio eased the Jeep into the streambed and out the other side without resorting to the lower gears. "You did that quite well," remarked Arturo.

"I think I'm ready for anything," said the new driver, "but those coffee trucks, they still bother me."

"I know what you mean," the other responded. Pointing ahead, he added, "Germán's place is just up the road. Oh. There he is, waiting for the produce truck." Sergio stopped the vehicle just in front of the campesino. "Good day, Germán."

"Good day, señores." Without having to be asked, he blurted, "I have not heard from my brother. It's a month and I am worried, señores."

"Do you know where he went?" asked Arturo.

The man came over to the vehicle and put both his hands on the bottom of the window opening. "I have heard nothing from *him*, only the rumors in the South Forest that he went to Sulaco. What will a bumpkin like him do in Sulaco? I tell you señores, I'm worried."

Sergio started inching the vehicle forward. "We must get back, Germán. We'll let you know, if we hear anything."

"And let us know, if *you* hear anything," added Arturo as the forlorn brother turned back to his pile of watermelons.

CHAPTER 36

S ERGIO WONDERED IF HE'D BEEN completely out of his mind. He was at the outskirts of Nicoya on the final leg of the arduous trip from Catachoclo. His passenger in the Jeep, Jorge Washington

Quishpe, was completely oblivious to the anxiety of his chauffeur, which had resulted in the trip taking two hours longer than it would have with an experienced driver. Perhaps it was a blessing. Jorge, not usually given to idle chatter, recalled at various points some memory of his making the trip in his youth with his grandfather. The affection the leader of the beneficio union held for the older man was implicit in these stories. They provided the few times when Sergio could relax, but a coffee truck would inevitably interrupt the euphoria. It seemed he could never escape his nemeses.

Jorge was indicating the way to the Saenz residence. "You will be happy to see your fiancée, no?"

"Yes. It's less than three weeks to the wedding, and we have a lot to talk about." Having said that, Sergio was not sure what there was to talk about. Just seeing her was the only thing on his mind. The other reason for the trip was to get his driver's license. Galo had assured him that it would not be a problem. Problem or not, he would be with Margarita for two days.

The sun had just set as Sergio pulled the Jeep next to the 1956 Chevrolet sedan parked in the small paved area at the bottom of the steps at the side entrance of the Saenz's home. Maria was descending from the entrance door, followed by the doctor, as the two emerged from the vehicle. Jorge greeted his cousin. Paco shook hands with Sergio and turned to exchange a warm embrace with Jorge. "How long has it been since you graced our home?" he asked, still holding onto the taller man.

"It was the Day of the Race, last October."

"See? Almost a year. But, come. Leticia awaits. And your mother," he added, pointing to the figure of a woman approaching from the garden. Maria hurried ahead with the baggage. Paco motioned for Sergio to come into the house, as Jorge and Gloria embraced for a long moment, exchanging murmured words of affection, both with tear-filled eyes.

The host held the door for his guest. As Sergio entered, Margarita was standing just to the side with that impish look he was still getting used to. It had its effect. He was stunned, but only for a moment. They stepped into each other's arms. He kissed her gently on the lips and gave her a long hug. Paco moved next to his wife, who had risen from her chair. The engaged couple turned to their hosts. Sergio reached out for Doña Leticia's hand and kissed her on the cheek. "You seemed surprised to see Margarita," Leticia observed.

"Yes, I was. I didn't think you were arriving until later in the evening," he said, looking rather quizzically at his fiancée.

"Yes, later *yesterday* evening." She waited a moment before adding, "There was a change in plan, my darling. An Institute car became available." Sergio was spared further confusion by the entry of Gloria and Jorge.

After a flurry of greetings, Doña Leticia invited all into the living room. Taking one of the arm chairs and her husband the other, she insisted that the engaged couple use the sofa. Gloria and Jorge sat in chairs on either side of the fireplace. The warmth of the day did not require a fire, but the faint fragrance of the eucalyptus could still be detected. "Well, Sergio, how was the trip?" asked Doña Leticia.

"It took longer than I expected." Margarita slipped her hand in his as he spoke. He warmed to her touch.

"Well, a new driver," exclaimed the doctor. "I'm not surprised. I give you credit for undertaking it. And without a license," he chided good naturedly. "But we'll remedy that tomorrow. After we drop the ladies at the center, we'll go to the motor vehicle office."

Maria entered to lay a tea service on the low table. Margarita leaned forward, poured maté, and offered the drink around. The conversation revolved around the trip and how it had changed over the years. Jorge recounted the many times he'd made it with his grandfather. Paco described the ones he and Leticia had made to visit the clinic. Leticia, after noticing the vacant looks on the faces of the newly engaged, placed her cup on the table and announced that dinner would be served in an hour and a half, and that Sergio and Margarita had more important things to discuss. "Why don't the two of you visit our park right up the street? It's a pleasant walk."

Sergio almost leaped out of his seat. "I think that's a good idea." The others smiled at his hasty response. Margarita thanked her and retrieved a cardigan from the coat tree at the entrance. After an almost perfunctory taking of leave, they were out the door.

"THEY ARE SUCH SWEET PEOPLE," she remarked as the two strolled arm-in-arm to the park. She described her visit to the women's facility earlier that day. "And I've started learning Quechua!" she exclaimed. As they turned into the park, Sergio slipped his arm around her waist. They made their way to a bench secluded from the street by a row of hedges and facing a fountain that was not operating. Seated, he drew her close, and they surrendered to a passionate exchange of kisses. "I am so happy!" she declared. He offered her the handkerchief he now kept dutifully in his pocket. They remained silent in each other's arms. With her head resting against his chest, she said dreamily, "What were we going to discuss?"

"I don't know."

She straightened up. You don't know?" She gave him a playful punch. "It's less than three weeks away!"

"What is?" He was finally beginning to loosen up.

"Our wedding!" That was accompanied by another punch. "It's a good thing I talked to Maruja. Oh, Sergio, it's going to be wonderful."

THE ARCHITECTURE AND STREET ARRANGEMENT of Nicoya, a city of 70,000 people, reflected its Spanish roots with a patina of the Serrano Indian culture. The climate, warmer than the capital's, permitted a lively street ambiance into the early evening, somewhat like that of the even warmer Sulaco. The five sat enjoying a coffee in the late afternoon at a café table in the colonnaded street a half block from the main square and across from the women's center. Margarita was enthusing about the services she had observed during the two days of her visit. Sergio, who, with Paco, his driving license sponsor, had joined them after the prolonged process, was particularly impressed by the legal advice the women with domestic problems were receiving.

"Exactly what Golda commented on," remarked Doña Leticia. "She's already gathering information for us."

"It's the only program of its kind in Costaguana," offered Margarita. "On my next visit I'm going to invite Maria Gloria de Orska. She's one of our staff attorneys."

The passionate conversation continued until Doña Leticia put her hand on her husband's arm and whispered, "I think we should be going, Paco."

"Of *course*, my dear." He rose immediately to assist his wife. Gloria came around to help. "You've had enough excitement for one day. Come. The car is just across the street." He turned to look for the waiter.

"It's the new driver's treat," said Sergio. He and Margarita got up and expressed their concern for Doña Leticia.

"I'm all right. Just a little tired. It's been a longer day than usual," she said, taking the arms of Paco and Gloria. Sergio and Margarita watched the three cross the street and get into the car. They resumed their seats at the table and sat gazing at each other. The sun had set, and the lights were coming on; it was their special time of day.

GLORIA HAD BEEN UP EARLY and not taken breakfast with the rest. She was sitting on the bench in the patio at the side of the house when the door opened and Maria descended the steps with two traveling bags. She was followed by Paco, who opened the back of the Jeep. Margarita appeared at the top of the steps, followed by Sergio and Jorge. The two men turned back and bade farewell to their hostess, who remained in the doorway. They all descended to the patio. Jorge shook hands with his cousin and warmly embraced Paco. There were final comments about the proximity of the wedding while Sergio and Margarita stood side by side with their arms around each other. "Well. I guess we'd better get going," said the newly minted driver. He kissed his fiancée and whispered something in her ear. She smiled, pressed her cheek against his, and kissed him again. The two travelers climbed into the Jeep, and Sergio maneuvered to the street. Those remaining walked to the end of the driveway to watch the vehicle move down the road. The taller Margarita instinctively put her arm around the shoulders of Gloria, who clasped her around the waist. They both waved at the Jeep as it moved out of sight. The horn sounded in reply.

FILLED WITH RESOLVE, SERGIO HAD WRITTEN a letter to Margarita immediately after arriving back at the Hotel Sulaco. Though it had taken him until eleven to finish it, he was up at six. In the dining room, Patricio, the survey chief, briefed him on their progress. They had completed the layout of the beneficio and were almost to the South Forest with the survey line. With the help of Arturo, the crew was making progress establishing the property limits of the former squatters. Sergio resumed his seat, but Walter and George had not yet appeared. Carlos came over, and after ordering the usual, Sergio asked the waiter where his companions were. Carlos shrugged and returned to the kitchen without further comment. Sergio didn't have to wait long for an answer. The drillers arrived. "Oversleep?" he asked.

"No," Walter answered as they took their seats. "We were at the airport. Cosgrove wants the results ASAP. We've even sent packages up to Nicoya to expedite it."

"I wonder what the hurry is for a seismic survey?"

Walter only hesitated for a moment. "I guess someone's on his case."

Nice recovery, thought Sergio. "I suppose," he said and dropped the matter.

Carlos came back and took their orders. While George struggled, Walter announced that they had received invitations to the wedding. "They were hand-delivered by Señora Luzuriaga yesterday. I understand there's forty-three people from Catachoclo attending."

Sergio had gone over the invitees with Maruja the previous week but hadn't remembered that there were so many. "I guess that's about right," he said. He was getting nervous. Margarita hadn't seemed worried. But still. . . .

"Are you all right?" asked Walter. "You look a little pale."

"Yes. No. I'm fine. . . . Fine. . . ." Fortunately Carlos appeared with the food, and the wedding plans were put aside. Temporarily.

JUANITA ROSE FROM HER CHAIR TO GREET SERGIO. "Señor Fidanza, welcome back! How was your trip?" she asked, shaking his hand.

"I got my driver's license and visited with my fiancée. At the home of Doctor Saenz," he added. "We had a lot to discuss."

"I can imagine. We are so looking forward to the wedding," she exclaimed. "Señor Luzuriaga is in his office." She gestured up the stairs.

Pedro appeared at the door. "Thank you for the invitation, Don Sergio," he said. "Coffee?"

"Yes. Yes. I'll be with Galo."

"Welcome," Galo called out as Sergio appeared at the door. "You didn't have any trouble with the license?"

"No. They decided that the lack of a learner's permit could be waived," he said, taking a chair.

"Well, things are rolling along here. All forty-three of them."

"I didn't know I knew that many people in the town."

"You can check the list at lunch and see if anybody was left out."

"Lunch?"

"Yes. You have standing orders for lunch with Maruja at least twice a week. Whether I attend is not important. And we are to bring Sor Marillac today."

"By the way," Sergio said, "as I came across the plaza, I saw our army friends making their rounds."

"Yes. They don't miss a day," observed Galo. "Unfortunately, it hasn't been so quiet since the confrontation. I'm sure we can't attribute it to them, but it is. . . . "

The coffee showed up, but the message that accompanied it was disconcerting. Pedro announced that he had spotted Hugo Rigpe crossing the plaza. "I'll get another cup," he said before retreating down the stairs.

"Rigpe? What's this all about?" Galo wondered aloud.

"The drilling is progressing well," Sergio remarked. "I was talking with Walter and George this morning."

"We'll soon know," Galo said as their guest climbed the stairs, his machete clanging against the balusters. Sergio moved to the other chair, but remained standing.

"Greeting," said the newcomer, smiling broadly. "Greeting," he said again, and grasped Sergio's hand. He reached into the leather purse hanging from his belt and extracted a folded white envelope. He held it up and said again, "Greeting."

"I think he means, 'Congratulations,'" said Galo.

Sergio smiled and nodded. Galo motioned for them to be seated. Pedro entered with the coffee, and the ritual of consuming it took place. Hugo nodded his approval and placed the empty cup on the tray.

"Arra'o make blessing at church," he announced with great seriousness. Sergio nodded again and shot a quizzical glance at Galo.

"They've done it before," Galo said. "When was the last time, Hugo?"

"Wedding of daughter of schoolmaster. My son was student."

It seemed that Hugo's mission had been accomplished. But not wanting to miss the opportunity for hearing it directly from him, Sergio asked how the drilling was going.

"Good," he replied. "Earthquake men stay away ChiriYacu." No one commented further. The Arra'o chief rose, shook hands, and left.

"Blessing?" Sergio leaned forward and sipped his coffee to reduce the contents of the cup, which he was afraid of spilling if he were to pick it up in his present state of mind.

"It'll be a very pleasant experience," said Galo but would not elaborate.

THEY WERE FINISHING A DESSERT of candied guava shells and cream cheese. All during lunch Sergio had been listening to Maruja and Sor Marillac describe in some detail the planned events of the wedding day. "And at four-thirty," the nun concluded with an eloquent flourish, "the bride and groom and the guests from the capital will be led by the band in procession from the cantonal hall to the plane."

"Another parade," Sergio moaned.

"Listen to this, Sor," Maruja remonstrated good-humoredly, "the happiest day of his life and he complains of a little demonstration of the affection of his friends."

Sergio looked to Galo for support and found none. "It's lucky for you," his friend added, "that we arranged for a seat for you on the return trip."

"*Oui, mon ami*," put in Sor Marillac. "Margarita's *Mamá* filled *every seat* with guests. It was either put you in a box and ship you back as cargo or find a person willing to give up his place." Sergio laughed with the others. "Fortunately for you," she went on, "they prevailed upon a cousin, who will return via Nicoya with Doctor and Señora Saenz the next day."

"I'm very lucky to have such good friends," the groom-to-be said.

Maruja reached over and gave his hand a squeeze. "Fidanza, it is truly our pleasure."

"Oh! I almost forgot. The Arra'o will give them their blessing," Galo announced.

"*Ooh, la-la!*" exclaimed the exuberant nun. "*Quel beau geste.*"

CHAPTER 37

JUAN CHIRIBOGA AND FELIPE KRUEGER retrieved their bags from the luggage cart in front of the Catachoclo airport. "An interesting switch, Fidanza," remarked Chiriboga. "The last time we were here, *you* were arriving on the plane, and *we* were meeting Ribadeneira and that geologist fellow."

"Yes. And Dale Cosgrove created a stir, arriving in his own plane," observed Sergio. "Since this isn't about earthquakes, I guess we'll have to get along without his presence."

The deputy director of ICRAC smiled. "They're still insisting it's not oil." The two functionaries and their consultant crossed the street. As they reached the plaza and were heading toward the canton administration building, they were hailed from behind. "Fidanza." Victor Hugo Ramirez, his long black hair extending to his shoulders from his jipijapa bobbed up and down as he limped toward them.

"Ramirez." Sergio greeted the newcomer. "You always seem to know when to show up."

"This is where all the action is, my friend. I may have to take up residence."

Sergio made the introductions.

"We met on our last visit here," Chiriboga remarked, putting down his bag to shake hands with the reporter. "Your question regarding the existence of oil in the area changed the whole tenor of the meeting we were about to have."

"I'm still trying to find out."

"Well, if you'd been at that meeting you'd have heard Cosgrove reinforce his position on the issue in no uncertain terms. Wouldn't you say so, Krueger?"

"In *no* uncertain terms," the lawyer repeated with emphasis.

"And your opinion, Señor Chiriboga?" the reporter asked, extracting a notebook from the pocket of his guayabera.

"I have none. You'll have to pursue it with Cosgrove."

"I tried calling him yesterday. He's either left or is about to leave for the United States."

"Well, no matter. The drilling issues we were concerned about are settled, at least temporarily. Although," Chiriboga added almost as an afterthought, "his trip to the U.S. may have something. . . ." His voice trailed off. "But we're here on other business," he announced.

"The groundbreaking for the new beneficio, I understand," said the reporter. "Can we can expect a planeload of dignitaries tomorrow?"

"Yes," answered Chiriboga. "My director and several others from ICRAC, the minister of the interior and his deputy, several Point IV officials, and there may be a presidential candidate or two. I'm not sure how they're all going to fit, but that's my boss's problem. I have the local organizing to worry about, which, I understand from our representative here," he added, pointing to Sergio, "is all in place. I was a bit concerned that his planning for another occasion next week might have been a distraction."

"One of the reasons for taking up residence," quipped the reporter. "Catachoclo is fast becoming the center of the Costaguana social whirl." They all looked at Sergio.

"It's out of my hands," he said.

"Spoken like a groom-to-be," Krueger put in. "I've been married seven months, and it still seems to be out of mine."

As they were conversing in the middle of the plaza, the Special Forces daily patrol rounded the far corner and passed in front of the canton administration building. "There they are," said Sergio, pointing to the Jeep and personnel carrier. They all looked without comment as the convoy turned the far corner and disappeared from view.

Sergio broke the silence. "We're on our way to meet with Luzuriaga, Ramirez. He's organized the local activities."

"May I join you?" asked the reporter.

Sergio looked at Chiriboga. "I'm sure it would only enhance your coverage of the events," the deputy director replied. "We are very pleased with and proud of this project and want it made known to the broadest audience possible." They resumed their way to the office.

"Welcome, señores." Juanita came around her desk to shake hands with the visitors. "Señor Luzuriaga had to go out to the site. He should be here within the hour. Would you like coffee?" They all agreed and proceeded up the stairs. Sergio invited them to sit at the conference table at the far end of his office.

Krueger pulled a file from his case. "I have the deeds here for the settlers," he said, laying it on the table. "There's one for that fellow whose house was burned, Fidanza. I don't know what you might want to do with it."

"I'll hold on to it until we get some definitive word."

"I must congratulate Tapia for his good work," said Juan, looking at one of the documents. "How do you plan to present these, Sergio?"

"The director will do it after the laying of the cornerstone. Galo'll have the settlers brought up to the site in the produce van."

"You'll have to make a few trips."

"One should do it," Sergio remarked without elaboration.

Chiriboga raised his eyebrows but didn't pursue it. "How're we getting the dignitaries to the site? Not in the produce van, I hope."

Sergio laughed. "No. I don't think they'll fit."

"The settlers will fit, but the dignitaries won't?"

"You'll see," said Sergio. "For the dignitaries we're hiring a bus from the Flota Entre-Montes. In fact, it should be here this afternoon."

Pedro arrived with the coffee. After each had sweetened his drink to taste, Sergio suggested they wait for Galo to discuss the itinerary for the next day. "He has it all written up."

The deputy director took a sip of his coffee. "Hot," he commented. Sergio smiled at the thought of Hugo Rigpe swallowing a cupful non-stop. "Sergio," he started, setting down his cup, "do we expect any trouble from Palacios?"

"Yes and no. On the one hand, I always expect trouble. On the other, there's been no activity lately suggesting trouble. To preclude any problems, we've invited Major Bertrand Ulloa."

"It'll be interesting to see if he comes," remarked Juan. "Have you sent an invitation to Palacios?"

"We would have, but we haven't found anyone who'll deliver it. Seriously, Juan, you think we should have?"

"Probably doesn't make any difference. He knows it's going to happen. He can come on his own."

A knock on the door ended the speculation. Jean Kattah, the canton prefect, entered, followed by Pedro. "Good morning, señores. Sorry I'm late. An emergency meeting at the electric plant." The visitors rose to acknowledge the introductions by Sergio, who asked if the newcomer wanted a coffee. "I'd be delighted." Sergio nodded to Pedro.

"And you know Ramirez here."

"Yes, indeed. The press has always been gracious to me. However, on occasion they get the spelling of my name incorrect. My card, Señor Ramirez."

Ramirez took it. "I'll make a note and forward it to my editor."

"No need," declared the prefect, taking the chair next to the reporter. "Here's another." Addressing the group, he asked, "Will Don Luis be attending?"

"We were hoping you might extend the invitation," observed Chiriboga.

"Perhaps he will appear of his own accord," the prefect offered.

Sergio could not get over the lightheartedness of the conversation. He hoped it was a good omen. The banter continued until Galo poked his head in the doorway. "Good morning, señores. I'll be right there. I want to get the schedule I've prepared." A minute later he returned and handed out copies of the agenda. "The *very* good news is that Major Ulloa will attend." They all agreed.

Comments on the schedule were made and duly noted by Galo. Kattah expanded on the details of the luncheon reception in the canton hall after the groundbreaking. He was advised that the plane had to take off no later than four o'clock. Chiriboga asked if anyone had any other comments. No one did. "Well then," he said, "I'd like to invite you all to lunch at the Flamenco."

"Sounds like a good idea. Thank you," said Kattah. The others agreed. They rose to leave.

"If you don't mind, I'd like to call my editor," said Ramirez, gesturing to the phone on the desk.

"Of course," Sergio said. "Maybe you can catch up with us?"

"I'll try to make it."

As they turned to the door, Kattah said good-naturedly to the reporter, "Mind the spelling of my name."

Galo dropped the marked-up agenda with Juanita. The five squeezed into the Jeep for the short drive.

"You've only learned to drive since you came here?" remarked Chiriboga, as Sergio parked the vehicle.

"Ask Galo. He's my instructor."

"I'll vouch for that. Except for the coffee trucks, it's a good place to learn."

"And I drove to Nicoya the weekend before to get my license. Now, *that* was an experience. I *still* had to deal with the coffee trucks."

Yapa Flores was sitting behind the bar. "The same room as last time," he said when he recognized Chiriboga and Krueger. "Would you like to go up now?"

"We'll eat first," Chiriboga told him.

Later the kerosene lamp cast a glow over the table in Sergio's room. The words flowed onto the paper before him. He wrote of their last meeting at the Saenzes', how he'd felt when the time came for him to leave, how short the time before they would be joined forever. How San Andrés would be paradise. How much in love he was.

LUZURIAGA AND CHIRIBOGA WERE FLANKED by Krueger, Sergio, and Padre Philippe, on one side, and Kattah, Major Ulloa, and Capitán Barrios, chief of the carabineers, on the other, as they stood on the tarmac watching the TAMC plane taxi toward them. Behind them were arrayed the leadership of Cooperative La Esperanza, Quishpe and the executive board of the beneficio union, Victor Hugo Ramirez, and Hugo Rigpe's nephew. The plane stopped ten meters from where they were standing. When the ground crew had the wheel chocks in place, the door of the plane opened, the stairway unfolded, and the first passenger stepped out. "I guess the prophet didn't make it," muttered Galo as Arturo Jaramillo, the director of ICRAC and Chiriboga's boss, appeared at the top of the steps. He was followed by the minister of the interior, and his deputy, the deputy director of Point IV, two functionaries of ICRAC, and finally, Jim Braun and Charles Wiggins. Sergio was glad to see the last two. As the visitors descended the stairs, the receiving delegation moved toward them. A flurry of introductions, comments on the trip, and general remarks about the business at hand ensued until Galo got their attention and directed them to the bus that had pulled up between the plane and the airport terminal. Chiriboga mentioned something to Galo. "Oh, yes. If anyone needs to use the facilities, they're to the right as you enter the terminal. We'll pull the bus around to the front." Only the gringos took advantage of the offer.

After Braun and Wiggins took their seats, at Galo's direction the bus got underway. He stood at the front and, holding up his schedule of events, reminded everyone that they had received a copy before leaving the capital. The visiting passengers proceeded to search their pockets for the document. "I have a few extra, if they are needed." They all managed to come up with their copy, as did the local participants, who had received theirs that morning. "The ceremony will be brief," Galo continued. "The purpose is to raise the awareness of the community at large and the co-op members in particular of the commitment of the government and the international community to this enterprise." He proceeded to run through the items on the schedule, asking the major participants if they had any comments. There were none. Ceremonies of this kind were an almost weekly occurrence, and the dignitaries had stock speeches to draw from. The minister of the interior asked if there would be time for him to visit the site of the earthquake survey. Galo thought that it could be arranged, but the minister might have to forgo lunch. It was important that the plane's departure not be delayed beyond four-thirty. The minister had second thoughts. Galo suggested that they wait and see how the morning progressed. They all settled back for the remainder of the trip.

By the time the bus got to the site, Arturo Morales had already arrived with the settlers from the South Forest. Much to Chiriboga's surprise, six of the eight families and the older children were accommodated in the produce van. Two families had been selected by lot to stay behind to look after the younger children and to keep an eye on things. In each case the eldest son would accept the deed for the family. "We could have taken more," Morales explained. "They would have stood, that's all." Chiriboga shook his head in amazement.

The ceremonies took only an hour. By half past twelve the thirty-eight or so who had been transported in the bus were assembling in the canton hall under the fierce stare of the black-bearded military man whose full-length portrait dominated the room. They were congratulating themselves and each other for a job well done. Galo was singled out for his organizational work. Kattah invited everyone to partake of the buffet. It was a step above the humble fare of the countryside: rice and beans, deep-fried shredded pork, hard-boiled eggs, spicy sauces, a large bowl of *chicha*, and cool bottles of Orangina. Three tables were set up with more or less the same array of dishes. There didn't seem to be any attempt to segregate into the three groups represented; visitors, co-op members, and union members mixed. The guests arranged themselves around the tables and, with small plates helped themselves and ate standing in place.

Jim Braun, standing next to Sergio and Jorge, announced that he and Elizabeth were planning to attend the wedding. "We've made reservations at the Flamenco. We're getting a room with a private bath," he added enthusiastically.

"*The* room with a private bath," remarked Sergio. "It's the only one in town with a private bath," he explained in response to Braun's quizzical look. "We look forward to having you, Jim. And thank you for taking the time to make the trip." He and Jorge excused themselves to join Galo and Arturo, who had just arrived.

"Arturo has some disturbing news," Galo informed the two. He turned to his assistant.

"There may be some trouble brewing at the South Forest," he started. "Vidal and Ruiz, the two that stayed behind to keep an eye on things, reported that the Tres de Mayo pickup passed heading south about a half hour after I picked up the group this morning. The guy with the teeth was driving with two others."

"How could they have gotten by without your seeing them?" asked Galo.

"I can't figure it," Arturo answered, "unless they were hiding out halfway down there until we passed. In any case," he went on, "they passed by again, heading north, an hour later."

"That'd give them enough time to get to the army camp and back," observed Sergio. "And we didn't see them come by us on the return. I wonder if they're still down there somewhere."

"And that's not all," Arturo went on. "On top of the visit by Rafael, Raúl showed up. When they told him where everybody was, he said that they could keep his deed. He wasn't going to let them treat him like a dog again. Then he poked around his burnt out shack, apparently found what he was after, and left. . . . They're pretty nervous," he added.

"I think we'd better get down there," Sergio said, looking around. "Can you join us, Jorge?"

"Of course," he answered without hesitation.

"I'll come, too," said Galo.

"I don't think that'll be necessary," said Sergio. "Arturo will be with us."

"No. We've been in this together since we confronted Palacios the day they burned Raúl's shack."

"Okay. Arturo, can you arrange to stay there tonight?"

The assistant manager said that he could. Sergio caught Chiriboga's eye and motioned for him to join them.

"What's up?" he asked, still sipping a glass of *chicha*. "This is good stuff." Sergio filled his boss in on the developments. Chiriboga's countenance became very serious.

"It'll be all right, Juan. Arturo is staying the night. And they have a few hunting muskets there."

"We don't want any martyrs."

"It's just to scare anybody that tries anything. Anyway, what could happen in the black of night?" Sergio looked at his watch. "If we leave now, we can be half way back by dark." He surveyed the room. "Before we go, let's get Kattah and Barrios up to date," he said, nodding toward the two men who were in an animated conversation. "The carabineers have to keep a close watch on this, and I want it to come from Kattah. Arturo, get something to eat," he directed the other. "After we talk to them we'll be ready to leave." Sergio and his boss started across the room. "Oh, Juan, can you get this to Margarita?" Sergio asked, holding out an envelope.

"Of course. I'll hand-deliver it first thing tomorrow morning," Juan said, slipping the envelope into his inside jacket pocket.

"I THINK IT WAS MUCH ADO. . .well, about *next* to nothing," Galo commented. He was driving, and they had just left the last barking dog behind. It would not be much longer before the sun set behind Mount Balboa, the tallest of the coastal range. "And I'm not sure if it was a good idea to leave Arturo there," he added. "We can't be taking on the responsibility for their safety."

"You're right, Galo," Sergio agreed. "But they were really spooked." He rolled down the window on his side. "If we could only find some way to allay their fears." The three mulled the problem as the sun began its descent behind the north flank of Balboa. The shadows of tall trees crossing the roadway softened. Galo switched on the lights. The temperature dropped perceptibly. Sergio rolled up the window.

"We should get that patrol to earn its keep by stopping at the settlement when they pass," Galo mused.

"Hah!" The retort had come from Jorge in the rear seat. "Maybe we can get Palacios to send his thugs around to check up."

"No, Jorge. It could help," put in Sergio. "It would have to come from their comandante. I could have Don Camilo put some pressure on." They discussed the advantages and the disadvantages, the patrol's presence versus the spying they would do.

As they continued to talk, darkness completely enveloped them. Galo was distracted by something he saw in the rearview mirror. He turned around to peer briefly through the window in the rear door and, just as quickly, returned his attention to the road in front, which meandered through the rolling landscape, never providing an unobstructed view of more than a hundred meters. "I thought I saw a flash of light." Sergio lowered his head to look through the side mirror. Jorge turned in his seat. Galo picked up the speed. "Uh. There it is again." He stopped and opened his window. "Let's see if we can hear anything." Sergio lowered his. The unmistakable sound of another vehicle reached them. Galo resumed driving. "Not far behind."

He reached the ford in the river and began his descent. As he pulled up the other side the second vehicle was right behind. He pulled over to let it pass. A black pickup forced the Jeep off the road.

A man jumped out of the passenger side immediately followed by a second, both armed with rifles. Another emerged from the driver's side. His gold teeth glinted in the headlights. "Get out!" he shouted. Sergio was the first out on the passenger side. Jorge followed. "*You!* Out!" The order was directed at Galo.

Sergio strode toward the first gunman, who raised his rifle. He lunged to deflect the barrel but went down when the stock crashed across his head. Jorge reached to help. The second gunman fired. Jorge dropped at his friend's feet.

"Oh, my God!" Galo cried. The driver fired. Galo spun around and fell on his face. The driver then finished them off with a bullet to the back of the head.

CHAPTER 38

EL PORVENIR

Page 1 - THREE RURAL LEADERS FOUND MURDERED

By Victor Hugo Ramirez

    Catachoclo, September 17. After an intense search, the bodies of the two labor leaders and the manager of the Cooperative La Esperanza, missing since their Jeep was found abandoned at the side of the road to the South Forest yesterday evening, were discovered this morning about two hundred meters from the vehicle. The remains of Sergio Fidanza, Jorge Washington Quishpe, and Galo Luzuriaga were brought to the clinic in Catachoclo, where an examination was performed by the provincial coroner summoned from Nicoya. Doctor Garcia concluded from the nature of the bullet wounds in the heads of the victims that they had been murdered execution-style. Bruises about the head and face suggested that one of the victims had been beaten prior to being shot.

    The day before, the three men had participated in the ceremonial groundbreaking for the new beneficio to be constructed in Catachoclo. The processing plant will be owned and operated by the members of Cooperative La Esperanza and is a joint effort of ICRAC and Point IV. They consider it their most important project. Reached for comment, Juan Chiriboga, ICRAC deputy director for colonization, and Leonard Hazen, deputy director of Point IV, deplored the violence and promised that it would not affect the progress of the work. "Señor Fidanza was a personal friend," added Chiriboga, "and I grieve his senseless murder." Compañero Julio Chang Crespo, secretary general of

FLOC, and Doctora Golda Lederer, cofounder of the union federation, issued a statement:"We will not rest until the perpetrators of this heinous crime are brought to justice." Capitán Barrios of the carabineers would not speculate on the motive. The foreman for a coffee processor had been questioned. His employer denied any knowledge, suggesting that, if his foreman was involved, it was a personal vendetta. Barrios added that there would be no need to involve the provincial police at this time.

The families are devasted by the brutal crime. Maruja O'Neal de Luzuriaga, wife of the co-op manager, is expecting their first child. She is staying temporarily at the convent of the Sisters of the Holy Redeemer. Jorge Quishpe is survived by his mother, Gloria Quishpe of Nicoya, and a half brother, Andrés Puíg. Sergio Fidanza was engaged to be married to Margarita Bustamante, daughter of former president Camilo Bustamante and Doña Elena Aguirre de Bustamante. The wedding was to have taken place in Catachoclo next Saturday. Señorita Bustamante has gone into seclusion. The former president has said that he will do all in his power to bring the murderers to justice. Fidanza is also survived by a sister, Giovanna Fidanza de Arpe, a nephew, Danny Arpe, and a brother-in-law, Freddy Arpe.

A requiem Mass will be celebrated tomorrow at the Church of San Augustin. Interment of all three victims will be in the church graveyard. It is anticipated that the wedding guests, who were to fly by charter flight to Catachoclo, will still fly to the inter-Andean town to attend a memorial mass on Saturday, the 25th of September.

EL SEMINARIO
Page 8 - PLANS FOR BENEFICIO TO MOVE AHEAD
By Staff Reporter

Santa Marta, September 23. ICRAC and Point IV have announced that plans for a new beneficio to be con-

structed in the town of Catachoclo, the coffee center of
Entre-Montes Province, will move ahead in spite of the
untimely death of the manager of Cooperative El Esperanza, the planned owner of the coffee processing facility.
Galo Luzuriaga, the manager, and two local labor leaders
died suddenly of foul play. The details are sketchy.
Capitán Barrios of the local carabineers is in charge of
the investigation.

THE NEW YORK TIMES
Page 16 - PROSPECTS FOR OIL STIR UNREST IN COSTAGUANA
By Homer Bigart

Washington, October 14. Ambassador E. Graham
Carter, career diplomat currently posted to Costaguana,
spoke yesterday before the National Press Club. His timely
views shed light on recent unrest in this Latin American
country. Ambassador Carter described the area centered
on the town of Catachoclo as an isolated backwater whose
principal activity has been coffee growing and processing.

An ongoing seismic exploration in the area had been
recently confirmed to be for oil by the Walker Tool Company, the exploration arm of a U.S. syndicate. According
to the ambassador, prior rumors of oil exploration had
made the region a target for outside forces bent on desta-
bilizing the economy of the nation looking to the new re-
source as a way to solve its social problems.

Mr. Carter went on to describe what he characterized
as an egregious assault on the political security of
Costaguana, which has only in the past four months ex-
tricated itself from a military dictatorship. The event occurred mid-day on September 30. An army squad,
returning from patrol of Catachoclo and vicinity, was am-
bushed by eight armed and masked men. The sudden and
unexpected attack resulted in the loss of their arms, their
uniforms, and two vehicles, later abandoned and set afire.
The soldiers were stripped of their clothes and sent off

barefoot to their camp some ten kilometers south of the site of the attack. The ambassador indicated that it had all the earmarks of a Cuban inspired, if not led, operation. In a related incident, two weeks earlier three labor leaders were murdered. One of the victims had recently returned to Costaguana, having fled the country three years before when threatened with arrest by the then newly installed military junta, on suspicion of being part of a left-wing conspiracy.

Ambassador Carter concluded with the following observation:"Latin America presents a great opportunity for our nation to contribute to the growth and prosperity of an underdeveloped society through the Alliance for Progress. But the price of these newly gained opportunities is constant vigilance. Leftist ideology continues to inspire reckless measures to thwart the positive intentions of our foreign aid programs. In the final analysis we cannot permit another Cuba in the Western Hemisphere."

BRATTLEBORO REFORMER
COMMUNITY NOTES - October 14.
LOCAL GRAD JOINS PEACE CORPS

Cynthia Granger of Brattleboro is heading for Nicoya, Costaguana. Miss Granger joined the Peace Corps immediately after graduating from the University of Vermont in June of this year. She has completed her training and will leave immediately for South America. Her parents, Paul and Florence Granger, plan to visit their daughter next summer. "We are not at all surprised," said Mrs. Granger. "She's always been the adventurer."

Miss Granger received a master's degree in social work and will be assigned to a women's center in the provincial capital high in the Andes Mountains. In her most recent letter she wrote, "I'm looking forward to working with the women and hope that I can be of some help to them."

In mid-December, behind the Church of San Agustín, the four women, arms tightly clasped around one another, gazed at the three concrete slabs, one meter by two meters, marking the graves of Sergio, Galo, and Jorge, identified by brass plaques. A simple stone cross had been erected between the slabs and the wall of the church. On the wall three plaques had been installed by the Cooperative La Esperanza, the Union of Beneficio Workers, and FLOC, the Littoral Federation of Christian Workers. Two coffee trees, laboriously transplanted to either side of the cross, were in blossom and gave off the distinctive aroma of jasmine. Two white marble angels looked over the graves from the corners nearest the church. Blossoming peonies surrounded the individual grave markers. Padre Philippe and Doctor Saenz stood together at the corner of the church. Margarita, Maruja, Sor Marillac, and Gloria had had lunch with the two men. They were now taking leave of their loved ones.

It was Gloria's first trip to Catachoclo, and it will be her last. Doctor Saenz will take them back to Nicoya: Gloria to the Saenzes' and her work with Doña Leticia, Maruja to the home that she and Galo would have shared and to her artistic endeavors, and Margarita to her new job, director of the women's center.

For now they will have each other.

EPIGRAPH

HOPE

Hope is the thing with feathers
That perches in the soul,
And sings the tune—without the words,
And never stops at all

—*Emily Dickinson, 1830–1896*

GLOSSARY

AIFLD—American Institute for Free Labor Development. Established by the AFL-CIO to provide instructional programs in union activities (organizing, leadership, collective bargaining, union finances) and promote social projects (housing, credit unions, savings-and-loan co-ops, community development). The Institute is contracted to the USAID in most countries in Latin America to run its labor programs.

Beneficio—coffee-processing plant

Cafetero—a person or entity engaged in growing and processing coffee.

Carabineers de Campo—a rural police force

CCSL—Costaguana Confederation of Free Trade Unions

Chuchaqui—Quechua word for hangover, devastating in the high altitude

Day of the Race (Dia de la Raza)—the name for Columbus Day in South America.

FLOC—Littoral Federation of Christian Workers. A union federation inspired by "Quadragesimo Anno," the encyclical of Pope Pius XI, On Reconstruction of the Social Order; Antonia and Golda founded the federation, recruited existing unions in the coastal area, and organized others.

Guayabera—an embroidered cotton dress shirt worn outside the pants, with four pockets

ICRAC—Costaguana Institute for Agrarian Reform and Colonization. A state entity reporting directly to the president.

Jipijapa—a straw hat made in Ecuador, erroneously called a Panama hat

Malecón—a road or street along a waterway

Monte Christi—a *jipijapa* made in Monte Christi, Ecuador.

ORIT—Inter-American Regional Organization of Workers, the western hemisphere branch of the International Confederation of Free Trade Unions.

O. S. N.—Ocean Steam Navigation Company. A British shipping firm that had established Sulaco as its principal port of call on the Pacific coast of Costaguana.

Point IV—predecessor agency to USAID. Dealing with economic aid to developing nations, named for the fourth of four major courses of action proposed by President Harry Truman in his 1949 inaugural address. In the 1960s it had remained the informal designation for USAID in some countries.

TAMC—Costaguana Military Air Transport. A domestic airline operated by the military.

USAID—U.S. Agency for International Development

Walker Tool Company—A U.S. firm specializing in equipment and services for the drilling industry.

WCFTU—World Confederation of Free Trade Unions.